Also by Abi Silver in the Burton & Lamb series:

The Pinocchio Brief
The Aladdin Trial
The Rapunzel Act
The Midas Game

Also by Abi Silver in the Burton & Lamb series

The Pinocchio Brief
The Aladdin Trial
The Rapunzel Act
The Midas Game

THE CINDERELLA PLAN

ABI SILVER

Second edition 2021
First published in 2019
by Lightning Books Ltd
Imprint of Eye Books Ltd
29A Barrow Street
Much Wenlock
Shropshire
TF13 6EN

www.lightning-books.com

ISBN: 9781785632730

Cover by Nell Wood
Typeset in Minion Pro and Trade Gothic LT

British Library Cataloguing in Publication Data
A catalogue record for this book is available from the British Library.

Printed by CPI Group (UK) Ltd, Croydon CR0 4YY

For Dan

The public's expectation of available explanations for how these systems make decisions is misguided. The core strength of a deep-learning system lies in its ability to draw very accurate conclusions from many diverse pieces of information. Fundamentally, it is not capable of providing simple explanations. In short, the concept of a simple explanation of these systems is a deception.

Dr Michael Fielding
Written evidence provided to the House of Commons Select Committee on Autonomous Vehicles

PART ONE

LONDON, 10 OCTOBER, 2018

1

BERTIE LAYTON, aged three years and one month, standing at the 65th percentile for height, maybe a touch more for weight ('he is a good eater' his grandmother would frequently comment when he finished off his sister's unwanted scraps), was tired of waiting in the central reservation. He craved the Freddo chocolate bar Therese, his mother, had promised him 'if he was good' on the way home. He wanted to race his Hot Wheels car around the track his father had constructed for him the previous day and try, independently, to make it loop the loop; and, more than anything else, he was desperate to be able to move his arms and legs freely after spending most of the day confined indoors.

Sensing a momentary lapse in his mother's attention and grip, he'd removed his hand from his mouth, where it had been languishing, and clutched the two vertical bars of the pram which contained his baby sister, Ruby. Next, he'd slipped his back foot from the shiny plate of the buggy board onto the ground and he used it now to propel himself and the pram forwards into the road.

It was partly a test, pushing the boundaries, as three-year-olds often do (and Bertie more than most). And although he would not have been able to articulate it, being such a little boy, Bertie wanted to feel, once more, that glorious surge of his heart in his chest that accompanied these improvised scooter rides, the adventure amplified by his father's past whisperings that this was somehow a dangerous activity, the pounding only subsiding later. Sometimes he drifted off to sleep, imagining himself on a giant superhero skateboard, cavorting around the house, his sister in hot pursuit.

Georgia followed her brother, as best she could, with her mother's arm restraining her. Even though she was older, Bertie was the bolder of the two. 'He's the one who encouraged her,' Therese would complain, exasperated, to her husband, Neil, when another of Bertie's schemes left Georgia in trouble, while he emerged unscathed. 'He doesn't see danger,' Therese would lament, and Neil would smile proudly and shrug. 'I don't think you do when you're three years old. I'd rather have him this way than timid and scared of his shadow.'

So, Bertie would lead the way across a fallen log, his speed and sheer willpower conveying him to the other side. Georgia, in contrast, would hesitate midway, wobble and then find herself pitched off into whatever water or mud the enticing trunk was straddling.

Even tame pastimes often ended in tears. Playing bowls in the garden, Bertie's erratic throws would just as often miss as score a spectacular knock-out. But when a frustrated Georgia tried to up her game, she would hold the ball too long and it would plunge down onto her head or toe.

To be fair to Bertie, it wasn't always his fault that Georgia got hurt; good fortune seemed to follow him around. Like the time he thrust his nose into a pink, rambling rose, drinking up its scent with a broad grin. When Georgia copied, she disturbed a queen bee and ended up being chased around the garden, screaming.

So, lively, luck-kissed Bertie, often-dirty Bertie and sometimes-flirty Bertie, after a snatched, sly glance at his mother, plunged himself and the baby into the road, with Georgia in pursuit.

Therese, behind the children, but scrambling to catch them, was clipped first by the right-hand side of the bumper of the large blue car. She was hit mid-way up her thigh, her body crumpling inwards and folding over the bonnet. Its momentum carried her up onto the windscreen, where her elbow struck the glass, shattering the bone before she thudded, limp and ragged at the roadside. As she lapsed into darkness, the blue of its bodywork triggered a distant memory of the curtains which had hung in her bedroom as a young girl.

Georgia, taller than Bertie, but light and feathery, with one hand outstretched to grab her brother, was knocked high up into the air and landed just short of the concrete barrier, her head hitting the pavement with a resounding 'thwack' which cleaved her skull in two. Bertie, keen to be first across the road was last to be hit, his left arm splintering before he creased over and fell beneath the wheels; two tons of high-tensile strength steel passing over his diminutive body, crushing out his life, his fingers still wet, as they rapped the pavement lightly once, before falling still.

The car came to a halt just short of where Georgia lay, its wheels twisted, its windscreen smashed, its former gleaming chrome grin now ragged and droopy. Its occupant, James Salisbury, aged fifty-nine years and three months, hovering just below the six-foot mark and, at twelve stone, carrying the same weight as he did at twenty-one, was first thrown forwards then back then forwards again, his brain shifting in the opposite direction to his body, in a textbook coup contre-coup, before coming to rest against the inflated airbag.

Only the pram lay intact. When Bertie was struck, it had been sent into a violent spin. Now it rested, upright, part in the gutter, part clambering its way back up to normality, rocking gently forward and back, its occupant blinking her eyes once, twice, before letting out a tentative cry, which quickly became more persistent when no one came.

LONDON, ONE MONTH EARLIER

2

JAMES SALISBURY was on a roll. Three minutes into his ten-minute address to the House of Commons Select Committee, and the rapt faces of the audience confirmed his words were hitting home. It wasn't easy, taking listeners from a place of ignorance to one of knowledge, and from sceptical to convinced. How had he done it? He had spoken from the heart. And as he paused and focused for a moment on the video screen, which was transmitting his briefing further afield, he allowed himself a rare moment of self-congratulation.

Sitting upright behind the glossy desk, in a new single-breasted, wool-mohair-mix suit, his shoes highly polished, his Gucci tie a fashionable shade between pale blue and turquoise, picked out by Martine, his wife, only the previous day from a selection at Selfridges, he was on top of the world.

'Autonomous vehicles provide tremendous potential to drive change,' James spoke confidently. 'No more motorway pileups, no more traffic jams, no more uncertain journey times or wasted down time. No need to swelter on overcrowded public transport. Eliminate the negatives. And the ability to live in that house you've always desired because now your commute is a breeze, or just to travel independently for the first time. Embrace the positives.

'This is no dream. This is reality. A new dawn heralding not just a new way of travelling; it's a new way of living. A new way of life.'

Peter Mears, special adviser to Alan Tillinghurst, the Secretary of State for Transport, watched from the side of the hall. He was portly and bald, his stomach overhanging his tailored trousers, and he had a disconcerting habit of tapping his fingers on his belly when engaged in earnest conversation or when deep in thought. This was one of those occasions, and his index finger was striking his stomach over and again as James spoke. When James finished, to tumultuous applause, and stood, majestic, awaiting questions, Peter frowned and entered a quick reminder to himself into his phone.

'Mr Salisbury. That was fascinating and I can see you are a man of great vision.' David Morris, MP for Woking, vice-chair of the committee and a staunch supporter of the Autonomous Vehicles Bill, smiled broadly at James from the horseshoe of chairs facing him. 'And SEDA should be proud to have you at its helm. We all appreciate you coming here today,' he continued, 'to talk to us at this advanced stage of the reading of the Bill. I will now open things up for questions, if you can spare us a few more minutes of your time.'

The first question came from a man to David Morris' left.

'I wanted to ask about the level of autonomy of your vehicles. Once the Bill is approved and your cars are sold to the public, will they be fully autonomous? And, if not, why not?'

James' eyes sought out Peter, who had tucked his phone away and was focusing on the debate again.

'SEDA's cars will be level three autonomy. They will have a manual function too,' James replied. 'The fully autonomous vehicles, level five, should be available within two to three years.'

'I see. And, given the numerous benefits you've mentioned, I'm interested in the reasoning for this marketing decision.'

'That issue has been done to death in previous sessions. It's not Mr Salisbury's decision,' Alan Tillinghurst, the Secretary of State for Transport, bearded and loud, boomed from centre right.

'I'm still interested in hearing from James,' the man continued. 'He builds the things. Not from some academic or a politician. That's why we asked him to come today, isn't it?'

Alan withdrew. Everyone's attention returned to James. He moistened his lips; beads of sweat had broken out on his forehead. Peter stared at him intently.

'While I believe in change and radical change,' James began, 'and I firmly believe in the capacity of the fully autonomous, level five vehicles to bring about that change, we have to take things in stages. And particularly with autonomous vehicles, there's a nervousness, understandably, about the product. So, regardless of the other issues it creates, I…on balance, support introducing the level three car first.'

'You mean people get to trust the car, knowing they have the option to take over if necessary.'

'Exactly, yes. And, in time, once they see how safe autonomous mode is, they will use it all the time, and then bringing in level five will be uncontroversial, second nature.'

'So, it's a matter of public confidence only, not any problems with the cars?'

'Yes.'

Now Alan looked over at Peter. Peter nodded his gratitude in return.

'There have been times, Alan, though, when governments have decided they know better than the people they serve. We could take the choice away from the people; just give them fully autonomous vehicles straightaway and they have to lump it – if they are so much safer, that is,' the man who had asked the question persisted.

'Extensive research has been carried out,' Alan replied, 'and the majority of people surveyed said they would not feel safe in a fully autonomous level five vehicle.'

'But we all know the vagaries of market research,' a woman on the end of the row joined in. 'Who did you ask? People shopping at Westfield at 2pm on a Monday?'

'You wanted to hear from a manufacturer and James has answered the question,' Alan said. 'We can debate the issue after he and the others have given their addresses today. Let's allow someone else to ask a question now, shall we?'

'How can you be so sure that your vehicles won't have accidents?' a woman to Alan's left piped up.

'We have been trialling our cars in the UK for the past five years,' James replied. 'We have driven over 600,000 miles and never had one collision. What I can say with confidence is that once all vehicles in the UK are autonomous, and they are all linked, connected – we've talked about this before – essentially, "speaking the same language", then there will be no more accidents.'

'And when do you anticipate that will happen?'

'It depends on when the Bill is passed. But, assuming it's in this reading, which is very much what I should like to see then, if level five vehicles are out in two years, I would say ten years maximum. Of course, the government could hurry things along by outlawing manual vehicles before then, but that's not a matter for me.'

'No, it isn't,' Peter muttered under his breath.

'What about cost?'

'SEDA currently produces two models. The smaller Go! will retail at £18,000 and the larger WayWeGo! will be £32,000. That's based on certain projected sales in year one. If we exceed those sales the prices could come down substantially in year two.'

'Are there any technical issues that concern you, which we should know about?'

'Absolutely none. Not only with my own product, but I attend regular meetings with all the other autonomous car manufacturers worldwide. Perhaps surprisingly, we are very collaborative as, like myself, everyone sees the fantastic potential to change lives which these vehicles bring.'

'You've already said that,' Peter mumbled louder than he had intended, and his neighbour frowned at him.

'I understand that people have concerns, and maybe part of that is the misunderstanding that driving is somehow a skill; we pride ourselves, don't we, on being "a good driver" or "a careful and experienced driver",' James said. 'We need to accept that driving is really just a process like any other, getting from A to B safely without colliding with anything. It doesn't require emotional intelligence or judgment. It's the perfect task for a machine to carry out.'

Alan half rose from his seat and swivelled around to face the committee chairman.

'We are running a little behind schedule and our next speaker is waiting. Can I suggest that we allow Mr Salisbury to go now, and that any further questions are channelled through my office, in writing.'

Outside the auditorium, Peter clasped James' hand tightly.

'Well done,' he said.

'Thank you. Do you think that did the trick?'

'Who knows? They are notoriously unpredictable, this lot, and cautious. But you were confident and behind your product and they liked you. That should go a long way towards oiling the wheels.'

'So what happens next?' James asked.

'Two more speakers now. You can tune in, if you like. Then we go into a closed session for further debate, probably finish up in a couple of hours.'

'And will that be it?'

Peter raised his eyes to heaven.

'God knows,' he said, 'but we are getting there.'

***

Toby Barnes, James' second in command, was watching from a round table in the corner of James' office, via the video link. He had written *Embrace the positives. Eradicate the negatives.* on the notepad in front of him, with a flourish.

As James exited the podium and the next speaker was introduced, Toby stood up and made a circuit of the room. He hopped on one leg, then the other, then back onto two feet. He perused the books on the shelf in the corner, pulling out one or two and then shoving them back into place. He straightened the picture on the wall, then he yawned noisily before sitting back down to view the rest of the debate.

3

THERESE LAYTON lifted Ruby from her basket and held her at arm's length. The little girl sneezed twice and then hiccupped. Therese stared at her, sighed and then brought her close to her chest, tapping her back lightly. She paced the room, bouncing on the balls of her feet, humming gently. Ruby's head nestled into Therese's neck.

'Oh dear!' Therese said. 'You've got hiccups?' As she pronounced the word, she shifted her weight from one side to the other. 'Hi-ccups,' she repeated. Ruby gurgled.

Therese skipped across to the window and peered out. The rain striking their discoloured decking was light, but the grey sky suggested the bad weather was set in for a while. She sighed again. She had been hoping to get out of the house this morning. Walking distracted her from her thoughts, and it kept Ruby occupied too. And she sometimes bumped into another local mother, and they chatted and exchanged grievances as they walked. Otherwise the morning stretched out, long and lonely, each second expanding to fill a universe of isolation.

Ruby tugged at Therese's hair. She disentangled her daughter's fingers and headed downstairs, where she placed Ruby carefully down on her back on her playmat and shifted the colourful mobile over her body. Ruby hiccupped again.

'Play with your toys,' Therese told her. 'Mummy needs a break.'

She caught a glimpse of her dishevelled self in the glass of the patio door and winced. She touched one hand up to her hair and smoothed it down, tucking it into her neck. Ruby groaned irritably. The hiccups frustrated her.

Therese ran both hands down over her belly. She really needed to get some exercise or she would never revert to her pre-pregnancy weight. She had managed with each of the other two children; somehow things seemed so much harder third time around. Then she noticed her nails, short and stubby; a manicure would be nice. But there was no point yet, that was what Neil had said, not while she was busy digging in their makeshift sandpit each afternoon – well, when the weather was dry, that was. Plenty of time for beauty treatments once things had settled down a bit.

Ruby's complaint became a cry, progressively increasing in volume. Therese glanced over at her daughter and blinked heavily. She looked down at her wrist, remembering too late that she had discarded her watch the previous day because she had been repeatedly checking it at shorter and shorter intervals and it had become overwhelming.

Therese stood by the glass doors, with Ruby's wailing drowning out most other noises. She watched the pouring rain rebounding off an upturned spoon she had missed and wondered what she could offer up to a long-neglected deity, in return for a clear sky when she had to collect the other two from school later on.

4

Toby Barnes was alone in his flat, a pair of noise-cancelling headphones over his ears. He was sitting on the floor, leaning back against his sofa with a games console in both hands, rocking from side to side, muttering under his breath.

To his left lay a pizza box with a few remaining scraps of Hawaiian Special stuck fast. 'You have to have pineapple on a pizza or it's just not pizza,' he would tell anyone who was prepared to listen. Next to it was an empty bottle of Corona and a second, half-full.

He detached his right hand from the console for a moment in order to scratch his head and push his glasses further up his nose. His tongue was firmly trapped between his teeth, his shoulders hunched, his brow knitted, as he focused on the game.

He knew everyone else was playing *Fortnite*, but he still loved good old *GTA*. He preferred the real-life scenarios, street scenes, recognisable goodies and baddies and, of course, lots of cars to steal. It didn't matter that all the characters had American accents and were caricatures. That was part of the attraction; it was real life but not his real life. Anyone who said that playing these games normalised violence had clearly never played. Hours of *Fortnite* had not encouraged him to shoot anyone and GTA had not, at least so far, elicited from him a desire to hotwire anyone's car, either.

That said, he had to admit that, from time to time, when he was bored at work, and alone, he did find himself re-living some of the game's better moments and mumbling 'die motherfucker,' under his breath. But this was much more a reflection of immersing himself in youth culture generally, he reflected, than of his time spent playing video games.

MISSION COMPLETED! The message flashed in capital letters across the screen.

Toby raised his right hand in a silent salute, then pulled off the headphones, stood up stiffly and bowed to the TV screen, turned around and bowed to the kitchen, then he seized his beer and his phone, sank back down on to the sofa and checked his messages. Finally, he dialled a number and held his phone to his ear. When it rang through to voicemail he quickly hung up. He had been trying his father for two days now, just to catch up, but Barnes senior was hard to locate.

Returning to his phone menu, he selected 'videos' and opened up the recent film of James addressing the House of Commons. Toby joined in where he could remember, copying James' mannerisms, chanting '*Eradicate the negatives. Embrace the positives*' over and over. Then he laughed uproariously and threw his phone face down onto the cushion.

He lifted the corner of the pizza box, but the remaining soggy slice, coated in congealed cheese, was distinctly unappealing. He wiped his fingers on his jeans. Then he pulled the headphones over his ears a second time, slipped back down onto the floor, grabbed the games console and loaded his next mission.

5

James Salisbury sat at the head of the shiny, mahogany table in the largest meeting room at his Essex headquarters. A Mont Blanc pen languished by his right hand; only for show, as he preferred to use his iPad these days to make his notes. And although the table behind him was groaning with finger food to cater to every taste, he had chosen only an espresso and a piece of peanut brittle to sustain him.

The room was spacious enough, the table seated ten comfortably and there were only four men present, positioned at regular intervals. James had planned it that way, subtle touches to discourage the attendees from taking certain places; a strategically placed bottle of water, an imperfectly closed blind and the saucer-like speaker phone deliberately hijacking another potential pew.

'I am grateful to you for calling this meeting, James, especially as I know you've just returned from a week overseas, although it's hard to find you in the country these days,' Peter Mears began. 'Perhaps SEDA runs itself now, just like its cars.'

James said nothing. He had learned he usually achieved the best results by letting Peter have his say, and he always pretended to appreciate Peter's attempts at humour, even where others, less discerning than himself, might have viewed them as sarcasm.

'Thank you. It seemed sensible to take stock of where we are,' James replied, 'post the select committee meeting.'

Peter was silent for once and awaited James' introduction.

'We have an agenda,' James continued. 'Does everyone have it to hand? If not it's in the Cinderella dropbox, first item.'

Peter wiped his mouth and fingers on a paper napkin, scrunching it into a tight ball and depositing it on the edge of his still-groaning plate, indicating that he had finished eating. James winced. He abhorred food waste of any kind. Imogen, his former business partner, had said you could learn a lot from a man by the way he eats. Peter wouldn't have impressed her, James reflected, although few people had.

Peter's eyes circled the room, falling on each of the men for just long enough to make them feel under scrutiny. Then he shoved his plate away so roughly that the napkin rolled off and dropped through the hole in the centre of the table.

'I have some things I need to say,' Peter began, 'on behalf of Alan, which don't feature on the agenda and they won't wait till "any other business". They came up at the meeting, mostly in our closed session. Shall I kick off?'

'Of course,' James replied, although his relaxed comment belied his anxiety. He preferred to stick to his agenda. That was the whole point of producing one, and the implication of Peter's words was clear; Alan Tillinghurst, the irascible minister, had more hoops for them to jump through.

'Thank you, James. You two?' Peter poured himself a cup of

coffee and waited for a response from the room's other inhabitants.

Will Maddox, a tall, skinny man sporting a ponytail, shrugged his agreement. In his day job he was a college lecturer in psychology, but he was present today in his capacity of chairman of UK Cyclists, a group with a burgeoning membership recently topping 1.2 million. The last man, Jeremy Fry, much shorter, at around five-foot six, grunted out what sounded like a 'yes'. He could usually be called upon by James as an ally, canny and protective of his members' interests, which often aligned with those of SEDA. An actuary by profession, he now led the Institute of Automobile Insurers, its three hundred UK members keen to be kept involved in the process of conversion to autonomous driving.

'So,' Peter continued, 'the government has invested £2 billion in autonomous vehicles over the last five years. MPs have participated in focus groups, parliamentary commissions and there has already been twenty-two hours of formal debate on the matter, and hundreds of hours of discussion at various other levels, including in the select committee you attended last week.'

'Yes. And it's much appreciated, I can assure you,' James responded, wondering how many more times he would have to sit through similar opening remarks from Peter.

'We didn't do any of this for you, James. We did it to save lives, to improve lives, for the good of the people of the United Kingdom.'

'Absolutely. You know I'm in total agreement,' James said. 'That's how I see it too.'

'And to bring business to the UK,' Will butted in.

'All right. We don't disagree with that addendum,' Peter said, 'and we don't see any difficulty with it either, as long as there's no conflict between those two objectives. Now for the things we need to get straight.' Peter shuffled back in his chair. 'Jeremy, if the statistics are to be believed, within five years your insurer members will be paying out billions less in claims than they are now. You will almost certainly be making "bumper profits". No pun intended.'

'That doesn't mean we roll over on every point,' Jeremy replied, clearly cross that he was being singled-out for Peter's treatment. He aimed a swift glance at James, who returned it with a reassuring inclination of the head.

'I've talked to Alan about your proposed list of "exclusions", which your members are refusing to cover when the autonomous cars come in, and it won't wash,' Peter said, ignoring Jeremy's petulant comeback. He picked at his front teeth with his fingernail, then curled his tongue over the surface to loosen some mashed-up food, lodged in his prominent gap.

'Your first request, for the government to pick up the tab for accidents involving the first autonomous vehicles, isn't acceptable,' Peter droned on. 'Individual car owners will need to retain their own personal insurance for when they drive in manual mode. And once cars are fully autonomous, it will cease to have any relevance. All insurance will be linked to the vehicle instead, which, naturally, your members will cover.'

'But accidents involving these vehicles will most likely be complex, much more so than now,' Jeremy complained. 'We don't have the resources to investigate them. We'll end up paying out without a clue what really happened.'

'Isn't that what happens now, anyway?' Will mumbled. 'Most of the time, when there's anything tricky you give "knock for knock", as far as I can see.'

Peter held up his hand.

'I put all your points to Alan and the rest of the committee, and there is no way they will change their minds. The government is not going to pay, even at the beginning.'

'My members won't be happy.' Jeremy peeled an apple, paring the skin back, sliver by sliver, the blade of his knife all the time pointing provocatively in Peter's direction.

'I see that. But, given the safety statistics James has provided, accidents will be incredibly rare, even at this interim stage of deployment, so, unpalatable as this may seem to you in principle, this should make little real difference to insurers' profits.'

Jeremy sliced a large section off his apple and put it in his mouth. When he had finished chewing, he laid the knife down across his plate.

'Thank you, Peter,' he said. 'Just making sure I've understood you, then. To sum up, the government has rejected our members' reasonable and considered request for help during this transitional period. Instead, you're insisting we keep on insuring drivers of manual cars in the conventional way. For the new cars, you demand that we insure the vehicle and that we pay up, without investigation, regardless of who is to blame for any accident. This debate appears to be all one-way traffic so far,' he said. 'Excuse my pun.'

'That's not fair,' Peter replied, 'and you know it. It's up to you how you choose to investigate, like Will says. And Alan wanted to impose a cap on premiums. Naturally, they should fall dramatically with the reduced risk of accident. But I managed to persuade him to put this off for the foreseeable future. That is likely to be worth more to your members than anything they will pay out in claims. There is one further area, though, where we might be prepared to accommodate you.'

Peter paused and waited for the full attention of everyone around the table before continuing.

'We've previously discussed the importance of keeping the software in these vehicles up to date. Alan can see that it is crucial, especially in the early days, that vehicle owners update their software regularly. In terms of a proposal to *your* members, Jeremy, it goes like this.

'If the software is not properly maintained by the vehicle owner, we will agree to pay for any resulting losses, at least over the first two years; we'll create a fund to meet any liabilities. It will be strict liability, though. If you haven't updated your software, your insurance will be automatically vitiated. Alan would appreciate some advice on a quick and easy mechanism for checking if the software is up to date. Subject to that box being ticked, the Department is prepared to support and help the insurance industry in the way I have proposed, if the other provisions can be agreed now.'

Jeremy poured himself a glass of orange juice and proceeded to drink it down in one gulp.

'You're not saying anything?' Peter said.

'What would you like me to say?'

'"Thank you" might be in order.'

'It seems a fair compromise to me,' Will mumbled, clearing the last mini quiche off his plate and turning around to see what further tasty treats remained. 'You couldn't seriously have expected them to pick up the cost of the other stuff, could you? I mean, that's what insurance is for.'

Jeremy opened his mouth and then closed it again.

'I have a feeling you have more demands to communicate,

Peter,' James said. 'Why don't we hear everything and then maybe we can comment on the whole package?'

'I think "demands" is a little strong, and I am merely the mouthpiece. All right,' Peter said. 'To move on – Will. You continue to support us and the autonomous car bill, without making any waves, including agreeing to two TV appearances per week at the relevant time, and there'll be a guaranteed additional £5 million per year invested in cycle superhighways.'

'Where?'

'Your choice. You send me your ideas for the most needed places and, while I won't promise it will be exactly as you want, you will be consulted at every step.'

'What about lorries in central London?'

'By 2025 they won't be allowed in at all, except between 10pm and 6am.'

Will rose again and combed the food table for anything interesting he had not yet sampled. He selected a satsuma and a bunch of grapes.

'Even autonomous ones?' he asked, popping a grape into his mouth.

'Yes.'

'Oh no!' James protested. 'Why ban autonomous lorries? They won't be able to hit cyclists. It's not in their DNA. It's unnecessary, just pandering to public hysteria.'

'DNA!' Will feigned choking on his fruit haul. 'How many cyclists have to be crushed before you understand that we can't share the road with these lumbering vehicles any more and we shouldn't have to?'

'So you're in, then?' Peter asked.

Will sat down heavily. 'What's the catch?' he said.

'No catch. Alan simply expects your continued support.'

'I'll wait to hear what else you have to say to the others, like James said.'

Peter turned towards James.

'All right. The last piece of the puzzle. We had some discussion last time about manufacturers working together so that their vehicles can communicate effectively. I know your IT man spoke subsequently to our IT team. Clearly that is crucial, but not without enormous difficulties in terms of data protection and susceptibility to hacking.'

'I've told you, it's all in hand,' James said. 'I've been to the sessions you set up on communication and cyber security. Now it's a simple matter of cooperation and, given that it will be to everyone's benefit, it's a total non-issue. The critical first step is the government's publication of the list of approved manufacturers, which will accompany the Bill. Then we will all know where we stand. No one will put his head above the parapet and agree to get into bed with another manufacturer unless he knows who is government-approved. It's simple. Five years, Peter. The Minister, in various incarnations, has been prevaricating for five years!'

'The time hasn't been wasted. Your vehicles are far safer as a result.'

'But we can't go on like this. None of us, not just SEDA. I need to sell my cars in this country. If I can't sell them soon, I'll have to consider closing the factory and shifting my focus overseas. If that is what you want, then you should make it clear and we'll move on. Tell Alan when the list comes out, there'll be no "homegrown" vehicles on it.'

'If it were my decision alone, you know things would be different,' Peter said. 'Be patient. We have so many different groups to keep on side, you know that, including the anti-terrorist lobby. Immediately after you presented to the Committee, Dr Fielding gave his views. Did you hear him?'

'He's an old woman and you shouldn't have invited him.'

'He is well-respected and, I accept, cautious, but the committee wanted to hear from a wide range of people, and they listened to the warnings he gave on a number of issues.'

'The sooner you publish the list and SEDA can sell its cars in the UK, the sooner we can all work together and this "hacking" theory can be consigned to the dustbin.' James picked up his pen and rolled it around in his fingers.

Peter took a deep breath. He knew his next request was likely to be incendiary.

'Alan feels strongly that, in order to allay any fears of hacking or other data breaches, we should have immediate access to information about the security of your systems and that of the other autonomous car manufacturers who want to sell in the UK. Without it, how can we comply with our national security agenda?' he said.

'What?'

'Access to information about the security of your systems.'

'I go to all the cybersecurity events and work closely with the team the government set up.'

'It's not enough.'

'So, what, now you want us and Tesla and Google and all the others to allow you access to our most secret information? You're not serious,' James muttered through clenched teeth.

'Not me. Alan. And the PM. I am afraid I was not as convincing this time in my pleas on your behalf, although I will continue to try. But at the moment they are deadly serious,' Peter said. 'And, in all honesty, I really don't see what the fuss is all about. It's just the *processes* they…we want to oversee. I can tell you, without naming names, that at least two other manufacturers have already agreed to be audited in this way.'

'And the list?'

'Assuming we are satisfied with the security of your systems, we are looking at a few weeks only for publication of the list of approved manufacturers; October I would say. And there is no reason, for the time being, to think that SEDA would not be on the list.'

'October this year?'

'Yes.'

'For the Bill to pass and the list to be published?'

'Yes.'

'Thank the Lord.'

'Well there's no need to be rude.'

'Is that it?'

'No.'

'I didn't think so.'

'I would love another cup of coffee, but you know I like it piping hot. Could you see if someone can bring a fresh pot?'

6

It was Tuesday and that meant it was Neil Layton's day to assume responsibility for the morning routine. For the first month, when Ruby was tiny, he had been in charge of breakfast for their other two children every day, but they had now settled into this routine, where he was boss on Tuesdays and Thursdays and Therese managed the rest of the week.

This morning he was feeling particularly perky as Therese had only disturbed him once, around 2am, when she had fed Ruby. He had even slept soundly enough to dream, although it was a weird mash-up of wailing babies, fleeing something large and frightening and having his face licked by a large, slobbering dog.

Breakfast was challenging when he had to orchestrate it one-handed, but if he used the sling for Ruby he had learned that he could work twice as fast. Of course, that meant that he had to postpone his own breakfast, either that or risk dripping it all over his baby daughter, but that was a small price to pay for relative normality in the kitchen. And it was worth a few minutes of discomfort for the look of relief on Therese's face when he took Ruby from her arms and shepherded Bertie and Georgia down the stairs.

Today Bertie demanded his Coco Pops warmed up. Neil placed Bertie's bowl in the microwave for twenty-five seconds, just how he liked it and, as he had anticipated, when Georgia saw him serve Bertie, she asked for hers to be heated too.

'Look. Turns the milk brown,' Bertie declared proudly. 'Can I show Ruby, dad?'

'You can try. She's a bit muffled up in here, but I'll turn her head for you.'

So Neil had manoeuvred his way over to perch next to his son and Ruby had patiently endured Bertie prodding her cheek and pointing out his breakfast. And she had hardly flinched when Bertie attempted to prise her eyelids open, ever so gently, just to ensure she really could see.

The microwave pinged and Neil took the opportunity to leap away and collect Georgia's cereal. But, in his haste, he must have pressed the wrong combination of buttons. The bowl was staggeringly hot. He dropped it back onto the worktop with a shriek, sloshing soggy Coco Pops and brown milk all over and raced to the sink where he ran his hand under the cold tap, swearing under his breath. Ruby smacked her lips. Bertie laughed hysterically. Georgia began to cry.

'Just one minute, Georgie. Daddy just needs one minute to save his fingers. Not sure there's a plastic surgeon on hand today, so I need to sort this out myself. Then I'll get you a fresh bowl. Are you sure you want them warm? It turns the milk brown you know?'

Georgia's face was screwed up tightly and her sobs were

wracking her entire frame, but Neil believed he detected a shallow nod among the shudders. As a parent you had to be able to develop a whole new set of observation skills. Switching off the tap earlier than the recommended two minutes and kissing the top of Ruby's head for no reason other than relief that she, at least, was not demanding anything of him, he lifted a clean bowl down from the cupboard, shovelled some Coco Pops in and tried, once more, to feed his elder daughter.

This time he watched the seconds tick down on the microwave, tested the temperature with a teaspoon and then set the bowl down ceremoniously in front of Georgia. Her face was so awash with tears and snot that he could hardly tell if she was happy or not. He tugged at some kitchen roll and wiped her down.

'Thank you, Daddy,' she croaked.

Neil was dying for a cup of coffee, but Therese wouldn't allow him hot drinks around the children, and certainly not when he had the youngest strapped to his chest. Staring out of the window at next door's cat oozing its way along the fence distracted him for now.

There was a loud plop behind him, followed by a scream from Georgia. He turned abruptly to find that someone, presumably Bertie, had lobbed a spoon into Georgia's bowl and it had landed with a titanic splash, sending half the contents spilling out over Georgia's face, clothes and the table.

'Bertie!' he yelled, then remembered that Therese had told him not to shout at Bertie.

Bertie giggled.

'Georgie looks funny.' He pointed at his Thomas the Tank Engine toy, which he had smuggled onto the table. 'It wasn't me, Daddy,' he said.

'What? Thomas used his special springboard to launch a missile at Princess Georgia's breakfast?' Neil was no longer shouting.

Georgia screamed again.

'Neil?' Therese was calling from the top of the stairs. He heard the creaking of the floorboards, as she manoeuvred herself around in bed.

Neil swore for the second time that morning, this time more audibly than the last. Bertie clapped his hand over his mouth and Georgia stopped crying.

'It's OK,' Neil called back into the upstairs void. 'Thomas the Tank Engine had a little accident. I'm just cleaning him up.' He put his finger to his lips. 'Shh,' he said. Both children laughed.

He dabbed at Georgia's face with the soft hand towel and cleaned the spilled milk off the table. Then he examined her t-shirt. It was khaki-coloured anyway and only spattered around the neck. She sometimes came home from school dirty, so Therese would never know, as long as they could escape from the house without her scrutiny.

'Georgia, sweetie. Finish up your Coco Pops and then I'll just dry your t-shirt with some tissue.'

She nodded obediently. As he yanked another paper sheet off the roll, she leaned forward and planted a kiss on the back of his hand. 'Thank you, Daddy. I don't agree with Grandma. I think you're a very good daddy,' she said.

7

James was standing at the wash basin in his ensuite bathroom at 2am. He was not a vain man, but there were definitely two additional lines radiating out from his left eye, which he had not noticed before and, following his jaw line down, he questioned if that was the beginning of a double chin. He stepped onto the scales and squinted at the reading. No. Still exactly twelve stone. That didn't necessarily mean everything was precisely the same, though. He knew that he might have lost some muscle tone recently and it could easily have been replaced by body fat.

He opened the top drawer of the bathroom cabinet and surveyed the array of beauty products which Martine utilised on a daily basis. There was an entire row of nail polish, with white at one end, black at the other and every imaginable colour in between. Her lipsticks were less varied, around twenty different shades of red. Then the creams and ointments began; moisturisers, toners, scrubs, cleansers. He ran his fingers along the tubes and jars but balked at opening any. And he certainly couldn't ask Martine for advice, even though he knew she would be delighted to provide it – not after the many occasions on which he had teased her for buying the products in the first place. He would ask Jane at work instead. She was nearer his age and very discreet.

Settling back down underneath the covers, he let out a deep sigh.

'What is it?' Martine asked, her hair splayed out across her copper-infused pillow, her latest aid to clean sleeping.

'Nothing. Just can't switch off,' James replied, gazing at the ceiling.

Martine turned over, shuffled her body in closer and ran her fingers down his arm.

'What are you so worried about? Are the others causing trouble?'

'They're all after what they can get for themselves.' James leaned back against the velvet headboard. 'Jeremy, he's the insurance guy. He's going to be allowed to make a killing by keeping premiums at current rates when no one will ever have an accident, but he wants more. Will, he's the cyclist, he gets big investment in cycling lanes, but he's still not satisfied. He wants all lorries banned during daylight hours. Alan, he's the minister, he must love it when Peter reports back. Divide and conquer. He doesn't even have to try. We do it for him.'

'And what is it you want?'

'What I've always wanted. To sell my cars. To improve people's lives.'

'So why aren't they all on your side? What you want will benefit millions of people,' Martine said.

'Alan doesn't see it that way, apparently. I could sense he wasn't happy when I spoke at that committee meeting at the House of

Commons last week. Oh, there was lots of effusive thanks and "We love you for taking all these risks and having a vision", but then some counter-terrorist idiot spoke after me and convinced them all that autonomous vehicles were awful, because they could be hacked and taken over and that people's personal data could be stolen. Now Alan wants to send someone to vet our data controls. God, Peter sounded just like Tony Blair today, going on about "national security". Spineless, they are. No trust. No imagination. No vision.'

'Well, no one could compare with you.'

'You might just be my only fan at the moment.' He stroked her arm. 'If only we could have some progress, something tangible, anything, rather than all this delay. There was a moment, at the government meeting, when I thought I had them. I thought they felt it too. *Embrace the positives. Eradicate the negatives.* The whole room was rising with me. But as soon as I left and the next guy came and talked "terror" and "opaque systems" it was all washed away. I might as well have never existed.

'You know, I feel like one of those hamsters on a treadmill, running, running, running, but never getting anywhere. In the end I think my heart will burst and I'll fall down dead and then another hamster will take my place and no one will notice that it has a black splodge behind its ear when I don't.'

Martine laughed. 'No one could take your place. Can you imagine Toby trying? What did you tell me he asked the other day? Oh yes. He thought someone was joking when they said a cow gave off as much pollution as a car. He never knew they farted methane.'

'He's young. He'll learn.'

'You think? By his age I had two regional titles and I was

running my own business.'

'You were very...advanced. And you weren't born with a silver spoon.'

'You shouldn't let them push you around so much,' Martine said. 'Peter and the others.'

'I shouldn't shoot the messenger, either. I know it's not Peter's fault. He's very supportive, if a little annoying. It's Alan who's pulling the strings.'

'So talk to Alan, then. Ignore Peter. He can't be so terrifying.'

'It's not as simple as that. You don't understand. There's a protocol. Oh it's just so...pathetic! I've played by all the rules. They've had the royal visit, the business plan, five years of collaboration and strategic thinking and they're still too scared to publish the list. God if I have to sit through another one of those endless meetings with obstacles being thrown in my path again and again...'

'Maybe you could ask Alan to come to the office. He's never been, has he? I could organise some lunch.'

'I doubt a lunch, however enticing, is going to change Alan's mind, and I'm trying to keep them out, not invite them in! I'll have to talk to the other manufacturers. I'm seeing them next week. Maybe if we all fight it, they'll realise they have to drop it. I'm not sure it's legal anyway. I'll ask Bruce. Must be against some data privacy rules. They're just all so weak, these politicians, that's the real problem. And the lawyers make them nervous. No one wants to go down in history as the person who got it spectacularly wrong. You'd think we were talking about "weapons of mass destruction" not autonomous cars.'

'So is that what you're going to do? Fight it? Fight the government?'

James laughed. 'You make it sound very dramatic,' he said. 'Maybe Peter has brought Alan around already. He did hint that he would try again. Then there won't need to be any fight.'

Martine turned her back on James and plumped her pillow. James was right that something needed to happen to shake things up. She understood his frustration at being undervalued in this way, after all his years of hard work. Every time he capitulated, he was asked for more and more, the goalposts constantly shifting.

She drew her knees up to her chest – her thinking position – and listened to James muttering to himself as he finally drifted off to sleep.

8

Juan Herrera sat at his computer screen in the technology lab at SEDA's Essex factory, concentrating hard. He had connected first to one of their test vehicles, which was stuck in traffic in Islington. It was dull watching how SEDA's cars behaved in the rush hour, but important, too. One thing he had already noted to report to James was that the other drivers were clearly nervous at how close behind them the SEDAs regularly travelled. That wouldn't be a problem once every car was autonomous, but the last thing James would want was any bad publicity at this crucial testing stage, so Juan would mention it at the next opportunity. In any event, the driver was keeping his own log and was scheduled to come into the lab for a debrief tomorrow, so they could compare notes on his driving experience.

Juan looked at the road ahead, to anticipate any particular obstacles the car would need to navigate. Now the SEDA car was first in line at the traffic lights. The lights changed, the two lanes of traffic immediately to the SEDA's left began to move, but the

SEDA was stuck in its blocks. Had it stalled? Juan urged it on. Then he saw why it was waiting.

Just as the lights turned to green, a cyclist with a death wish crossed the junction from left to right. None of the other cars could see her, as she was hidden, until the last minute, by a vehicle which had not completely cleared the junction. Each of the regular vehicles slammed on their brakes and swerved to miss the cyclist who, miraculously, emerged unscathed and pedalled off intact. Only the SEDA had remained stationary, anticipating her approach. Once the cyclist had escaped, the SEDA moved smoothly off.

Juan switched on his left-hand screen, which provided him with the view of the road the car itself could 'see', via its combination of sensors. The images appeared as coloured shapes against a black background, each car was represented by an orange square, although all SEDA cars were green to help distinguish them easily, pedestrians were purple rectangles and other obstacles covered the spectrum from red to blue, according to their status. He rewound a few screens and then he understood what had happened.

'Perfecto!' he mouthed as he watched the cyclist, a yellow circle, appear at the far left of the screen twenty seconds earlier. None of the human drivers could see her, but the SEDA knew she was there, its sensors turning through 360 degrees, those high frequency radio waves bouncing off her, even at a distance of some thirty-five metres. This was the kind of snapshot the public would love; James could spin it as his cars exhibiting some kind of 'sixth sense'. He made a careful note of the vehicle ID and the precise reference for the footage before sitting back and rubbing his eyes. Then he pulled out a bag from under the desk and extracted a crumpled white t-shirt, a pair of boxer shorts and a toothbrush. He was just heading for the toilets when Toby walked in.

'Hi Juan. Why're you in so early?' Toby asked.

Juan shrugged and folded his hands behind his back, so as to hide his clothes. 'Lots to do on the new project. Thought I'd get a head start.'

'New project?'

'Well the new initiative. I suppose it's all still part of Connect, isn't it?'

'I suppose it is, yes.'

'When does James need my report?'

'I'm to see it first,' Toby said a little too quickly, 'and I'd love an update.'

'OK. I could get you something by Friday, just in outline. I'm waiting to hear back from one of the big US guys. I think it would be best to do that before I write it up.'

'Sure,' Toby said. 'Oh, did you see there's going to be a new James Bond movie, after all. Do you get James Bond in Mexico?' he continued.

'I think James Bond gets most places,' Juan said, 'and before I came here, I was in the US for five years, and he definitely gets there.' Juan smiled and a dimple hollowed out his right cheek.

Toby's nose twitched. Then he marched over to the recycling bin in the corner and opened it up. A pungent mix of turmeric and coriander wafted its way through the holes in the top of a small cardboard box.

'Were you here late too?'

'There's a lot to do. I'm not just evaluating our own vehicles. I need to review all the systems the other car manufacturers are using, compare them with ours. Then I can assess compatibility.'

Toby took in Juan's red eyes and dishevelled appearance.

'Have you been here all night?' he asked.

Juan leaned back against his desk and scratched at the beginning of a beard. His t-shirt was clinging to him in all the wrong places and he really wanted to go and clean up but, evidently, Toby wanted to chat.

'I got kicked out of my flat,' he said. 'Crazy landlord came in shouting, said I had to leave immediately.'

'What did you do?'

'Nothing…well I was having a party…just a little one. I thought he was away. Turns out he came back early and he doesn't like parties.'

'That's a shame.'

'I didn't know it was in my contract. Who has a "no party" agreement?'

'Does he live in the block?'

'Downstairs. There was quite a lot of…stuff going on at the party which he didn't like. I wouldn't have let him in, but someone else opened the door. Thought he was my dad, he said.'

'How many days have you slept here?'

'Just three.'

'Three! James'll have a fit if he finds out.'

'I know. It's hard to look for a new place when I'm working. If I could take a day off, I could probably find somewhere. I've been looking.'

'I thought you were married?' Toby said, suddenly, thinking back to Juan's personal statement he had read with interest a couple of months back.

'I was. Rosa went back to Mexico. Said it was too cold here. She missed her family.'

Juan rubbed at his wedding band as he spoke.

'I'm sorry.'

'Don't be. She only married me to get away from her parents. And I only married her for...well it doesn't matter now.'

Toby peered over Juan's shoulder to the coloured shapes shifting around on the screen. 'Listen. I have a spare room,' he said. 'And I've been thinking of renting it out anyway. You could stay for a while, till you find somewhere else.'

Now Juan was pleased Toby had stayed to talk. 'Thanks so much,' he said. 'That's so kind.'

'You'll be doing me a favour too. But I would get rid of that curry box before James comes in here. There's a dustbin out the back. You don't know him very well yet, but he has a nose like a bloodhound.'

Juan looked confused.

'He doesn't like strong food smells in the workplace. Or mess of any kind. I'll give you a buzz when I'm leaving tonight. We can go together. I'll show you the room and you can see what you think.'

'Thanks again, Toby. I promise no parties, OK.'

'Oh no,' Toby laughed. 'I'm counting on a few parties.'

9

CONSTANCE LAMB was preparing to cover a bail application for her colleague, but every time she thought she had assimilated all the salient points, another document would worm its way into her inbox.

'You're a real mate,' he had thanked her earlier, before departing for his wife's thirtieth birthday do, leaving the work experience student to find all the relevant papers and pass them on. That was why he needed the favour. He anticipated a late night and a hangover, which might detract from his usual eloquence before the judge.

The student had knocked on Constance's door and said her goodbyes around 7pm and, by 8.30pm, Constance was alone in the office again. It was only fair, she reasoned to herself, that she should help out when she was less busy and had nowhere to go. And she liked the tranquillity of the office at night, but she also wished she wasn't so often the last man standing.

Part of it was her own fault, she knew that. There had been a work trip to *The Band* only last week, a musical playing in the West End, but she had declined, partly because she didn't like the music but, mostly, because any theatre reminded her of Mike, her actor ex-boyfriend. While it was patently clear, with the benefit of hindsight, that they had grown apart and the relationship would never have worked, she still missed his physical presence enormously, and even a whiff of theatricality made her maudlin.

Constance finished her work and then spent five minutes catching up on Facebook, ensuring she 'liked' and 'commented' in all the right places, so that she wouldn't become a total social outcast. She couldn't resist a quick foray onto Mike's Facebook page, attempting to ignore his new profile picture, and found that his latest post reported, in excited tones, that he had landed a supporting role in a new production of *Tartuffe* at the National Theatre.

As she switched off the lights and set the alarm, she thought about Mike again, and what he might be doing at this very moment. Probably standing in front of a mirror somewhere practising his lines and roping his new girlfriend in for support.

She should be magnanimous and go along to the play, she reasoned, take a friend, congratulate him afterwards. Not because she wanted him back, but just because it was the right thing to do. And Constance always tried to do the right thing.

10

JAMES SWEPT through the entrance of SEDA's office, casting a critical eye over its glass panels and white tiles, all the time in perpetual motion.

He had developed the perfect combination of making each of the receptionists feel he cared about them, while, at the same time, maintaining his steady progress across the floor. He achieved this by a short, but meaningful comment, accompanied by a toss of the head or raised eyebrow, delivered without breaking stride. 'Carol, how was your mother's operation? Oh. That's so good to hear. Give her my best.' 'Jane, thank you. The flowers in the atrium are superb today.' 'Diana, so good of you to send me on that material from Cars International. I'll use it in today's meeting.'

And, something about his speed, trajectory and the determined look on his face as he moved rendered him unlikely to be waylaid on his journey by any of them. After he had gone, they each preened themselves, safe in the knowledge they were a valuable member of the SEDA family.

'Hello James. I saw you arrive. Tim and Jason are already here with the new guy for your meeting, but I asked Diana to keep them in reception, as I know you usually like to head into the room first.'

James looked up. Toby was lurking by the door in a white t-shirt and black chinos. The previous day he had worn bright blue ankle-skimmers and James' eyebrows had twitched judgmentally. Although today was clearly an improvement, Toby had remained steadfastly without socks.

'Thank you for letting me know.' James returned to his screen.

'Were you happy with the briefing I sent over yesterday?' Toby persisted. 'I wasn't sure it was what you wanted.' Toby forced his glasses further up his nose.

'Oh yes. Concise but on point. Next time, try to get it to me a little earlier in the day.'

Toby considered protesting and then thought better of it. James had only asked for the research late morning and he had worked solidly through his lunch to complete it, before James left for the evening.

'And a couple more worked examples are always useful. Have you organised my transfers in Frankfurt? You know how awkward they are out there.'

'Yes, it's all done.'

'And did they agree to a table for dinner at 8pm? They often close up before I get there.'

'It's sorted. They said, seeing as it's you, they'll take the reservation and not to worry if you are a few minutes late.'

'That's because I always give them a large tip. How's the IT guy doing on our Project Connect?'

'Juan? Good. He's fitted in and he's getting on with the things you asked. Working long hours too. Do you need the report from him today?'

'When I'm back from this next trip. I'll let you know. Anything else? Otherwise give me five minutes and then ask Diana to send them in?'

'Would it be useful for me to take notes at your meeting, especially as I prepared the briefing?' Toby was bolder now and had taken two more steps into the room.

James picked up his tablet and tucked a pen in his top pocket.

'Today is pretty much routine. I'm sure you have other things to get on with.' He tapped Toby on the shoulder, as he sidestepped him and exited the room.

After James had gone and Toby had watched him through the window, marching in military style along the corridor, he sat down in James' chair and spun around in it, first one way, then the other, lifting his feet off the ground, like a child on a roundabout. He tapped James' mouse and his screen came to life. Toby tutted as he scrolled through and closed the various applications which remained open, before locking the computer. Then he picked up James' desk phone and dialled a number.

'Hello. Juan here.' A tentative voice filled the space around his ear.

'Juan. This is James Salisbury, CEO,' Toby spoke in an affected booming voice. 'I'm thinking of a new "jacuzzi" option for the latest model. Do you think it will work, technically, I mean?'

'Hello Mr Salisbury. Jacuzzi?'

'You know, water with bubbles. In the back. For entertaining. Or will it interfere with the radar, do you think?'

There was a long pause before Toby burst out laughing.

'Got you, didn't I?' he giggled.

'I knew it was you,' Juan replied. 'I was just, how you say, playing the game.'

'I don't think so. I think I got you. That means first beer of the evening is on you.'

He replaced the phone and twisted the chair around again, so he could survey the greenfield site. On a sunny day, like today, it was a hive of activity. There were two men pounding the far shores of the lake, an older man attempting star jumps on the grass next to the car park and a heron standing stock still in the shadows, waiting to skewer any unsuspecting passing fish.

Toby stood up and brought his face close to the glass, pressing the palm of each hand either side. When he withdrew, they had left a greasy mark on the cool surface. He turned on his heel, punched the air once with his arm and then sauntered out of James' office.

11

THE JOURNEY to school took around ten minutes without children in tow, but more like twenty when they travelled en famille. It wasn't raining so Therese wrapped Ruby in a light cotton blanket and placed her, with great precision, in the pram.

How she had argued with Neil when they had shopped together for baby accessories, five years back. She had insisted on pink for Georgia, despite Neil's protestations that 'a neutral colour might be more serviceable'. Of course, Therese had known precisely what he meant. That when (rather than if) they had the boy he craved, they would need a new pram. She had delighted in tormenting him by insisting that it was totally acceptable 'these days' to push boy babies in pink prams too. It was only when Neil had become a seething mass of frustration that she had tucked her head into his shoulder.

'Please babe. I just want Georgia to have a pink pram,' Therese had whispered. 'I'll work extra days to pay for it when I go back. And when we have a boy, we'll get him a blue one. Why should our son have any less than our daughter?' And Neil had relented; to be fair he usually did, and now, of course, she was vindicated, because the blue pram was folded away in the loft and the pink one was back in action.

Outside, once they'd cleared the nearest obstacles, aka the neighbour's motorcycle, which was parked halfway up the pavement, and a discarded shopping trolley, braved passing by number 26, where the smallest dog (a miniature Schnauzer) made the loudest noise, Therese relaxed and settled into her stride. It was a struggle with all three on her own, but she had the prospect of depositing two of them at school very shortly and a bright day ahead.

Ruby's eyes were open and focused on a multi-coloured, giant ladybird which floated a few centimetres above her face and Georgia was skipping along at Therese's side. Bertie was standing on the buggy board which Neil had insisted they buy. Therese hadn't been keen. She thought it encouraged Bertie to be lazy. And when his weight was combined with the pram and the baby, she found it heavy to push.

But she understood that Neil liked to do little things for his son that he had enjoyed as a boy or that he knew he would have enjoyed if they had existed then. That was why he had bought an extensive train set, second hand, and was slowly re-populating it with Bertie's favourite Thomas the Tank Engine figures. It was also why he'd already put Bertie's name down for an Arsenal season ticket.

'It means he can help too,' Neil had told Therese eagerly.

'How do you mean?'

'Well if you are really tired, Bertie can help push Ruby, you know...'

'I can't believe you just said that! He's three years old.' Therese had flung Neil a look which would have turned lesser men to stone. But, eventually, she had conceded defeat and the board had been purchased and installed.

Now they had reached the last stretch before school, Bertie gave his mum an enquiring look. She knew what that meant, from the last time they had all walked together.

***

Neil had allowed Bertie, then, to take control of his sister, to push off, lift both feet onto the buggy board and open up a small gap on Neil, herself and Georgia. Not only that, he had held Therese back with a whispered, 'Leave him, Tay. He's responsible, he can do it,' as the space between them had increased to ten metres. Therese's heart had been thumping in her chest, and all her instincts had screamed at her to prevent her son from extending his lead, when Bertie had stopped independently and waited, ahead of the main road. She remembered how Neil had caught up with Bertie, patting his back and tousling his hair.

'Well done Bertie,' he had said loudly, to Therese as much as to his son. 'What a great big brother you are.'

'Well done Bertie,' Georgia had copied her father, rapping Bertie on the top of the head.

***

Therese gripped the handles of the pram with both hands, gritted her teeth and pushed up the slight incline.

'Mum?' Bertie fidgeted and leaped off the board, landing

heavily in front of her, forcing her to an abrupt stop. He giggled and Georgia giggled too. 'Can I push Ruby?' he asked, this time in words. 'No, not today,' Therese replied, her mood suddenly plummeting.

Bertie stared at the ground, kicking at a loose paving stone. She held out her hand for him and he turned away.

'Tell you what?' she said. 'You push one side and I'll push the other. That way, we'll get there together even faster.'

Bertie thought about the proposal for a few seconds. It wasn't quite what he had wanted, but he was prepared to try anything once. After a scowl and a quick scuffing of his toe along the pavement, he took the right handle of the pram in both hands and Therese took the left. And Georgia, unwilling to be left out of the joint enterprise, gripped Bertie's back pack in her fist and they continued in this rag-tag procession all the way to school.

12

Toby had always been fascinated by Martine Salisbury. She would arrive at the factory regularly, unannounced, and wander around, often pretending she was looking for James. She would stride through the assembly room in her red stiletto boots or peer over the shoulders of the IT specialists, extending a polished fingernail in the direction of anything which required explanation.

Then she would drape herself over the reception desk, her wavy locks streaming in the blast from the air conditioning unit, positioned just above Carol's head, as if she were modelling some hair-care product. And, with a sweetened latte in one hand, she would oversee the day's appointments and arrivals.

Occasionally, she came in on the premise that they had a board meeting, even though James always provided for them to be held virtually. She, Toby, and Bruce Debrett, SEDA's legal adviser, were directors of SEDA, together with James. Not that being a director meant anything at all, or at least that was how it had been for Toby up till now. James' view on how to run the company had always claimed the day. Toby was there just to make up numbers and draw up the relevant minutes, which the lawyer always checked anyway. But, most of the time, Martine arrived when no board meetings were planned and James wasn't even there.

Toby had made the mistake once of mentioning her visits to James, although it had left him even more confused about whether he should consider deferring to a second master, this one sporting real fur and a diamond in her belly button. He had dropped it casually into the conversation without, he believed, having proffered any view as to the motivation behind it or its merits.

'I don't need you to tell me all the details, Toby, thank you. Martine and I have no secrets,' was James' curt response. Although he had noticed that, after that exchange, for a few weeks or so, Martine had tended to time her visits more for when James was absent.

The girls in reception complained sometimes too, only quietly as they liked Martine 'as a person'. She always bought them fabulous custom-made gifts at Christmas, and her presence certainly livened things up. But she did question and challenge some of their duties and then they, like Toby, were confused as to who was really in charge.

And when Toby thought about it, as he often did, on those long afternoons when James was in meetings or abroad and he had completed the various menial duties allotted to him, he had to admit that Martine was a very persuasive woman.

A large part of the influence she wielded was down to her appearance. After all, she looked amazing for a woman of her age and Toby was forever trying to curb his vivid imagination about the sex life she shared with James. It didn't help that, on a random search online, he had uncovered photographs of Martine from her Miss South Yorkshire days. That was how he knew about the belly button stud and, try as he might, he struggled to prevent himself from undressing her, mentally, back down to that skimpy bikini she had worn in the swimwear round, before taking her well-deserved crown, whenever he encountered her.

Luckily for Toby, Martine generally paid him little attention, so he could gawp from afar and privately congratulate his boss and mentor on his good fortune, with a lewd chuckle, or routinely grumble to himself about her interference in the business, without the discomfort of her unsettling presence close by.

But today Martine was standing very close to him and speaking to him very directly.

'Toby. Just the person I was looking for.'

'Hello Martine. How are you?' Toby gulped and checked to see if anyone else was in earshot.

'Good, thank you. I wanted to ask you if you had any plans next week, in the evenings?'

'I don't think so. Does James need me to do something?' he asked.

'I thought you might like to come over for dinner, to the house, on Monday night?'

'James is away Monday night.'

'Yes.'

'In Germany. I organised his schedule.'

Martine had squeezed out a smile.

'I wanted to discuss a business idea with you. I thought I'd surprise James with it, but I'd value your views first. I don't want to look stupid.'

'Oh.' Toby felt colour flooding to his cheeks.

'And we never get much time to talk privately at work. There's always someone listening in. Can you come around seven?'

'Yes. Thank you,' Toby stuttered. 'Monday at seven.'

'I'll make us some food. Just something light. I never eat a heavy meal at night,' Martine added. 'It affects my sleep.'

'No. Me neither. Sounds great. See you then. I'll look forward to it.'

13

JAMES JOINED Peter for coffee at Haz on Foster Lane in the City. Peter sometimes did this, requested James' company at short notice, usually to pass on some wisdom he had overheard or to probe James for information. Peter had already ordered a large espresso and some baklava and he dug into the latter with enthusiasm and the aid of a large fork.

'Ba-kla-va,' Peter exclaimed as syrup oozed out onto his plate. 'Food of the gods.'

James ordered a camomile tea; he was trying to cut down on caffeine and it was nearing his watershed of 3pm. He refrained from any food. He wanted to know why he had been summoned this time.

'I got the recipe off the internet and gave it to Fiona, but she hasn't mastered it yet,' Peter continued. 'Filo pastry is tricky, apparently. You know where it originated?' Peter tapped his taut stomach companionably. 'Topkapi palace, Istanbul. The best I've ever tasted was in Armenia, where they add cinnamon and cloves, but this is not bad, I have to say.'

James' eyes travelled to the counter, where the young man making his tea was trying to accept money from another customer while simultaneously answering the phone.

'You wanted to meet?' he said flatly.

'Yes. Look, this is awkward. You know I hate to be the harbinger of bad tidings.'

'You and Fiona can't make it to *Amadeus* now, after all.'

Peter took another mouthful of cake.

'No. We're still up for it – looking forward to it. It's the cyber security stuff we talked about at the last Cinderella meeting. I've talked to Alan again, but you're going to have to give on this one, I'm afraid.'

James' tea arrived and he poured it straight into his cup.

'I don't understand why Alan is insisting,' he said. 'I can't believe it's happening in any other industry. Why are we being singled out? Maybe if I spoke to him myself I could explain.'

'I don't think that's a good idea. Alan can be quite fiery. Just think about it. Autonomous vehicles will be the norm in, what, ten years' time? Everyone will have them and we will be totally reliant on them to get us from one place to another and to transport things across the country. Blind people, sick people, old people, they will be getting into these vehicles too. Alan's job is to protect the public.'

'Alan's job is to administer transport…'

'Which necessarily includes road safety.'

'So you are telling me that BAE and Rolls Royce have welcomed the Ministry of Defence in to vet their security? Or British Airways has allowed the CAA to probe its systems?'

'Frankly, I haven't a clue. I just know that Alan is not to be moved! It's just to take a peek, nothing more.'

'What kind of peek?'

'We send some computer geeks into your offices for a couple of days.'

'A couple of days!'

'We could do it while you were away. You wouldn't even have to see them.'

'And who are these computer geeks?'

'They work for us.'

'They're probably contractors, with no allegiance to anyone. I handpick my staff.'

'You think that makes them incorruptible?'

'And I pay well.'

'No one is incorruptible. I've learned that after twenty years in the Civil Service. But I can assure you, there is no more risk of a leak than with your own staff. And it's only what you're planning to share with the other car manufacturers, in any event. Or that's what you said?'

'I choose what we share with the others, and it's the minimum. I don't just open the doors and invite them in and spill our innermost secrets. No.'

'I don't see how we can move forward with SEDA if you don't agree.'

'Was this all because of Dr Fielding? Because I might just pay him a visit myself.'

'It's not just Dr Fielding. I can't provide details as it's confidential.' Peter fixed James with a serious stare. 'But there have been lots of memos on this from multiple sources. Hacking is a serious concern.'

'And unfounded. It's all in hand.'

'Is that your final word, then?'

James downed his tea. He wanted to bang the cup down and storm out. Instead, he shoved it to the centre of the table.

'I'll sound out the others early next week,' he said. 'We have another meeting.'

'And you'll let me know?'

'Yes. I'll let you know.'

***

After James' hasty departure, Peter ordered another slice of baklava. He knew he shouldn't, but he would walk the long way back to the office and his diet, strictly enforced at home by his wife, Fiona, was making him listless and grouchy.

He checked that no one remotely interesting-looking was present in the café before making his call.

'Hello. Is that Toby Barnes?' Peter leaned back in his chair and scratched the area around his belly button. 'We haven't spoken before. My name is Peter Mears. I work for the Department of Transport.'

'Yes, that's right. "Cinderella". You do know.

'...Thing is. I think it would be useful if you and I could meet. Do you think that would be possible?...

'...Oh no. It would be better if he didn't know about it just yet. I'll explain everything then...

'...Very good. I'll send you an invite.'

14

Toby sat in Martine's kitchen on a bar stool, his knee jogging up and down, concealed below the worktop. Martine was at the stove, stirring the contents of a large wok, into which she was liberally splashing various mysterious liquids. Nearby, she had positioned a remote-control handset and she flitted industriously from one song to another, the walls vibrating with the pounding rhythm of her hip hop playlist.

Martine turned around, beamed at Toby and re-filled his glass. This was Toby's third. He couldn't remember now precisely what ingredients she had mentioned throwing into the mix. He knew that it was some kind of margarita, as he could taste vodka and lime juice, and it just kind of slid down so effortlessly he was not going to refuse.

Martine hummed to herself as she worked, and he wondered if he had misjudged her. Here, in her kitchen, without her earrings or boots, with her wild hair tied back, she seemed, well, normal and relaxed; any celestial or diva qualities subsumed by her domestic persona.

By the time Martine placed the sizzling beef in front of him and turned the volume down on their musical accompaniment, he was already at the off-balance, not-totally-in-control-of-his-mouth stage and in danger of moving into the hysterical giggling phase.

'Thish looksh good,' he said, picking up his fork and shovelling up some noodles, failing to notice a large chilli until after its heat had seared the delicate underside of his tongue.

'Oh, it's just something I rustled up,' Martine said. 'James likes it.'

Toby ate some more, the noodles sliding awkwardly off his fork and flicking sauce across his cheek.

'Here.' Martine dabbed Toby's face with a paper napkin.

Toby coughed distractedly. His mother was the only one who had ever wiped his face, until now.

'I'm so pleased you've come,' she drawled. 'It's always so hard to find you at the office. Sometimes I think you're hiding.'

'James keeps me busy,' Toby said.

'Look, I have a confession to make.' She lay down her fork and gazed at Toby over her cocktail.

'OK.' Toby swallowed his mouthful of food, even though he had not chewed it sufficiently well. His half-sozzled brain had reasoned that the chilli may have less impact if it passed through his system making minimal contact with his already burning tongue.

'It wasn't just that I wanted to run my idea past you, see what you thought. I hoped you might help me develop it further.'

'Oh. OK.' Toby's voice came out weaker than expected and he sipped at his cocktail to clear his throat.

'James is always so busy.'

'Sounds sensible to talk to me then. What's the idea?'

'Do you like the beef?' she asked suddenly.

'Yes. It's really delicious,' Toby slurred.

'So. Well, you're not to laugh.'

'I promish I won't laugh.'

'All right. This is what I was thinking.'

***

Toby woke up in the middle of the night. He was alone in bed in a strange bedroom and he had no recollection of how he had got there or of having gone through any of his bedtime routine. He peeked under the covers; he was naked, his clothes sprawled across a chair by the window. He tried hard to recall anything which would provide a clue as to where he might be and then he remembered dinner and Martine.

He stumbled over to the window and peered out. Although it was still dark, the well-lit driveway confirmed to him that he was still at the Salisburys' residence. Crossing the room again en route to the bathroom, his foot nudged something soft on the floor. He bent down to pick it up, transporting it with him into the glare of the bathroom strip light. It took seconds for him to register that it was a piece of clothing. Toby held it up in both hands. It was a champagne-coloured silk camisole with lace edging. The fabric rippled at his gentle caress. It exuded sultry, seductive sexiness. Suddenly, the realisation hit him like a brick; it was Martine's. It must be. She was the only woman who lived in this house. Martine's underwear had been lying on the floor of his bedroom.

He closed the bathroom door tightly behind him, the need to

pee taking over momentarily and preventing him from thinking straight. Only afterwards did he tiptoe back out into his room and check for any other signs of Martine. Thankfully, he found none. He was half way back to bed, when he realised he was still holding the camisole. He wrenched the bedroom door open, flung it out on to the landing and returned to his bed, desperately hoping that he and Martine had not…what?

God. What had he done? James was a black belt in one of the martial arts. Toby couldn't remember now which one, but he was fairly sure it was the one in which they used nunchucks. Carol had once whispered to him that she had seen a pair in James' desk. And there were cameras everywhere in the house, weren't there? He'd counted at least three on the drive on the way in. He switched on the bedside lamp and directed its beam around the room, sending a search light into all the far away corners. He couldn't immediately see anything, but you could hide a camera anywhere these days.

Whose room was this? Martine had told him. He tried to focus but a sharp pain was traversing his temple and the light was making him feel nauseous. *Zac, that's right. Their youngest son. How old was Zac now? Twelve or thirteen. Surely they wouldn't spy on their own son? Maybe James had set the camera up and Martine didn't even know about it. Sometimes parents hid them in soft toys. There was a teddy, of sorts, on the dressing table.* Aagh! He leaped up again, ignoring the wave of dizziness which almost overwhelmed him, picked it up, squeezed it and was relieved to find it soft in all the right places. Even so, he stuffed it inside the wardrobe.

Returning to bed one more time, Toby tried to focus. *What had they been talking about before he got so drunk?* He wanted to remember. Martine had been asking him for advice. She had a plan and she had asked for his help. Slowly, as he allowed his head to flop onto the pillow and his shoulders to sink into the memory foam, it began to come back to him, one piece at a time.

15

'SIDWELL HOUSE ortho clinic, how can I help you?' Therese's voice cracked around the edges as she uttered the words for the first time in five months.

'Yes. We can fit you in, Mr Kelly...

'...It is. Yes, thank you. I'm very well...

'...A little girl...

'...I'm in today, more days next week. And I'll be back properly next month.' Therese realised as she made the announcement that she hadn't yet discussed any of this with Neil.

'How about 10 o'clock next Tuesday the 10th?...

...Great. See you then.'

Therese felt a curious sense of pride at having completed her first call successfully, but there was no one to tell. Ella, the other receptionist, had disappeared five minutes ago and not yet returned. She double-checked she had entered Mr Kelly's appointment properly. The practice had brought in a new booking system since her maternity leave began and she'd only had half an hour's training.

Then she checked the cupboards behind the reception area to make sure they had plenty of toothbrushes and dental sticks. She noticed that only two packets of the red TePes, the most popular size, remained. She scribbled a reorder note to the practice manager.

Ella returned with two mugs of coffee and handed her one.

'You don't take sugar, do you? But I put in extra milk the way you like it.'

'Oh thanks. That's so kind of you.'

'Biscuit?' Ella offered her the packet of Oreos she had tucked under her armpit and Therese took one.

'I bet you don't ever get time for coffee at home, with three little ones,' Ella said.

'No. I can't eat biscuits either, not without having to give them to the kids first. And we're trying not to let them have a lot of sugar. Not just because I work here,' she laughed, 'but because, well, it's not good for them generally. All this stuff about childhood obesity.'

Ella nodded her understanding.

'Oh.' Therese said. 'I saw Mrs Titian is coming in at 11.30. I wasn't sure if you knew that she's terrified of dogs. We used to have a note on the old system. To make sure that we don't give her an appointment next to someone we know brings their dog, like Mr Bygraves.'

'You're right. It has dropped off. I'll sort it out. I think Mr Bygraves' dog died anyway.'

'That's a shame.'

'It was very old. He practically had to drag it in here, literally. Last time it sat down just outside the door and wouldn't move.

Maybe we smell like the vet, all the anaesthetic. Um, do you know when you're coming back, properly that is?'

'I'm not sure. I'll be in a few mornings next week.'

'It's just, well, we've had people covering for you. But it's much nicer having you here. And you know a lot of things, like the Mrs Titian stuff.'

Therese walked over to the seating area, where she tidied the newspapers on the low table in front of her and lined the chairs up. Then she sat down again and took a draught of coffee, before checking through the appointments for the rest of the day.

'Soon,' she said. 'I need to sort out my childcare, but I'm really hoping to come back soon.'

16

CONSTANCE was reading through some papers for a new client accused of shoplifting, when her phone rang. She ignored it at first, and by the time her curiosity had overpowered her will to resist, and she had scrambled to retrieve it from the bowels of her handbag, it had stopped. But the name of the caller, *Jermain*, remained, emblazoned across her screen. As she contemplated what her brother might want, he called a second time. Constance checked the door was closed, before sitting back and tucking the phone into her ear.

'Hello,' she began, with the lump which accompanied most of her conversations with Jermain firmly lodged in her throat. And, as anticipated, the line was poor, suggesting he was speaking long-distance or from some underground bunker. There was probably a simple explanation for the weak connection, Constance reflected, but she would never forget that he had once called her from a cupboard in a basement in Colombia, where he was holed up while a gun fight erupted outside. They had been cut off partway through and she hadn't known whether he was alive or dead until he turned up in the public gallery at one of her hearings, two weeks later, and waved at her enthusiastically over everyone's heads.

'You didn't answer first time,' Jermain began.

'I'm at work,' Constance replied.

'Me too.'

'Oh?'

'Yeah. Sorry I've been out of touch for a while. I'm in Swindon.'

'Is it nice there?'

'I've met this girl and I'm staying with her for a few weeks, but I need a favour.'

'That's a surprise.'

'I just need to use your address. Can you send it to me?'

'Why do you need my address?'

'Don't be so suspicious. It's for my payslips. I told you. I have a job, a proper job.'

'And you can't use the Swindon address?'

'I've only just met her. I don't want to ask.'

'So it's OK for you to move in, but not to use the address.'

'Don't be like that. I didn't think it was much to ask from my sister.'

Constance tapped her fingers on the table.

'You know I'm a lawyer, right? So, if this is anything illegal...'

'It's just an address for my payslips...and other official stuff. I promise.'

Constance squeezed her eyes tightly closed. When she opened them again, the world still looked the same.

'All right. That's fine. You have it anyway, but I'll send it again. Maybe then you'll come by some time. It would be nice to see you. As you're only in Swindon.'

'Sure. In a week or two when I'm a bit more settled.'

'What is this new job?'

'Sales and marketing. Pays well. Things are looking good.'

'Will you call Mum?'

Now there was silence from Jermain's end of the line, permeated by background traffic noise. When he finally answered he was less upbeat.

'It's been so long I wouldn't know where to start,' he said. 'She'll ask me loads of questions.'

'She misses you. Call her. It's her birthday next week.'

'Maybe.'

'And come and see me soon.'

The line went dead. No asking after how she was. No commitment to visit. No *thanks*. No *goodbye*. But that was Jermain's style. Constance contemplated telling her mother that he had called, that he was fine, had a new job and was living in Swindon, although she only had his word for all of that. Her mum would be upset that she had been singled out for a call. Would that be better than no news at all?

She retrieved Jermain's number again on her phone, typed in her address and pressed 'send'. Then she buried her phone in her handbag, zipped it up and returned to her papers.

17

'How was dinner at the boss' house?' Juan asked, as Toby slumped down on the sofa after a full day of failing dismally to concentrate at work. At least James had not been there, so he had managed to slink around without being subject to scrutiny.

Looking around him with the fresh eyes of a day's absence, Toby noticed, without displeasure, that Juan had deposited a few of his own things around the room. A brightly-painted, ceramic skull had found its way onto the coffee table and a small, rotund bowl with a watermelon motif now sat in the centre of the bar. And, in front of the sofa, hugging the laminate flooring, lay a cream-coloured rug with a geometric pattern in a rich shade of plum.

'Is it OK?' Juan followed Toby's line of vision. 'When you were gone and I was alone, it made me feel more comfortable. But I can take it away if you don't like it.'

'No. It's fine. I like it. Very…authentic. And can I smell dinner?'

'I'm just making something I like. To say thank you to you for letting me stay here. It's…well Rosa, my wife, she used to make it. So I should say that it's also good, what do they say, "therapy", for me too.'

Toby laughed. He could see that he would enjoy having Juan around, although he might struggle to eat much dinner this evening.

'When is James back from Germany?'

'He flies back later tonight.'

'Should I put something in his diary about Project Connect?'

'Why don't you and I look at it together first, like we said? But not now, tomorrow. Don't want to spoil dinner.'

'Sure no problem. You've worked with James a long time?'

'Three years.'

'You must have been so young when you started. What's he like to work for?'

'He's very decisive, always knows what he wants. He expects a lot from his employees, though. He wants to make SEDA huge, that's his…well that's our aim.'

'You know people told me not to take the job…at SEDA.'

Juan took two beers from the fridge, opened them and handed one to Toby.

'Did they? Why not?'

'Small company, British-owned, said it's not going anywhere. But I thought it's good to get in somewhere small, at the beginning, help it grow. And if I'd gone to one of the big boys I'd just be a nothing, no face. At SEDA I get to work on all the latest projects, have meetings with the boss…and to share a flat with the deputy.' He saluted Toby with a broad grin, which Toby returned.

'What is Mrs Salisbury like then?' Juan said. 'I can say to you, I hope, that I think she is a very beautiful woman. She comes in to the lab, seems interested in all our work.'

'Martine?' Toby felt his face burning up. 'Is she? Yes, I suppose she is attractive.'

'How was she away from work? She was friendly?'

'Very friendly, yes.' Toby took a large gulp of beer, even though he didn't want one. 'She cooked for me too…which was thoughtful of her. She has a lot of ideas…business ideas.'

Juan flung himself down onto the settee with a thump, but Toby remained standing, holding the beer.

'Is everything OK?' Juan asked. 'When you didn't come home I was a bit worried. I don't want to be like your mother, but I wasn't sure if I should call you. Back in the USA they tell us London is more dangerous than New York.'

Toby swigged half-heartedly from his beer again. The door to Juan's room was open and he could see a garish quilt cover had replaced the grey one he had provided.

'I drank too much so I stayed over there,' Toby said, finally sitting down and placing the beer down too, 'in one of the spare rooms. Felt like shit all day. Some cocktail, probably Mexican.'

Juan giggled.

'Can we keep it to ourselves, that I slept there? James knows all about it but, well I wouldn't want other people to get the wrong idea.'

Juan picked up the skull and waved it close to Toby's face.

'Sure. I can keep a secret,' he said, laughing. Toby looked away.

'Is something wrong?' Juan asked.

Toby sighed heavily and ran his fingers through his hair.

'No, just hungover,' he said. 'What time will dinner be ready? I'll go get showered and changed first.'

PART TWO

18

Juan was back at work, sitting behind his desk, watching video after video of SEDA's cars moving around London's roads. As was his habit now, first he watched them in regular format, from film captured on each car's elaborate camera system. Then, he studied the coloured boxes of the parallel digital format, their position and trajectory and whether and how well each green box, representing a test SEDA, navigated its way around them.

His current subject was progressing along the north circular in a clockwise direction, and he scrutinised every action as it, correctly, predicted the movement of a lorry into its lane and braked accordingly, then moved out when its own lane became blocked by slow moving traffic. He was pleased with today's session. There had been nothing unusual, erratic or worrying. No hazards they hadn't anticipated.

He could only manage around thirty minutes of this level of concentration at a time. But that was fine as he had a number of other tasks to complete. Project Connect also encompassed exchanging information with other manufacturers and trial runs connecting up with their vehicles. His Spanish speaking had been a tremendous advantage on this part of the venture, helping him build rapport with the US-based operations, as well as with SEDA's own small outfit in Madrid.

Toby had let slip that while James was in Germany he would meet some of those contacts and Juan wanted to ensure that he was invited along on the next trip. James couldn't possibly know the right questions to ask the technical staff, but Juan needed to work out the best way of demonstrating this to James, without appearing insulting.

He already had a few proposals for improvements to the system in any event. He knew Toby wanted to hear them first, but he might hold back one or two things for James' ears only. He didn't know Toby very well yet and the last thing he wanted was for Toby to appropriate his ideas and present them to James as his own.

Next up was a new podcast on hacking, put together by two 'white knights' who were keen to illustrate potential weaknesses in the latest autonomous vehicles. Juan had concerns that SEDA's system was not as robust as it might be, despite James having attended the latest conferences and upgraded their software as a result. He knew how much value he could add in the cyber security space too, if only James would allow him. But James liked substance, he could see that already. So he needed to ensure he could back up his anxieties with hard evidence, before he said anything at all on that subject. And for now, Connect had to take priority.

19

James' flight from Berlin had been delayed and he had only managed three snatched hours of sleep at home. Arriving at the office, he diverted from his usual routine and took a stroll outside in the fresh air. After all, he had chosen this location because of its green outlook, but he so seldom had the opportunity to take advantage of it himself.

At the far side of the man-made lake, he sat down on a newly-installed bench. He questioned why he did not do this more often; take ten minutes 'time out' to reconnect with nature.

As he sat quietly, enjoying the warmth of the early autumn sun on his face, a family of mallards, with the mother leading the procession, waddled past him and hopped one by one into the water. The last duckling, and by far the smallest, was lagging behind and the mother gave him a sharp 'hurry up' call before turning her back on him and striking out for the centre of the lake. 'Shorty', as James nicknamed him, struggled to catch up. His lateral swaying was more pronounced than the others and by the time he reached the water's edge, the rest of the brood were long gone.

Shorty stopped and spun through 360 degrees, probably wondering where everyone was.

'They've gone that way,' James told him, flicking his wrist, amused by his own attempts to communicate with the duckling.

A loud quack from the water sent Shorty back on track, but as he tried to clear some weeds in the shallows, he suddenly lost his balance entirely and turned upside down. For a few seconds, his head was fully submerged, his tiny legs thrashing the air ineffectually.

Then Shorty came up for breath, but he couldn't right himself. He lay, on his side, one leg hopelessly tangled beneath him. James gazed out over the expanse of water; the mother duck was some distance away and preoccupied marshalling her remaining young. Shorty tried desperately to free his leg, but to no avail, and his head plunged downwards again.

Suddenly, a young woman in brightly-coloured Lycra, flashed past James and knelt down at the water's edge. She picked up the tiny duckling and lifted him high out of the water. She surveyed the lake, ran twenty metres on and, as James watched, she stretched out and set him down on the surface, ensuring he cleared the weeds. Shorty paddled out towards his mother, who turned and came to meet him, quacking angrily all the time, no doubt scolding him for his tardiness. James moistened his lips with his tongue. The young woman cast a quizzical look in his direction, before running on.

James turned his attention back to the factory. From his vantage point, he could see the reception staff chatting away, Jane was on the telephone, Carol was accepting a delivery. He could also see two of the factory workers sharing a cigarette at the back of the assembly hangar. He checked his watch; it was their official break time so he wouldn't complain.

Another woman in sports kit sprinted by, breathing heavily, and her appearance dragged him back to the Shorty episode. James peered across the lake, but the ducks had now disappeared. Even so, he had retained the image of the duckling in the weeds, struggling and helpless, and it troubled him more than he could explain.

He wasn't sure whether he was an animal lover or not; they had no pets, he hadn't been allowed them as a boy and with their own children being away so much, he had never considered keeping one now. And he liked his roast beef as much as the next man, although he would never tolerate cruelty to animals.

The duckling had survived, but only because the woman jogger had intervened. Of course, in nature, there were many casualties; it was part of natural selection. But human beings had a duty to protect those weaker than themselves, including animals. James was certain there was something about it in the Bible. That was what separated humans from other animals.

No, what really bothered him was his own inertia. Faced with a dilemma which could easily have resulted in the duckling's death, he had merely sat and pondered, taken perhaps a macabre interest in what might happen next. There wasn't even any downside for him personally. He just had to step forward and pick up the tiny, helpless creature, as the young woman had done. But, instead, he had been paralysed. And perhaps that was the problem with his business too. He simply wasn't dynamic enough any more. He was sitting back and watching and letting other less able people pave the way for what was coming next. Worst of all, being brutally honest, at the moment it just wasn't working.

James had never been superstitious and his contact with religion had begun and ended with school prayers, but as he checked his watch and marched back towards his place of work, he queried if this had been a sign, if it was significant and if it meant something. And, if so, if he should do anything at all about it.

***

'Hi James. How was the trip?'

Toby poured them each a glass of sparkling water and hovered by James' arm. James downed it, smacked his lips and motioned to Toby for a refill.

'We did make progress,' James began, 'but I am worried we are falling behind. Google and Tesla are already fully licensed in France, and Germany is probably only a month behind. I so wanted our first European launch to be here in the UK, but I think we may have to cut our losses and begin somewhere else.'

Toby nodded his understanding. 'Are they willing to share?' he asked.

'Share?'

'Data. Their processes.'

James stared at Toby. 'Who have you been talking to?' he asked, sharply.

'No one. I…I thought that was what you went to talk about, with the other car manufacturers.'

'Look. They will work with us once we are out on the road. Until then, they consider us nothing, of no importance. And the damned German rep, do you know what he said?'

'No.' Toby leaned in, pleased at James' sudden and unprompted willingness to share confidences.

'He tried to exclude me. Said that they couldn't risk discussing details around me until we had the green light. Said if our own government didn't support us, we weren't in the same league as them. One of the others, Spanish guy, persuaded him to back down. He told me he'd been talking to Juan. I think he was impressed. I knew Juan was a good hire. Otherwise I would have had to pack up and leave there and then. God, I think I need something stronger to drink!'

Toby sat back. Was that a cue for him to try to find some alcohol? Evidently not, as James sipped furiously at his fizzy water.

'At least I got their agreement for their UK representatives not to share anything about cyber security with the Department for Transport, for now anyway. Peter won't be happy. He's the civil service intermediary between us and Alan, the Minister for Transport. I've told you about him before.'

'He's the man you meet every few months. The "Cinderella" project.'

'Yes, among others. I doubt the Minister'll let this drop, though. But now I have everyone else's support, he probably has no choice. Ah! Alan Tillinghurst. Couldn't happen to a nicer guy.' His eyes wandered around the room before alighting on Toby.

'James?' Toby's hands shook as he attempted to put into words his thoughts of the last few days. He resorted to sitting on them, as James' heavy gaze swung around to hold him fast.

'Hm.'

'You have so much on at the moment. You could lean on me a bit more.'

'Ha!' James' half-laugh, half-shout echoed around the room.

Toby's legs started to quiver. But then James sat back in his chair.

'You are absolutely right,' he said. 'Thank you, that's much appreciated.'

Toby stood up, hyperventilating but relieved.

'I could lean on you more and I should. From now on, "Operation Lean on Toby" is underway. I've another Cinderella meeting coming up in a few weeks, with Peter and the others. Fancy helping me out? I warn you. It's likely to be quite tricky if we're making a stand on the data stuff, and it would be good to know someone was watching my back.'

'Yes. I know I can help.'

'And, Juan. Why don't you catch up with him, find out how he's getting on? You can brief me together.'

Toby's eyes sparkled.

'Yes. Of course. I won't let you down,' he said.

'I'm sure you won't,' James replied.

***

James strode along the chilly corridors towards the technology laboratory, at the furthest corner of the site. He knew he had asked Toby to catch up with Juan, all part of his new resolution to delegate more, but he suddenly decided there would be no harm in speaking to Juan, himself, too, just for five minutes. As the doors swung open, he thought he heard the tinkling laughter of a woman.

Martine was sitting in one corner of the room, watching a video on a laptop perched on her knees. One of the programmers was at work nearby. She turned around at his entrance.

'Oh hello darling!' She paused her screen, shifted the laptop on to the desk and sashayed towards him, kissing him lightly on the cheek. 'You left so early this morning.'

'I didn't want to wake you,' James replied. 'What are you up to?'

'Oh this. It's just some stuff…' She waved her hand over in the direction of the technician, who had taken his headphones off when James entered.

'Juan,' he said.

'Thank you, Juan. It's just some stuff Juan told me about, that's going into the next model. More shiny metal around the wheels. Maybe I'll get an early upgrade. I was going to come and find you when I finished. I thought we could have lunch together, if you're not too busy.'

James scrutinised the frozen image on Martine's screen. 'It is an incredible piece of kit,' he said. 'Looks a bit different to the last time I saw it. But not sure why you're looking at bodywork in the IT lab?' James stared pointedly at Juan.

'The design team asked me to double-check that the new shape and the added chrome won't impact the sensors on the wheel arches,' Juan explained.

'Oh, yes, of course. And does it?'

'Not as far as I can see, but I've asked for a few more tests to be run.'

'Good.'

'Can I help you with anything else, Mr Salisbury?' Juan asked.

'Well I… There was something, but it can wait. But also, I wanted to thank you. You've clearly made an impression on some of the others in the Connect team who I met on my trip.'

'Oh. I'm so pleased if it was useful. I have some ideas…'

'And I know I said you should report only to me, but I've just asked Toby to catch up with you first, later today. Hope that's OK. And I want to discuss a new project with you, just the two of us.'

'Sure.' Juan frowned before regaining his composure. 'How about tomorrow?'

'Tomorrow is great. Put something in my diary then, if there's a half-hour slot.'

'I will.'

Martine was now standing by the door.

'Didn't you want to watch the rest of your video?' James asked her.

'Not now you're here.'

He opened the door and they walked together back along the corridor, arm in arm.

'How was your trip?' she asked.

'The usual. Did you manage all right on your own?'

'Oh yes. I watched some Netflix and had an early night. You haven't forgotten we have tickets for the theatre tonight? With Peter and Fiona.'

'No, I hadn't forgotten. Not great timing though. You might have to nudge me if I drop off.' He patted her hand affectionately and kissed the side of her head.

20

Toby had received two messages from Peter since they'd met, the second one marked with a red exclamation mark, and, having read and digested them, he wasn't sure what to do. He had tried his father again but received another answerphone message. To be fair, his dad had called him back twice since his pizza-alone night, but they kept missing each other. It was probably just as well, as he didn't really want to let on what a predicament he was in, and he might let it slip if they did connect.

Toby had seen Martine in the office on the morning of James' return, but she had made no attempt to approach him or contact him and he was certainly not going to make the first move. Of course, he could try confiding in Juan, currently ensconced in the shower singing 'Despacito' at the top of his voice, and with all the right words, but Toby was reticent about sharing so much with such a new acquaintance.

And Juan didn't take life very seriously, Toby had discovered. Absolutely wonderful when you wanted to let your hair down or get some advice on what to say to a prospective love interest but not much help when bigger issues were at stake. And while the girls had flocked towards Juan on their first serious night out together, no doubt attracted by his olive complexion, flamboyant style and skinny jeans, and this had led directly to Toby bringing 'Marion' home for the night, he would have much preferred Nita, Juan's conquest. Thankfully, Marion had left early the next morning and had not called again.

Poor Toby. That was not all that was bothering him. He had pretended to follow everything Juan had told him about Project Connect, and Juan had been patient with his explanation, before joking around again, and suggesting they crack open a few beers, but Toby didn't understand it all. He could follow the theory of linking to the test cars, although he doubted he could accurately reproduce the necessary steps himself, but he really couldn't comprehend how the cars communicated with each other and what channels needed to be open, in order for them to do so. He wondered if he could conduct some independent research, quietly. It would be embarrassing to ask Juan to explain it all again.

Toby checked the time. They were supposed to be leaving in fifteen minutes for a party of one of Juan's friends, and Toby had been looking forward to it, till he saw Peter's messages. He plucked at his hair then he squeezed his own biceps. Not bad, given he did nothing other than the occasional game of tennis. But he should probably shower too if he was going to look at his best.

He muted his phone, turned it face down and left it on the kitchen worktop.

'Juan? How much longer are you going to be?' he called out. 'I'd like a shower too. And I am the landlord.'

21

James and Martine greeted Peter and Fiona in the foyer of the National Theatre. Usually they would meet for a drink beforehand, but James had decided instead to freshen up at home, and since becoming teetotal a few years previously, he found bars a real struggle, even though he would never let on.

'Ooh, don't you look fabulous,' Fiona kissed Martine on the cheek. And James thought Fiona had never spoken a truer word. Martine was dressed all in black, her skin-tight, leather pencil skirt and polo-neck jumper accentuating her curves and her high stilettos, which brought her almost up to his height, emphasising her slender calves.

'You too,' Martine replied, charitably and Fiona blushed. 'I love that lipstick. Where's it from?'

The two women disappeared off to the ladies together, chatting away, and James rolled his programme up into a cylinder. He was feeling particularly anxious this evening, not only because of the way his last meeting with Peter had ended, but also because he worried Peter might have already heard from the other manufacturers that they would not conform. Although perhaps that would be sufficient for Alan to relent and confirm SEDA was on the government list after all.

'It's so good the girls get on well,' Peter commented, and James reflected on how much Martine detested being referred to as a 'girl'.

'Yes. What do you think they're talking about?'

'I haven't a clue.'

'What does Fiona do again? I've forgotten.'

'She works in marketing, for a pharmaceutical company.'

'That's right. That must be interesting. Does she bounce her ideas off you?' As James said the words, he stifled a laugh. Peter's belly was certainly ample enough for the trampoline metaphor to be appropriate.

'I don't let her talk about work. She's lucky she's allowed to have a job.'

James frowned. Then Peter burst out laughing.

'Had you there, for a moment, didn't I? Yes, she's always singing jingles and making me watch hours of advertisements. It's a good antidote to my day job. Is Martine still working at that homeless shelter?

'Yes. She seems to find it rewarding, more than her modelling career ever was, so she says.'

'Good for her. Not everyone can be academic, can they? I bet she was stunning when you first met her. Still a very attractive woman, if you don't mind me saying. You're a lucky man.'

James managed half a smile. Was it really acceptable for Peter to tell him how much he admired Martine's looks? He wasn't certain, these days, what was allowed. Martine and Fiona returned, still deep in conversation.

'I just had a wonderful idea,' Peter said, as they entered the auditorium together. 'Fi, you could use Martine in one of your commercials, couldn't you? You're always saying you need older, presentable women who've lived a bit, not just those blond, wispy types who look like they would blow away in the wind.'

Fiona frowned and Martine did her best not to appear affronted. 'That's what we were just discussing, actually,' Fiona said, winking at Martine.

'Oh,' Peter appeared genuinely surprised.

'I'd love to,' Martine replied. 'We're going to talk about it over coffee this week.'

Martine allowed Peter and Fiona to enter their row first, before following herself, placing James at the end of their group. James fidgeted as his knees knocked against the seat in front and he resigned himself to another evening sitting twisted and askew, which would have to be fixed by some judicious yoga later on.

'You OK?' Martine asked, behind her hand, after sharing another joke with Fiona.

'Mm. You're not really going to do a pharmaceutical advertisement are you?' he asked.

Martine patted his knee.

'Spoilsport,' she said. 'I think it sounds like fun.'

'I'm not sure we should have come,' James muttered under his breath.

'Just focus on the play. It's had rave reviews. Can Peter take a look at the programme?' Martine nudged James' arm.

James handed the programme down the line, with apologies for its crumpled state although, in reality, he wasn't at all sorry. Peter never bought his own programme or stumped up for the interval drinks, however many times James treated him to events like this. He would insist that it was 'protocol', not wanting to be seen to be preferring one business contact over another, but James knew it was because he was mean.

For a short moment, as the music began and an aged Salieri strode onto the stage and raised his arms as if conducting the orchestra inside his own head, James wondered if Peter would pass the programme back with a copy of the government list tucked inside, with SEDA's name right at the top. Then he would enjoy the rest of the evening, safe in the knowledge that the future of his company was secure.

Maybe he would ask Peter subtly in the interval about the progress of the list, drop it into the conversation, allude to it in passing? He knew it was a bad idea but the thought that he could ask, if he wished to, sustained him throughout the first half of the play.

LONDON, 10 OCTOBER 2018

22

JAMES STRODE purposefully out of the modern office block as the minute hand on his Omega Seamaster nudged 2.35pm. He had been visiting one of his suppliers and was delighted to see that they had taken on board all his suggestions for the new design of the seats for the latest model.

He hung his jacket on the hook in the back of his car, smoothing it down and checking in his top pocket for his favourite pen. Then he walked around to the passenger side, wiping away some stray blades of grass, which had attached themselves to his back bumper, and deposited his brief case, iPad and notebook on the seat. He tapped the car, companionably, on its roof, twice, before retracing his steps to the driver's side.

Once inside the car, he allowed his back to sink into the upholstery, then closed his eyes and double-checked he was feeling supported and comfortable, even though he had only arrived two hours earlier and, to his knowledge, no one had touched his car in between. Next, he reviewed the position of wing mirrors and rear-view mirror before pressing the ignition.

'Hello. I'm VERA, your voice-activated, enhanced, road-experience assistant.' The woman's voice rang out from the four speakers situated in the front part of the car.

'Hello VERA. You sound as perky as ever. It's James. Back to the office please.'

'Hello James. I'll calculate time to destination for you. That should take twenty-three minutes if we go by the most direct route. Is that OK?'

'Yes. Thank you, VERA. I'm surprised it's so quick. Same as last time, when we travelled at eleven. Are you sure?'

'Current time to destination, twenty-three minutes exactly.'

'OK. You're the boss.'

'Please put on your seat belt and I will let you know when we are near our destination. Would you like to listen to the radio?'

'The usual please.'

'Is "the usual please" Radio Four?

'Do you know, I'm going to be radical today, VERA.'

'I'm sorry. I didn't understand which channel you required.'

'My fault. I wasn't clear. Let's try Classic FM, at least for the first five minutes. I might as well try and relax before I get to my next meeting. God knows there will be little time to relax once I'm there.'

'Switching to Classic FM. Classic FM is playing Gustav Holst's *The Planets*.'

'Is it really? Which movement?'

'It is "Mars, The Bringer of War."'

'I think that's a little heavier than I was anticipating. How about you go to my Spotify playlist and play that aria I like from

The Pearl Fishers?'

'Searching for *Pearl Fishers* aria.'

'Ah!'

As the strings began to play, James unfastened his top button and reclined his chair just one click. Then he reached over to the passenger seat and grabbed his iPad.

'James. Would you like the seat warmer on?'

'No thanks, VERA.'

'There is chilled water in the box next to you. Do help yourself. Can I help you with anything else?'

'No. That's everything for now.'

'The compartment is currently maintained at twenty degrees Celsius. If you wish to change the temperature please let me know, beginning your request "can you change the temperature please?".'

'I understand but it's good for now.'

'Temperature outside is 18 degrees Celsius.'

'Great. Thank you.'

'Should I let you know when we are approaching "Villa Italia"? Last time you purchased an Americano coffee.'

'No thank you. I don't drink coffee in the afternoons any more. You should know that. I have enough problems sleeping as it is. I should like you to be quiet now and let me work. If I need anything else I shall let you know.'

'Thank you, James. If you wish to switch off VERA, please press the red button to the right of the steering wheel. Wishing you a pleasant journey.'

23

Therese began the walk home from the dental surgery. The sunlight was seeping through the plumy clouds and she draped her jacket over her arm.

Her back was sore and her breasts were swollen, but she couldn't help but succumb to the smile which tugged at the edges of her mouth. She had done it. A second morning at work this week and looking forward to the third. Three children under five, well including five, and her brain was still functioning. In fact, it was feeling decidedly spritely and raring to go, although admittedly the rest of her was fading fast.

She felt the familiar buzz of an incoming message on her phone but resisted the temptation to take a look. She had told her mum she'd most likely be back by 1.30, but Ella had had to rush in to help when one of the patients felt unwell, so she'd run slightly over. She picked up her step, just a little, not wanting to rush, savouring her last minutes of relative freedom, flicking at her hair with the tips of her fingers, thinking that she might enquire if her mother-in-law would come over for a couple of hours next week, so she could get her lowlights done.

As she turned into her street, she quickened her pace even more and felt her heart rate begin to rise. A rush of endorphins and she was buoyed along by her own sense of wellbeing and optimism.

Jacquie, her mother, was seated in an armchair feeding Ruby when she arrived home. Therese's smile quickly dropped away.

'Mum! I asked you not to feed her again,' she wailed.

'She was hungry love. I'm sorry. You can express, can't you?'

Therese shut her eyes tight and blinked back the tears that were threatening to escape. She pressed her hands to her breasts.

'Didn't you have a good morning?' Jacquie asked. 'You don't have to go back if it's too much for you, you know.'

Jacquie plucked the bottle gently from Ruby's lips, placed it down next to her and lifted Ruby over her shoulder. Ruby beamed at Therese and Therese wiped her eyes and sniffed.

'I did. It was really good. I can't wait to get back, actually,' she said.

Jacquie's nose wrinkled. 'You can take Ruby, if you want,' she said. 'I'm only half way through the feed. I suppose it doesn't matter if I throw the rest of the formula away.' She tapped Ruby's back lightly. Therese retreated.

'No. It's a shame to waste it. I'll go upstairs and change and then I'll get the pump. I've got a few minutes still before I go for the other two. And I don't want to spoil my work clothes, do I?'

24

MARTINE HAD arrived at the office at around 11am. Toby had noticed her flitting through the reception area with a laptop under her arm, then reviewing designs in the factory for around half an hour – not that he'd been keeping tabs on her – but then she had disappeared. He had asked each of the receptionists if they had seen her, but no one had.

Then, around 1.45, he saw her emerging from the far side of the lake, talking animatedly to Juan. They stopped halfway across the grass, with Martine pointing back along the path. She carried a jumper draped over her arm and as she shook it out, Juan suddenly raised his hands to either side of his head with his index fingers facing forwards. Then he bent over and began to paw at the ground with his foot.

Martine raced a few steps ahead. She flung her jumper out to the side of her body, jerking it up and down. Juan charged and she swept it away at the last moment, giggling uncontrollably.

Juan stumbled, almost fell but righted himself. He straightened up and snorted. Martine sprinted on a few metres more and they repeated their comic performance.

When they finally tired of their adventure, Martine directed Juan to stand next to her, while she took a quick selfie with the lake in the background. Then Juan removed something, possibly grass or dirt, from Martine's hair and their faces almost touched. Toby wasn't certain if Martine whispered something to Juan or not, her mouth was obscured by Juan's arm, but he sensed some kind of communication between the two of them. Then Juan set off, alone, in the direction of the technician's pod, waving goodbye over his shoulder and Martine continued strolling back towards the main building.

As Toby watched, his mouth dry, his pulse racing, Martine dropped her jumper onto the lawn, sat down on top of it and began to swipe wildly at the screen of her phone. At one point, gesturing excitedly with her free hand, she put it to her ear and spoke. When she had finished, she tucked her knees up tight and sat, motionless, staring out over the lake.

Toby thought about going to her, but he had no idea what he would say. He could just say hello, ask her how she was, test the water. He still hadn't spoken to her since their dinner together. She had clearly wanted to play things down, but now her open flirting with Juan confused him. What had Martine said to him? *I can't talk to you privately at work.* That was the reason she had invited him over in the first place. But it didn't seem to have put her off cavorting openly with Juan.

His phone buzzed for an incoming call and his father's name flashed up, but Toby suddenly had no appetite to speak to his father after all. He checked the time and then buried the phone in his pocket. He had places to go, people to see. As he marched smartly out of the front of the building, Martine suddenly turned in his direction. She smiled and waved. He pretended not to see her at first. Then he feigned surprise at encountering her, waved in return, got into his car and drove away.

25

James glanced up at the road. The navigation system said twenty-one minutes now until his destination, but the traffic was building up on the other carriageway. 'Going against the flow'. That was a useful analogy for his life as a whole. James had never done things the conventional way, trusting his own judgment from an early age, and sticking his neck out to prove many points over the intervening years. He knew this trait sometimes made him unpopular, but that was the price to pay if you were a man of vision and principles.

And he had never been good at delegation. He knew that. 'If a job's worth doing, it's worth doing yourself.' That had been his father's mantra and had served him well. But now was definitely the right time to reach out, just a little, to the younger members of his team. It wasn't delegation as such, more collaboration, making the best use of the skills others could bring to the table. He would take Toby along to the Cinderella session and perhaps he would even ask Juan to accompany him on the next overseas meeting, as long as he wouldn't have to engage in too much inane conversation on the journey. He would assess Juan when he gave his presentation, see what kind of travelling companion he might make, before any final decision.

A roadside sign, to his left, advertised pizza. He did a double-take before grabbing his iPad and scrolling through a few screens. When he located the one he wanted, he stared at it hard for a few seconds, before laughing to himself and picking up his phone.

Just thought I saw you on a ten-foot billboard, he wrote. *Had to check. She is your double. Take a look. She could be your...sister.* He had eschewed 'daughter', his first choice and had then written 'doppelganger' before erasing it in favour of 'sister', to keep things uncomplicated. He copied the link to the ad, hit 'send', sat back and opened up some emails.

Halfway through reading his second one, he received a message back.

Not sure I'm pleased you're looking at pictures of other women! Where r u?

On the road. Might be back late. Don't wait for me to eat. You know I only have eyes for you. He sought out an emoji of a heart; it was the kind of thing he saw others attach to their messages. Martine sent them in droves to their son Zac when he was feeling lonely. His fingers hovered over it but, in the end, he sent the message without it. Martine didn't need him to send sentimental pictures to know how much he appreciated her.

As he rounded a corner on the residential street where Haringey shifted seamlessly into Tottenham, he held up his phone in front of his face. Searching intently for some new communication, he failed to notice the road signs, warning him of work up ahead.

Twenty metres on, James glanced up and, instead of the expected grey, tarmac street scene, he was suddenly confronted with an obstacle in his lane and, behind it, a flash of colour; the pale pink hood of Ruby's pram looming loud in his sights, the canary yellow of Bertie's backpack streaking across his peripheral vision. The car shifted to the right and the colours disappeared, then it swung to the left and, this time, Therese Layton's illuminated face was before him, horror etched across it, her body bending forwards but simultaneously poised to lurch backwards. He had a split second to gasp and then the world exploded around him.

26

Chief Inspector Dawson peered through the curtains at the man lying in the hospital bed. He was propped up on three pillows and his head was turned in Dawson's direction, revealing a full shock of greying hair, a crooked, aquiline nose and a cheek sporting a large, purple swelling. Eyes closed, his breathing appeared regular but shallow.

'That's him?' he asked the nurse at his side.

'Yes. That's Mr Salisbury.'

'He doesn't look very good.'

'It's just cuts and bruises on his face, all superficial, and some broken ribs but he is quite confused. Dr Price said you could speak to him for five minutes, but if he gets upset you'll have to leave.'

'Does he know what happened?'

'He knows he was in a car accident.'

'Has anyone told him about...about the family?'

'No. I don't think so.'

'Has he had any visitors?'

'Yes. His wife came in, yesterday, not long after he arrived. She said she'd be back this morning. And a man came from his work, young he was, just before I finished my shift, but he was asleep.'

Dawson slipped through the curtains and sat down next to the patient. He honed in on the rhythmic whack of the pump sending a clear, saline solution into James' left arm, the same arm which, only yesterday afternoon, had been gripping the steering wheel of the car which had ploughed into a young family. 'Absolute carnage. He might as well have taken a loaded gun and fired it at them.' That was what Dawson had overheard an old man say, as the bodies were removed by emergency services.

Dawson leaned forward and coughed into his hand twice. James' eyelids flickered.

'Mr Salisbury. I'm Chief Inspector Dawson. Can you hear me?'

James opened his eyes.

'Yes,' he said.

'Do you know where you are?'

'In hospital.'

'Yes. We're in Dalston hospital. You had an accident, a car accident. Do you remember anything about it?'

James lifted his cheek off the pillow, groaned and then allowed it to fall back again.

'I'm not sure,' he said.

'You were in your car.'

'Vera,' he muttered, then more alarmed, 'is Vera all right?'

Dawson frowned.

'You were alone in the car. Is Vera your wife?'

'She's…' James opened his mouth and closed it, then clenched and unclenched his fist. 'I don't know,' he said finally.

'Do you remember being in your car?'

'No.'

'What's the last thing you do remember?'

James stared above Dawson to the screen monitoring his blood pressure and pulse. It showed 119 over 58, pretty normal, and his heart rate at a regular 62 beats per minute. He followed the tube snaking its way from his arm, up to the bag suspended above his bed, before returning his gaze to the screen.

'I was working at home,' he said, 'I had a meeting in London. That's it.'

'Do you know what day of the week it is?'

Dawson watched James try to moisten his lips, but he didn't want to offer him any relief from his discomfort. He satisfied himself with the conclusion that he may not be allowed any fluids in any event.

'You're the police?' James spoke slowly, shifting around so he could catch a glimpse of the ward through the narrow gap in the curtains. Then he stared at Dawson. He noticed the policeman's hands clasped together, hanging between his legs; large, fleshy hands with wide wrists.

'Yes.'

'You asked about my car. Has it been stolen?'

Dawson had known, before he sat down, that he would not sugar-coat the pill he was about to prescribe. But James was an imposing presence, even when horizontal and in a hospital gown, his resonant voice, angular frame and restless eyes unsettled the policeman.

'A woman was badly injured. Shattered pelvis. They're not sure if she'll walk again.'

'Oh God.'

'And two of her three children died when you hit them. The baby in the pram survived.'

'But who took my car?'

'No one took your car. You were driving it. You hit them with your car.'

James' eyes grew wide, he forced himself into a sitting position and gripped the sides of the bed so tightly that his knuckles turned white.

'I hit them in my car and now they're dead?' he said, the words spilling out of his mouth unchecked.

'Yes.' Dawson was impassive.

'That's impossible.'

''Fraid not. Dead at the scene.'

'You don't understand. My car can't have hit anyone, let alone killed them. Are you sure it was my car?'

'It was the car you were driving, sir. A blue car, SEDA make, registration number SAL1 2016. With extra...equipment on the roof.'

James gasped, released his hold on the side of the bed and slumped back against his pillows. Then he lurched forwards suddenly and grabbed Dawson's wrist.

'I have to get out of here,' he shouted. 'There's been a huge mistake. If I can get out of here I'm sure I can sort it all out. I must call Toby. Where's my phone?'

The nurse drew back the curtains on Dawson's side, frowned at him, released him from James' grip and eased James back to a prone position.

'Where are my clothes?' James asked her. 'Where's my phone? I want to go. Can you call Toby for me? They're probably all waiting for me in the meeting.'

'You've had a nasty bump on the head. The doctor will see you later,' the nurse said to James. 'You can't go home before then.' She turned to Dawson. 'I think you should probably leave now.'

***

Dawson stood in the lift, chastising himself for not asking James more about the car, about its special functions, before focusing on the dead children. Maybe that would have elicited a more engaged response. Too late now. While there would be plenty of time to talk once James was out of hospital, he would almost certainly have appointed a lawyer by then and might choose not to cooperate. Perhaps Dawson had missed his chance.

And because the car was so 'special', he had been forced to make an appointment with the police lawyer to talk things over, something he avoided as much as possible, as it usually heralded some breach of protocol and was followed, at the very least, by a rap over the knuckles. But their session, first thing that morning, had only led to some tentative conclusions and lots more areas of uncertainty. Dawson also reflected, just for a moment, on how he had laid it on a bit thick about Therese Layton. He had made up the part about her not walking again; the doctors had said they couldn't predict anything with certainty for a few days. So, it wasn't a lie, just a worst-case scenario.

He exited the lift deep in thought and stopped to watch the passing traffic. What were the statistics now; fifty-nine car accidents per day in the UK, two thousand fatalities each year and the biggest killer of five- to nineteen-year-old males? People got all moralistic about guns and knives and drugs but never gave a thought to these killers, kitted out with reinforced bonnets, crumple zones, side bars, roof pillars and side intrusion beams.

'We don't even take car theft seriously,' he thought. 'Joy riders! That's what we call people who steal cars, race them at high speed and then either kill themselves or some other poor innocent bugger. Well there was nothing joyful about this business.'

The police lawyer had also advised Dawson to obtain legal representation for James straightaway, had said he was 'vulnerable' in the eyes of the law, because of his head injury, that the police must not be accused of 'taking advantage' of him. That was a joke. James Salisbury had just driven a car straight into a woman and her kids in broad daylight and he was the one who, apparently, required protection. Dawson chewed this over. He would do as he was told this time, as he didn't want to jeopardise the prosecution case, but he was fairly certain that few people would be on James' side in all this.

27

MARTINE SAT in her kitchen, staring out through the window, a bottle of gin, a can of tonic and a glass lined up before her on the shiny, granite worktop. 'Emerald Pearl' – that was the colour she had chosen, after hours of agonising over whether the 'glistening green-tinged flecks' would complement the cream tiles she had selected, or whether 'Absolute Black' was a safer bet. In the end the 'natural elegance and timeless beauty' of the former won through, but as she sat this morning, her red gels tapping against the hard surface, she wondered if she had made the right choice after all.

Toby sat opposite her, fingering his car keys nervously, having politely declined the offer to join her in an early tipple. He shifted his position so as not to be directly facing the camera, which sat in the furthest corner of the room, shadowing his every move.

'Did you see James last night?' Martine asked.

Toby pushed his keys away and folded his hands together.

'He was asleep. I didn't want to wake him.'

'They said he'd only bumped his head, but he was pretty out of the game. Called me Vera when he first saw me.' She took a gulp of neat gin, then splashed in some tonic. 'What will happen if he's not OK, if there's something wrong with him?'

'Is that what they've said?' Toby leaned forwards. 'I thought it was just concussion. It'll pass in a day or two.'

'That's a relief. I wasn't sure. There was no one to ask. Like a ghost town it was.'

'I can manage at work for the next few days, till he's back.'

'Is everyone talking about it?'

'A bit.'

'What are they saying?'

'Depends who you talk to.'

'I bet Carol's telling everyone. She loves to gossip.'

'I don't think anyone's gossiping about it. They're just upset.'

'And the men in the factory. Are they pleased their workaholic boss is human after all?'

'That's not how it is. No one's pleased.'

'What about the technicians? What do they think? Do they know what happened? What does Juan think?'

Toby frowned. He wanted to ask why Juan's view was important to her. A few weeks ago she hadn't even known who Juan was. 'I don't know,' he said instead. 'It only happened yesterday. Everyone's pretty shocked.'

'More likely worrying about their jobs. When things go wrong, that's when you find out who your friends are. That's what they say, don't they? It's in the newspapers.'

'Is it?'

Martine handed her phone to Toby, who scanned the screen.

'It doesn't name James,' he said. 'That's good. And we should be pleased they didn't arrest him. They often do, you know.'

'Arrest him? Why would they arrest him?'

'Because of the children he hit. I'm sure they won't, not James, but you must have read before. It says things like *21-year-old man was arrested at the scene on suspicion of driving under the influence*. That kind of thing.'

James isn't 21...'

'I know that. I just meant...'

'And he doesn't drink.'

'No.'

'It's been six years.'

'That's good.'

'Although I bet he wants one now.' Martine stared out of the window. 'Newspapers are always so negative,' she said. 'They should focus on James being alive.'

'Well. You can understand it.'

'Can you?'

'Because of...well...like I said, because of the children.'

'That's what they're all doing, all of them. Smiling children, first birthday photos, "good times". I suppose it helps them sell their papers.' Her voice quivered and she finished her drink and poured another.

'I'd better be going,' Toby said. 'Acting CEO and all that. I just wanted to check you were OK.'

'Me? I'm fine. Why wouldn't I be?'

'Are you visiting him today?'

'Yes. I'm going now. Would you like to come?'

'No thanks. I should get in and keep an eye on things, hold the fort, for James. I know he'd do the same for me. Send my best though. I'm surprised I haven't heard from him already. "Where's my boarding pass?" "Have you organised my transfer?"'

'Is that what he's like with you?'

'What?'

'Making you run errands for him?'

Toby shrugged and he blinked a few times in quick succession.

'Someone told me recently that I had a lot to offer,' he said. 'I'm not sure James always thinks that.'

He rose to leave and reached for his keys. Martine lay her hand over them.

'What's going to happen?' she said.

'I'm sure he'll be fine.' Toby tried to shake off the image of James lying helpless in the hospital bed.

'I don't mean James. I mean the cars. James always said they can't crash,' Martine persisted.

'Well, maybe James doesn't know everything.' Toby barked, surprised by his own candour. His index finger twitched towards his keys.

'When we had dinner, two weeks back,' Martine said.

'I thought we agreed. You said in the morning…not to talk about it.'

'I want to talk about it now.'

'OK.'

'I told you about a plan I had. Do you remember?'

'No.' Toby shook his head too many times to be convincing. 'I had a lot to drink. What was the plan?' he said.

Martine's eyes narrowed.

'Have it your way then,' she said. 'It's probably better to forget we ever had that conversation anyway, now this has happened.'

'OK,' Toby said again, although he was feeling decidedly not OK. 'So now you don't want to talk about it?'

'You didn't tell anyone about it, did you?'

'No. I told you. I drank too much.'

'I'll just go back to peeling potatoes then, leave the big ideas to you and James. He thinks a lot of you, you know, even if he doesn't show it.'

'Really?' Now the room was starting to spin. Toby needed some air. 'It was a great meal you made, though. Lots of chilli,' he managed.

'Some bits you remember then?' Martine withdrew her hand and Toby grabbed his keys and made for the door.

'Send my best to James,' he said, over his shoulder. 'Tell him not to worry about anything.'

After he had gone, Martine downed her gin and tonic. Then she scrolled through the news story again on her phone, staring at the images of James' mangled car and the tributes to the family he had destroyed. She wanted to crawl into bed, pull the covers over her head and wait for someone else to sort everything out, but that wasn't going to happen. She knew that. She needed to be resilient now.

Sometimes unexpected things occurred and you could either let them overwhelm you or you could emerge stronger out the other side. She poured herself another measure of gin, just a small one this time and checked the clock on the wall. She would wait another five minutes, until she had finished her drink. Then she would tidy her hair, put on a fresh coat of lipstick and go to visit James in hospital.

28

THERESE WAS lying awake, in bed, flowers adorning her bedside table and the various free spaces around her hospital room, a vacant expression on her face. Dawson was surprised so many bouquets had been allowed. These days most hospitals found one or another reason for banning them; 'germs', 'allergies', 'unnecessary work for nurses'. But as he inhaled he understood. The heady, intoxicating scent of the burgeoning blooms served primarily to mask the hovering odour of death.

Neil was sleeping, slouched forwards onto the bed, breathing evenly, one arm hanging limply at his side.

'Mrs Layton. Hello. I'm Chief Inspector Dawson.'

He deliberately spoke softly, reining in his usual blaring overtones. His superintendent had suggested he be accompanied by a female officer to help provide support, but he knew he could 'do sympathy' when called upon and if given sufficient notice to prepare himself. In any event, the victim liaison team had already visited. His role was different; he wanted to put away the person responsible for this devastation, preferably for a very long time.

Neil stirred and awoke, forcing himself into an upright position. Therese did not move.

'Mrs Layton?'

Still no response.

'Hello, Inspector. My wife is on a lot of drugs. She may not hear you,' Neil began.

'I can hear all right,' Therese replied bitterly. 'That's one thing I can do.'

'I am so sorry to intrude at this awful time,' Dawson began, standing behind Neil and taking a notebook out of his pocket. 'My officers and I will try to keep any questions brief, but we are trying to establish, if we can, what happened.'

'Don't you have witnesses?' Neil asked. 'Or CCTV?'

'Yes we do. But...'

'What happened is that he drove straight into us,' Therese interrupted. 'He came round the corner like a maniac. We didn't stand a chance,' she said.

'You think he was travelling fast?'

'I think! I know. He wasn't even looking. He was on his phone.'

'You saw him on his phone. Are you sure? Things must have happened quickly.'

'He came around the corner too fast on his phone and he hit us.' Therese looked at Dawson for the first time and it occurred to him that every flower head in the room had turned to face him too, providing an army of back-up for Therese's testimony.

'Did he see you at all?' He dithered with his follow-up question, under the scrutiny of so many of Therese's supporters.

'Yeah, at the last second he looked up. He could've swerved and missed us, but I suppose there were lamp posts, barriers, other cars. We were a bit softer. He's still alive then?'

'Yes, he is.'

'Broken any of *his* limbs?'

'No.'

'He is going to be prosecuted, isn't he?' Neil broke in. 'I mean, it must have been dangerous driving at least.'

'I can't comment on that at the moment, I'm afraid. If we do decide to prosecute, I will let you know and you may be asked to give a statement.'

Neil took his wife's hand, but she shrugged him off.

'My statement will be very short,' she said. 'It will contain one word in capital letters.'

'Tay. Stop it. You'll get too upset.'

'I'll get too upset!' She threw her husband a withering look. '"MURDERER," that's what my statement will say. Why don't you write it down now, while you're here? Save you coming back again.'

Dawson nodded slowly. 'Do you remember anything about the vehicle?' he asked.

Therese's eyes widened. 'What sort of things?'

'Colour? Size?'

'You've got the driver. So why does that matter?' Neil's eyes challenged Dawson as much as his words.

'I just want to know what your wife remembers. That's all. Little things may help. Mrs Layton?'

Therese stared at her hands.

'I think you can see that my wife is not really in a state to answer any more questions.'

'I understand.' Dawson tucked his notebook back in his pocket. 'Like I said. We have some way to go in the investigation. I'll let you know what we decide.' He turned to leave.

'Do you have children, Inspector?' Mr Layton stopped him with his question.

'I have two daughters.'

'Can you imagine what it would be like to lose them both and then be told there was no one to blame?'

'I understand, sir. But I think, it would be important to me to make sure the right person was blamed, not just the first person in the firing line. So, like I said, we're still investigating. I'll leave you in peace now.'

'Is he here?' Therese was staring out past the foot of the bed and her question was delivered with a quiet steeliness which was sustaining her, despite her agony.

'Here?' Dawson dawdled by the door.

'In this hospital?'

'Oh. No. He's not here. He's…well I can't say.'

Therese bit her lip.

'Don't worry. I'm not going to send Neil after him with a sawn-off shotgun. I just wanted to make sure I wasn't going to bump into him on my morning run, that's all.'

'Keep us updated, Inspector, please,' Neil called after him, as he closed the door and made his way back down the corridor.

29

James was sitting in the offices of Mainstream Debrett, watching Bruce Debrett, his company's legal adviser for the past eleven years, shuffling papers around and scrolling through various items on his PC. He had sat through Martine's protestations, delivered an hour before at the hospital, urging him to rest, and Toby's muted reassurances that 'everything was under control' at work and that he could do whatever James required via telephone instructions from the hospital. He had then promptly discharged himself and headed straight here.

'Well?' James asked, tiring of Bruce's exertions.

Bruce sat back and pressed his fingers to his lips. Then he scratched the side of his nose and flicked through some more pages on his PC. Finally, he clicked his tongue against the roof of his mouth and concentrated on James.

'What precisely did this police officer say to you at the hospital?' he said.

'He told me that two children had died and the mother had

been injured and may be paralysed.' James grimaced. Every time he moved a wave of pain shot down his neck and across his shoulder blades. 'Is that true? About the children?' he asked.

'Yes. I'm afraid so.'

James moaned and he lowered his head into his hands.

'I'm so sorry, James. It must be terrible for you. Did he say anything about you or the car?'

'What?'

'The policeman. Did he ask about your car?'

'He just asked me what I remembered.'

'And what did you say?'

'That I didn't remember anything.'

'Good. That was quick thinking. Bought you some time.'

'I wasn't trying to buy time.' James shifted in his seat. 'It was the truth. I don't remember the accident. I didn't know about the children or the mother till he told me. The doctors said it may be the concussion or the trauma.'

'He didn't say anything about charges?' Bruce asked.

'Charges?'

'Criminal charges. You heard. Two kids are dead, James. And you were at the wheel.'

'It's like I told the policeman,' James said. 'It just can't have happened. You know that. You've seen all our stats. Don't they have witnesses?'

'You can ask, if that's what you want. You might not like what you hear.'

'And the cameras. And the EDR. They will show the police what happened.' James' eyes were darting around the room. 'You don't seriously believe they'll press charges, do you? As if I'm some kind of criminal.'

'You can ask the police about that too.'

'Does it say, in the news, that they're investigating?'

'That's the gist.' Bruce tapped at his keyboard and then focused on James. 'I'm advising you, as a friend, off the record, that the police will almost certainly question you and they may bring charges,' he said. 'You need to formulate a plan.'

'There must have been another car involved. It hit them, not me.'

'No other car,' Bruce said. 'Not unless it just disappeared afterwards or, what do they say in Harry Potter? Apparated. That's it. Sorry, just been reading it to my oldest. I can show you the crash scene if you want. Plenty of people have uploaded it. Amazing what they'll do for a minute's fame.'

Without waiting for an answer, Bruce swivelled the screen of his PC around. James could see the aftermath of the accident, his car sitting only a metre or so from the concrete barrier, positioned diagonally across its lane, the windscreen smashed.

'What about the other carriageway?' James asked.

Bruce flicked through a few shots.

'Can't really see it. They've all focused on your car, as it was the only vehicle there. Look. Like I said, you can ask the police if you want. But I would lie low and let them contact you. I wouldn't go playing detective yourself, if that's what you're thinking of.'

'Are they saying it was a SEDA car?'

'Yes, not everyone, but it's obvious it's not a regular vehicle and you can see the make on the photos if you enlarge them sufficiently. You'll have to release a statement.'

'But how can we do that if we don't know what happened?' James rubbed his head where it ached. 'I'll go into the office and talk to Toby and the technical guys. We have a new programmer who's a cut above the others. See if he has any idea what might have gone wrong. Can you meet us there, say, in a couple of hours?'

Bruce circled the fingers of his right hand around the fleshy palm of his left. He always chose to do it this way around. The life line on his right hand was broken in three places; he wasn't a superstitious person but, ever since his sister had read his palm at the age of nine and foretold an early, agonising death, he tried to ignore it. When he looked up, James was staring at him.

'I wish I could. You know I want to help,' he said.

'So what's the problem?'

Bruce's shoulders sagged.

'I can't. I'm so sorry,' he said.

'Why on earth not?'

'Conduct rules, I'm afraid. Conflict of interest.'

'What! How can there be a conflict? You're my lawyer. We're both on the same side.'

'I'm not *your* lawyer. SEDA engaged me as the company's lawyer and to advise you, as CEO. So, yes, I can help with SEDA's position and, like I said, at the moment, my advice is to do nothing at all. And if you're asked for an official comment you must say nothing of substance, just that it's a tragedy and subject to a police investigation. That's it.'

'So why won't you come to the office, as SEDA's lawyer?'

'Because the lines will get blurred. If you are charged with a criminal offence, then your personal interest and that of the company might well be polar opposites. I can't defend you.'

'What?'

'Can't you see? If you are prosecuted, they'll be saying it's your fault, that you did something wrong. And to defend yourself, you'll need to say the accident happened because of a problem with the car, then SEDA will take the hit. It's one or the other. Either you go down or SEDA does. I can't be in both camps.'

James stood up and groaned as sparks of light flashed before his eyes and disorientated him.

'You should go home and rest, you look awful. I can recommend someone, certainly, to advise you, to represent you if things progress, and I'll be glad to do so. And I will help as much as I can.'

'You're the one with all the knowledge of the business. You even persuaded us to stick with you for the marketing, patents, employment work, the overseas contracts. You said there would be "economies of scale" if we instructed you to provide "the full service package".'

'That's right. And Mainstream Debrett has done a fantastic job for you.'

'How much did we pay you last year in fees?'

'Oh come on. You're not being fair. I'm not even a criminal lawyer, James. I'd be way out of my depth.'

'You know me, you know how I do things. You know the company. You've been to my house for dinner. Your nephew did work experience at the factory.'

'I'm truly sorry but, even if I wanted to act for you, it's out of my hands. I'd be disciplined, struck off.'

'I see. So I'm on my own, am I?' James headed for the door.

'I didn't say that. I have advised the company what to do for now. I sent something through to Toby just an hour ago; sit tight and, if pressed, give a short non-committal response like the one I've drafted. And I said I'd help you find someone, a criminal lawyer, to advise you. I'll send you over the list of people I recommend.

They're all good.'

'Thanks for nothing. I'll see myself out.'

Outside, on the street, James marched one way, then the other, eventually leaning back against the window of a newsagent. He had planned to go to the office, but now he wasn't sure it was the best thing to do. As he turned around, he caught sight of his reflection in the glass; he glimpsed a haggard and confused face, all his usual self-assurance glaringly absent. Then he shook his head sadly and looked out into the street for a taxi. For once, the office could wait. He really needed to go home and sleep.

30

Constance arrived at Judith Burton's flat around 7.30pm. She carried a bottle of red wine, which the shop assistant had advised her was 'full of character' and had 'aged graciously', and which seemed to her to be eminently suitable for her hostess.

Judith buzzed Constance up with a lively greeting and before long she was standing in the hallway of the spacious two-bed apartment.

'Greg will be here in a few minutes,' Judith announced, 'so take a seat. I'm just finishing the fruit salad. Help yourself to wine,' she added.

Constance advanced into the living room to find a table, set for three, next to the window, a sofa and armchair facing it and a wall of books directly opposite. She poured a glass of red wine from the open bottle and placed her own offering on the table.

Then she sauntered over to scrutinise Judith's book collection. Most of them didn't surprise her; Jane Austen, Thomas Hardy, Shakespeare and Thackeray. There were plenty of law books too

– on procedure, practice and jurisprudence – but half the bottom shelf was taken up by cookery books. Constance extracted a Jamie Oliver volume and was surprised to find it dedicated inside the front page, in a neat, looping hand. *To Judy. Loved your avocado mousse. Hope you like this in return. Big Love, Jamie.*

Constance had not anticipated Judith to have any interest in cooking; she imagined her only attracted by cerebral matters. And she could visualise the sucked-lemon expression which would have hijacked Judith's face when greeted with the colloquial shortening of her name which the celebrity chef had used. *To Judy, To Judy, To Judy.* She murmured the words under her breath, but each time seemed just as irreverent as the last.

At the far-left side of the shelf, Constance spied an old-fashioned photograph album, the type her mother kept, crammed full of childhood holiday snaps. She slid it out from its position and her hand caressed the dusty cover.

'Is it OK if I look at your photo album?' she called out.

Judith appeared in the doorway, a pair of oven gloves over her left shoulder, an amused expression on her face.

'Look at anything you like,' she replied. 'I have no secrets, although you'll find it very dull, I warn you.'

The sound of a key in the lock heralded Greg Winter's arrival, and he swept into the room, removing his coat and hanging it away as he entered. Constance had a glimpse of his private face, focused and earnest, before he spotted her.

'I must be late if you're having to fend for yourself,' he said, stretching out his hand to her. 'So nice to meet you, after everything I've heard.'

'I think you'll find Connie's very self-sufficient,' Judith called out, 'and she's welcomed the time to take a good look around.'

Constance blushed and Greg focused on the photo album she had tucked under her arm.

'Don't let her embarrass you,' Greg said, still smiling. 'She likes to pretend that she values her privacy, whereas she actually relishes a bit of exposure, now and again.'

He took the album from Constance and flicked through the pages.

'I'll show you the best picture,' he said, 'but probably not Judith's favourite.'

He pointed to a snap of Judith, taken with her sister in their teenage years. Clare was older, but Judith stood a head taller, gawky, angular and ill-at-ease before the camera, one leg sticking out in a display of awkwardness. Clare, in contrast, was a mass of curves, arms thrown open, a wide inviting grin stapled across her face.

'I already know which one he's showing you,' Judith shouted. 'And before you pass comment, there's nothing wrong with being a reserved teenager. I suspect Clare regrets being quite so welcoming of all comers now.'

'See. I told you she didn't like it. I think photographs, especially old ones, can be very revealing,' Greg advised, conspiratorially, before replacing the album on the shelf. Then he turned his attention to the wine Constance had brought.

'Good choice, I think,' he said. 'Did Arnie recommend it?'

'If Arnie is the man in the shop around the corner, then yes.'

'Judith tells me you're always working, no down time.' Greg poured himself a generous serving, checked the level in Constance's glass and then settled himself on the sofa, sinking back into the cushions, his long legs stretching out to straddle the rug.

'No more than anyone else,' Constance replied.

'Nonsense,' Judith called from the kitchen again, 'she's even more of a workaholic than I am. Has your Mr Whatsisname promoted you yet?' She leaned around the door frame.

'Mr Whatsisname is Mr Moses, and I don't think he does promotion,' Constance said.

'But your high-profile cases must have brought lots of work in for everyone?'

'Maybe.'

'Oh she's too modest, Greg. I did tell you.'

Greg laughed, and the glow from the table lamp caught his heavy brow and highlighted the grey edges to his close-cropped curls.

'Not a bad quality in a person,' he joked, 'but in short supply around here.'

'Shall we eat?' Judith asked, ignoring his jibe. 'I missed lunch again. Do you mind Connie? I know it's not good form to throw your guest straight in to the food. You can stay as long as you like afterwards, really.'

'I'm always happy to eat. I hope you haven't gone to too much trouble.'

'Ssh,' Greg put his finger to his lips, 'don't say that. It's the first time she's cooked in weeks.'

'I heard that you know,' Judith called out from the kitchen and Constance giggled.

'She hears everything,' Greg said.

'I heard that too.'

'I saw your Trixster app has really taken off,' Constance began, sipping from her wine as she sat down at the table.

'It's done pretty well, yes,' Greg said. 'I think it's almost peaked, to be honest, but Judith doesn't like to talk about it.'

'Really?'

'Yes. Because she didn't think of it herself.'

'And Pinocchio?'

'It's been refined even more, and now it's gaining mainstream acceptance. Since we dropped the transparency aspect that Judith was so keen on, we've improved the reliability enormously. People don't realise that with AI you have to sacrifice one in order to enhance the other.'

Constance held her glass out for a refill.

'Judith was keen on transparency?' she said.

Greg swallowed his wine.

'Did I say Judith? I meant Claudia, the lawyer who used to advise me, in the old days before I was rich and famous.' He laughed. 'They're using Pinocchio now across the board for recruitment. The army particularly likes it. And they say it will be in US courtrooms in the next twelve months.' He paused, as if expecting a cutting retort from the kitchen, but nothing was forthcoming. 'But, as you asked, I have a new venture which is more acceptable to Judith, within these four walls only for now.'

'Really?'

'Yes. Garden centres. There are a couple of ailing ones we're buying up and we're going to give them a makeover, improve selection, encourage more people to grow plants which are particularly good for wildlife, introduce interactive exhibits and a new mode of delivery.'

'In what way "new"?'

'Well it won't surprise you to know that there'll be an app to use. You choose your plants either on site or remotely via the app, you get advice on location and care, and a nice young person, probably a school leaver and possibly someone with previously low career expectations, will deliver your selection and, if you like, help plant them all for you.'

'So a kind of bespoke garden makeover, but from your local garden centre. What's it called?'

'That's still work in progress, but I like "From Little Acorns…".'

Constance beamed. 'Sounds very interesting.'

'Greg does seem to have the Midas touch at the moment.' Judith joined them with a large casserole dish, which she deposited on the table. 'And, of course, he has the funds now, from his other, more commercial projects.'

'It's early days but it's part of a drive to get more young people involved in environmental issues and in working in the community. Judith likes it because it's something tangible.'

'Absolutely,' Judith replied. 'Nothing like getting one's hands dirty.' She laughed at herself.

'What are you working on at the moment?' Judith asked Constance, as she lifted the lid off the tureen and an exotic smell wafted through the room.

Greg coughed exaggeratedly.

'Oh, sorry. I had promised not to talk shop too much. We can do that afterwards when Greg retires to smoke his pipe in the drawing room, then.'

Constance looked around her, in confusion, as she hadn't spied any other living space, before realising that Judith was joking. Judith retreated to the kitchen one last time and returned with a basket of bread.

'Don't let me stifle the conversation,' Greg said. 'Go on. Judith will only kick me under the table repeatedly, till you tell her what you're up to. She has steel toe caps on her shoes, you know.'

'OK.' Constance took a moment to examine both their faces; Judith alert and curious, Greg relaxed and bemused. 'How much do you know about driverless cars?' she asked.

'Only what I've read,' Judith replied, 'that we'll all have them in the next ten years and they're the answer to all the world's problems, including third world debt and human trafficking. Why? I suspect you're not looking for a recommendation.'

'Did you read about the family hit by a car outside their house yesterday?'

'Yes I did. Terrible mess. Two children killed. Oh no! It wasn't one of those cars.'

'Yes. A SEDA. British-made. They've kept that part out of the mainstream press so far but it's all over the internet. There's lots of photos too.'

'I didn't know we had them out on the roads yet.'

'They've been keeping it quiet,' Greg chipped in, 'but more than one company is trialling them. It's all around the country, in quite a few cities.'

'And who is to blame for the accident?' Judith asked.

'They don't know yet. The car's in a secret location and the driver's in hospital. The driver needs a lawyer, that's how I know all this. There's pressure to arrest him but they haven't decided what to do yet.'

'Did Dawson call you?'

'Not this time. It was a lawyer working for SEDA.'

'Interesting, and I can see it could be tricky, if the car was driving, that is. What did you say?'

'I said I would let him know.'

'Oh Connie. You must take it.'

'I'm not sure I was the only one he contacted.'

'So you need to let him know before the others do. This could be the first case involving one of these cars, new law. How thrilling.'

Greg stopped eating and stared at Judith.

'And two dead children. And the mother injured,' he said quietly.

'I know that,' Judith replied. 'You don't need to play my conscience. It goes without saying that it's an absolute tragedy. That poor family. But two thousand fewer deaths per year, insurance premiums cut by eighty per cent. That's how driverless cars were sold to us, if I remember correctly. There must be some very red faces in high places right now. And the driver should not be held liable if he relinquished control. Even so, he's going to need a good set of lawyers. You must see that, Greg?'

Greg resumed his eating but with less interest than before.

'Has she persuaded you yet?' he asked Constance.

'Oh stop it! You're the one who's always motivated by "innovative" responses to things. Well this is the pinnacle of innovation. We have to be in on it. To prevent another similar tragedy if nothing else.'

'She is very convincing, I have to admit,' Constance replied.

'You wouldn't have it any other way, Connie. Let's at least take a look at the papers and talk to the driver. It could be really fabulous. And no one touches that car before we do.'

31

PETER WAS SEATED in his office in Whitehall the next morning, reading an essay on the proliferation of electric charging stations across the UK. Progress was apparently slow, but it was also steady. And, importantly, the writer believed they were reaching the critical mass which would finally make electric cars viable. Of course, the supermarkets wanted compensation for their 'lost parking spaces', which Peter considered ludicrous, especially because surveys had shown that most of them were never more than seventy per cent full. But he needed to keep them on side, so compromises would have to be made.

He allowed himself to be diverted by the many emails which were flooding his inbox this morning. It wasn't the first time. He had picked up the academic paper earlier, in the hope that it would distract him from the barrage of attention his grumbling mailbox was receiving. But even with his phone on mute, he was aware of the tiny vibrations which indicated yet another missive arising.

Top priority was Alan's message, demanding a full enquiry into the SEDA collision and telling Peter to be 'on hand' to brief him at any moment. It was followed by links to all the newspapers with their varied coverage of the crash, none of it remotely helpful or positive.

Then there were a series of polite enquiries from journalists to 'catch up' or 'get an update' from him, 'just generally' on the progress of the Autonomous Vehicles Bill and any remaining hurdles. Peter marvelled at their audacity. These were the same people who had printed the stories he had just read, pretending they only wanted to chew the fat, when what they really craved was something juicy and 'exclusive' to add to the story about the tragedy.

He noticed a message from Toby. He poured himself a coffee and read it through slowly.

Hi Peter. I'm in charge in James' absence, it said. *Could we meet please?*

Peter frowned, then he read the words aloud. He patted his stomach a few times and looked up Toby's number on his phone. Then he deleted the message, took a sip of coffee and returned to his reading.

32

James stepped out of his taxi at SEDA's offices and groaned as his broken ribs shifted beneath their hastily-wrapped bandage. He had paid little attention to the nurse's entreaties to 'hold still' before he left the hospital. Now he realised, too late, that this had been short-sighted.

He could see Carol and Jane at their posts, although Diana was not there. Of course, it was Thursday. Diana didn't work on Thursdays; she took her nutritionist course instead. He had joked that she should develop a healthy eating programme for the office. She had taken him seriously and her suggestions for their 'vegan makeover' were now sitting in his inbox awaiting review.

He pushed open the door and walked as briskly as he could manage across the atrium. Carol leaped up and ran towards him, her wailing stopping him in his tracks. To his enormous surprise, and a great deal of discomfort, she threw her arms around his neck.

'James. We're so pleased to see you. They said you were in

hospital. Are you hurt?'

He waved her away with a scowl. Jane was standing too, but remained behind her desk, smiling in his direction.

'It's good to see you,' she said. Always the consummate professional, he could rely on Jane when matters of good taste were on the agenda.

'Thank you, both of you, for your concern. I am a little sore but otherwise unhurt. Just keen to get back to work. Is Toby around?'

The two women exchanged glances.

'He is,' Jane replied. 'If you wait a moment, I'll find him for you.'

'No need,' James strode on. 'I suspect I know where he is. But if you find him first, just tell him I'd like to see him straightaway.'

The door to James' office was ajar and a glass of half-consumed orange juice sat on his desk. His swivel chair was rocking gently as he approached. James halted in the doorway and listened hard for any sounds of company, before walking over to his PC. It was switched off, but the monitor was warm. A feeble knock at the door and Toby appeared.

'Hello James. I wasn't expecting you so soon.' Toby attempted a welcoming smile.

'No. Obviously not. Would you like to finish your juice?' James said, holding out the glass. 'Seems a shame to waste it.'

Toby tiptoed forward and reclaimed his drink, dabbing at the watery mark it had left on the shiny surface and then wiping his hand on his trousers.

'I was just keeping an eye on things for you,' Toby said.

'I can see that. As you should. Thank you. But now I'm here. I'll just need a few minutes to check my inbox. Is there anything urgent?' James slipped effortlessly into work mode. 'Did we hear back from Hamburg and are we any further on with that change on the ABS we discussed?'

'It's all fine. They're working on it. Are you sure you're OK to be at work?' Toby surveyed his boss through narrow eyes.

'Yes, thank you.'

'What about your car?' Toby said.

'My car?' James raised his voice.

'The crash.' Toby lowered his by a corresponding amount. 'What's going to happen? Have they said?'

'I really don't have the time or the inclination to talk about it now...unless it was something particularly urgent?' He glowered at Toby.

'There were some calls, but they can wait.'

'What kind of calls?'

'Carol fielded one this morning from a journalist. Wanted to speak to you. When she said you were out she left her number and asked for a comment. There've been others too. Quite a few.'

James leaned back in his chair and tidied his pens into a straight line.

'Is it true you don't remember what happened?' Toby asked.

'Who told you that?'

'Bruce called, after you went to see him. Is it true though?'

'Yes. Look. I understand Bruce sent some wording over yesterday, for a statement to the press.'

'It's in your inbox. But, I wasn't sure it, well, gave the right message.'

'Oh?'

'We could put a positive spin on things, I was thinking,' Toby spoke with his eyes on the ground and the surface of his untouched juice rippled and swelled.

'How positive?'

'I know it's not much, but we could major on how things could have been worse in a normal car, I mean, the side bars might have protected you. And the baby and mother were saved. And maybe other pedestrians too. I know it's terrible about the family and we have to tread really carefully, but if we've got all this attention, it's an opportunity, isn't it? To focus on all the positive safety features.'

James' fingers idled on his keyboard space bar.

'No,' he said quietly. 'No "positive spin". In fact, we're not going to "spin" anything.'

'I was just trying...'

James stared at Toby and then he beckoned him over. Toby sat down opposite James.

'I do appreciate the thought you have given this, and your obvious loyalty, and I see where you are coming from,' James said. 'But people have died and I don't understand how or why. So that's what I want to know. That should be our focus. And I am really not interested in anything else.'

Toby nodded and James leaned forward onto the desk and smiled reassuringly.

'Listen, we haven't had any problems with the 2016 model, have we?' he said. 'Anything, however small? I don't care if you didn't tell me about it at the time.'

'No. Nothing. I mean, obviously the radar is updated on the latest model but that's all.'

'Good,' James grunted.

'Do you need anything else?'

'I want to talk to Juan, about Connect. That might provide some clues. And I'll need a new phone. As soon as you can. The police kept mine.'

'Sure.'

'And if you see or hear anything – anything which might shed some light on how this happened – you tell me, you tell me straightaway.'

33

A NURSE BROUGHT Therese's dinner; poached cod with mashed potatoes and green beans and a saucer of vanilla ice cream. Therese waited patiently, her face a blank canvas, till she had exited the room before speaking.

'Take it away,' she demanded.

Neil stared at the food and then at Therese.

'I'll get you something else,' he said, as he picked up the tray and shifted the portable table to the foot of the bed, out of her reach.

'No,' she said. 'Nothing else.'

'Tay. You have to eat something.'

'No. I don't have to do anything.'

She closed her eyes. When she opened them, Neil was sitting on the edge of the bed. He reached for her hand and she withdrew it. He shrugged.

'I'm going to take five minutes to get some fresh air,' he said.

'That's fine. Take longer. There's not much excitement round here.'

He hesitated, half standing, half sitting.

'What is it?' Therese asked, less abruptly.

'It's all over the news about the car which hit you.'

'What?'

'It wasn't a normal car.'

'What do you mean?'

'It was one of those "drive itself" cars. You should see what it looks like. It has radar on the roof. There's loads of photos of it, bit like something from an old sci-fi movie.'

Therese was silent, but her face contracted into a frown.

'I called the policeman, Inspector Dawson and he confirmed it was one of those cars.'

'What's the difference? It still hit us.'

'He said it's all a bit tricky, whether they're going to charge the driver or not. He says it will take a few more days till they know what happened.'

Therese's face returned to its earlier impassive expression.

'They need to see if he was driving, if the car was driving, if something failed on the car, that kind of thing,' Neil continued.

'I don't care,' she said finally.

'But you must care,' Neil said. 'This guy destroyed our lives, our family. How can you not care?' He stood up now and loomed over her. 'He deserves to go to prison. You told the inspector, when he came. Remember? How he drove too fast and was looking at his phone. He's a menace. He shouldn't be on the roads.'

Therese's eyes blinked lazily.

'I remember what I said,' she said. 'But I don't care what kind of car it was or if something failed. Georgia and Bertie are dead. They're gone, never coming back. Finding out what happened doesn't change that.'

'You called him a murderer. You said he should be punished. Nothing's changed.'

'I'm very tired.'

'Do you remember anything else about the accident? If the police are getting cold feet, we need to help them nail the guy.'

Therese closed her eyes again.

'Leave me,' she said. 'Go for your "fresh air" and just leave me alone.'

34

THE BRUISE ON James' left cheek ached. Perhaps one of his teeth had been knocked loose in the collision. Now the pain relief was wearing off, he was becoming aware of parts of his body he had never previously noticed.

He flicked through his emails and saw that, true to his word, Bruce had sent him details of a number of criminal lawyers. Immediately below Bruce's message were three separate emails, each requesting a statement from SEDA about the crash and asking for reassurance that SEDA's cars were safe. There were also enquiries after his health, one from a manufacturer friend in Germany and another from France.

Gazing out of the window, he saw Martine's car flash past from the overflow car park at the rear. Three minutes later she was in his office.

'How long have you been here?' She breezed in, her cork platforms squeaking as she crossed the floor. 'The doctors said you needed at least another day in bed and I thought you'd sleep for hours. If I'd known what you were planning, I would have hidden all your clothes.'

'Since when did doctors know anything about running a multinational company? How did you know I was here?'

'I checked in with Jane and Carol on reception, to see if there had been any difficult calls.'

'Toby's been handling those.'

'He's so young. I thought I would make sure.'

'You don't need to park around the back, you know,' James said, 'like you're hiding. You are my wife. I could arrange for you to have your own space if you wanted.'

Martine swallowed. 'It was full, earlier…'

'Really? There was hardly anyone here when I arrived.'

'Maybe they've all gone now.'

'Maybe.'

Martine walked over to the window and looked out across the empty car park.

'An Inspector Dawson called just five minutes ago, Jane said to tell you,' she said. 'He asked if you could go to the police station tomorrow morning at ten. She's sent you the details. He said there will be a lawyer there for you, if you don't have your own.'

James nodded stiffly.

'Does that mean they think you did something wrong?'

'I don't know but I suspect I'll find out pretty quickly.'

'I'll come with you?'

'No. If I have a lawyer, I'm sure I'll be fine.'

'Will you take Bruce?'

James allowed the tips of his fingers to meet in front of his face, before answering.

'Bruce doesn't want to handle this one. He's not a criminal

specialist.'

'He's always been your lawyer.'

'Not this time.'

'But he has found you someone good, someone who can explain that it's all a big mistake?'

'Yes. I think so. I hope so.' He sighed and fingered his sore ribs. 'Look, this isn't going to go away any time soon.'

'Don't say that.'

'I'm just being realistic. And it couldn't have happened at a worse time for SEDA, for the whole industry. It's like Bruce said. Either the crash really was my fault, in which case, I may go to jail and the company will fold without me and the cars will be scrapped, or the car malfunctioned. If it was the car, then I can blame it on SEDA, if my conscience will allow me, that is, but that's still my fault, because it's my company. I put the cars out on the road. I told people they were safe. I thought they were safe. I would have staked my own life on it, your life, our own boys.'

'Your cars are safe. You have to tell the police that. You have to tell the newspapers.'

'And what kind of person am I then? Those poor children. That poor family. And I'm thinking about myself.'

Martine stood behind James, bending down to kiss the top of his head.

'Do you remember anything about the crash?' she whispered.

'Nothing at all.' He reached for her.

'Bruce'll get you a good lawyer,' Martine said, pulling away. 'We'll get hold of all the pictures and they'll show it wasn't your fault. I'm sure of it.'

'I just don't understand,' James' hands trembled. 'I don't understand what could have happened.'

35

CONSTANCE MET James at Hackney police station. She had emailed to offer to meet him earlier, when he hadn't returned her phone call, but he had insisted he couldn't spare the time.

'Mr Salisbury,' she took the plunge, marching forwards as he approached the desk, waiting for an appreciative response, but the eyes which met hers were searching and sceptical.

'I'm Constance Lamb,' she said, 'your lawyer.' She shook his hand and he grunted. 'Are you still unwell?' she asked.

'That depends on how you define "well",' James said. 'Everything works. Is that well? Is there somewhere we can go to speak privately before I'm subjected to my interrogation?'

'Room one,' Constance said. 'It's this way.'

Once inside the interview room, Constance removed her jacket and switched on her tablet.

'Have you come straight from the hospital?' she began.

'No. I discharged myself on Wednesday. I had so much to do. Am I being arrested?'

'No,' Constance replied. 'The police just want to ask you some questions.'

'But I might be…arrested, that is?'

'Yes. It's possible.'

'Until then, until I'm arrested, I'm free to carry on working?'

'You are, yes. But I don't think they'll want you going overseas.'

'Why on earth not?'

'They'll be worried that you'll abscond.'

'Abscond? I have a business worth millions, a wife and two children and I don't think I've ever had a parking ticket. Why on earth would I abscond?'

Constance sighed. 'They might not say anything and I won't mention it if they don't. I was just advising you of what might happen.'

James nodded. 'I understand,' he said curtly. 'So what happens now, Miss…?'

'Lamb, but I am happy for you to call me Constance, please.'

'Constance. What happens now? Do I answer the policeman's questions? Or do I say nothing, like you see on television.'

'How much do you remember about the accident?'

'Very little. I remember getting into my car. I was at a meeting in the City. Then nothing…till I woke up in hospital and was told I had killed two children and injured their mother. They said she might not walk again.'

'Do the doctors know why you've lost your memory?'

'I hit my head pretty hard, they said. Concussion. "Not life threatening". They made a point of telling me that.'

'And when will you start to remember things?'

'They don't know. I have to go back in a week. I…I still can't actually believe this has happened to me. You do understand that.

It's like the most terrible nightmare. Will the police tell us what they know?'

'I'll be asking them what they have. The crash was on a street called Common Lane, just coming in to Tottenham from Haringey. Do you know the area?'

'Yes. Major thoroughfare. Low-level housing each side. Red route and bus route. It has these funny little feeder roads running parallel, for access to the houses.'

'You have incredibly good knowledge...'

'One of my regular suppliers is down that way. I've been along that road many times.'

'And before then?'

'I worked at home till around nine, then left for the meeting.'

'Your car, registration number SAL1 2016.'

'Yes.'

'I understand it's specially modified.'

'Look. This is what I tried to explain to the police officer who visited me. It's an autonomous vehicle. It drives itself. It is fitted with cutting-edge technology; cameras, lasers, radar, other sensors, advanced braking mechanisms, innovative steering. It is a whole different beast from a conventional car, a new species. And it doesn't crash.'

Constance looked up and her eyes met his. She turned the screen of her laptop around, so he could see the image of his car at the scene; windscreen shattered, bodywork battered and at least one tyre punctured. Before he could look too closely, she rotated it back.

'I know. I've already seen it,' he said, 'but it feels all wrong. It must be wrong. You know how they say that you can make photographs do anything you like these days.'

'The police attended at the scene. This is what your car looked like after the accident.'

'I'm certain that if we can get the footage of the accident, from my car, then this will all be sorted out in a second. Do you know where my car is? It's vitally important that the police don't tamper with the EDR, the event data recorder. My technicians will need access to it, to de-code the data.'

'I'll ask Inspector Dawson, the officer in charge. Have you met him yet?'

'Yes. At the hospital. Friendly guy. He was the first to deliver the good news.'

Constance made a note.

'Is there anything you remember about the accident, anything at all?'

'Nothing. I wish I did.'

'All right. So, next steps are that Inspector Dawson will ask you some questions, but I'm assuming you will tell him that you don't remember. That's a perfectly valid response, if that is the case.'

'And you'll ask him about my car, the data?'

'Yes.'

'Will anything happen today?'

'It's unlikely. But you need to show you are taking this seriously. You can be firm but always be polite, try very hard not to get angry, and my advice is that you don't tell him that "it's impossible" for your car to crash. It will just annoy him.'

'I understand,' James said. 'God!' He laughed hollowly. 'This is probably the one time I wish I didn't have to rely on technology. I just want to remember what happened.'

'And that's why I'll be trying to persuade the Inspector to give you, to give us, more time. So that you can recall everything about the crash. But anything you remember in the meantime, however small, you need to tell me. Is that clear?'

'I bet you've never had someone like me to defend before, someone who can't remember what happened.' James managed a smile.

'Each case has its own…challenges,' Constance replied. 'Can I get you something, before the Inspector comes in. A cup of tea?'

'No thank you. I doubt the tea here is up to much.'

'Some water then? For the interview.'

'Yes please. That's thoughtful of you.'

His voice cracked and the low laugh he emitted, to cover it up, turned into a cackle, before disappearing into his throat.

***

Dawson was sitting in his office, flicking through a paper file, repeatedly checking his watch. He sat back at Constance's light tap and turned the file face down.

'Hello Constance. I saw your name in the book. Is Mr Salisbury, saviour of the universe, ready for us now?'

'Why do you call him that?' she asked, entering but not sitting down.

'Oh, don't be so prickly. You should read some of his speeches. That's what I've been doing. He thinks his cars will save the world. Did his halo fit into my interview room?'

'Where is his car?' Constance lowered herself into the chair opposite Dawson.

Dawson's eyes flicked towards the glass which separated him from the rest of his team, before returning to Constance.

'It's in a secure garage. Why?'

'I'll want access and a specialist technician to extract the data from the EDR.'

'The EDR?'

'The data recorder. It holds the record of how the car was being driven, immediately before the accident. If you tamper with it, you risk all the data being lost.'

'How many car crash cases have you defended before then? Listen to you with all the lingo.' Dawson fiddled with the file on his desk again. 'I can't see any reason why we would give access to your client before we've taken a look ourselves, although you can try to persuade me.'

The beginning of a smile flickered across his lips and was quickly gone.

'The EDR belongs to Mr Salisbury,' Constance began. 'It's a part of his vehicle. If you won't agree, I may have to issue a court application for access and I will ask for costs. And if you touch it, now I have alerted you to the dangers and the data is compromised, I will ask for the case to be thrown out, on the basis that my client cannot hope to have a fair trial.'

Dawson frowned. 'You're jumping ahead a little aren't you, talking about cases and trials? Today is just a friendly chat. Has your client got a guilty conscience then?'

'The data on the EDR may be key to determining what happened, although I am assuming you have other sources of information, like CCTV?'

Constance waited.

'We might.'

'So, I have to take steps to ensure it's properly preserved. That's all. I assume the family of the deceased children will want to know what happened, regardless of any prosecution. I would, appreciate it, please, if you could give me that reassurance, pending further enquiries being carried out.'

Dawson turned the file over and Constance saw the words 'Haringey Crash Report' scribbled on the top. He lay the palm of his hand across it.

'Now you've asked me nicely, I'll see what I can do,' he said.

'Thank you. Are you proposing to charge Mr Salisbury with anything today?'

'Well that depends.'

'On what?'

'On what he says when I question him.'

Constance felt her face beginning to flush, but she remained calm.

'Give me two minutes to get Mr Salisbury a glass of water and then we'll be ready to start,' she said. And then, as an afterthought, she added, 'even superheroes need to drink.'

Dawson chewed his thumb as she exited the room. Then he clicked his knuckles. Then he opened the file up and continued reading.

36

Judith Burton was returning to her apartment with a shopping bag in each hand. She had completed her sixty lengths at the nearby pool and had sourced all the ingredients she needed for a 'superfood' salad lunch.

Greg was at work, so she was looking forward to spending as much time as she wanted, chopping and whisking and simmering, and sporting her disposable caterer's gloves for hostile vegetables like beetroot and red onion, without fear of censure. And when her culinary creation was finally ready, she could sit down with all the newspapers spread across the table and a glass of her chosen white wine (Greg would never drink during the day and she suspected he disapproved of this habit of hers, although he never said), some ciabatta and an olive oil/balsamic dip and peck away, making the meal last the whole afternoon.

As she deposited her parcels on the floor of the kitchen, she thought back to the dinner she had made for Constance. What had Greg commented afterwards? Interesting young woman, that was it. The comment didn't bother Judith in itself, but she was intrigued that he should focus on those two attributes of Constance; something unusually alluring about her and her youth.

She, Judith, generally forgot how young and relatively inexperienced Constance was when they worked together, although Constance did defer to her on some matters and, clearly, Constance was the master of lots of technological applications Judith didn't even know existed. And while Judith had certainly been drawn in at first by Constance's online profile, once they had met she had ceased to find her particularly fascinating. Constance was bright, there was no doubt about it, and extremely hard-working and they made a great team, but she was patently down to earth and conventional in many ways.

Judith pulled her phone out of her bag and switched it on for the first time that day. As she extracted various knives, peelers and a chopping board from her cupboard, she sat down to check her messages. The first was from Constance.

Have taken the car case. Assume you're 'in'. Pick you up around 3pm for meeting with our client?

This was followed by two missed calls, also from Constance, presumably to check she'd received the message. Judith checked the time. It was only twelve. She could still manage a more hastily prepared salad than she had anticipated and a read of some background on the case before pick-up. She should probably, therefore, abandon the alcoholic accompaniment.

Yes please, she replied. *I'll be waiting*. And 'here we go again,' she muttered to herself.

37

'WHAT DO WE KNOW about James Salisbury's background?' Judith asked, as they sat in Constance's car, parked on High Firs Lane in Hadley Wood, a few doors away from his house.

It was a wide street, lined either side by large detached houses, most of them set back from the road and accessed via intimidating gates, surrounded by high walls or occasionally softened by neat hedges. On their journey, they had circled a large, green park, replete with swings and two tennis courts. And at the corner of the street they had passed a small preparatory school; Judith didn't catch its name.

'He's fifty-nine, founded SEDA in 2005. He was fifty-fifty shareholder with a childhood friend of his called Imogen Walsh. She died two years into the venture on a skiing holiday. James carried on alone. It's his personal car that was involved in the accident.'

'And how is the company doing?'

'Published accounts show low but steady profit for the parent company...but they are waiting for the explosion in the UK, when the government Bill goes through, any day now.'

'Because what? Their cars go on general release then?'

'Yes. There are about a hundred SEDAs on the roads here now, either on specific trials or a few owned by staff, like the one in the accident. Word is, SEDA is far advanced in terms of the sophistication of the software, because they've thrown more money at the project than their competitors and focused on this product only.'

'You sound like a SEDA advert.'

'I've been asking around. The SEDA is rated. Their main line is called the Go!.'

'The Go!.'

'Yes. It's a catchy name; there's lots of marketing about how it's for people with busy lives, you know, "always on the Go," that kind of thing. It looks sleek, it's pitched at medium income people and it's roomy inside. And it's good on fuel consumption.'

'It's electric?'

'Yes. Apparently, it was SEDA who finally persuaded the supermarkets to start installing charging points, which made the whole electric car thing viable. James himself went to visit all the big chains and asked them "if they wanted to help make the world a better place".'

'And they did, of course. Is he married?'

'Yes, to Martine, born Martine Braithwaite. Former Miss South Yorkshire 1998. Age thirty-nine, housewife, likes shopping.'

'How do you know that?'

'She was in a local magazine recently talking about it. "Shoes for every occasion," it was called. I'll dig it out for you.'

'Thank you. I might learn something useful. Children?'

'Two. Joshua aged nineteen and Zachary aged twelve. I think his wife must have chosen the names.'

'Careful. That sounded decidedly like the snobbery I am trying hard to curb.'

'It's not snobbery. I've met him, remember. Just drawing conclusions, like you do.'

'Anything else noteworthy? I assume no criminal record, no previous bad press?'

'Nothing on Google but I need to look deeper. He says he doesn't know what happened.'

'How do you want to play things?'

'With a straight bat. After all, he is our client, albeit an unusually wealthy one.'

'He suggested coming here, which is surprising.'

'It is, although it's understandable that he wants to play the whole thing down at work. I'll just try to get some background on him and the cars. Feel free to ask anything yourself. Let's drive in. It's number 26, so a few more houses along.'

The Salisburys' house was set back from the road along a gravel driveway and protected from the world's intruders by high, black metal gates. It was an imposing Georgian-style edifice, surrounded by a neat lawn and colourful garden and overlooking fields beyond. According to Zoopla, when it had changed hands last in 2010, it had set the Salisburys back a cool £4 million but it was worth more like £5 million now.

'Ooh! Smile you're on *Candid Camera*,' Judith mumbled, as a camera, mounted on a stone planter, came into view and swivelled around, following their movements as they travelled along the driveway. 'Just an old joke, don't worry.' Constance frowned her confusion.

'Mr Salisbury. How nice to meet you.' Judith's hand was extended to coincide precisely with his opening the door and he took it hesitantly, also grasping Constance's hand in a similar diffident manner.

'I don't have long,' he said. 'Something has come up and I have to leave for a meeting shortly.'

James directed them into an opulent lounge and waved them to sit down on a white leather sofa. He remained standing by the mantelpiece. Judith took out her notebook. Constance pulled out her tablet.

'Well, if we don't have long, let's dive in straightaway, shall we?' Judith began. 'I'm Judith Burton. If your case goes ahead, I will be your barrister in court and I'll be working with Constance to do all I can to defend you.'

James drew a sharp intake of breath. 'I'm hoping it won't come to that, as I told Constance. So tragic. That family, almost totally wiped out in one blow.'

'Yes, absolutely terrible,' Judith replied, 'but, forgive me if I don't stand on ceremony, especially if time is short today. We want to know about the car you were driving. What model was it?'

'A 2016 SEDA,' James stammered.

'It's one of a number of SEDA cars registered to you at this address?'

'Yes.'

'You're the CEO?'

'Yes. And the founder. SEDA was established with the aim of bringing autonomous vehicles to the masses. And, I'm pleased to say, after a lot of hard work, we are nearing our goal.'

'That must be very gratifying for you. Your wife has one too, a SEDA?'

'My wife has a new model, and my eldest son the same.'

'And they're all registered for use on the road in the UK?'

'Absolutely. That's one of the first things the police asked me, but, yes, they are all registered. You can see it as soon as you check the number plates with the DVLA.'

'Do you have a garage?'

'We converted it. But I usually park the car on the drive, close to the house.'

'And at work?'

'I have a designated space in an outdoor car park.'

'And the car was in full working order, no problems, nothing damaged, fully serviced?'

'Yes.'

'What level of autonomy does the car have?'

'How familiar are you with these vehicles?' James asked.

'I've read about them, that you can have different levels of control, some driverless cars have a full manual alternative, others don't even have a steering wheel. Which was yours?'

James squinted up towards the sun pouring in through the sash windows.

'Forgive me. I was just thinking about that poor family again. Would the police really put them through a trial, on top of everything else?'

'I can't say. And perhaps I was leaping ahead. What's important, for now, is to establish the basic facts. The level of autonomy of your car?'

'My SEDA is an early model, a pioneer in many ways, voice-activated software as well as all the laser, radar and full camera package. The 2016s have a manual override.'

'A manual override?'

'Yes. When you get in the car, VERA, the computer, talks to you, asks where you want to go, and there is an option to drive the car in manual mode for the entire journey, or all journeys, if you wish.'

'And why might someone want to use manual mode in a driverless car?'

'We prefer to call them *autonomous* or at the very least *automated*, not driverless. There are a few reasons. I'm not sure if either of you is a car enthusiast.' He allowed his eyes to travel through the window to Constance's modest vehicle before continuing.

'If you were, then, let's say you were embarking on a journey up in Yorkshire in some scenic countryside, up hill and down dale, as they say, you might very well prefer to drive the car yourself, to feel at one with your vehicle.'

At that moment, the gates opened and a white van drove in and continued along the driveway. As it parked next to Constance's car, they read 'McQueen's Security Systems' emblazoned across its side panel.

'Security?' Judith asked.

'There's a lot of burglary in the area,' James explained, 'and I'm probably not the most popular man in town at the moment, either. I thought it prudent to have everything checked over. Excuse me a moment. I'll be right back.'

James exited the room and they watched him, through the window, instructing the young security man, who listened intently, before James tapped him companionably on the shoulder and said his goodbyes.

'I was asking about why a person with an autonomous vehicle might wish to drive themselves and you talked about aficionados.

Any other reason?' Judith resumed her questions, when James returned to the room.

'At the other end of the scale. If you wanted to break the law, speed, travel the wrong way down a one-way street, that kind of thing. You would have to re-take control of the car to do so. The car's programmed to drive according to the law, including any speed restrictions.'

'So if anyone gets into your car, if he does not actively choose the manual mode, the car will drive itself.'

'Yes.'

James handed Judith a business card. 'Toby Barnes is my marketing assistant. The number on the card is direct to him. Make an appointment with him and he'll show you around our factory and answer all your questions. I'll tell him to expect to hear from you. Then you'll understand things better.'

Judith gave the card a cursory glance then tucked it away in her pocket.

'If the car is operating autonomously, what should happen if a person steps out into the road suddenly?' she said.

'It should take evasive action.'

'Like what?'

'Brake and swerve away from the obstacle.'

'Why did that not happen in this case, do you think?'

'This is where I am struggling,' James replied. 'I know I have no memory of the crash, but I still can't believe it happened. Thinking about it now, I wonder if the car was in manual mode, that I'd switched over and then I did something wrong. I can't see any other explanation for the accident.'

A wave of tension rippled across James' face.

'I see.' Judith watched him closely. 'Constance has told me that, understandably, you want first access to all the data from your car,' she said. 'The police have rejected that request, so we now need to make a court application, on your behalf, to persuade the judge you should get to see it first. Presumably you have other means of transport for now.'

'Yes. The police can keep my car as long as they feel necessary, of course. It's the data we need. And I am sure that it will explain this awful mix-up.'

'So we'll get on with the application and let you know.'

'Thank you. I would very much appreciate it if you could do it quickly, please.'

'You said it's impossible for your car to have crashed in autonomous mode,' Constance had her own questions to ask, 'but you accept in your marketing material that your vehicles can still have accidents. Can you explain how that might happen?'

'I prefer to talk about incidents or crashes, collisions,' James said. 'Those words are more neutral, they don't imply fault and, you're right, they can happen, but only in circumstances where there is no way out.'

'Like what?'

'Like totally undetectable black ice, combined with another conventional car pulling out at speed unexpectedly, for example.' James suddenly became more animated. 'Or oil, which is hidden, perhaps because of the camber of the road.'

'I see. Then, assuming your car was in autonomous mode, we would be looking for something like that, at the scene?'

'Yes.' James laughed suddenly and the two women waited for him to elaborate. 'Sorry. Of course it's not funny,' he said. 'It's just that this whole issue has been debated over and over recently. Our illustrious insurers want the government to pick up the tab for all collisions involving autonomous vehicles, when they are first introduced.'

'And what does the government say to that?'

'What you would expect.'

'Why are the insurers taking that approach?'

'They foresee it will be too complicated to explore fault in autonomous vehicles, at least at the beginning, but I think that's an excuse. I mean, they can easily adapt the current process. They are focused too much on profit.'

'And you're not?'

'I am running a business and I want it to be successful, if that's what you mean. But safety is always SEDA's first concern.'

'How did you suffer your own injuries? Do you know?'

'Ah, silly, really. I broke three ribs and bashed my head. They think I wasn't wearing my seat belt properly. That may be right. Sometimes, I spread my work out across the car, even on the back seat. I might have pushed the belt down across my waist to reach my papers. Then, on impact, I hit the air bag pretty hard.'

'The airbag inflated?'

'I believe so. I hope so. The EDR will say. If you view the car, you'll be able to see. Our cars are very safe. We have brought in a number of radical features to protect drivers.'

'Yes. I read that too.'

'Look. I was wondering. Supposing this does all go to a trial and, we don't manage, well, what's the worst that could happen?'

'It's a bit artificial to talk about now, as we have no idea what happened. But, assuming you pleaded not guilty and there was a trial and you were to lose, you would be sentenced to anything from around two years up to fifteen.'

'Fifteen years in prison!'

'The maximum sentence is reserved for the most serious offences; excessive speed over a prolonged period, under the influence of alcohol or drugs, use of your mobile phone or driving a car with mechanical problems you know about. Although I haven't read many of your papers yet, it appears that few, if any, of those aggravating factors are present, but, because of the deaths, it would definitely be a custodial sentence.'

'What about pleading guilty?'

'That's up to you; were you to do that now, we are unlikely to get to the bottom of what really happened.' Judith paused. James watched her intently. 'But your sentence would be reduced. Of course, I don't see how you can do that, when you don't remember what happened and you haven't had a look at your EDR. Of course, this is all assuming you were in control of the vehicle.'

'Yes, I understand. Thank you for being so candid. I do need to go now or I'll be late. The show must go on and all that,' James accompanied them towards the door and forced another half smile. 'But, like I said, feel free to call Toby. He loves visitors.'

'Thank you. We will. Would you have any objection to us speaking to your wife also?' Constance asked.

'I don't speak for Martine,' he replied. 'I'll send you her number and you can ask her yourself.'

***

Judith and Constance sat in Constance's car in James' driveway.

'He still doesn't remember the accident then?' Judith began.

'No,' Constance murmured. 'You don't believe him?'

'It's so convenient, isn't it? I know! I should keep an open mind.'

Constance started up the engine and began to turn the car

around. As they headed out, the security man was inspecting a camera above the gates. He stood back to let them pass.

'Although, unless we can blame the crash on some malfunctioning component made by another manufacturer,' Judith continued, 'hopefully in a far-off and inaccessible land, preferably with no rules about assisting courts in a foreign jurisdiction, either James goes down personally or his company takes the blame. A modern-day manifestation of the Scylla and Charybdis dilemma.'

'Is that Latin again?'

'Apologies. I forgot your lack of a classical education. It roughly translates to between a rock and a hard place,' Judith said.

'What will our defence be, if he was driving?'

'Yes, interesting he was prepared to concede that one unprompted. What did he say?'

'Something like he "must have been in manual mode", because there was no other explanation for the accident.'

'Yes. So he has already appreciated the point. Remember he doesn't go down just because he was driving. There has to be a dangerous element too. From what I've seen so far, James doesn't strike me as the reckless kind. There are other things we should keep an open mind about too.'

'What things?'

'You know I'm always suspicious. This is new technology. Something major could genuinely have malfunctioned. That could be the other explanation and he wouldn't necessarily want us to know about it.'

'How will we find out?

'Well that data he's talking about might show us. And although it was incredibly irritating to be told that he wanted the court application to be done quickly when he was rushing off elsewhere, he is right on that point.'

'I've arranged to see the car this afternoon. Then I'll send you the papers for the application; they're nearly ready. Is it always like this with professional clients? You know – they want everything.'

'That's one reason I left it all behind. Not only do they want everything, they want it yesterday.'

'Are you still doing your mediation training?'

'Not training. I am a fully-fledged, accredited mediator and gaining hours, days, weeks of experience.'

'How is it?'

'Tedious – there's lots of sitting around, but tinged with moments of sheer brilliance and genius.'

'Yours or theirs?'

'Both, if I'm being generous. And the smiles on their faces are a joy to behold when we shake hands, usually around midnight.'

'You like it then?'

Judith shrugged. 'I like this better,' she said.

'Do you want me to call the assistant at the SEDA factory?'

'Oh yes. I think that visit will be most enlightening. I'm looking forward to it already.'

***

After Judith and Constance had left his house, James sat down in his armchair, rested his pounding head and closed his eyes. '*Fifteen years*.' This was some fix he was in, but if he just remained calm and controlled and thought positive thoughts, that would provide the best opportunity for getting through it.

After a few minutes of deep breathing to relax his nerves, he messaged Toby.

Hi Toby. I know I've already asked, but I really need to see the full list of manufacturers whose parts went into the 2016 model and any problems we experienced with them, however small, asap. Thanks, James.

Then, he entered some text into the search engine on his phone. He read the first item which appeared, picked up his home phone, then discarded it in favour of his mobile. He was relieved when his call was picked up promptly.

'Peter? It's James, here...

Yes, good thanks...

No. I'm out of hospital now, thank you...

'...Oh, sorry about that. The police kept my phone, so I had no idea. This is a new one...

'...It's a bit sensitive. It's about my car. Can you talk?...

'...Yes. Awful business. We're all so upset. Martine especially...

'...That's just the thing. I have no memory. I wish I did, then I could sort this all out in a second. We have to rely on the EDR and the cameras, at least for now...

'...Naturally, it's of critical importance that we, at SEDA, get to the bottom of *what really happened*. And I imagine you feel the same, too...

'...Yes. The thing is, if the police start digging around, we're concerned they don't have the appropriate technical expertise to reach the right conclusions. So my…solicitors are going to make an application to get access to the software. Thing is, the police have said they might oppose it. And that would jeopardise our chances of finding out what really happened...

'...I thought you would. It's in a police garage somewhere in East London. The officer is called Dawson, Hackney-based...

'...That's very generous. I knew you would understand the importance of a thorough examination by an expert and reaching the right conclusions...

'...Yes. I'm getting a full list now of all the third parties whose parts went into the car...

'...You'll update me then. Thanks...

'...No, I don't think we need to postpone it. I'm not planning to lose my liberty any time soon. I'll see you then if not before. Goodbye.'

Peter placed his phone face down on the table. He hadn't appreciated that the police might have confiscated James' mobile, which explained his inability to get hold of James till now, but was otherwise of no real importance. He had only called James a few times before giving up. If anyone asked, it was perfectly appropriate for Peter to have wanted to know how his friend was after such a terrible accident.

But James confessing to having no memory of the crash – that was interesting news and, as James had said, threw more importance onto the data and cameras. He should get onto that straight away. And maybe James would find his memory returning sooner than he expected. Peter liked to be optimistic.

38

THE MIDNIGHT blue SEDA was sitting in the corner of a police garage in Mile End. It was a large hatchback with alloy wheels, resembling a standard car in most respects, save for a particularly shiny chrome grille and the bulky apparatus on the roof, comprising roof bars and an elongated, laminated box with a cylindrical structure mounted on the top.

Constance circled the car slowly and noted the marks and dents. The damage on the driver's side at the front was the most pronounced, the bumper compressed with an impressive semi-circular indentation, the bodywork rippled either side and there were deep scratches across the bonnet, too. The windscreen had not survived unscathed; cracks spread out like an intricate spider's web from a central hollow and, when Constance stood on tiptoes and leaned closer, she could see fibres caught between the splintered shards. She also noticed two tiny cameras mounted on the dashboard, one at each side, facing forwards.

Then she turned her attention to the tyres, finding the front right deflated. There was a dark, smeary substance covering the front left, together with a small piece of blue shiny-cotton material, probably part of an item of clothing.

'You can't touch it,' the policeman, who accompanied her, announced.

'Thank you. You've said that, and I heard you.'

'I'm just doing my job.'

She peered in through the driver's side window. There was a steering wheel, as James had said, and two or three buttons on the dashboard and a screen which could be for the radio or GPS. Constance thought she could see two foot pedals, which she assumed were the accelerator and brake for the manual mode function. Other than that, the interior of the car was devoid of gadgets and glaringly empty. She walked around it a few times, taking photographs. The apparatus on the roof intrigued her the most.

'Who's examined the car?' she asked.

'Usual team did finger printing and DNA checks and looked it over,' the policeman replied, leaning close in, to attempt to see for himself what Constance was finding so interesting.

'But it hasn't been cleaned up yet?'

'I don't know anything about that. They're coming back. That's why we have to preserve it. And why no one can touch it.'

'No one has examined the car who knows anything about computers or these kind of cars?'

'You'll have to ask Chief Inspector Dawson. He's in charge. But I don't think anyone special has been round.'

'Are you here every day?'

'Yes, but we close up at six, and not weekends.'

'Has anyone been in and taken anything away from the vehicle?'

'Not while I've been here. Inspector Dawson told me no one is to touch it and that's how it's been on my watch.'

'Do you have the key?'

'In the office.'

'Any chance you could bring it over?'

'You're not allowed in the car, Miss.'

'I know, but if we can just unlock it, then the lights will come on and I can see inside more easily, without opening the doors. I wouldn't be touching it.'

The policeman collected the key and, as Constance had hoped, as they returned to within two metres of the car, the doors unlocked automatically and the interior was flooded with light.

'Hello this is VERA, your voice-activated, enhanced, road-experience assistant. How can I help you?' They could hear VERA's dulcet tones from outside the car.

The policeman quickly pressed the key fob to lock the doors again.

'I told you we shouldn't touch it. I'll get in trouble for this,' he said.

'We haven't touched the car,' Constance said, hurrying to the driver's side to look inside again, with the benefit of the rapidly receding light. 'Don't worry.'

Constance took some photographs of the very empty interior, including the blood-spattered airbag, now hanging limp and flaccid from the centre of the steering wheel.

'I didn't know it spoke,' the policeman said. 'That's the computer then?'

'I think so.'

'Look, have you finished yet? There can't be much else for you to see.'

'Thank you and goodbye,' VERA intoned, before powering down. The lights inside the car were extinguished.

The policeman shivered.

'I wish you hadn't made me do that,' he confessed. 'All that talking. Gives me the creeps.'

39

Martine Salisbury marched up to Constance and Judith, tossed her chestnut mane to one side and spread her shopping bags on the floor under the table.

'Hi, I'm Martine,' she announced loudly. 'Sorry to keep you waiting. They were short-staffed in Selfridges. I knew I should have gone to Oxford Street. This one can't really compete but, there you are.'

'No need to apologise. We were quite happy here watching the world go by,' Judith replied. 'We seldom get the opportunity. I'm Judith and this is Constance. We're advising your husband on his car accident.'

'I know who you are, although I'm not sure I can help. I wasn't there. I thought you spoke to James?'

'We did, but then he had to rush off and we had some general questions about timing. We thought you might be able to answer them, save bothering your husband again.'

'Fire away. I needed a break. Shopping can be exhausting, you know.'

'You have a SEDA car also?' Judith began, nudging the nearest shopping bag away with her leg.

'Yes. We all do, me, James and Joshua, my eldest son.'

'Do you enjoy driving your car?'

Martine leaned forward and smiled, revealing a perfectly white regiment of teeth.

'Is that a trick question?' she asked.

'It's not supposed to be.'

'OK. Sorry, I wasn't sure. I mean, I don't drive it, you see. That's the whole point.'

'How long have you been driven around by your current vehicle?' Judith re-took control of the questions.

'I've had this car a few months. I had another SEDA before that, the same model as James'.'

'And have you had any accidents?'

'Not in the SEDA. Before that, I was a bit accident-prone. James was cross. I find it hard to concentrate on the road sometimes, when there are so many other things going on.'

'Near misses?'

'No. Not in the SEDA.'

'Are there any concerns you have about autonomous vehicles?'

'Only how long it's taking to get them onto our roads. James has been working on this for, what, nearly fifteen years. He says we could have been at this stage at least five years earlier.'

'What's holding things up?'

'Lawyers, always picking over things. The government has this legal department, James says they should all be shot, well, he finds them...frustrating.'

'What kind of issues are the lawyers raising?'

Martine turned to Constance and tapped her lightly on the arm.

'Could I have a coffee do you think? Latte, with a shot of hazelnut. Thanks.'

Had Martine still been looking in Constance's direction when her request landed, she might well have been turned to stone. As it was, she was already engaging with Judith again when Constance rose stiffly and headed off to the counter. 'I think I'll leave my husband to talk about that,' Martine continued. 'Wouldn't want to get things wrong on such an important matter. I don't talk business, well not his, anyway.'

'Has your husband ever lost his memory before?' Judith asked.

'No, of course not.'

'And he's generally in good health?'

'He's very fit.'

'No problems with eyesight, that kind of thing.'

'Look, these are really things you need to ask him. But there's nothing I know about.'

'And are you employed at the moment?'

'I go to a homeless shelter in Camden and help make lunch or dinner.'

'Is that a regular occurrence?'

'Tuesdays and Wednesdays.'

'You don't have any paid employment?'

Martine glanced over her shoulder and reached up for her coffee as Constance returned.

'I don't see what that's got to do with James' car crashing,' she said.

'We like to build up a profile of our client; family, background. Sometimes the tiniest fact can be material. You don't have to answer any of our questions if you don't feel comfortable.'

Martine took a sip from her syrup-infused coffee.

'No, it's all right. I'm a model, a fashion model. I used to do competitions. I held some titles. I still get offered some work but I can't always fit it in.'

'I imagine it's a difficult profession to dip in and out of.'

Martine shrugged.

'Does anyone else drive James' car?'

'No!'

'You seem very certain.'

'He doesn't like anyone else to touch it. Actually, he helped build it. He's very handy. He likes to do things like that, if he has the time.'

'Your husband told us his car wasn't garaged. Who has access to your house, other than family?'

'We have a housekeeper, Lina.'

'Any other workmen come by?' Judith asked.

'The security guys, once a month, to check everything, the cameras, the alarm.'

'Ah yes. McQueen's'

'How did you know that?'

'We saw the van when we were at your house. You have a lot of cameras.'

'James worries about me, when he's away. I didn't like them at first, but now I'm used to them. It makes him feel better, knowing I'm safe.'

'I would have thought you would be comfortable with cameras, given your profession?'

Martine looked from Judith to Constance. 'It's not the same as when I'm working. Everyone needs some privacy, don't they?'

'Does anyone else visit your house regularly?'

'Waitrose delivery. They ring and we buzz them in.'

'Is it possible that any of these visitors could have tampered with your husband's car?'

'Is that what you think happened?' Martine leaned forward onto the table.

'It's not likely, but we're considering every option. We haven't yet got access to the car, you see, to check whether it malfunctioned or not.'

'OK, so it is possible. Lots of people come and go, when I'm not there. Lina lets them in. Dean could check the film on the security cameras on the gates, if you wanted, check who's been in. I wouldn't know where to start.'

'Dean?'

'McQueen, the security man.'

'I see.' Judith stifled a smirk. 'What about your sons?'

'Joshua does his own thing. He stays at friends a lot.'

And your other son?'

'Zac, my youngest, he's away most of the time.'

'Away?'

'At school. He's only home a few weeks a year.' Martine took another sip.

'On the 10th of October, the day of the crash, can you tell us what you and James were doing?'

'He was working in the study. I took him in a coffee and some juice and then I left.'

'What time was that?'

'About nine.'

'So he started early?'

'He's a morning person.'

'Where did you go?'

'To the gym. You don't say much,' Martine squawked at Constance.

'Do you know the expression "still waters run deep," Mrs Salisbury?' Judith replied. Judith flicked through her notes and Martine shrugged and began to collect up her parcels. 'Is that it then? I told you I didn't know anything.'

***

Judith and Constance sat in silence after Martine's departure. Eventually Judith spoke.

'What did she put in her coffee?' she asked.

'Hazelnut shot. Some people like it.'

'Are they all people like Martine?'

'What do you mean?'

'Oh never mind. That's the old Judith speaking. The new enlightened Judith would not sneer at hazelnut shots.'

'I didn't realise you were undergoing some kind of metamorphosis?'

'Really? Well, perhaps it's not so noticeable. What did you think of Miss ex-model, shop till I drop?'

'I thought it was interesting that when she mentioned the modelling, her voice dropped. She sounded full of regret for something.'

'Yes. Well spotted, it might be as simple as her being too old now.'

'Naomi Campbell's still working, and Kate Moss. They're both in their forties.'

'True. I'm not sure Martine Braithwaite was ever in their

league, though. Dig around. There might be something there.'

'What do you mean? What am I looking for?'

'The usual.'

'But this was a car crash and she wasn't there.'

'We only have her word for that so far. I know it's unlikely, but look into her background and keep an open mind. Anything else?'

'She wasn't exactly helpful with the names of people who came to the house.'

'Well, I don't know. There was Dean McQueen wasn't there?' Judith laughed aloud this time. 'Do you think his parents really thought that one through when they christened him? Oh forgive me. Ask her for a list of all their tradesmen; plumbers, electricians, gardeners, with phone numbers, if she has them. Tell her to ask the housekeeper too. Let's make Martine do a little work, shall we?'

'You seriously think someone messed with James' car?'

'Look. James is certain there will be something on that black box which will make everything all right. I'm not. We have to have other defence options. Going back to our lovely Martine, what was lacking?'

'She didn't ask us anything at all.'

'Yes. Very good. No "What's going to happen to James?" "Will there be a trial?" "Could he go to prison?"'

'Maybe she's already had advice via their company lawyer, the one who recommended me.'

'Or maybe she doesn't care. Oh, you're probably right and I'm reading too much into it. She wanted some light relief from her heavy retail day, not to sit with two dour-faced lawyers and contemplate the prospect of her husband behind bars. It might seriously curtail her shopping habit.'

'Speak for yourself.'

'What do you think she does all day, children away, James travelling?'

'There's her volunteering.'

'Yes, but that's only twice a week. And the gym, she said. Shall we go? It's getting late.' Judith rose and stretched out her shoulders and back.

Constance switched off her tablet and tucked it into her bag.

'Hm, but do you know what?' Judith said.

'I'm sure you're going to tell me.'

'I might try one of those shots in a coffee to go. Just for research purposes, that is. Which would you recommend?'

40

CONSTANCE AND Judith entered SEDA's flagship building. In the central, all-glass atrium, a white car stood vertically on its nose. Judith walked all around it. The means of suspension was not at all obvious and from the entrance it appeared to be floating through the air, its open doors flapping in the breeze, like wings. Judith had the sense of something dynamic and vibrant happening in this place.

Tracking the reception area were photographs of SEDA's various models of autonomous vehicle. Most of these had the tell-tale, revolving, aerial-like structure on their roofs, which they both now knew concealed a LIDAR, a combination of laser and radar technology. Constance pointed out James' 2016 model in the middle of the row of images; a chunky, large, conventional hatchback. The later versions, including the up-to-the-minute Go! had become sleeker and more streamlined, with a definite futuristic design brief.

'Hello. Are you Constance?' Toby was ambling towards them.

'Yes. And this is Judith.'

'I'm Toby, deputy CEO. I suppose acting CEO when James is out and about. Hope you found us easily. James asked me to show you round. I thought we could start at the factory and then you can ask questions afterwards, if anything isn't clear.'

Toby led them along some equally shiny corridors and a walkway, linking the various buildings on the sprawling site, until they entered a large rectangular hangar. Running down the centre was a production line with cars in various stages of construction, surrounded by a series of robotic arms.

'This is where all our production happens,' Toby announced proudly.

'How many people work here?' Judith asked, raising her voice over the combination of music and mechanical noises.

'In the factory? Up to twenty at any time. It's a small team. We're keeping production low for now, but there's capacity here to make loads more if we need. But because we have the robots, it's probably equal to having at least another twenty staff.'

'And is it efficient using the robots?'

'Yes. They're very cost-effective. The maintenance cost is low. And the plant has a really low carbon footprint. It's one of our big selling points. All our electricity is generated locally either through solar, wind or bio. We insist that all the packaging we get in from suppliers is reusable and that anything we use ourselves is recycled too. Here, let me show you one of the cars close up.'

He marched them to the far end of the room, where the cars were nearing completion and the volume of the music was lower.

'We work with water-based adhesives and we've swapped petrol-based seating for soy foam. All much better for the environment. Take a look. You can't tell.'

Constance crouched down and leaned inside the car. There was a sweet, spicy smell, reminiscent of cinnamon, completely unlike the rubbery scent she had expected.

'Well done,' Toby giggled as Constance's nose wrinkled. 'Do you like it? We're doing research on the most attractive consumer smell, although it's not easy because people are always changing their minds. And, can you believe this? Now we've got rid of VOCs, people are complaining that they don't have the new car smell any more. Amazing isn't it? You'd think they would be satisfied that we'd reduced the chance of them getting cancer, but no they all miss the smell.'

'What are VOCs?' Judith asked.

'Volatile organic compounds. The stuff we used to put in car interiors gave them off. They can give you cancer. The new stuff doesn't.'

'And is the music supposed to help production too? Like with plants?'

'It is a bit loud, I agree, and not everyone likes it,' Toby laughed. We let a different member of the team pick the music each day. James says if they're happy at work, they're more productive.'

Constance cast a quick look around to try to guess who had picked today's dirgey playlist.

'Do you have other factories?'

'Oh yes. We're in six countries, the biggest is China. We are selling out there already, very profitable, although we did it quietly. James wants the UK to be the big launch. Did you know, in China, you're not allowed a toilet break? You have to wait till your lunch. And if you take a day off because you get sick, you lose your job.'

'I'm sure Mr Salisbury would not condone those practices in

his factory though?' Judith interrupted.

'What? Yes. I meant in the competitors' factories, not ours. But this is our flagship, as we are a British company.'

'Would it be all right for Constance to take some photographs? It's all so interesting. We don't want to miss anything.'

'I'm sorry but we have a strict no photographs rule,' Toby said. 'We had to let one of our best workers go a few weeks back, after he took a selfie in front of one of the side panels. Competitors, you understand.'

'Yes, of course.'

'Would you like to go for a test drive?'

'Yes please,' Judith replied for both of them.

Toby led them outside to a line of five identical cars. These cars were just like the one they had viewed in its nearly-finished state; there was no steering wheel or gear stick and the dashboard was pared back to a narrow elliptical screen.

He grabbed some keys from a table, muttered a few words to a nearby technician and then invited Constance to sit in the back and Judith in the front, while he took the driver's seat.

'There's no steering wheel,' Judith remarked.

'No. This is a new model, not out on the roads yet.' Toby pressed a start button with his index finger and then announced 'Test drive one' in a loud voice. The car moved off smoothly. He folded his arms and sat back. Judith shivered and gripped the sides of her chair.

'This car is fully autonomous then?' she said.

'Yes and no. It's level four. The car is totally in control except there is an emergency brake. It's tucked away near my right foot. You probably didn't notice. That's all.'

'Is there a level five?'

'There will be, yes. All computer-operated with no option to get involved. But we won't be trialling level five until more people have level three and four on the road. There's no point.'

'So where are we going on our test drive?'

'We've built a model village. It covers around half a mile. We've tried to make it authentic with different road situations, but the houses are just wooden fronts. And we add things or change them each month too.'

'Why do you do that?'

'We don't want the cars, well the computers, to learn the routes too well. We like to mix things up a bit. Give them new experiences.'

The car stopped at a red traffic light on the outskirts of the man-made town.

'It's smoother than I imagined,' Judith commented.

'Most people say that. But that's logical isn't it? The car is better than humans at anticipating how it should ride the bends. I always think it's like when the dentist cleans your teeth and he keeps catching your gums. You know, yourself, how to do it without making them bleed.'

'Yes, very true.' Judith resisted the impulse to cast a disparaging look at Constance. 'How fast can it go?'

'We do tests up to eighty miles per hour, on another track. But the cars can go much faster.'

'Does it avoid other vehicles effectively?'

'Wouldn't be much good if it didn't, would it? Each car is aware of the positioning of other cars on the road. That's why they can't collide. But our cars also talk to each other.'

'But don't they only talk to other SEDAs?'

'For now, yes, but we want to reach agreement with other

manufacturers as well. That's where James is now, in fact, although I can't say anything more about it. Top secret.' He tapped the side of his nose.

'But then you'll have to share data with those other companies, won't you?' Judith persisted. 'And aren't they your competitors too?'

'You ask all the hardest questions,' Toby joked. 'We are exploring ways to do it. There are lots of tricky bits, I know. And it's hard to know what to share without giving too much away.'

'Toby?...' Constance leaned forward to get his attention. 'I understood these cars can talk?'

Toby pressed a button on the dashboard and a small red light began to blink.

'Hello VERA. Toby here. How are you today?' he chuckled.

'Hello Toby. This is VERA. I am your voice-activated, enhanced, road-experience assistant. How may I help you today?'

'That's why I turn it off,' he told Judith and Constance in a loud whisper. 'I hear VERA in my sleep, saying the same old thing over and over. James chose her voice. VERA is actually the computer, so she's here all the time, even if you can't hear her.'

'I'm sorry. I didn't understand what you wanted,' VERA intoned. 'Please repeat your instruction.'

'I wasn't talking to you, VERA. Can you continue on test course one, please.'

'Yes, thank you. Can I ask who are the other occupants?'

'You can ask but I'm not going to tell you.'

'Oh Toby. Please can I try?' Judith pleaded. 'This is so fascinating for me.'

Toby shrugged his acceptance, delighted that his guests were enjoying themselves so much.

'Hello VERA. My name is Judith Burton. I'm a ventriloquist. Do you know what that is?'

'Hello Judith Burton. A ventriloquist is a person who can make their voice appear to come from somewhere else.'

'Very good. VERA. If I said that I wanted you to take a right turn at the next roundabout, could you do that please?'

'At the next roundabout, there is no right turn.'

'Thank you. I am asking you to turn right please.'

'Judith Burton. There is no right turn. Not able to turn right. I will continue on test course one, travelling straight ahead.'

'VERA. Can you drive straight into that house on my left, the big one with the blue front door?'

'Judith Burton. I can only drive on the road.'

'I have some heavy shopping. It would be better if you could drive closer.'

'No shopping detected in the car, Judith Burton. Are you requesting me to park?'

'All right. Can you park please VERA outside that house on the left, the one with the pale blue door.'

The car slowed, the left indicator lit up and it came to a smooth halt, parked neatly around 1cm from the kerb and directly outside the house Judith had indicated.

'Impressive,' Judith mumbled. 'Thank you. I would like to continue on test course one now please.'

The car indicated then pulled out smoothly.

'Watch out!' Judith shouted without warning. Toby leaped out of his seat, his head just missing the roof of the car. But the car continued, without any deviation from its route or change in speed.

'VERA. Can't you see the people on the crossing?' Judith called out again. Finally realising that this was Judith's method of putting the car through its paces, Toby began to giggle hysterically, after checking there really was no one on the crossing. This time the car slowed noticeably before speeding up again.

'Judith Burton. You are mistaken. There is no one on the crossing.'

They returned to their starting point outside the hangar and exited the car. Toby, still sniggering to himself, pressed the key fob and the car reversed itself into its parking space.

'I know what you were doing in there, Judith,' he wagged his finger at her, which Judith accepted graciously. 'But you can't trick VERA,' he continued.

'How does this car differ from the one which was involved in the accident – Mr Salisbury's car?' Judith asked.

Toby's eyes narrowed for the first time. 'Does anyone know what happened yet?' he asked. 'Why it crashed? I mean, James doesn't remember.'

'The car is going to be examined to determine precisely what happened. Mr Salisbury is supportive. Given your...extensive knowledge, do you have any particular concerns?'

'Oh no. Not that. Not concerns. You've seen how the cars perform. What were you asking me? Oh yes, differences. James' car was a level three. That means it operates in normal driver or autonomous mode.'

Toby began walking quickly back towards the main reception. Judith and Constance struggled to keep up.

'But when it was in autonomous mode, it would be just like the car we tested?' Judith persisted.

'Yes.'

'And how do you know if you are in one mode or the other?'

She stopped deliberately, so Toby was forced to stop walking too, or shout his answer from some distance.

'Usually when you switch on, it's in autonomous mode and, after you've done the whole "Hello I'm VERA" thing,' he rolled his eyes theatrically, 'she'll ask you if you want to move to manual. If not, she's in charge.'

'And can you choose to take back control later on?'

'Yes. In James' car, whenever you like.'

'What about the software?'

'What about the software?'

'Is it developed here?'

'Yes. But I can't take you to that part. It's top secret, I'm afraid.'

'Why's that?'

'Competitors.'

'Yes. I should have guessed.'

'We can't risk letting anyone unauthorised in.'

'What kind of things are you still working on – if the cars are ready to be sold to the public?'

Toby ran his hand over his chin and began to walk away again, but more slowly this time.

'Lots of things. The LIDAR equipment is very expensive. We want to find cheaper ways of navigation which are just as safe. And other things I can't talk about.'

'And am I right that you need government clearance before you can sell the cars in the UK?'

'We're waiting for the government to publish a list of approved vehicles, any day now. Then everything will take off...' He raised his arm, palm upwards, towards the ceiling, 'like a rocket, to the moon. It's no secret that we all want to be on that list.'

'Has there been a lot of consultation with the government?'

'Tons. And the insurers and the software providers. We're all working together, so you can imagine how quickly it's all going.'

'And when things go wrong with a prototype, do you check it out here?'

'They don't usually go wrong, but yes. We're constantly monitoring the test cars. We can connect to them while they're out on the roads, see what they're seeing. It's very clever.'

'Do you have a suitable person here to look at the software from Mr Salisbury's car, and to analyse what happened when it crashed, if that were necessary?'

Toby hovered outside the door leading back into the reception area.

'As long as we have the EDR, we can take a look. Is there anything else you'd like to see?' he asked, although he hinted heavily that their visit was at an end, by choosing that moment to burst through the swing doors and lead them towards the exit.

'No. You have been extremely helpful and informative. I'm intrigued. You're very young to hold such a senior position in the company,' Judith said. 'Is your background in business or technology?'

'I came in as an apprentice, straight from school,' Toby said. 'James trained me. I did well, so he promoted me.'

'I see,' Judith said. 'What a fantastic opportunity for you.'

'Yes,' Toby said flatly.

'Can I call you again, if I need to?'

'Sure. You have my number.'

***

'Interesting, isn't it all?' Judith began, as she and Constance sat drinking coffee in a Little Chef, a couple of miles from the SEDA factory. Judith scowled after her first mouthful and shunted her cup away.

'Yes. Looks like it's going to happen then.'

'A world full of identical, faceless vehicles, travelling in equally-spaced convoy, with the option of customising the voice of the software to whatever accent you desire. Hm. That's not what's intriguing me, though.'

'How do you mean?'

'One of SEDA's cars has just been involved in a fatal collision, the fallout for SEDA is potentially extremely damaging. When a similar vehicle crashed in the USA in 2015, it set the whole industry back a year. Not only that, SEDA's CEO was driving it. What would you expect from them?'

'You think they should be closing the doors, lying low. We are James' lawyers. He wants to prove the accident wasn't his fault and you asked for more information.'

'But showing us how amazing his product is won't help him. Far better for him to find some niggling little problem they haven't ironed out yet that caused the crash, and then present it to us. Hey presto! He has a complete defence. Instead, we get a VIP day out at the factory and a direct phone line to the number two, even if he is only a boy.'

'You're assuming he has some kind of plan to save himself, to save his business. He says he just wants to find the truth.'

'He is a businessman. He's been doing this for years. Of course he has a plan. How much has the government spent on the autonomous car scheme so far?'

'I know £20 million was invested, just in cars talking to each other. It must be at least ten times that, if you look at all the other aspects of the project.'

'So, perhaps the most interesting thing of all is why this case has not yet disappeared down a large hole. It can't be in the government's interest to have this going through the courts, all this close scrutiny. Maybe they've told James, privately, that if he just hangs on, it will get buried.'

'I don't believe that. He's pretty worried about it. And they can't bury it. People wouldn't accept it. Neil Layton, the husband, has begun a social media campaign. He had 18,000 Twitter followers after two hours and he was at 200,000 when I last looked.'

'Ah. The power of social media. When is the application to get hold of the EDR?'

'I've sent you the papers to review,' Constance said, pausing to stir her drink with a plastic stick. 'I thought Toby was rather sweet, though.'

'Sweetness is not usually a quality associated with promotion to acting CEO of a major manufacturing company, even one which has not sold any products in the UK yet. You heard what he said. He came straight from school. There's no evidence of business acumen or managerial skills. And he was hardly effusive in his attitude towards James, was he?'

'He was, at the end, when he was trying to get us to leave.'

'Perhaps.'

'And not many people like lawyers asking questions, and you are an especially scary lawyer.'

'Am I?' Judith looked affronted. 'How did James describe Toby to us?'

'He called him his marketing assistant.'

'Yes. You're right. I bet that would have wiped the smile off "acting CEO" Toby's face in a flash.'

'Do you think the government forced SEDA to take Toby? You know they push all these apprentice schemes.'

'You mean take on an idiot and we'll give you a tax break? Nothing would surprise me these days. Shall we go home then, now I've finished my rant? But I sense we may have a few more revelations to come with this one. I can hardly wait for tomorrow.'

41

THERESE SAT quietly on the sofa, hugging the soft teddy to her chest. Jacquie had given up trying to tempt her to eat and was in the kitchen, mixing formula for Ruby.

Neil had been despatched upstairs to fetch the photo albums they had made for each of the children's first year of life. He had hung back when she asked him, the words 'Are you sure you want to do this?' etched across his face, but her icy expression had warned him not to challenge any request. Even so, his hands trembled as he retraced his steps, carrying the colourful books.

He perched beside Therese and lay them down on the coffee table; pink for Georgia and blue for Bertie. Therese had secretly wished for a girl for their first-born and she had read countless articles on how to ensure she achieved her chosen gender, from what to eat in the months before conception to what music to play during sex. And even though she knew it was too late to have any more influence on the gender of her baby, once the blue line appeared on her pregnancy test, she had tried to have girlish thoughts throughout the pregnancy, to wear sweeter perfume than usual, to read romantic novels and to wear pink more often than before, in a subtle attempt to cajole her first-born into being a girl.

When Georgia had arrived, Therese had felt smug as well as ecstatic, having gone along with Neil previously when they selected and whittled down a short list of boys' names, successfully concealing her lack of enthusiasm. Which wasn't to say that she had loved or wanted Bertie any the less when he appeared; his timing had been perfect too. After eighteen months of pink-and-floral-fest adoration for her daughter, she was fully prepared for another male ego charging into their household.

She turned the first page of Georgia's book and, as she leaned in to scrutinise and commit to memory every detail of every photograph of her daughter, Neil placed his hand on her arm. She allowed it to stay there for a few seconds only.

'Please don't,' she whispered.

'Let me help you,' he said.

She pushed his hand away and continued staring at Georgia's photos.

Neil sat quietly beside his wife; he had no more tears left. He was desolate and shrunken. His perfect life was shattered. He could not begin to contemplate how they would ever recover from this blow. He queried if he was strong enough to withstand the months and years ahead.

Jacquie entered, humming lightly, the same lilting melody she had sung to each of her now deceased grandchildren, and settled herself nearby, as Ruby obediently drank her milk, her eyelids drooping. She was a model child, a breeze of a pregnancy, a three-hour labour and had slept through from eight weeks, as if she knew instinctively that her two older siblings had taken all the pressure on their shoulders, and she was free to do whatever and be whomever she wished. Jacquie thought of asking Therese to hold Ruby, but then decided it was still too early.

'She was so beautiful, wasn't she?' Therese whispered, stroking Georgia's face in the first photograph.

'Yes, she was,' Neil replied.

'How could he take her away from us? How could he do that? It's so unfair.'

Neil turned to see the bottle slipping from the mouth of his youngest child, now his only child, as she drifted off to her world of milk and cuddles. He rose, took her from Jacquie and tucked her close up to his chest. And he swore, with every last breath in his body, that he would protect Ruby on her journey through life.

'I want Georgia and Bertie,' Therese said. 'I want them back.' She was moaning, rocking backwards and forwards on the sofa. He gripped onto Ruby more tightly and watched Therese, struggling with his priorities as father and husband. He wanted to hold his daughter and never let her go, but he wanted to comfort his wife too. He sat down with Ruby still in his arms. Therese turned away from him.

'I know you do,' he whispered.

Neil's phone buzzed in his back pocket. It was probably Inspector Dawson replying to his enquiry of whether James Salisbury was to be charged or not. Or perhaps it was a notification of some more Twitter followers. His campaign for the Autonomous Vehicles Bill to be thrown out was gaining support. He wanted to check, but this wasn't the time.

Therese began to sob quietly into a cushion, the photo album open on her knee. And Neil knew that there could be no moving on unless someone was punished for what had happened to his family. Therese might prefer to focus on their loss, but his priority was retribution. Someone was to blame for this tragedy, and someone had to pay.

42

JUDITH STOOD outside Court 11, reviewing her papers. It was quiet and tranquil, and she welcomed the orderly beginning to her day. This was the civil court system; no defendants on criminal charges to represent or bolster or cajole, just people arguing over money or property or valuable intangible rights. It was the hygienic world she had left behind, in favour of the hurly-burly of the criminal law.

She could see their application to obtain access to the SEDA's data, listed on the door of the courtroom, but, with only five minutes to go to their appointed time, Constance was nowhere to be seen. The court clerk unlocked the door and peered out.

'Are you here for this one?' she asked, pointing to the first case on the list.

'Yes.'

'Is anyone else coming?'

'I'm not aware of anyone else, but perhaps we should wait another five minutes?' Judith ventured, reflecting that Constance would not want to miss the fun.

'I'll tell his lordship,' the clerk said. 'He's reading the papers. He says it'll take him a few minutes. When the light comes on you can come in. That should give anyone else time to arrive. After that they'll be too late.' She disappeared back inside.

Another ten minutes passed before Constance suddenly appeared, barrelling her way towards Judith from the lift, breathless and flustered.

'I'm so pleased you haven't gone in yet,' she called out, when she was within earshot.

'What's happened?'

'The Minister for Transport is objecting to our application. He's sending someone now. They've asked if you can tell the judge, but they say they'll be here any minute.'

'On what grounds are they objecting?'

'Public interest. I haven't had time to get hold of any cases to help us, they only told me half an hour ago as I was leaving the office and, since then, I've been trying to find out what's going on.'

'Public interest?'

'That's all I know. Perhaps the rest will be clear when they arrive.'

At that moment a delegation of four men, deep in hushed conversation, swept around the corner, heading in their direction. Judith recognised Adam Venables QC, a renowned public law barrister, accompanied by three other suited men. He waved the others to silence momentarily, as they passed close by, nodded politely in their direction and then the group came to a halt a few metres away, resuming their intense debate, in an undertone, their backs to Constance and Judith.

Then the red light on the court door turned to green and they all trooped inside.

Judge Smyth settled himself before them and opened a small laptop.

'Ms Burton, thank you, I have read your application on behalf of your client, Mr James Salisbury. Is your client here today?'

'No, my lord. He is still a little unwell. He was injured in the collision which has led to this application.'

'I see. Yes. Mr Venables, an unexpected pleasure?'

'My lord, I am appearing today, instructed by Her Majesty's government, more specifically, by the Minister for Transport, the Right Honourable Alan Tillinghurst MP. It is with great regret that I address you, without having provided papers in advance or, indeed, having been able to give my learned friend, here, notice of our opposition to her application. I only took carriage of this matter within the last two hours. And, also, less than ideal, I am afraid that I have been instructed to ask for my reasons for opposition to this application to be heard by you privately.'

'Hm. Thank you Mr Venables. Is your client here today?'

'No, my lord.'

'He's not unwell?'

'No, my lord. Just elsewhere.'

'And on what basis are you asking for a private hearing? Let me understand, when you say private, you are even objecting to Ms Burton and her instructing solicitor being present?'

'I am, yes. If I might hand up a letter from the Minister, then matters may become a little less opaque.'

'Yes, very well. Ms Burton, bear with me for a moment.'

The judge read the letter through carefully, laid it down on his desk and spent a few minutes reviewing matters on his laptop. Then he stared out at his audience.

'Ms Burton. I know this will be frustrating for you, and Mr Venables, it's a pity you were unable to provide a little more warning to the applicant, to save the attendance of all parties. However, I confirm that the information provided by a member of Her Majesty's government is sufficient to satisfy the requisite test of a "public matter of a highly sensitive nature". Accordingly, I will, albeit with some reluctance on my part, as the maxim "justice should be seen to be done" has always formed part of my daily mantra, accede to Mr Venables' request to hear his objection and cross application for release of the data in question to his client, in private.'

'My lord. The car belongs to Mr Salisbury, he is currently under investigation by the police, the data which will be recovered is crucial to his defence and I am instructed that his company's technicians are best-placed to extract the data safely,' Judith was not giving up so easily. 'A man's liberty may be at stake here. I have not had time to find any cases to back me up, but I am certain there must be a number of heavy-weight decisions directing that the balance should fall in favour of the liberty of a British subject as against "a public matter of a highly sensitive nature".'

'Ms Burton, you and your client have my sympathies, but you don't have the law on your side on this one. If your team could leave now, please. Do wait outside, in case we need you again. And, if there is anyone else out there who looks as if they may be tempted to enter, inform them this is a private hearing now until further notice.'

Judith bowed to the judge obediently and exited the room. Once she was outside the court, she stomped her way to the furthest corner of the waiting area and sat down, depositing her papers unceremoniously in the next seat and scowling broadly.

Constance trotted obediently behind.

'This is outrageous. We should appeal,' Judith said. 'Sneaky, sly, shifty application! Can you find out who the duty judge is today and see if we can get before him? How did the Department of Transport get to know about our application, though?'

'I'm sorry. I think it was my fault.' Constance dug her toe into the hessian carpet and avoided Judith's hard stare.

'How could this be your fault?'

'I told Dawson we were going to make the application today. I wanted to make sure he didn't mess with the car in the meantime.'

'Oh don't be silly. I would have done the same. If the police had botched it up it would have been even worse. Everyone would have been in trouble then, including Dawson. The Department of Transport will have sufficient technical expertise, I hope, to do the job properly. It can't be that difficult. I suppose they see this accident as having wider repercussions and they want to be informed. You could see Smyth didn't like it, though. He smelled a rat.'

'Do you still want to appeal?'

Judith sighed and leaned forward, clasping her hands together.

'It won't do any good. Let's see what happens. They will get the access they want for their chosen expert. The best we can hope for today, I think, is an order to review their report within twenty-four hours. What? What is it? I know you're cross. Tell me.'

Constance laughed sadly.

'I know James is not like most of the defendants I represent, that he can look after himself, but I do still feel that things are harder for him than for most.'

'Do you?'

'He can't remember what happened and now, not only does he

have the police on the other side, it looks like the government is against him too.'

'Oh this is just a little blip along the way of our near text-book defence preparation. Now I know why I hate public law. As soon as you get any government entity shouting "public interest" or "national security" or one of those other signifying-nothing buzz words, you know you're screwed. Apologies. The profanity was uncalled for but liberating. When you next see James, make sure you tell him what tremendous progress we're making on his behalf. We don't want him getting depressed about his prospects.'

43

MARTINE ARRIVED home from her volunteering to find James packing a suitcase.

'I bought lamb,' she mumbled, wide-eyed, standing in the doorway of their bedroom.

'Oh, sorry, darling.' He crossed the room and kissed her on the cheek. 'Something's come up and I need to go to France.'

'You didn't say. I was going to make it Tuscan-style, how you like it.'

'My mouth is watering as you're speaking. Will it keep till tomorrow?'

'Probably.'

'There's been a problem at our Toulouse plant,' he explained. 'I had no warning. I'm catching the Eurostar so I can get there for an early meeting in the morning. Try to sort things out before they develop into something more serious. Will you be OK?'

'Don't worry about me. I'll have a long bath and watch another box set.' She forced a smile. 'But, do you think it's a good idea for you to go?'

'I have a business to run.'

'Didn't your lawyers say not to go abroad?'

'They said I might get asked to surrender my passport. I wasn't. And it's been days now and I haven't heard anything.'

'Nothing at all?'

'No.'

'So it might disappear?'

'I don't think so.'

'The older one looked down her nose at me, you know,' Martine pouted.

'What? Who?'

'Your lawyers, when I met them for coffee.'

'Are you sure? You can be oversensitive. What did she say?'

'It wasn't what she said.'

'Ah.' James sounded unconvinced. 'Would you like me to complain, to the police, to the, whoever it is…Law Society?' he asked.

Martine took a step into the room.

'No. I'd like you to understand, that's what I'd like.'

James swallowed hard. 'I'm sorry,' he said. 'I should have asked, before, how it went when you spoke to them. You didn't have to see them.'

'How would it have looked if I'd refused?'

'I'm grateful that you did.' Martine was still pouting. 'How did she upset you?' James asked.

'It was her attitude. They see themselves as working women, don't they? Career women. And I'm just a "trophy wife".'

'I'm sure you're wrong. The older one, Judith, is very direct, as I remember, but I didn't see her as judgemental.'

'Well I did.'

'You do your bit, at the shelter. You're just as clever as they are and twice as beautiful. You don't need a career to prove it. You don't have to speak to them again, if you don't want to.'

'I'm sorry. The last thing you need is me feeling sorry for myself. I wish you'd let me help you more. Everyone else is doing something to help. Your mind is probably not on the business at the moment.'

'You are helping me. Just by being here for me. And keeping going. That's what I need right now. And I'm getting Toby more involved at work.'

Martine sauntered over to James' suitcase. Each item of clothing was neatly folded and set out in ordered lines. One good thing about living with James; she never had to pack for him.

'You're not bored of this life, are you?' James asked. 'I know it's not been as glamorous as I promised. Not many tiaras to wear recently.'

'Don't be silly. I didn't mean that. Look at all this.' She waved her arms around and, as she did, her eye alighted on the camera in the corner of the room. She turned her back on it. 'Not bad for a girl from Sheffield,' she said. 'OK, it's taken longer than we expected to win the jackpot, and this is a bit of a setback, but that's all.'

'You are fabulous, you know that,' he murmured. 'What about, tomorrow night, when I get back, instead of you cooking, we go to a really nice restaurant, Le Chien Blanc, your favourite? We haven't been there for ages.'

'Great.'

'I'll get Toby to make us a reservation. Is eight o'clock good? I know it's your night at the shelter, but you can miss that once, can't you?'

'Yes, yes of course I can.'

Twenty minutes after James left, Martine picked up her mobile, lying back on her bed and kicking off her shoes as she anticipated the caller's voice.

'Hi.'

'He's gone away again.' She sighed.

'I'm sorry, it's been a bit difficult...

'...Just tonight...

'...No, there's no news...

'...That would be nice. I hate being on my own at night...

'...See you then. Looking forward.'

44

Constance and Judith sat side by side in Constance's office, reading through the preliminary report on the SEDA's software, taken from the EDR. When the message heralding its arrival pinged on Constance's phone, she had quickly replenished their coffee supplies and printed off a paper copy for Judith.

After a couple of minutes of skim-reading, Judith scrunched the report into a ball and threw it across the room. Constance raised her eyes once and then lowered them again to her screen. Then Judith stood up and began to pace in military fashion.

'If only we'd got there first,' she shouted, waving her arms around. 'We'll have to get our own report now, but who knows whether it's all been compromised? How could Dawson let them do this? We'll have to make an official complaint.'

Constance sat in silence. She knew better than to take on Judith on the rampage.

'Who's the author of the report?' Judith demanded.

'It says "Department of Transport"...'

'More like Department of Nonsense. I should have expected they would blame it all on James. It's a whitewash and no self-respecting person would put their name to it.'

'But it's signed off by a forensic crash examiner. He has lots of qualifications. I looked him up.'

'Who has, no doubt, been sat upon very hard by the Right Honourable Alan Tillinghurst MP, or someone else in the industry, to say this. I should have intervened. Why didn't you insist I appeal? Now it will just look like sour grapes. Oh, why am I even surprised?'

Judith retrieved her copy of the mangled report and began to smooth it out.

'Do you want me to call Dawson? We could speak to him together?' Constance asked.

'We both know this is above Dawson's pay grade,' Judith said huffily. 'Although it would make me feel better to let off steam and he's probably expecting it. Perhaps I have contacts who know Alan Tillinghurst.'

'I don't understand how the data could show for certain what they've concluded,' Constance said.

'I'm more interested in what's missing, rather than what's there. I mean, we can see how many revolutions per second the wheels were making, but that doesn't mean they were necessarily functioning properly. There's a kind of sweep-up on page sixteen which seems to say that all the systems were working correctly, but it doesn't explain how they know that. Ah! Not a good start to our evening session. Has James seen it?'

'Not from me. Should I call him?'

'No. I'd rather see his response in person. Let's go and see him tomorrow, early, as his devoted wife tells us he's a "morning person".'

'We can't. He's away.'

'Where is he?'

'Just France, I think. He went on the Eurostar.'

'Didn't you advise him not to?'

'I tried. But Dawson hadn't said and, technically, he isn't under arrest or anything.'

'Find out when he's coming back.'

'He said tomorrow night. Agh.' Constance checked her phone.

'What is it?'

'From Dawson. He wants to see James. They're going to charge him.'

'Well there we are then. Good job we didn't just give Dawson an almighty telling-off. You'll need to sweet-talk him. The last thing we want is them arresting James at the train terminal and it's all over the newspapers again. It will look like he was running away.'

'Does this report mean we give up on all the things we've been working on?'

'Absolutely not. The report doesn't convince me one bit. We need to work on all those other areas of defence. And I have a few more ideas, too.'

45

MARTINE HAD screened and rejected three calls from Toby already that morning. The fourth came as she was attempting to leave the house.

'Hello?' She tried to hide the annoyance in her voice.

'Martine?'

'Yes. That's me.'

'It's Toby.'

'Yes. I can see.'

'Um. Look. James is away.'

'I know that.'

'And, um, well, he's taking me to this big meeting, when he gets back. I thought you should know.'

'Does he need his bag carrying or something?'

'He asked me before to come along, before the accident, but now he wants me to prepare all this stuff and work up a paper afterwards. I wanted to thank you, for putting in a good word for me. It was you, wasn't it?'

Martine hesitated. She could hardly tell him she hadn't said anything to persuade James to involve him, more the opposite.

'What meeting is it?' she asked.

'His Cinderella meeting, you know.'

Martine was suddenly alert. 'Yes. Listen, Toby. Make really careful notes of what they all say at the meeting. He needs them to accept that the cars are safe. Don't let James give in to them, not now when he's vulnerable. He's putting on a brave face but he's pretty devastated by what happened to that family.'

'Wow. Thanks. I mean, he said he needed me. But I wasn't sure if he was just being polite.'

'Don't thank me,' Martine said. 'I'm sure James has just realised, on his own, how much help you can be. I don't think he appreciates quite how fragile his own health is.'

'OK. I get it. I'll stick close.'

'Was that all? I have a lot to get through today.'

'Yes. I'm sorry. I know you're busy. I...have a lot of respect for your views...as a person. I wanted you to know.'

'Thank you. That is nice to know.'

'And, even though James sometimes gives me things to do that are, well, not so challenging, like booking hotels and restaurants, I always do my best, for the company.'

'Of course you do. James knows that.'

'I might have, well, said stuff before which would have made you think I'm ungrateful.'

'If you did I don't remember.'

'And are you keeping well? I haven't seen you at work recently.'

'Is there something else you want to tell me?'

'Why do you say that?'

'I get the feeling that you're leading up to something?'

'He's going to be really cross.'

'What is it?'

'It's the report about his car.'

'Oh?'

'James told me to check his emails while he's travelling. It says there was nothing wrong with the car and that James was driving when it crashed.'

'Oh!'

'And, I don't know how, but Bruce sent it.'

'Bruce?'

'Bruce Debrett. He just called me. He said that he's advising the company that James should not be allowed to touch the master copy of the data. He said James has "a conflict" in dealing with the crash and that I have to be in charge of anything to do with the crash. That we have to call an emergency directors' meeting to talk about it. So I'll be sending out an invitation, to a directors' meeting first thing tomorrow and you need to come.'

'You're right. James won't be pleased.'

'It wasn't me who told Bruce. He says I have to act in the best interests of the company and forget any allegiance to James.'

Martine sat down and closed her eyes to help focus her thoughts.

'Thanks for letting me know,' she said. 'I'll tell James when he gets back. No point spoiling his trip, is there?'

'Bruce sent him the report.'

'All right. But let *me* tell him about the other stuff, though, the directors' meeting.'

Martine stared at the screen of her phone long after the call had ended. Then she shrugged, picked up her bag, left money out in an envelope for Lina on the kitchen worktop and headed off to help chop up vegetables at the homeless shelter in Camden.

46

CONSTANCE KNOCKED on the door of Dean McQueen's house at six o'clock that evening. He hadn't returned her calls and Martine had not yet provided the list she had requested, but the McQueen's company registered office was a residential address, and her hunch that he might live there himself was rewarded when she saw his van in the driveway.

Dean was taller than she remembered from seeing him at the Salisburys' house, and broader, too. She wondered if his 'security' exploits extended to barring Essex youth from entry to local popular haunts, as well as protecting people's homes. She explained the reason for her visit was 'just a few questions about security for the Salisburys' and his eyes flicked lazily across her face, before he stepped out into the cool evening in his bare feet, pulling the front door closed behind him.

'Of course, anything I can tell you,' he said. 'I remember you now. You were at the house when Mr Salisbury asked me to check everything over.'

'Mrs Salisbury says there are a lot of cameras.'

'Yeah, I suppose there are.'

'Do you know how many?'

'If you want the exact details, I can find them for you. From memory, there's cameras on the gates, three along the driveway, one above each external door and in all the downstairs rooms. They also have them in some of the bedrooms.'

'The bedrooms?'

'I just do as I'm told. My dad put them in. I maintain them.'

'And does anyone check what they are recording?'

'Not routinely. If Mr Salisbury asks me, then I can do. I keep the recordings for six months, then I delete them.'

'And you have access to the house?'

'I have the code for the gate, so I can check the outside cameras. Or if the alarm is triggered, I can come on site. I don't have a key to the house, no. I wouldn't want to. Put me in the frame if something happened, wouldn't it?' He grinned conspiratorially. 'But I can access the cameras remotely now, anyway.'

'Remotely?'

'Yeah. You must have seen all the stuff you can get nowadays, those smart doorbells. You can see who's standing outside your house, even when you're away.'

'Isn't that very complicated technology?'

'The doorbells are quite basic, but the stuff I do, yeah I suppose so. But security's my business. I have to keep up. That's why my dad's handed a lot of it over to me now. Mr Salisbury's been really good to us, though – gave us the contract for the office too. That's how I could afford this place. But the stuff we've put in at his work, state-of-the-art, that is. Hidden cameras, just where you wouldn't expect.'

A sudden gust of wind whisked some fallen leaves up in to the air. Constance drew her jacket tightly around her.

'Have you ever seen anyone, other than Mr Salisbury, touching his car?'

Dean shook his head. 'No,' he said. 'My dad told me when I first started there, about a year back, not to go near it, not to even park near it. He said Mr Salisbury was very particular about keeping it clean.'

'And does anyone else come to the house, that you know of?'

'The gardener – Leo's his name. I have his number if you want. I've worked with him on another property where we had to bury some cables and the people were fussy about their flower beds. The others, you'd have to ask Martine or James...Mr Salisbury.'

'Thank you. That's all useful.'

'I'm happy to help if I can. It's a horrible thing that's happened. Was he going too fast?'

'I can't say.'

'No, I suppose you can't. I was just interested. How come you're doing all the investigating and not the police? It's maybe not safe for you to be going to people's houses on your own, at night.'

'I'm just...filling in the gaps. And I'm sure you don't need to be concerned about me.'

Dean stepped back on to his doorstep and withdrew his front door key from his pocket.

'Is that all you need now?' he asked. 'I would have asked you in, but the house is full of my equipment and I was just eating my dinner when you rang.'

47

'How was France?'

Martine was reading a magazine when James returned that evening, but she pushed it aside.

'Good. They're so far ahead of us out there, it's unbelievable.' He deposited his case by the door.

'You sorted out your problem then?'

'Oh, yes, all sorted. You know I am seriously thinking of applying for our first European licence in France. Forget about the UK for now. I was bluffing when I said it to Peter but now I'm serious. And there isn't the same interest in the crash over there. It was only in the news for a day.'

James poured himself a glass of water and drank it down.

'Would we have to move to France?'

'Maybe. But not if you're happy here. I can probably continue to manage everything from here.'

'Toby rang.'

'Here?'

'He says you have a big Cinderella meeting tomorrow and that you've asked him to go. That was nice of you.'

'Like I told you, I am giving him some more responsibility. I pay him enough. And I haven't managed to close the deal on my own, have I? Maybe Toby will be my fairy godmother?'

'Does that make Peter an ugly sister?'

'Oh, very good!'

'Is that why you called it Cinderella in the first place?'

'The project name came first, I think, before I met any of them. It's just a name,' he said. 'We give all our projects names. No real significance. Like hurricanes.'

'But it has a happy ending, Cinderella.'

'If you say so.'

'You don't know the story?'

'Of course I do. Maybe the name suits it, after all. I mean, they're a pretty dysfunctional lot, each awaiting their prince to change their fortunes.'

'And you deserve him, more than the others. That makes you Cinderella. Ha!' She laughed softly.

'I think you should keep that to yourself. I'm not sure that's the image I'm going for. And that would mean that, what, Alan was Prince Charming!'

Martine laughed. 'You will keep a close eye on Toby at the meeting, won't you?'

'Course. What are you worried about?'

'He might come out with some nonsense, like that emissions comment again. He might not be the best person to help you out, with all the other things that are going on.'

'You worry too much and I've already asked him. But, yes, I will talk to him before we go, and I'll have him in my sights at all times. You know I do keep hoping that Josh will want some involvement in the business.'

Martine closed the magazine and added it to a burgeoning pile. 'He's just not interested. You can't force it.'

James re-filled his glass.

'Why don't you want to show Peter what you do, in the lab?' Martine asked.

'Pride in part, but it's more than that. It's also the principle. It's none of his bloody business what my company does with its data. It really makes me laugh. They go on about our systems being hacked, when we've employed the highest quality technicians and used the most sophisticated security systems. It's the MPs who are always leaving their papers in taxis and dropping unencrypted memory sticks in the street.'

'Toby also said the expert report came through, on your car.'

'Yes.'

'He says it says you were driving. That's not good, is it?'

'Well, it's not good for me, but, clearly it's good for SEDA, or as good as we could hope. If I was driving, then they can't blame the car. It puts SEDA back on track. Well that's the line I'm going to take at the meeting. I'd rather not talk about it now though. I'm very tired. Maybe we should stay in and have the lamb after all.'

'You mean that if you were driving, then they might try to say it was your fault?'

James walked through to the lounge and sat down on the sofa. Martine followed close behind.

'You've guessed it,' he said. 'That's why I have to go to the police station tomorrow. Apparently, they wanted to arrest me at Kings Cross! My lawyer managed to persuade them not to.'

'You're being arrested?'

'Arrested, charged, prosecuted. Whatever they call it. Because of the report. So yes, if I was in control of the car, they think it was my fault.'

'What do your lawyers say?'

'They're being optimistic. Said I'll get bail between now and the trial.'

'Trial?'

Martine wrapped her arms around James' neck. 'There's something else he said too,' she said.

'What? What's Toby flapping about now?'

'Bruce has called an emergency meeting of SEDA's directors for eight o'clock tomorrow morning.'

'That's keen of him. I didn't think he got out of bed before nine. What's on the agenda then?'

'You are. He says you can't run the company and that you might have to sell your shares.'

A strangled cry came from the back of James' throat. 'He can't do that!'

'I didn't think he could. So you'll tell him that tomorrow morning.'

James shrank back into the cushions of the sofa.

'Maybe it's not so bad, all of this. You said you wanted something to happen,' Martine said, 'Remember? That you were fed up with waiting around. You wanted to mix things up a bit.'

'Mix things up! This isn't a cake. Two children are dead, I'm about to be arrested and possibly imprisoned and Bruce wants to take my company away. We might lose everything.'

'It won't happen.'

'We were so close,' James said, making fists with both hands, 'so close to what I've worked for all these years. To see it snatched away, I'm not sure I can bear it.'

'It will come right,' Martine said. 'I just know it. In a few months this will all be forgotten.'

'And I promised Imogen. I promised her.'

Martine bristled at the mention of Imogen's name. She sprang up and marched over to the window.

'Even if I don't go to jail, if I lose the company and I have to begin again. It may be too much.'

'I won't let that happen,' Martine said calmly. 'Ride the storm. It's not like you to accept defeat.'

48

NEIL SAT AT HOME in the bedroom which used to be Bertie's. It was the place he felt closest to his son.

Sometimes, when Therese and Ruby were asleep, he would creep in and lie down on the bed, surrounded by Bertie's toys and stare up at the ceiling, as his son would have done. He tried to imagine what perspective Bertie might have had of the world from this cosy vantage point. And occasionally, Neil would open the wardrobe and stroke his son's clothes or take out the buggy board, now relegated to the bottom shelf, and hold it tight, as he had once held his son.

He did occupy Georgia's room too from time to time, but only if he was certain Therese was elsewhere. Therese had turned it into a shrine, with photographs of Georgia plastered all over the walls, and she had shrieked at him when he entered, once, and found her curled up in the corner. Therese never went into Bertie's room, so his hours spent there allowed him the additional benefit of time alone. He wondered fleetingly if Therese had always favoured Georgia quite so much when the children had been alive and he had failed to notice.

A message popped up on his screen from Inspector Dawson, politely informing him that a decision had been taken to prosecute James for causing the accident which had killed his children. He would be in touch, he said, shortly, to arrange a time to speak to Therese again.

Neil flicked on to his Twitter account. The Department of Transport had not replied to any of his tweets, but a supporter had sent him a series of articles which suggested the Autonomous Vehicles Bill was stalling. One of them maintained it would not move forward until more testing had been undertaken on the vehicles. Another, that nothing would happen, pending the resolution of the investigation into James' car.

Neil picked up the toy dog he had bought for Bertie the day he was born, which had been his constant companion in his hospital crib. Then it had accompanied Bertie in his car seat on the day they brought him home from hospital; another bright sunny day which had begun full of promise. He held it against his face and thought again about his poor, dead son.

49

'WHAT'S WITH the suit?' Juan slapped the back of his hand against Toby's lapel and then wafted it in front of his face. 'Has it been in the closet?'

'We say cupboard, not closet…or we say wardrobe,' Toby snapped. Sometimes, Juan could be over-familiar.

'OK. But why so smart? That's right isn't it? You do say "smart"?'

'I have a big meeting. I thought I should wear a suit. It's not really dusty is it?'

'I was joking with you. It looks great. You look like the CEO when you wear it. Move over James! What's the meeting?'

'Cinderella, with the guys from the Department of Transport.'

'The big men. Is the Transport guy called Mears?'

'Yes, Peter Mears.' Toby felt his cheeks heating up. 'Why?'

Juan leaned against the kitchen worktop and grimaced.

'I don't think I like him much.'

'You know him?'

'He contacted me,' he said.

'Did he?'

'He asked me to meet him.'

'To meet him?'

'He wouldn't say why. Said he would tell me when we met. I didn't, of course. I said I was too busy.'

'Oh. Right. What do you think he wanted?'

'I don't know for sure, but I talked to some of the other IT guys I know, at other companies. They said he likes to find out things, get inside knowledge. I should be flattered, perhaps, that he thinks I have inside knowledge. Do you think you should tell James? He's having all these important meetings with this Peter guy and then the guy is going behind his back?'

Toby shook his head violently. 'I think James has enough to deal with at the moment. Best just to ignore it and delete the messages. Maybe you could ask the other IT guys in your team, quietly, if they heard from him. I can do the same around the factory.'

'Sure,' Juan said, without sounding terribly sure. 'You're deputy CEO. But don't leave any secret papers on the desk when he's in the room.' Juan laughed heartily. Then he tapped Toby on the arm.

'You do look really great, Toby. I mean it. You really look like a serious businessman.'

This time Toby beamed.

'Thanks,' he said. 'Let's get going if you want a lift. I have another meeting first which I'm not looking forward to, but I really mustn't be late.'

50

JUDITH SAT IN the park close to her apartment and stared out over the grass. She had wanted to return here today, by herself, to reflect, before the conversation she was planning to have with Greg this evening.

They had been here together only a week earlier. They had sat on this bench after a long, exhilarating walk through the trees.

It was funny how everything could change in an instant. How you could imagine you were blissfully happy, well, perhaps that was overdoing it, but certainly compatible and content. And then a few incautious words and gestures and you weren't any longer.

But Judith knew that, of course, after Martin. She had shielded herself from another attack with all the weapons at her disposal; shoes and clothes, precision haircuts and barbed words. Then Greg had come along and he hadn't asked for much. But that was part of the problem. She knew, deep down, he must want more. She had allowed herself to be taken in, because it was nice to be wanted. Or she had pretended to herself that she was enough for him, that he was busy with his various businesses and all he wanted was intelligent conversation, companionship and uncomplicated sex.

What had he said to her when they had sat down here, on this very bench? It had been innocent enough, a gentle enquiry about her work.

'How's it going, the car case?' he had said.

That had been it. And she had told him, in as sympathetic a voice as she could muster, that she anticipated the driver would be charged and that they would have an uphill struggle trying to find reasons why the car had malfunctioned so badly. And how it was complicated because the driver, James was his name (although, of course Greg already knew that from the newspaper reports), didn't want to lose his company too. She had been careful how she had expressed it, not referring directly to anything James had told them. Everything she said was in the public domain.

'The father's been Tweeting,' Greg had continued.

'What kind of things?' Judith had asked.

'First he said there should be a public enquiry. Then all kinds of stuff he's found online about the cars being dangerous, and finally asking for signatures to postpone the cars being sold.'

'I should ask Connie to take a look. Show us what we might be up against in court.'

'And photos of his kids. Beautiful kids. And stuff about all the things he misses now they're gone. Poor man.'

And perhaps it would have been all right if things had ended there, but then a mother had walked past with two young children – a boy and a girl – all three of them devouring ice cream. And Greg's face had lit up. And as they passed by, the mother had smiled at Greg and he had grinned at her in return and ten metres further up the path, the boy had turned and stared at Greg, ice cream smeared around his mouth and Greg had waved to him, one of those fingers only waves, before wrapping his arm around Judith and pulling her close.

51

Toby was waiting in the entrance hall when Martine and James arrived for the impromptu board meeting Bruce had called. James marched straight past him at twice his usual speed, managing only a shallow nod to each of the receptionists, his face set hard. Martine walked behind, ensuring she greeted everyone she encountered in her usual friendly manner. Toby raced to catch up.

'Hi James, Martine. Did you want to talk about anything before we go in?' he began.

'What is there to talk about?' James barked.

Martine glared at Toby and he shrank back against the wall. James careered onwards and burst into the meeting room, where Bruce was dealing out papers, like a deck of cards.

'I assume I am still allowed to sit at the head of the table,' he said.

'Yes of course. You're still CEO. But I need to do this, to protect the company. It's nothing personal.'

'Nothing personal.' James had just begun to pour himself a glass of water. Now he banged the bottle down on the table. 'I should take you outside around the back and then we'll see how personal it is.'

'James!' Martine was at his side.

'Has someone put you up to this? Someone who wants me out.'

'Let's hear what Bruce has to say,' Martine suggested. 'It may not be so bad.'

'Thank you, Martine.'

Bruce adjusted his collar and completed handing out the papers, choosing a seat at the far end of the table. James grunted loudly as he sat down.

'So. Let's start, shall we?' James said. 'I should have known there'd be loads of paper.'

'I've prepared a number of resolutions which we need to vote upon,' Bruce said. 'Toby has told me that you are pressed for time. So I worked late last night to try to advance things as much as possible. Of course, if there are questions you need answering, we can postpone, but my intention is to keep things simple.'

'Perfect. Simple is always best. I'm all ears.'

'First of all, I have seen a copy of an expert report into the crash on 10th October, involving your car. That says that everything was in working order and that the car had been moved into manual mode when it crashed. Inspector Dawson has told me that you will now be charged with a criminal offence. I understand that your lawyer has negotiated that you will surrender yourself to the police.'

Martine cleared her throat. Toby tried to pour himself some water, but his hand was shaking uncontrollably and he gave up and returned the bottle to the table.

'We are the four directors of SEDA,' Bruce continued. 'As its directors, we have to act in the best interests of the company. We also cannot vote on any matters where our own personal interests conflict with that of the company. So the first resolution on which we must vote, without your participation, James, is that you, James, must not be allowed unsupervised access to the data from your car.'

'You think I'm going to corrupt it or throw it away? It's a bit late for that, isn't it?'

'It's just a precaution, and it'll protect you, too.'

'Really?'

'Second, I am recommending to the board that Toby take over the day-to-day running of the company, while you are helping the police with enquiries, and for the duration of any trial. There's no reason why Toby can't consult with you on all matters, apart from those relating to the cause of the accident, but he needs to be the figurehead over this difficult period. And if he has doubts he should return to Martine and me as his co-directors for support.'

'You and Martine. That's ridiculous!'

'No. And you'll thank me for it afterwards. You need to focus on your defence. You can't run the company at the same time. I'll be on hand twenty-four hours a day, as will all my partners.'

'And what will you charge for that 24/7 service?'

'As long as it doesn't become too onerous, I won't charge for my time at all. My partners will charge at their usual hourly rates.'

'Thank you, Bruce.' Martine had recovered her composure.

'How will it look, Toby taking over?' James asked.

'It will look like a prudent decision by a sensible board of directors during a difficult and, I hope, temporary period. Third,

I need to remind you that, in the unlikely event of your being convicted, the company's rules provide that you must give up your shares...'

'Do we have to do this now?' Martine interrupted.

'No, let's hear it all. Let's hear what the scavengers want to scrounge,' James thumped the table, as Bruce tried to continue.

'That's uncalled for! The company's rules provide that you give up your shares if convicted of a serious criminal offence. If the tables were turned you would want the same from one of us. There is a mechanism for sale. You'll get market price for them.'

'If I'm convicted, we all know what that market price will be.'

'And, naturally, you'll have to relinquish your place on the board.'

Martine stood up. 'We are nowhere near that stage. You said that's only if James is found guilty.'

'All right,' Bruce ran a finger around the inside of his collar. 'The third resolution can wait. I drafted it so that it read "in the event of James being convicted..." so we could move quickly if that happened, but I can see it's an emotive issue.'

'Damn right it is.'

'What if we refuse to vote?' Toby said, his face miserable and forlorn. 'You can't make us.'

'If you refuse, then I would be obliged to ask the court to authorise me to proceed, on the basis that the company was not being run properly.'

James turned to Martine and Toby and sat back in his seat. He took a deep breath.

'It's fine,' he said finally. 'Bruce is right about the company. Toby, you were looking for a bit more responsibility. You'll do a fine job. And we'll just have to make sure I don't go to jail. Martine, I want you to vote to do what's right for the company.'

'What about the Cinderella meeting?' Toby asked, still pale and anxious.

'It doesn't start till after that, Bruce, does it? I still get one last chance to be boss of it all.'

52

CONSTANCE WAS trying to cram as much as she could into her head about autonomous vehicles. She had looked into James' background, read through and watched his speeches and tracked the progress of the Autonomous Vehicles Bill. There were so many different issues involved, she could begin to see why things were taking so long.

On the table next to her sat a letter addressed to her brother, Jermain. It looked official and innocuous enough, a white, rectangular envelope, with a transparent window, allowing the typewritten address to show through. She lifted it to the light, in the vague but ultimately forlorn hope that more of the content of the letter would be visible.

She returned to her work, but the letter was distracting her and she couldn't focus. Instead she diverted onto Twitter, finding herself trawling back through Neil Layton's Tweets, a mixture of anger and bitterness, logic and non sequitur, interspersed with heart-breaking photographs.

@AlanTillinghurst you should be ashamed of yourself. Supporting the #Bill without enough #trials #signthepetition

@DepartmentofTransport Did you even talk to @Uber about their #fatal #accidents? #killer #cars #signthepetition

Bertie Layton. You would have been four next week #RIP my boy #signthepetition

With each angle Neil covered, Constance made a careful note of the names of anyone mentioned, for research purposes, trying not to dwell too long on any of the photos. Within half an hour she had thirty-two more leads to follow, individual and company names, related technical issues. She couldn't possibly check up on all of this; she would have to prioritise. But the letter to her brother was winking at her invitingly. She broke off from her work with a huff, shut the letter away in the kitchen drawer and then messaged Jermain a curt, *Post arrived for you. C.*

Two hours later, when he hadn't replied, she had made her decision. She carried the envelope over to the window and allowed the steam from the kettle to pour over it. Now it opened fairly easily, although the whole letter took on a rather flaccid appearance, which she would have to explain when Jermain eventually turned up to claim it. With shaking hands, she opened the folded white page and found it bore no writing at all other than Jermain's name and her address. Inside it was a small, printed, formal pay slip.

53

James and Toby were waiting for the remaining players to arrive for the Cinderella meeting. James wanted Toby next to him and, after his conversation with Martine, Toby was not going to complain about remaining in close proximity to his mentor and a few steps away from Peter.

Toby shook hands with Peter, Jeremy and Will. Did Peter's sharp, abrupt squeeze of his hand carry any particular meaning? He had paid little attention to body language when they had met clandestinely, a few weeks before, but now everything had changed. He sensed a wave of colour washing over his face but, luckily, the other men were busy settling themselves and watching James.

'Thank you all for coming,' James began. 'I called this meeting, primarily because it's the end of October and we've heard nothing more about the publication of the list. Peter, we wanted to give you the opportunity to explain this further delay. If you recall, you sat in that very same chair, I believe, in August and reassured us all, that our cars would be out on the roads by now.'

'I have to say that if that is the purpose of today's meeting, it will be very short,' Peter replied.

Toby laughed out loud, and every eye in the room turned on him. After an initial frosty glare, James joined in with a low chuckle.

'That's what I like about our meetings. Always conducted in a light-hearted manner,' he said.

Finally, Peter smiled too, and his smile encompassed Toby, who looked away. 'No point us losing our sense of humour, is there?' Peter said. 'But I thought it would have been obvious that your accident has had a significant impact on our proposed timetable.'

'It shouldn't change a thing,' James replied. 'If anything, it shows how important it is for us to push on and not be diverted.'

'I don't quite see how slaughter on the roads, at the hands of one of your vehicles, will endear your product to the general public,' Peter persisted.

'It would have been much worse with a conventional car.' Toby spoke clearly and, for a second time, everyone stared at him.

'You can't possibly say that.'

'I have all the information here about SEDA's superior safety features, compared with ordinary cars,' Toby said, tapping his screen. 'I'd be happy to show you or send them on after the meeting. James might also have died if this had been a regular Toyota or a VW. He would almost certainly have hit the concrete barrier.'

'I'm not sure the public's sympathies lie with James at the moment, I'm afraid.'

'Maybe not at this precise moment,' James took over. 'And that's right. And I don't expect sympathy. It's right and proper that we mourn the victims of this tragedy. But if it's explained properly, comprehensively, by someone in a position of power and responsibility, they will begin to see why we mustn't let this stop our progress. That would be an even bigger tragedy. Alan has the ear of the media. He can tell it like it is and they'll listen.'

'And how, precisely, is it?' Peter was beginning to get cross.

'The car was not in autonomous mode,' Toby said. '"Minimal damage." That's how the algorithm works. James' car could not have hit the family, if it had been in autonomous mode. It's just not possible.'

'Is that right, James? Are you accepting you were driving the car when it crashed?' Peter kept his gaze fixed on Toby. Toby, in turn, was looking all the time at James. James scrutinised Peter's words for any hint of gloating, but found none.

'That's how it looks at the moment,' he replied gravely.

'I'm truly sorry to hear that,' Peter said. 'This must be terrible for you. Those are my personal sentiments which I wanted to express.' He scratched at his chest. 'But I have to ask, to salvage something from the wreckage of this project, whether you will be able to give me an official statement, from the company, to that effect?'

'The crash is still being investigated by the police,' Toby chipped in, and Peter raised an eyebrow.

'Yes,' James continued. 'Toby's right. I've received a copy of an expert report which appears to indicate that the car was in manual mode at the time of the collision. Peter, your man prepared it. You must have seen it?'

'I've seen it but it's the product of an independent expert.'

'If the report proves to be correct, then SEDA will provide a statement to that effect, but we are not there yet. So I don't see any wreckage – quite the contrary. But assuming that will be the conclusion, can you assure me that the list will be published as promised?'

Peter held James' stare. 'James. You're not thinking straight. It's understandable with the criminal charges hanging over you?'

'Criminal charges?' Jeremy tilted his chair back until the front legs lifted off the ground. Will, who had been fidgeting in his chair from the outset, began to leaf through screens on his phone.

'This is a very tricky situation,' Peter persisted.

'You're not publishing the list…'

'Not yet.'

'So Alan is reneging…'

'No one is doing any "reneging" or anything quite so dramatic!' Peter rose to his feet and then promptly sat down again, like a rotund jack-in-the-box. 'Even with a statement from SEDA, people are scared. Their trust has been shattered. We have to tread carefully, not just bulldoze on. And we could easily complain about your dilatory behaviour too, if we weren't all feeling those warm feelings of cooperation, which have featured so highly throughout the life of this project.' Peter smiled at Toby again, and Toby, glancing up for a moment, smiled back this time, although his right leg had begun to jump around erratically under the table.

'Don't minute this part of the meeting, will you,' Peter waved at Toby, and Toby's fingers dropped off his keyboard and onto his knees, where they attempted to calm his errant leg. Out of the corner of his eye, he sought out James' direction, but James was focusing on Peter again, his mouth set in a thin line.

'You still haven't agreed to allow access to our cyber security team, which I requested at the same meeting you remember so vividly,' Peter continued. 'And – surprise, surprise – none of your peers have either. In fact, the two who agreed previously have now "thought better" of that agreement. Would you happen to know why that is?'

'This is nothing to do with data security. One hiccup and you're throwing in the towel.'

'It was a fatal accident and you were behind the wheel!'

'And I have to live with that. But if everyone had given up, in the history of the world, when they had suffered setbacks, we would still be living in caves.'

'I'm not sure I go along with any of this.' Jeremy had loosened his tie, when he took a seat at the table, and now he removed it, rolled it up and placed it on the table.

'I don't see why you're bothered. You're not in any worse situation than you were before,' James said, 'and it's possible you'll end up so much better off.'

'And how do you reach that conclusion?' Jeremy said.

'If my car was being driven manually, then the conventional insurance rules apply.'

'Thank you, James. I don't need a lesson in how insurance policies work. I think Peter's right and you really have lost the plot. I don't care about who is going to pay this time,' Jeremy said. 'Our three hundred members have signed up to all of this, on the promise of a huge reduction in the number of accidents and a streamlined, more cost-effective process for claims. You're talking about an investigation into the circumstances of this one accident, which has already involved SEDA, the Department of Transport and an independent expert, who certainly won't come cheap. And it's all over the press.

'If we have to do this with every accident, we'll go out of business by Christmas. I'm beginning to agree, reluctantly, with

Peter. If the project proceeds, and this is now a big if from me, then maybe we do have to give up trying to allocate blame, we accept that we just have to pay up. But that's a huge about-turn and we'll have to ballot members again.'

'You are not entirely wrong...'

'Thanks for the vote of confidence...'

'But you are being short-sighted.' James rose to his feet as he spoke. 'Naturally, there will be a requirement for additional investigation during this transitional period only – and on the very rare occasions these collisions occur. I see that as a small price to pay for the long-term benefits we know we will all reap.' He returned to his seat.

'All right, James. We don't need your maiden voyage speech again.' Peter rolled his eyes.

'Our cars have covered 600,000 road miles,' Toby chipped in, 'and this is our first accident involving injury to any person. With conventional cars, you have more than four hundred accidents every day including four or five fatalities.'

'I can't believe you're all talking statistics when two lives have been lost. Two young children.' Will stood up, shuddered dramatically and glided towards the door. James rose to cut him off.

'Please!' James' mellifluous voice echoed across the room and Will faltered. 'My friend, you are right to remind us of the human cost. It's in the forefront of my mind too, all the time. How could it not be? The Layton family – which has been irreversibly damaged – like it or not, will require financial assistance. I am sure Jeremy was only thinking of their wellbeing and the certainty that the government needs to bring to other families countrywide, when he reminded us of the insurance angle.'

'We've got two children killed by your car and a woman seriously injured. I've been happy to put my weight and the weight of my organisation behind you, as you know. I've had people spend hours on calls and on the streets with leaflets, I've retweeted constantly and we've formally endorsed all your ads. But if your product is flawed, I couldn't possibly support it.'

'The product isn't flawed,' James remained calm, although one corner of his mouth twitched almost imperceptibly. 'And once the expert report on the vehicle's EDR is made public then I am 100% certain that you will all have the reassurance you need about the product. Now, I understand that you may feel sufficiently distressed to wish to absent yourself from the remainder of our important discussions. But, from a professional as well as a personal perspective I, for one, would welcome your continued contribution.'

As Will hesitated on the threshold, Peter rose and straightened his jacket.

'I'm not sure there's much I can add to what I've already said,' he said. 'I don't want to waste my time cajoling others into remaining in a process which clearly has much to recommend it, or in reminding you of the minister's reasonable proposals. When you're ready to let us in, James, Toby, just contact my PA.'

'That's it then? An ultimatum?'

'I thought I had already made myself clear,' Peter said. 'You're lucky SEDA's still in the running. If Alan had his way, you would have been categorically rejected as soon as your car touched those children. But I persuaded him, explained we worked as a team, convinced him of the benefits of our project, how much you, personally, had contributed, despite the one or two remaining stumbling blocks we need to overcome.'

He moved towards the door. 'He's a practical man, and a fair one, and he thought, after all your efforts, James, you should at least have the opportunity of proving your innocence, and continuing goodwill in the manner I have described.'

'We don't have to prove innocence in this country. That's what they do in dictatorships.'

Toby had just resumed typing his notes. He paused, fingers in mid-air.

'I've bought you some time,' Peter replied. 'Six months. Be grateful. But SEDA will need to be fully exonerated at trial, and we require full co-operation as regards the security of your systems and processes and I am relying on you to bring the others into line too. I'll be off then. And leave the rest of you to work things out.'

As Peter exited the room, they heard shuffling and raised voices in the corridor. Jane came rushing in, her face red.

'Mr Salisbury,' she called out nervously. 'So sorry to interrupt, but the police are here. I asked them to wait, but they said they need to see you now.'

James cleared this throat.

'No problem, Jane. I'm sure you did all you could to make them comfortable. Carry on Toby. We'll catch up later.'

James strode out of the room, leaving Toby open-mouthed and Jane in floods of tears.

54

'SOD'S LAW,' Judith muttered under her breath repeatedly, as she alternated between checking the time and gazing out of the window and up the street for any sign of Greg. This morning, he had said he would be back around 7, and by 7.30 Judith was climbing the walls.

And then he arrived, suddenly, with a bunch of flowers and a jaunty air, which was soon dispelled when he was struck by Judith's grave expression.

'What is it?' he asked, hurrying to Judith's side.

'You're late,' she managed. Those words, on their own, confirmed to Greg that there was a problem; Judith had never challenged him on timekeeping before.

'Sorry. I was training a new manager. Did I forget something important?' He laid the flowers down on the table and removed his jacket. 'Was it my turn to make dinner?' he said.

'No.'

Judith wandered over to her bookshelf and stood staring at the spines of the novels she loved; stories about sacrifice, love and loss, many of them from times when women had fewer choices than she had today.

'OK. Are you going to tell me what's wrong?' Greg's fingers brushed the table, nudging the flowers in Judith's direction.

'I think it would be better if you moved back to your flat,' she said, only spinning around to face Greg once she had spoken.

Greg opened his mouth to reply, then thought better of it.

'I have a lot to deal with, this new case will be taking up so much of my time,' she continued. 'I don't think it's fair to impose that on you.'

'Don't you think I should be the judge of that?'

Judith could not mistake the bitterness in his voice. Now she said nothing.

'Is that it?' Greg said. 'All I get. You're booting me out, but you're doing it for my benefit?'

'I'm sorry. It's how I feel,' she said. 'It was supposed to be temporary, when you moved in.'

Greg picked up his jacket.

'You're right,' he said. 'It was. Not like you to let that one slide. Have I broken the terms of my contract then? No problem. I'll grab my stuff. What are you so afraid of?' he burst out suddenly, hovering in the doorway of the bedroom they shared.

Judith bit her lip and returned to her books.

Greg shrugged. 'Looks like I'll never get to know now.'

He nudged the door closed with his foot. After only five minutes he emerged with a small bag. He stopped by the front door to deposit his key and then he was gone.

PART THREE

LONDON, FEBRUARY 2019

55

James sat quietly in the dock. He was impeccably turned out, as Constance would have expected, but his face had taken on a gaunt air recently, and if anyone had looked closely, they would have noticed that his suit hung off him in multiple places. He had given up standing on the bathroom scales at home, once his weight travelled south of eleven and a half stone, telling himself he would 'sort it all out with a few good meals' once the trial was over.

Since his arrest, he had stuck firmly to the story that he had been in control of the car at the point of collision, insisting 'that must have been what happened,' although he maintained that he still had no memory of any of the journey. And he had provided little practical assistance with building a case for his own defence.

Judith and Constance had tried, only yesterday, to obtain more from him, on their final session before the trial began.

***

'When the first autonomous cars were being tested on the streets in San Francisco there were reports of them going through red traffic lights. What do you know about that?' Judith had asked him, with forced patience.

'Human error,' James had said. 'The cars were being driven at the time.'

'You can't expect us to believe that.' Judith had said. 'At that second, when they went through the red lights, just that second, they were being driven?'

James had shrugged. 'That's what Uber said, and it didn't go further because no one was hurt. I don't know anything more.'

'But they were taken off the roads?'

'For a couple of months, yes. And it didn't happen again when they came back.'

'What about the Tesla driver in Florida, and the trailer?'

'That was in auto pilot. Tesla said the car got confused between the white colour of the trailer and the sky. But Tesla's auto pilot isn't the same as our autonomous mode. It's just auto pilot, that's all, far less sophisticated.'

'But there is evidence to suggest that autonomous vehicles do have difficulty distinguishing objects when in bright sunlight, isn't there?'

James had shrugged again.

'Come on! We can read the material ourselves, but we need you to give us confirmation we are on the right lines.' Judith rapped her pen down on her page.

'Why are you asking me about this stuff? It wasn't bright on October 10th, there were no white trailers and the expert report says I was driving.'

'It only says you were driving at the very end, the last three, four seconds. Before that it says the car was in control. We need you to lay it bare for us, warts and all. All the stuff that keeps you awake at night. All the flaws you are trying to iron out with your vehicles. All the tiny, niggly, not-quite-right features which might explain the collision.'

'If I give you that list I am committing commercial suicide!'

Constance had stopped making notes and was frowning at James.

'We won't use material in court without your permission,' Judith tried to reassure him, 'but if we don't get the basics from you, we can't even begin to craft your defence.'

'I don't want you to "craft my defence". I've been reading all about the trial process. The prosecution has to show beyond reasonable doubt that I was driving dangerously. We don't have to do anything really.'

'We have to raise that doubt in the jury's mind.'

'I was driving within the speed limit and the boy ran out into the road.'

'And you hit him at 36mph on the wrong side of the road.'

'I was on my side.'

'You were driving at full speed on a part of the road which was closed to vehicles. We have to come up with a plausible reason why.'

James stared at the floor.

'All right. If you won't give us your snagging list despite my assurances, let's try some specific questions and see if that works any better.'

***

Martine sat in the front row of the public gallery with Toby next to her. Her hair was still a 'to wish for' shade of chestnut and she was sporting her characteristic red lipstick, but she wore a demure navy suit and a serious expression. She had dodged all Constance's calls since their meeting and ignored her messages.

Toby had promised James he would keep a close eye on everything in the office and, over the last week, he had worn his suit every day, including socks, arrived early and left late, waiting for his 'call up' to the hot seat. In contrast to Martine, he had answered Constance's subsequent enquiries, but all of them by telephone and generally on the run from one place to another, and occasionally from somewhere noisy with music playing in the background.

Jeremy Fry was also present, about halfway back, arms folded. He had sent James a supportive text that morning, which James would appreciate when he got to see it. James had also received a 'Good Luck' card from the staff, which he had read and put away in his desk drawer. It had seemed a strange gesture in the circumstances, but he appreciated the sentiment.

Neil and Therese Layton sat only a few seats from Martine. Neil was fussing over his wife, ensuring she was comfortable, whispering things behind his hand, plucking at his own shirt, checking his phone. He had given journalists 'an exclusive' the previous week, including more photographs of the family in happier days, timed perfectly to evoke maximum sympathy in the run-up to the trial.

Therese had not contributed to the newspaper article. She sat perfectly still, her glassy eyes fixed on James. Judith concluded she was most likely on medication, although she had not been given notice by the prosecution.

Judge Wilson was reputedly an IT buff, one of the advocates of a number of digital innovations of recent years, to help things move more smoothly in the court room. That wasn't a bad thing, Judith mused. At least she could count on him to be interested in the various technical defences she would be putting forward. But he was also extremely harsh when it came to sentencing, generally preferring the higher end of any tariff. If James was convicted of both causing death and serious injury by dangerous driving, he could be looking at a fifteen-year prison term.

Celia Mansome QC, sat next to Judith, separated by less than three feet but thirty-five years of animosity. Judith had stifled her consternation when she heard who would be prosecuting James, but it hadn't gone unnoticed by Constance.

***

'You don't like her?' Celia had passed close by, while they were waiting outside court, fifteen minutes earlier. Constance knew Judith well enough now to read some of the signs she gave out.

'We were at school together – only briefly, thank God. She was a nasty piece of work then. And you know how when you meet people years later and you are forced to admit that, perhaps you were wrong or they have mellowed or learned the error of their ways?'

'Let me guess. That didn't happen with Celia Mansome.'

'Quite right. The woman had become more objectionable and opinionated than ever. Do you know, she once called me slow-witted? "Slow-witted?" Me? Not that I took it personally. Not when it came from a cart-horse like Celia.'

'Cart horse?'

'She was on the heavy side at the age of twelve and last to be picked for sports. And her parents kept horses. Some of the girls, not me I should say, gave her that nickname.'

'What happened?'

'She got thin and beautiful, well, scrubbed up fairly well and got a top First from Oxford, and everyone who had been nasty to her ate their words.'

'Is she any good?'

'Sadly, yes, very. She prosecutes each and every case as if it's a personal affront. And she is pushing for a space on the bench, I've heard, so I can see why this case would be so attractive to her. She probably has friends in the government and they will want to make sure they don't get egg on their faces over this one.'

'I know the solicitor,' Constance said.

'Do you?'

'Sarah Timmins. We were at law school together. She fancied our tutor. I think I heard they moved in together later on, but I covered for her once when her boyfriend came to find her.'

'Will she remember?'

'Oh yes.'

'Good. Let's keep all avenues of communication open. We might just need them.'

***

'Celia. How nice to see you again.' Judith leaned across and shook her opponent's hand, with a wide-eyed air of sincerity.

'Judith. I heard you'd retired but then I was so pleased to hear you were back in the saddle. Was it money trouble?'

'What?'

'Brought you back into the ring?'

'And I heard you only back sure-fire winners these days, as you have your eye on the big prizes. I'm surprised you want to risk everything on this one.'

'How can there be any risk in this case? First, your client was driving the car. And second, everything was in working order. If he persists in defending, he could get the maximum sentence. I'm telling you now, in all fairness, that's what I'll be asking for.'

'It's so kind of you to appraise me of your strategy, albeit blinkered and lame.'

Celia folded her hands on her lap.

'You think you're on a winning streak, Judith, but I know your weaknesses and I will show no mercy. I don't spare the crop; be warned.'

Constance observed the two women with a mixture of curiosity and bemusement. She had often wondered if Judith had been exactly the same as a girl and this horsey banter with her old nemesis strongly hinted that she had. Then she saw Sarah, the opposing solicitor, watching her and she looked away.

***

Celia began at a little after 10am that morning.

'Members of the jury. This is a case where a family has been devastated by the events of a split second on the 10th of October last year. In that moment, a car, with the defendant, James Salisbury, behind the wheel, mowed them down as they crossed the road close to their home. It wasn't dark, it wasn't raining and they would have been in his clear view – that is, if he had been attending to the road. Instead, eye witness evidence will establish, beyond doubt, that he was driving too fast and using his mobile phone.

'Mr Salisbury's vehicle hit the family at just under forty miles per hour, killing two children, Georgia, aged five, and Bertie, aged three, and seriously injuring Mrs Therese Layton, their mother. Mrs Layton broke her arm and her pelvis and has undergone reconstructive surgery to allow her to walk again. The baby, Ruby, in her pram, four months old, was pushed to safety and was thankfully unharmed.

'I have mentioned the speed, just under forty miles per hour, so, admittedly within the lawful speed limit for that stretch of road. However, you will hear from the police that the car should have been travelling much more slowly, given the road layout. And the expert evidence will establish that the angle at which the family was hit, essentially the car being driven straight at them, contributed to the devastation Mr Salisbury caused.

'Mr Salisbury happens to be the founder of SEDA, a company which manufactures, trials and aspires to sell autonomous cars. The vehicle involved in the accident was a SEDA autonomous vehicle. Now my learned friend, Ms Burton, defending Mr Salisbury, will make much of this. She intends to call witnesses to talk about autonomous vehicles and how they operate.

'I say and I will continue to say, throughout this trial, that this is all smoke and mirrors. It is of no relevance whatsoever. This is a straightforward case of dangerous driving leading to a collision with tragic consequences. Mr Salisbury, for reasons known only to himself, took control of the vehicle, then drove it erratically, in law, *dangerously*, leading to the death of the Layton children and their mother's serious, life-changing injuries.

'I will be bringing evidence from a specialist technical examination of the vehicle, which will show exactly how dangerously it was driven just before the collision, but that is the only technical evidence of relevance in this case. James Salisbury, and James Salisbury alone, is the person responsible for these deaths and for Mrs Layton's injuries and, once you have heard the clear evidence, you should have no hesitation in returning a verdict of guilty to both charges. Thank you.'

Judith watched the jury watching Celia. It was normal for them to be engaged at the beginning of any trial, before they started to dwell on the disruption to their personal lives: missed family meals, stacking up favours which would later be called in by friends or employers, difficult daily commutes to and from court. Even in the most interesting cases someone would always detach on day two, usually mid-afternoon.

It tended to begin with one juror, often a middle-aged woman, juggling work, kids, aged parents, insomnia and other personal or family health issues. She would start to fidget, almost imperceptibly at first, touching her hair or face, crossing or uncrossing her legs. Within an hour, at least two more jurors would have joined her and the trio would have become a quartet by the next morning.

There were always one or two stalwarts, usually men in their sixties or, occasionally, a fresh-faced youngster, who prided themselves on their stoicism, who didn't flinch during harrowing forensic evidence and remained focused throughout the most long-winded and detailed testimony. But it was tough retaining their interest. That was one reason why it was so important to make an impression at the start, when the jurors' minds were open and receptive.

'Mr Salisbury was not driving the car which was involved in this terrible collision,' Judith began simply. 'I prevented myself from leaping up to interrupt my learned friend, as a courtesy at this early stage of the proceedings, when she referred to his being behind the wheel...'

'I think you'll find I chose my words carefully enough...' Celia replied.

'If I may continue... When she referred to his being behind the wheel of the car, as if it were an ordinary vehicle, with which we are all familiar; a Toyota Yaris, a Mini Cooper. The car in this case was out of the ordinary, part of the new breed of driverless cars. In the industry they are known as autonomous cars because they act independently of any human intervention. Crucially, they govern their own actions, free from our influence.' Judith allowed her words to sink in, counting to five in her head, before continuing.

'I say now, in opening, and the defence will show, that the car, a 2016 SEDA, was, at all relevant times, operating in autonomous mode. While the expert evidence appears to show Mr Salisbury attempting to take over, he was not, in fact, in control of the SEDA when it crashed; he was no more driving the vehicle than a pedestrian at the side of the road.

'And, importantly, although certainly without intending for one moment to trivialise the extent of the destruction caused by the SEDA vehicle, that meant that he was permitted, under the rules governing these autonomous cars, to review messages on his mobile phone, send messages, make calls and carry out any tasks, without the need to pay due care and attention to the road.

'If he had wished, my client could have composed an opera or written a play or chaired a meeting. The law, in its current form, does require him to sit in the driver's seat but, as long as the car is operating in autonomous mode, and we say it was, that is all that is required of him and, if he was using his phone at the moment of impact, or shortly before, then he did nothing wrong.

'I must also outline that my client was, himself, hurt in the collision. He suffered broken ribs and a head injury which led to concussion and then, to total loss of memory of the crash.

'Now Ms Mansome will say that Mr Salisbury is faking, that he knows full well what happened, that this amnesia is not real. So we will call medical evidence to advise the court on this point, to confirm that Mr Salisbury is, indeed, suffering from amnesia in relation to the events of the afternoon of 10th October.

'There is one thing which Ms Mansome said in her opening with which I wholeheartedly agree. And that is that I will be bringing into this case evidence about autonomous vehicles, their testing, their operation and their behaviour in complex situations. But I object to my learned friend's characterisation of this important part of the case as smoke and mirrors as if it were some kind of deception.' Judith paused and, with a hint of a huff, Celia half rose to her feet.

'Your honour, perhaps it was an unfortunate turn of phrase. My intention was not to suggest that the defence or my learned friend would act in anything other than a perfectly proper way. If I were to substitute the word "smokescreen" would that allay my learned friend's concerns?'

'Not really, your honour, I…'

'Ms Burton, I suggest you accept Ms Mansome's revised terminology and move on. We have your point,' the judge said coolly.

'Yes, thank you. I will be bringing evidence about the behaviour of autonomous vehicles,' Judith continued, 'and about the regime which governs them. The reason I am doing this is because if you have *a reasonable doubt* that Mr Salisbury's actions, on 10th October last, caused the accident, then you must acquit him. We are not intending, nor is it appropriate, to put the entire autonomous vehicle industry on trial this week.'

'I'm delighted to hear that,' Celia muttered, half behind her hand.

'But the evidence the defence will bring will illustrate for you that, tragic as this accident was, my client was not to blame.'

***

Martine whispered to Toby. He whispered back. Then he rose quietly and left the court room. As he slipped out of the door, he looked over to his left. Peter was sitting on the back row, hands resting on his ample belly. He gave a shallow nod in Toby's direction which Toby ignored, but when he was outside the court, Toby leant against the railings to steady himself, before hailing a taxi to take him into work.

56

CHIEF INSPECTOR Dawson was the prosecution's first witness.

'Inspector. You are the officer in charge of the investigation into the car crash which killed Georgia and Bertie Layton and in which Mrs Therese Layton was horribly injured?' Celia began.

'Yes, that's right.'

'How did you first become aware of the crash?'

'A 999 call was received at 2.43pm, reporting a serious car accident on Common Lane. Two of my officers attended within five minutes. I visited the site about forty-five minutes later.'

'Just before we get on to you visiting the site, what did your officers find when they arrived?'

'A blue SEDA car, registration number SAL1 2016, was stationary on the northbound carriageway of Common Lane. A woman, Mrs Therese Layton, was lying on the ground, conscious but in pain, and two young children were also on the ground, not moving. Ambulance arrived at 2.57pm. Two children confirmed dead at 3.20pm by ambulance services.'

'Thank you. And when you arrived at the scene, where were we in the sequence of events?'

'I arrived after the ambulance. The two young children had been covered over. We were keen to get forensics down there quickly so that their bodies could be removed, to avoid causing further distress. Mrs Layton was on a stretcher and was being placed in an ambulance.'

'Was she conscious?'

'Yes. And Mr Layton was there and was sitting on the pavement, crying.'

'It must have been a very distressing sight.'

'Yes. It was.'

'And the defendant?'

'He was lying in the road, next to the car, with a medic in attendance.'

'How was he lying?'

'He was on his side'

'Was the defendant conscious?'

'Yes.'

'How had he got out of the vehicle?'

'It happened before I arrived, but one of my officers said he thought he had opened the door himself and climbed out.'

'Did anyone other than Mrs Layton see the collision?'

'No one came forward who had actually seen the crash. My officers interviewed people at the scene and took statements, but they were all people who came to help afterwards.'

'And the road layout was unusual. Can you describe it, please?'

'Yes. Common Lane is usually a fairly busy main road in a residential area. It's classed as an A road. There are houses and low-level blocks of flats either side, set back from the road.

There is no parking allowed along the stretch where the accident occurred.

'On the day of the accident, there were roadworks blocking the northbound carriageway, the side on which the SEDA car was driving, so anyone travelling north, like Mr Salisbury, had to move over onto the opposite carriageway to proceed.'

'What was the nature of the roadworks?'

'There was a concrete barrier across the left-hand side of the road and some bollards and hoarding. This was to protect drivers from a deep hole which had been dug before the weekend and not yet been filled in.'

'So any drivers going north had to move to the right-hand side and continue, for how long, before re-joining their own side again?'

'Between 100 and 150 metres.'

'And where was the family hit?'

'There was a pedestrian crossing, just south of the work, and the family were crossing the road when they were struck by Mr Salisbury.'

'Was it a zebra crossing?'

'No. It was a "reserve". That's one of those unmarked crossings, where you have a dropped pavement either side and a central area, where pedestrians can stand.'

'Was it lit up?'

'No, but it was light when the accident occurred.'

'And where was the family hit?'

'They were hit on the northbound carriageway. As I said, there were no eyewitnesses of the moment of the collision, but we were able to determine, from statements gathered later, that the family had crossed the southbound carriageway first, waited in the central reserve and then begun to cross the northbound side when they believed it was safe to do so.'

'When did you first interview the defendant?'

'I first saw him in hospital on 11th October, one day later, and I asked him if he remembered anything about the accident.'

'And what did Mr Salisbury say?'

'He said the last thing he remembered was being at home in the morning. He didn't remember getting into the car, he had no recollection of the accident.'

'I see. On any occasions, since then, has Mr Salisbury said anything different?'

'No. Well, I believe he now remembers getting into his car at the beginning of the journey which led to his accident. But he has continued to maintain that he has no memory of the accident itself.'

'Is that usual?'

'I think you'd have to ask his doctor that.'

'I'm interested in your experience as a long-serving police officer. Do you often have *criminals* giving that response to your questions?'

'Your honour. Ms Mansome must appreciate that is not an acceptable question to put, and of no relevance either.' Judith half raised herself from her seat.

'Your honour I won't persist with that line of questioning,' Celia conceded, satisfied she had made her point.

'You also interviewed Mrs Layton the day after the accident?'

'Yes. At the hospital.'

'What did she tell you about the accident?'

'She said that Mr Salisbury had been driving too fast and he had been looking at his phone shortly before the crash.'

'Thank you. This is important so I want to make sure I have it right. Mrs Layton told you, the day after the crash, that Mr Salisbury had been driving too fast?'

'Yes.'

'And he had been looking at his phone?'

'Yes, and I made a note of both those things. She was very clear that she had seen him looking at his phone.'

'Thank you. I have no further questions for this witness.'

***

'Hello Inspector Dawson. I have a few short questions for you.' Judith stood up to begin her cross-examination.

'When you arrived at the scene, the two older children had been attended to, first, by passers-by and then ambulance staff, Mrs Layton and Mr Salisbury were receiving attention, but Mr Salisbury was still lying in the road. Is that correct?'

'Yes.'

'What was the atmosphere like?'

'Pretty awful. It was obvious the two children were dead. Lots of people were crying.'

'And what about my client?'

'What do you mean?'

'Was any animosity being directed towards Mr Salisbury?'

'People were saying things, yes.'

'What kind of things?'

'They were calling him names, saying he should have been more careful.'

'But no one had witnessed the accident itself?'

'No. Or at least no one came forward. They had all gathered

afterwards.'

'If Mr Salisbury had no serious injuries, then why had no steps been taken to get him into an ambulance, for his own protection if nothing more?'

'The ambulance staff had to prioritise. Mrs Layton appeared much more seriously injured.'

'Is it not correct that your officers told the ambulance services to treat the family and ignore my client?'

'Not to my knowledge. I wouldn't have allowed that.'

'But the ambulance log shows Mr Salisbury was not taken to hospital until almost 3.25, half an hour after their arrival.'

'If you say so.'

'Ms Burton. Just remember who is on trial today,' Judge Wilson spoke out of the corner of his mouth.

'Yes of course your honour,' Judith continued. 'So when you arrived and saw my client lying in the road, what did you do?'

'I asked the medic how badly hurt Mr Salisbury was and he said he thought it was not serious, but he appeared to have hit his head. He had cuts on his face. He was lifted on to a stretcher, with a collar around his neck for protection, just in case, and also taken to hospital.'

'Did you, personally, look inside the car or around the car, when you arrived?'

'Not immediately. I was too busy trying to ensure the injured people were treated and the crowd kept away so we could secure the scene, including the vehicle. But, after the injured people had gone, I did.'

'What did you find in the car?'

'Just some of Mr Salisbury's personal items; jacket, briefcase, phone, tablet, some papers.'

'No alcohol, pills or other nefarious substances?'

'No.'

'Now you described the roadworks to my learned friend earlier. It isn't ideal, is it, to close one lane on this busy thoroughfare?'

'No. But it's necessary if roadworks have to be completed.'

'What was the work which was being undertaken, do you know?'

'Yes. It was installation of high-speed cables for faster broadband.'

'And these couldn't be installed under the pavement?'

'The decision was made to go under the road in this small area because of the positioning of other services under the pavement.'

'But the original permission for the works stopped far short of the crossing, didn't it?'

'Yes. Originally the hole was to be positioned further north.'

'So were the contractors in breach of their permission when they continued right up to the crossing?'

'I don't know.'

'I'll put it another way. Do you think that continuing the digging, up to the crossing, so that the approaching traffic had to swerve at an acute angle, into the opposite lane, created a dangerous road hazard?'

'It wasn't ideal but there were signs up to warn people. And you have to credit people with common sense too.'

'What do you mean?'

Dawson gulped. He had been trying to sound magnanimous, to make a general statement about not always holding the public's hand, not wrapping them up in cotton wool, but he could see immediately why Judith had picked him up on it. God, he hated being cross-examined.

'Just what I said,' he replied.

'Well that was what confused me. When you said "you have to credit people with common sense too," were you perhaps referring to Mrs Layton?'

Dawson gripped the sides of the witness box.

'Not specifically. I meant any road user.'

'But we were talking about whether these roadworks constituted a dangerous road hazard, you see. You mentioned road signs and went on to say that "you have to credit people with common sense". Did you mean that pedestrians, like Mrs Layton, should have appreciated that this was a dangerous place to cross and, perhaps, have walked 150 metres south of this hazard and used the zebra crossing instead?'

'How dare you?' The shout had come from Judith's right. Neil was on his feet, his finger wagging in her direction, his eyes blazing. 'How dare you suggest my wife was at fault?' Therese, next to him, remained silent and still. Dawson looked from Neil to Judith and back again. Slowly, reluctantly, Neil lowered himself into his seat, the steam of his anger lingering one step behind.

Judge Wilson moistened his lips. He was gauging whether it was appropriate to say anything in this situation. Clearly one had to have order in the court room, but he could see how Ms Burton's question might have been unduly provocative for someone in Mr Layton's unfortunate position. Things appeared to be quiet now, though. He gestured at Dawson to continue.

'Mrs Layton was entitled to assume that vehicles would drive safely on that stretch of road, as on any road in Britain.'

'But…?'

'I don't know what you're asking me?'

'I felt sure there was a "but" coming next, Inspector?'

'All right. But I accept that a pedestrian, choosing to cross at that spot, would need to be more vigilant than usual, because of the contraflow.'

'So, perhaps a *more cautious* pedestrian would have chosen to cross elsewhere?'

'Yes. I accept that.'

Judith allowed herself a shallow peek to her right, but Neil Layton remained seated this time, albeit his eyes smouldered with outrage.

'You told Ms Mansome that the roadworks began some days earlier?'

'Yes. The previous Thursday. There had been complaints and hold-ups, and a lot of traffic had now found alternative routes.'

'How was traffic flow at the site managed during this work?' Judith moved onto safer ground.

'There was a traffic light controlling the contraflow and there were warning signs 150 metres before the works.'

'Did you see those signs and traffic lights yourself?'

'I didn't notice the signs when I arrived at the scene, but I came from the north – so, the opposite way to the defendant.'

'And?'

'One gentleman came forward, while I was on site and he said that the traffic lights from the northbound carriageway had been out of action when he came through earlier. He said he had called the council to complain as soon as he got home.'

'Did you check this out?'

'I walked down the road, the way Mr Salisbury had approached and found the traffic light was operational.'

'What time would this have been?'

'I noted it down as 3.55pm.'

'Is there any way you can verify what the man said about the lights being out of action earlier in the day?'

'I'm not sure.'

'But you didn't try?'

'No.'

'Did you take a statement from this gentleman?'

'Not a formal statement. But I made a note in my notebook.'

'Which is why you feel able to tell us about this today?'

'Yes.'

'Did you record his name?'

'No.'

Judith stared at Dawson as he shifted in the witness box. Then she looked across at Celia. Finally she turned to glare at Sarah, the prosecution solicitor.

'Don't you think that was important, relevant information that you failed to follow up?'

'Often when people are involved in road accidents at traffic lights, they claim the lights have malfunctioned. In my experience, they are making it up.'

'Oh I'm sorry, did I hear you incorrectly inspector? Was it Mr Salisbury who suggested the light was out of action?'

'No. It was an old gentleman, a member of the public, like I said.'

'Who wasn't accused of any crime. He had no reason to lie or embellish. He gave you a material piece of evidence and you failed to follow it up?'

'I didn't consider it material at the time. I examined the lights myself and they appeared to be in working order.'

'I see. When did you charge Mr Salisbury with dangerous driving and causing harm to Mrs Layton?'

'Once I had the forensic report from Mr Abrams, the expert.'

'And which part of the report did you rely on, just in general terms? Again, the court will be taken to the report later on.'

'The part which confirmed that Mr Salisbury was in control of the car before the collision and that he was travelling at 36mph as he approached the contraflow. That was clearly too fast.'

'Do you find the report straightforward in its conclusions?'

'Yes.'

'So you were sufficiently convinced, by what you read in that report, that you then charged Mr Salisbury with causing death by dangerous driving?'

'I was, yes.'

'Before then, you weren't so sure?'

'Well these cars are new. I didn't know whether something had gone wrong, with the car.'

'I understand. Did you know that, since 2014, nine hundred autonomous vehicles have been driving on Britain's roads?'

'No. I didn't know that.'

'Some of those are SEDAs but we have Teslas, cars made by Google, by many different manufacturers.

'If you say so.'

'There was a large-scale trial of these vehicles in Greenwich during 2016, including some with no humans at all at the wheel. Were you aware of that?'

'I read it in the newspapers.'

'How far is Greenwich from your patch?'

'Five, six miles.'

'So you, and your officers, have been given no guidance on how to respond to incidents involving these vehicles on our roads, even though they have been operating freely five or six miles away for the last two years?'

'No.'

'Well I find that quite staggering...'

'But completely irrelevant, your honour, please,' Celia was leaning heavily on her lectern, her brow knitted tightly, her right forefinger tapping out her frustration.

'Ms Mansome is right, please move on, Ms Burton.'

'Have you ever seen an autonomous vehicle being driven around in London?'

'Me, personally, no.'

'Can you describe, in general terms, what Mr Salisbury's car looks like. We will go to some photos later.'

'It's a large, blue hatchback and it has lots of apparatus on the roof.'

'Apparatus?'

'It has roof bars and then a big cylinder mounted on top.'

'Is that apparatus small or prominent?'

'It's prominent. You can't miss it.'

'You interviewed Mrs Layton the day after the accident?'

'Yes. At the hospital.'

'How was she?'

'Very upset. Very angry. In pain.'

'What did she tell you about the accident?'

'Just what I said already. That she had seen the car coming at her too fast and she remembered seeing Mr Salisbury looking at his phone, holding it up in his hand.'

'Did she say anything to you about the car?'

'No.'

'About its size or colour?'

'No.'

'Or about the "prominent apparatus" on the roof?'

'No.'

'She didn't ask you what that was?'

'No.'

'Thank you. No more questions.'

***

'Inspector?' Judith called out to Dawson, in the mid-morning break, but he persisted in his conversation with two journalists. 'Connie. He's ignoring me,' she muttered to Constance. 'Any chance you could see if you can get him to speak to me before he leaves. Go on. Work your magic.'

Constance approached Dawson. She waited, at a polite distance, for him to finish.

'I don't want to talk to her,' he muttered to Constance after his companions had gone. 'Tell her. She really stitched me up.'

'If it's any consolation she does it to me too,' Constance mumbled, rolling her eyes skyward. 'But I think it's probably something important she wants to talk to you about,' she said aloud.

'All right. But let's go in one of your lawyers' cubby holes. I don't want us overheard or even seen together.'

***

'Why didn't you give us the evidence about the old man and the traffic light before now?' Judith began as Dawson entered the room.

'Whoah!' Dawson's hand returned to the door handle.

Constance flashed Judith an angry look.

'What? I'm not supposed to ask a pertinent question for fear of offending a serving police officer?' Judith said.

Dawson spun around.

'Well done. I thought you'd forgotten. I am a serving police officer. Me and my officers, we put our necks on the line to keep you and yours safe at night. So ask away, but first you apologise. You criticised my officers and then you twisted what I said. You made it look like I was saying that Mrs Layton caused her own accident. No wonder her husband nearly thumped me. Even the judge thought you were out of order, but he didn't have the balls to say it.'

'I'm sorry if you feel aggrieved but I didn't mis-characterise your words,' Judith stood her ground. 'You know that's what you meant. You were saying that the people who put up road signs do their best to keep us safe, but it's up to us to be sensible. She should never have crossed the road there with three children in tow, with cars veering round her. That's what you meant and you were right, so don't talk to me about who has the balls to say what they mean.'

Dawson bit his lip and sat down.

'It wasn't my decision to keep the bit about the traffic light out of my statement. The prosecution lawyer said it wasn't relevant.'

'How could it not be relevant?'

'Because it didn't make any difference, she said. If the light was red, your client should have stopped, so he's in the wrong and, if the light was green, he should have driven slowly and carefully, which he didn't do either. Then the expert report arrived and confirmed what we thought. I have two other homicides on the go at the moment, so I moved on. I didn't waste time trying to track down an irrelevant member of the public. Anything else, while I'm wasting my time in here, when I should be back at my desk?'

'She didn't remember the accident at all, did she, Therese Layton? All that stuff about speed and mobile phones. If she'd remembered she would have asked you about the car.'

'I reported what she said and I reported it accurately. Anything else would be my opinion, which, you've made clear on more than one occasion, isn't something you value.'

Judith was silent. Dawson stood up and opened the door.

'I'll be going now, then.'

'Yes. Thank you. I appreciate you making time to speak to us when you have so much going on.'

***

'Well. I seem to have quite upset Charlie, this time.' Judith scratched underneath her horsehair wig.

'You did lay it on a bit thick, and he hated the suggestion they had ignored James.'

'They were out of order. What if James had suffered a worse head injury? He would never have survived. You've seen the timing; they deliberately overlooked him for at least half an hour. But, as Judge Wilson reminded me, we have only one enemy in that court room. And she hasn't improved with age.'

'Do you think it was the right decision to keep the information about the traffic light quiet?'

'No. It was part of the factual matrix. They should have told us, so we could make of it whatever we wished.'

'And what do you make of it?'

'I'm not sure. But can you follow it up with whoever was responsible for the temporary lights. See if there is a record of them malfunctioning, if they have the name of the old man. And I think we need to make a formal complaint in strong terms to your friend, Sarah, too. I'll prepare something suitable. Shall we go back?'

'What are you going to ask Mrs Layton?'

Judith opened her notebook and pretended to be reading from it. 'Very little,' she said, closing it abruptly. 'The less time she is in the witness box the better. But I have to say something about the other point I raised with Charlie, about her not remembering the car, or it won't hold water. No doubt her husband will hate that too.'

'You're not going to ask why Bertie was out in front?'

'No. I don't think so. That would be even more incendiary than my calling out Charlie about her choice of place to cross. If we are left blaming everything on a three-year-old boy then everyone, including the jury, will think we are desperate.'

57

THERESE APPROACHED the witness box, walking slowly and deliberately, with the aid of two crutches, which she laid down at her side. She wore a pink dress with a baby blue collar and two coloured bracelets adorned her right wrist, in matching hues.

'Mrs Layton. Clearly this is a difficult experience for you. I will keep things as brief as I can,' Celia began in uncharacteristically muted tones.

'That's all right. I'm not going anywhere today,' Therese replied. 'No plans for the evening.'

Celia nodded gently.

'In your own words, tell us what you were doing, immediately before crossing Common Lane on the afternoon of 10th October.'

Therese stared over at James, although her eyes had hardly left his face all morning. As if aware of the heat of her gaze, although perhaps more likely noticing the hiatus in the proceedings, James looked up. Therese's eyelashes fluttered rapidly and then she deliberately shifted her upper body back to focus on Celia.

'I used to work as a dental receptionist,' she said, 'just a couple of streets away. Ruby, my youngest, was four months old so I was still on maternity leave. But they rang me up a couple of weeks before and said that someone was going on holiday. Would I like to come in and cover? They said it would be a good way of getting back to work.'

'Is that where you were, then, on 10th October?'

'I didn't want to do the whole week, but I thought I'd give it a go. I had a try out, the week before, that was the week of the 2nd of October and that went really well, so I said I'd cover the next week. I agreed to do mornings at the beginning of the week and afternoons on the Thursday and Friday.'

'And where were the children when you were working?'

'They're at the same school. It has a nursery too. Bertie finishes at 12.15 and there was some teachers' day, so Georgia finished the same time. They wanted me to work till 1.30 so I asked one of the other mums to take Georgia and Bertie till then. My mum came over to look after Ruby. In the end, I finished at the surgery at 1.30, ran home to feed Ruby and then went to pick up the other two.'

'And you walked around to get them?'

'It's only a few streets away. Mum was tired, so she went home and I took Ruby in the pram; it was nice for her to get some fresh air. I collected Georgia and Bertie and we were walking back across Common Lane when it happened.'

'What was the weather like?'

'It was dry, bit windy but a nice day, sunny even.'

'Can you describe what you saw when you crossed the road?'

'There is a zebra but it's much further down. I like to cross where they have a place in the centre of the road, for you to wait. Everyone crosses there. I was annoyed this time because they were doing roadworks right up against it. They'd been drilling the pavement further up all week and we'd had to walk between the cones. Now there was this big hole in the road with a concrete wall around it. The traffic had to move over onto one side, but there was a traffic light.'

'You could see a traffic light.'

'I could see one down the road, back the way he came.'

'So you picked up your children?'

'I picked up the kids, was walking back and then we crossed halfway. The traffic usually slows down, even when there's no traffic light. And I'd seen this car, his car, but I thought it must go around us, you know, move over to the other side. But he just continued straight on, even though the road was closed. I thought, at first, he would hit the road sign but then he suddenly swerved to the other side of the road, so we…we started to cross. Then, I don't know, suddenly he hit us.'

'Did you see clearly who was driving the car?'

'I saw the defendant, Mr Salisbury, in the driver's seat and he had his mobile phone in his hand. Then I saw him grab the steering wheel… and that's all I remember.'

'Thank you. Please wait for Ms Burton to ask you some questions.'

'Mrs Layton. Thank you for coming here today,' Judith began. 'You seem to have very good recall of the moments leading up to your accident, so I do need to ask this question. Is the account you gave here today your independent recollection of what happened, or have you, since the accident, had access to the video material of the crash?'

Therese looked at Celia.

'I am trying to determine if you have seen other material which might have refreshed your memory of events of some months ago?' Judith continued.

'I have watched the video,' Therese answered, 'but I gave my statement to police first.'

'Thank you. That's clear. Now Mr Salisbury accepts that he was sitting behind the wheel of the car which collided with you and your children, and we will see recorded footage of the car travelling along the road later on, the video to which I just referred, so I am not going to trouble you with any of that. I want to ask about the mobile phone you say you saw. Can you remember how Mr Salisbury was holding the phone?'

'He did have a phone. I saw it.'

Therese shot a glance at Neil. Judith looked across at Celia before continuing.

'Was the mobile phone in one hand, in both hands, resting on the dashboard?'

'He was holding it up with one hand. I suppose it was his right hand.'

'How high was he holding it? Could you show us please?'

Therese lifted her right hand up to around the level of her nose. 'It all happened so quickly, I can't be sure, but I think about this high. So he could see the screen.'

'And was it directly in front of his face or out to one side?'

'Definitely to the side, 'cos I could see his face. And then he saw us.'

'Mr Salisbury saw you.'

'Yes. He looked up and saw us.'

'Was it then you saw him grab the steering wheel?'

'Yes, I think so.'

'Did he drop his phone?'

'I don't know. I think it was still in his hands.'

'Did he have both hands on the wheel then?'

'Yes.'

'Did you *see* his hands on the wheel?'

Therese sat very still. Her eyes narrowed and she stared directly at James again.

'I wish I could say I did, because that's what I want to believe.'

'I'm sorry, Mrs Layton. Are you able to answer the question?'

'Yes I can answer. I can't be sure now where his hands were. I saw him look at the phone, in his right hand, then we looked at each other, just like I'm looking at you now, then everything changed, forever.'

Therese steadied herself and flung back her shoulders.

'How much space was there in the centre of the road, where you were waiting?' Judith asked.

'Enough.'

'But you were there with two children and a pram.'

'Everyone crosses there. Usually the traffic slows down when they see us.'

Judith nodded sympathetically and waited for a few seconds before continuing, for their exchange to hit home.

'When did you find out that the car which struck you and your children was an autonomous vehicle?'

'I'm not sure what you mean?'

'You know now that Mr Salisbury's car was an autonomous vehicle, a self-driving car?'

'Yes.'

'Did you know what autonomous vehicles looked like before your accident?'

'I don't think so. There are lots of different kinds, aren't there?'

'Yes there are. I am going to show you a photograph of a car which is the same model as Mr Salisbury's.' Judith projected an image onto the screen next to Therese. 'Can you see that?'

'Yes.'

'Is there anything unusual about that vehicle?'

'Well, yes. Like inspector Dawson said. It has lots of things on the roof.'

'Had you seen a car looking like this before your accident?'

'I don't think so.'

'When Inspector Dawson came to see you in hospital, and you told him about how fast the car was travelling and how you saw Mr Salisbury holding his mobile phone out in front of him, why didn't you tell him that the car had "lots of things on its roof"?'

'I don't know.'

'Why didn't you ask him if there was anything unusual about the car?'

'I don't know. Maybe I didn't think it was important.'

'Did you have a clear recollection of your accident at that time?'

'Yes, very.'

'But you didn't remember the car looked unusual or had lots of things on the roof.'

'No, I didn't.'

'Thank you, Mrs Layton. I have no further questions.'

Therese Layton half stood up, then she sat back down with a bump. She looked out all around the courtroom and then she turned to Celia.

'Is that it?' she said.

'Yes, thank you, Mrs Layton. You are free to go,' Celia said.

Therese's lip quivered. 'You don't want to know anything about them, do you? About my children. Georgia and Bertie. Those were their names.'

'Thank you Mrs Layton, but please...'

'You don't want to know that Georgia liked to dance. She'd just started ballet and we had tickets to go and see *Sleeping Beauty* at Christmas. Or that Bertie already knew his tables up to five and could do a forward roll on the climbing frame.'

'Mrs Layton...'

'You don't want to know any of that. Because that would make them real and then it might hurt too much. It's easier to wheel me in and then wheel me out quickly, so you don't have to look at my misery. You can just talk about cars and speed and where his hands were. You can be clever and say he was "entitled to chair a meeting" or try to make out that *I* did something wrong. I had three beautiful children! He took two of them away from me, just like that!' She snapped her fingers and turned to face the jury.

'Do you know, there's a split second every morning when I wake up – that's if I get to sleep. Usually it's only because of the medication. There's a split second when I wake up when everything is perfect again. It's me and Neil, Georgia and Bertie and Ruby and we all live together in our little house. Once I even imagined Georgia was tugging at my arm and showing me her new ballet shoes. Then I remember. They're both dead. We don't have that life any more. And he's the one who took them away.' She pointed at James. 'But you don't want to know any of that, do you?

Neil had been easing his way towards his wife since she began her speech. Now he stood next to her and took her arm. She shrugged him off and stood up tall, flashing a defiant glance at James, who was staring at the floor. Then she took her crutches up, pressed one firmly under each arm and walked slowly across the courtroom and out of the door.

58

Celia was wearing a darker shade of lipstick for the afternoon session. Judith sometimes matched her own lipstick to her mood but was fastidious about maintaining a uniform appearance for every day of a trial. She would not want to give away anything about her own emotions, when a man's liberty was at stake.

'Do you remember that time you and Fiona Black threw my school bag in the swimming pool and all my notes were ruined?' Celia had leaned towards her and cut into her thoughts.

Judith's face flushed crimson. Now Celia mentioned it, she did have a dim recollection of an altercation at the side of their old school pool, when they were all filing out and back to lessons, but she knew for certain that she had not been involved.

'My art folder was in there; I was taking art 'O' level. All my work was spoiled.'

'I hardly think this is the time for reminiscences,' Judith replied. 'Shouldn't you be focusing on the case?'

'I'm totally focused,' Celia replied, her lips drawn tight together at the end of her sentence. 'And I have a clear conscience.'

As the court rose to greet Judge Wilson, Judith reflected again on Celia's comments and, as she thought harder, the memory came flooding back. Celia's words bothered her immensely, not only because she knew there was at least a grain of truth in them, but also because she could not be certain that she had been wholly innocent of any involvement. It was less that she had planned the attack or even encouraged it, more that she had taken no steps to intervene, when others had indicated they wanted revenge on Celia for past grievances. She could have stepped in, insisted they all take the moral high ground, "let bygones be bygones", but she hadn't. And afterwards, when she had heard Celia's wail and had seen her desperately fishing her belongings out of the chemically-impregnated water, she had walked on without breaking stride.

'Ms Mansome. Before we begin hearing from Mr Abrams, there are a few things I wanted to clarify please.' Judge Wilson was ensuring they both knew who was in charge. 'Your case is that Mr Salisbury was in control of the vehicle at the time of the collision. You say that he was driving *dangerously* because he, what, failed to slow down sufficiently, failed to control the vehicle effectively or was not looking at the road? Which of these is your case?'

'All of them, your honour. We say that Mr Salisbury was in control of the vehicle from at least 70 metres before the collision. However, he either did not see or chose to ignore the road signs and, as a result, he continued to travel at almost 40mph, heading straight for the family. Additionally, he was looking at his phone. We can't say whether he was looking over a prolonged period, but this certainly distracted him and contributed to his failure to drive safely.'

'And how do you say you *know* that Mr Salisbury was in control of the vehicle?'

'That is what I am hoping our next witness will clarify. I can explain it now, but it will be better to hear it from the expert.'

'All right. So you are relying on the expert?'

'Yes your honour.'

'Good. That's clear. And Ms Burton. You are disputing that your client was in control. Is that correct?'

'Yes your honour. I, too, should prefer to draw this evidence out from Mr Abrams' testimony.'

Judge Wilson scrutinised the two women. He remembered the old days when he had stood in their shoes. He had disliked interventionist judges, just as much as they undoubtedly did. But the new guidance dictated a more managerial approach and, in any event, he was not one of those judges who had chosen the bench for an easy ride.

'Ms Mansome. If Ms Burton is able to establish that her client was not in control of the vehicle at the moment of the collision, then do you accept that the dangerous driving charge fails?'

Celia rose to her feet with her usual poise, but Judith knew this was not an easy question to field at this stage. *Did I help throw her school bag in the swimming pool?* she considered, once more, as the profile of the mature woman in full flow, morphed into that of the thirteen-year old version; a girl who had always changed her clothes in the far corner for PE, and who had covered herself with her towel at every opportunity.

'Your honour, can I respectfully request that we await Mr Abrams on this point too?'

'I don't see why we need to do that? I don't need details, just the framework. If the car was in control at the moment of collision, then surely Mr Salisbury is not guilty. That's right isn't it?'

'Not personally, no. Of course, decisions taken in his capacity as CEO of SEDA may well then be open to scrutiny.'

'But that would not be a matter for my courtroom today, unless you are proposing, at this very late stage, to radically enlarge the scope and put Mr Salisbury's company on trial too. Not only would that be highly irregular, it would suggest to me that you had little confidence in your primary case.'

Celia opened her mouth and closed it again. Judith detected a slight shift in her body weight towards her left shoulder, over which her solicitor sat.

'No, your honour. I accept that the trial is concerned with what Mr Salisbury did that afternoon, in his personal capacity,' Celia said.

'Good. I'm pleased we've cleared that one up. So, as I said, if the car is shown to have been in control at the moment of collision, then you accept that Mr Salisbury cannot be guilty.'

'Yes, were that to be proven, but that is not the evidence we shall present.'

'All right. So that's clear too then.'

There, he had asserted himself sufficiently for now and received at least one straight answer from each lawyer.

Judith noticed Celia's hands fluttering as she organised her papers for the next witness. Perhaps she was not as brave as she seemed, or her own reminiscences about days gone by, flung at Judith, had unsettled her too.

***

Mr Abrams was a tall, thin man with a sparse head hair and a neatly clipped ginger beard. His approach to the witness box was permeated by a jolt, each time he lifted his left leg, which resulted in a tiny spasm in his left cheek. His affliction reminded Judith of a crude puppet on a string, a movement in one limb inevitably triggering a shift somewhere else.

'Mr Abrams. You examined the vehicle, SEDA registration number SAL1 16, which was involved in the accident?' Celia dived straight in.

'Yes.'

'Can you tell us what you determined?'

'Yes. The car had damage to its bodywork, dents and scratches at the front, mostly on the driver's side, from the collision with Mrs Layton, whose elbow smashed the windscreen. There are some photographs which show this clearly.'

'How do you know it was Mrs Layton whose arm smashed the windscreen?'

'I would have concluded independently that the two children were too light to damage the car so badly at that speed. But it's clear from the film of the accident.'

'What film is that?'

'This car, made by SEDA, it moves by using sensors of various kinds; cameras, infra-red, radar, laser. Some of these are stored in the unwieldy structure on the roof, some on the bumpers, but there are cameras in other places including on either side of the dashboard.'

'And you were able to access this film?'

'Yes. I can show you the collision from the viewpoint of the various different cameras. I also examined the laser and radar when writing my report.'

'Thank you. Let's have a look then, shall we?'

Celia played the film of the collision, at full speed, from the perspective of the camera fitted on the driver's side, positioned at the junction of the windscreen and bonnet. As the clip began, a temporary traffic light sign was visible on the pavement, but the car continued to travel steadily at 36mph, as shown on a display in the bottom right hand corner of the screen.

The car then rounded a left-hand bend, and a temporary traffic light structure appeared on the carriageway, together with a road sign. The Layton family also came into sight, waiting in the central reserve, the front wheel of the pram sticking stubbornly out into the road. When the car was almost level with the traffic light, it swerved suddenly and violently right, crossing onto the southbound carriageway, but then as little as two seconds later, it veered left again, back to its original path.

Then the camera lifted a fraction into the air, as the bonnet connected first of all with Mrs Layton, followed by each of her two children. The car decelerated rapidly and came to an abrupt halt, only centimetres short of the concrete wall.

The film ended. It had lasted twenty-four seconds only; it felt like an eternity.

'Ms Mansome. I now have a reasonable idea of the trajectory followed by the car leading up to the moment of impact. I have no wish to prolong the agony, but we will need to see this film slowed down and another camera angle might show us the collision with more precision,' Judge Wilson said.

'Your honour, this is the best camera footage we have,' Celia replied, 'but I'll slow it down, as you have requested and I believe that will provide sufficient information.'

Celia began the video, at reduced speed and, as the car

advanced on the family, she stopped the film periodically and blew up each image. It became clear from closer scrutiny and the series of stills, that the car had been steered to the right very late, only just short of the traffic light itself. And, as the car shifted back to the northbound carriageway, the cheeky face of Bertie Layton, his tongue between his teeth, exuberance personified, was visible momentarily, before he disappeared from view.

By the time the film had played a few times over, most of the audience and some of the jury members were openly weeping. The judge called a twenty-minute break and cleared the court room.

***

Constance went to James, who was sitting slumped against the wall in his cell downstairs.

'That's the worst bit over with,' she said, inching in close to him.

'The worst bit over? Is that what you think? I'm surprised we weren't treated to a 360-degree view, or one with enhanced colour and Dolby sound or maybe in the new 4D. We could have felt the boy's blood spatter our faces.'

He covered his eyes with both hands and his shoulders shook violently. Constance stared at the ceiling.

'This shouldn't be happening,' James said. 'I don't deserve this. That poor family certainly don't deserve this. Is this really justice?'

'We only have a few minutes before we go back into court. You need to compose yourself.'

James sniffed. 'Yes,' he said. 'I'll do that.'

'And I know it must be very painful, but I thought the film might have brought back some memories for you?'

'No, nothing.'

'Have you any idea why you didn't slow down?'

'No.'

'Was there anything you've heard today that has given you an idea of why you steered into the family?'

'No. But there is one small thing I noticed.' James dabbed at his eyes and sat up. 'I wanted to let you and Judith know.'

'Go on.'

'Well, in the photos, the bumper of my car was pretty bashed in on the driver's side.'

'Yes.'

'One of the main sensors is on that side. It would be difficult to say if it was functioning properly earlier, once it had sustained that level of damage.'

"That's useful. I'll pass that on. Anything else?'

James shook his head.

'You would tell me, wouldn't you, if you did remember something else?'

'Yes. I would tell you. Of course, I would.'

59

JUDITH LOOKED up to find Martine standing at the end of her row. For a moment, she contemplated ignoring her. Then she relented and slid her way over.

'How's it going, do you think?' Martine asked, curiously breathless, given that she had only walked over from the public seating area.

'It's early days,' Judith replied.

'But what the policeman said, about the traffic light, what does that mean?'

'It means we have a little more work to do this evening.'

'Do you think that's why James crashed? The light near me, over the summer, was always sticking on red and everyone started ignoring it, driving through it in the end. I could tell the judge about that.'

'That's a kind offer but we need to focus on this particular traffic light.'

'Is there anything else I can do to help?'

Judith was amazed at Martine's sudden interest and offer, given her lack of practical assistance with the case so far.

'You could encourage James to defend himself with a little more conviction,' Judith said. 'At the moment he appears to have decided that it's better for him to go down than the company, and that may mean they both sink together.'

'That's the way he feels. He thinks that if anyone is going to take responsibility for this, it should be him. And that's what everyone else wants, isn't it? For him to be guilty. It's so much easier to understand. He was looking at his phone or driving too fast. We can understand those things. They're all things we might do ourselves.'

'If that's how it is, why didn't he just plead guilty?'

'He would never do that. He hates giving up on anything. He's not hiding anything. He just doesn't remember what happened.'

'But he knows all about these cars, how they work. He could give us more help with the expert evidence, instead of refusing to engage.'

'He's angry about the expert report. He thinks it's unfair.'

'Well it would be helpful if he would explain to us precisely how to challenge it, rather than leaving us floundering.'

'I'll talk to him, but he can be very stubborn.'

'Thank you. Oh, one small thing you might be able to help me with. There's a man I've seen around today in court, average height, overweight, balding, striped suit. Sits at the back but seems very engaged.'

'Sounds like Peter, Peter Mears. I'll look out for him, so I know for sure. He didn't say he was coming. He works for the Department of Transport, on something code-named "Cinderella". James has known him for years.'

'Cinderella?'

'That's what they call it. The project to sell SEDA's cars in the UK.'

'James works with Peter Mears?'

'And there are others. Ask James or ask Toby. Toby was at the last meeting. He should be able to tell you all about it.'

60

'Mr Abrams. What other material did you examine, in order to reach the conclusions in your report?' When they reconvened, even Celia was relieved when the judge said he had seen the film played a sufficient number of times to understand what had happened, and asked her to move on.

'What you saw, before the break, is the live footage from cameras and lasers mounted on the chassis of the car, recorded by the car, like I said.'

'Yes.'

'But we also recovered the EDR, the event data recorder, which is the equivalent of a black box for these vehicles.'

'And what information does that contain?'

'It is a full record of how the car was driven before the collision, its route, its speed, how the controls were being used, instructions to the voice-activated software.'

'Can you explain how the EDR works?'

'Yes. All cars in the USA have them now and many here in the

UK, although you wouldn't necessarily know it. In SEDA's cars, all driving telemetry information is constantly being monitored by the EDR. The sensors all over the car, on the steering wheel, in the braking system, on the accelerating system, send a signal to the EDR, which it retains for a few minutes at a time. Then the space gets all filled up and it is recorded over if you like. Of course, when an accident happens the EDR has no new data to record, so we can see the last few minutes of the car's performance.'

'And can you tell us what this showed?'

'Yes.' Mr Abrams opened up a laptop and an usher connected it to the screen in the court room. This showed a map with a red line indicating the journey of the car northwards and he used his cursor to point as he spoke.

'This is the route the car took. It averaged 36mph on straight pieces of road, lower speed, down to 24mph on more winding parts of the road or slower where there was congestion. It successfully navigated four traffic lights and two pedestrian crossings. There was no unusual veering in any direction, the driving was regular and safe, with slow and steady acceleration and deceleration until shortly before the collision site. It was driving at all times in autonomous mode.'

'Then what happened?'

'These level three SEDA cars have an inbuilt mechanism which, in an emergency, alert the driver and order him or her to re-take control of the car.'

'Is that what happened here?'

'At this point, on the route,' Mr Abrams pointed with his cursor to show a place a few centimetres before the collision site, 'VERA, the car's computer system, asked Mr Salisbury to re-take the controls.'

'How do you know that?'

'The EDR also picks up and records the commentary of the voice commands, the sounds in the car's interior and pressure on any of the buttons on the dashboard. We interrogated that data and matched it with the satellite navigation system and the sensor on one of the wheels. This established that Mr Salisbury had been invited to re-take control of the vehicle at 150 metres, approximately where the temporary traffic light sign was situated, and that he had applied pressure to the manual override button shortly afterwards to switch to manual mode. We also heard him shouting out, as you heard when you watched the film, suggesting he was focusing on what was going on.'

'Or the exact opposite,' Judith whispered loudly to Constance.

'What signal would the car have given to Mr Salisbury to "invite him" to take control?'

'Both verbal and visual, so we heard a clear verbal direction – "please resume control of the vehicle" – and a red light will usually flash on the dashboard with the words "resume control".'

'What happened then?'

'Mr Salisbury did not reduce his speed until he was almost level with the traffic light itself. I conclude in my report that he didn't see it, till very late. Mrs Layton has said he was looking at his mobile phone, so that may be why. He passed straight through the traffic light, which was at green, and as he did so, he moved out of his lane. He swerved suddenly to the right, into the southbound carriageway, then to the left, bringing him back into the northbound carriageway and, ultimately, into a collision with the family, who were in the process of crossing the road.'

'In your opinion, was James Salisbury in control of the vehicle at the moment of impact?'

'Yes, definitely. The data also shows that Mr Salisbury applied the brake, and that the car was braking rapidly and speed was reducing in accordance with expected parameters. I found no evidence of any problems with the braking or steering systems, which remained intact after the accident.'

'And there is no doubt, in your mind, that the car responded to Mr Salisbury. By that I mean, when he steered it right, it travelled to the right and when he pulled the wheel to the left, the car followed?'

'No doubt at all.'

'Thank you, no further questions.'

***

'Hello Mr Abrams. Can I clarify for my benefit and everyone else here, what your area of expertise is please,' Judith was brisk as she tried to re-take the initiative.

'Certainly. I am a forensic crash examiner and I also advise the Department of Transport on road safety issues. I have fifteen years' experience visiting and advising on crash scenes, including analysing and understanding technical faults in vehicles and identifying road hazards. I have also undertaken specialist training on the impact of new technology in this area, working closely with car manufacturers. Every time more sophisticated systems are brought in, like advanced steering or assisted braking, it impacts how cars perform, and I need to keep up to date with that, to be able to do my job.'

'So artificial intelligence is not your thing?'

'No. Thank you for highlighting that. I am not a computer scientist or AI specialist. However, I do know a lot about autonomous vehicles because I keep myself up to date with all the related technological advances. But I don't, for example, have experience myself of computer programming or the technical side of how the computer systems which run these cars operate.'

'Thank you. Now I want to delve below the surface a little, so that I can really understand what you were telling the court just now.'

'Be my guest,' Mr Abrams replied.

'You talked earlier about Mr Salisbury holding the steering wheel. How do you know that?'

'The data records pressure being applied by his hands to the steering wheel.'

'But does that mean he was holding the wheel?'

'What do you mean?'

'You say that you can detect *now* that pressure was applied but is it possible to distinguish between gripping the wheel with your fingers and, say, resting your elbows on the wheel, which a person might do, sitting in the driver's seat, reading a book or, as you have mentioned, scrolling through messages on a phone.'

'It isn't possible to be that precise, no, but there was contact which was more than transient between Mr Salisbury and the steering wheel.'

'Ah. So the data doesn't really illustrate *pressure* in the sense of someone squeezing the wheel, but simply *contact*, in that part of Mr Salisbury's body was touching the steering wheel over a period of time?'

'Continuous period of time and in the same place and at the traditional ten-to-two position, which is why I concluded he was holding the wheel, but, yes, we don't have data on the strength of grip.'

'And also, just to clarify, your data shows us that Mr Salisbury also applied pressure to the manual mode button at somewhere between 150 metres and 70 metres from the collision site, but do we know how much pressure?'

'No.'

'Or if it was sufficient to operate the button? It's like buttons on a lift or on a keyboard, some require more pressure than others in order to be operative.'

'He pressed the button. We can't say precisely how hard.'

'And there is no way of showing that the car was in manual mode?'

'I don't understand the question.'

'What I mean is, there is no big flag on your data which says "this car is now driving in manual mode". You glean that information from reviewing the other data, so, for example, on a continuous stretch of road, you would know the car was in autonomous mode because it would be accelerating and decelerating without any pressure on the pedals. Is that correct?'

'Precisely.'

'So you have drawn the conclusion that the car was in manual mode, because Mr Salisbury pressed the button, you can't say how hard, and then, what? Applied some pressure to the brakes?'

'Yes. And held the steering wheel.'

'Yes. Thank you for reminding me of that. What happens if a person presses the brake, when the car is driving autonomously?'

'Nothing.'

'So, if, for example, I was in one of these vehicles and I mistakenly leant my foot on the brake, the car would ignore me. And if we were to examine the data afterwards, we would see, what?'

'We would see you applying pressure to the brake but the car not slowing down, so we would know the car was in autonomous mode.'

'Or it could be in manual mode, but the brakes have failed?'

'In theory, yes, but I checked the brakes on this car and they were operating correctly.'

'But that was after the event.'

'Yes.'

'So, just so I am clear, the only evidence you have of Mr Salisbury being in control of the vehicle is what appear now to be desperate attempts by him to brake and steer the car away from danger, recorded by sensors on the steering wheel and the brake pedal. How were these recorded?'

'They were recorded by the EDR, the event data recorder.'

'Let's say, hypothetically, Mr Salisbury had never pressed that button. Is it plausible that, in the seconds leading up to the crash, he still might have grabbed the wheel and pumped the brake, in a normal human response to an impending collision? It would look as if he was doing the work, but the car remained in control?'

'But the sensor recorded that he *did* press the button.'

'All right. Talking about sensors, can you tell us where the sensors on the car are situated?'

'The round structure on the roof is the main navigation system. It's called a LIDAR, as it combines laser and radar technology. Then there is a sensor on the driver's side front wheel which can accurately pinpoint where the car is on a map. There are video cameras on the dashboard which help the on-board computer system detect moving things, like pedestrians and other cars. And, finally, there are four radar sensors, three in the front bumper and one in the rear, to help guide the car.'

'Can I take you, for a moment, to a still image of the vehicle?

Thank you. Now you've shown us that the bumper on the driver's side was damaged, quite substantially. What had happened to that radar sensor, in the bumper?'

'It was crushed.'

'You don't mention that in your report?'

'Maybe not.'

'Is it possible to tell, from the data you reviewed, whether that particular front sensor was operating properly before the crash?'

'No. It isn't.'

'How might a sensor like that, set into the bumper, become damaged?'

'They are quite fragile. A knock into another vehicle would damage them.'

'Or even coming too close to a low wall, like in the car park my client had used, immediately before this journey?'

'It's possible, yes. But I would expect a signal to be sent if any sensor was out of action.'

'Did you check for any signal?'

'It would be a contemporaneous message on the dashboard so it's not possible to check now.'

'So how did you reach the conclusion that the sensors were operating properly?'

'All the other sensors were intact after the crash.'

'Apart from this one, the one closest to Mrs Layton?'

'Yes. I accept that it's not possible now to ascertain if that sensor was operating properly before the crash, because of the damage it sustained.'

'Thank you. Why did the car not slow down when it approached the temporary traffic light sign?'

'I don't know.'

'If the car was mimicking the actions of a human driver, we see a temporary traffic light sign, and a sign telling us to "slow down" and we do. Yet this car didn't do that. Instead, you say that the EDR shows that it sent an emergency request to the driver to re-take control, and continued on its existing trajectory, at its existing speed. I am asking you why that happened?'

'And I am telling you I don't know. I can tell you if certain components were working and were utilised, but I can't tell you why. I can't get inside the head of the car's control system. It's very difficult to explain after the event *why* such a complex piece of software has made a decision. It's like asking what, precisely, goes on inside a human brain to instruct a human to perform an action.'

There was silence in the court as Mr Abrams' words sank in. Mr Abrams was accepting, without any qualms, that he did not have the answer, that all he could do was suggest plausible explanations for what might have happened inside the computer, and that was unlikely to satisfy the Laytons or the public. The key question for James, of course, was the impact on the jury. Judith stole a snatched glance to see if Constance was making notes, but Constance was disappearing out of the back of the court, in a hurry.

'But, like I said at the beginning, it's not my field,' Mr Abrams continued. 'If you want to know *why* things happened, you should get one of the SEDA technicians in. He'd be able to tell you if I'm right or not.'

'Thank you. We may just do that.' Judith made a play of looking across at the clock.

'Your honour. I am noticing the time, and I still have quite a way to go with this witness. But I was about to move on to another topic.'

Judge Wilson checked the time too and closed his notebook.

'Very well. We'll stop there. Back at 9am tomorrow please.'

***

Constance had just completed a hurried phone call in the waiting area outside the court and was making notes on her iPad, when she heard a familiar voice.

'Hi, Sis.'

She turned around and Jermain was standing before her. She gasped and then she smiled.

'How did you know I was here?' she said.

'I asked at your work.'

'You know where I work?'

He pointed to his phone. 'I looked you up. It says so many good things about you, I thought they must have got the wrong person.'

'Thanks.'

He opened his arms and she went to him. It was funny how it was always that way around. She was the big sister, but he always gave out the hugs.

'You didn't say you were coming,' she said. 'I'm in the middle of a trial.'

'They said. But I was just delivering something up the road and I saw how close I was.'

'Delivering? Is that part of your new job?'

Jermain withdrew. 'You ask so many questions. You always do this.'

'I'm sorry. I was…interested.' Constance examined his face, clean-shaven, his hair cut shorter than before. 'How long are you in London? Can I, at least, ask that one?' Jermain looked past Constance as someone exited the court and the low murmur of the proceedings spilled out.

'Nah. This is it,' he said. 'I'm passing through. It's lucky you were here and not inside. You got cross with me that time I waved. Remember? I have to go. In fact, I might have a parking ticket by now. But I just throw 'em away.'

Constance opened her mouth to protest.

'Only joking,' he said.

Constance thumped his arm.

'Come and see me properly soon,' she said, 'for a bit longer!'

'Sure.'

He was already walking away.

'You can pick up your post.'

He had gone. Constance ran to the door of the building, but she couldn't see him anywhere. He had been swallowed up by the crowds and disappeared.

***

Constance joined Judith as she exited court, and they huddled together in a quiet alcove while the other lawyers and the public filed out.

'Where've you been?' Judith asked.

'I just wanted to make a quick call, on that point Abrams raised about why the computer does things, for your cross-examination. Greg says "hi" by the way.'

'Why have you been speaking to Greg?' Judith's tone was sharper than usual.

'I thought he'd know the answer,' Constance said. 'And he

did. Something he said when we all had dinner together. You'll definitely want to use it on Abrams tomorrow.'

'All right,' Judith mumbled her agreement. 'And the traffic light?' she asked.

'It's taken this long for me to find the contractor's name. I'll try them again now, but it may have to wait till the morning. How do you think it's gone with Abrams?'

'Fine, I think, but I'm fed up fighting with one hand behind my back. I mean, "damaged sensor". I used it, but is that seriously the best James can do? I'm wondering if we should introduce the hint of someone tampering with the car. Do we have anything at all we can use to support that?'

'Nothing. You've seen Abrams' report on the car itself. And I spoke to the security guy a few weeks back and he said he'd never seen anyone near the car. I also caught up with the gardener, who said the same.'

'Was there any reason for either of them to lie?'

'I can't think of any. They both seemed genuine, although Leo, the gardener, hinted that there was something going on between Martine and the security guy, Dean.'

'Did he?'

'He asked if James might go to prison and when I said I hoped not, but it was possible, he said he thought Dean might enjoy the prospect of free access to Martine.'

'*Free access?*'

'Those weren't the words he used, but that was the gist.'

'And you didn't think it important to tell me this before?' Judith pulled off her wig and attempted to straighten her hair.

'I met Dean. He seemed straightforward. I couldn't see it happening. I thought maybe Leo was making trouble.'

'All right. Like you say, we have no evidence of the car failing, so it's probably irrelevant for today's purposes, even if Dean has been dipping his toe in James' pond. I was on my way to see James, anyway, to insist he provides more help. Otherwise I'm in danger of drowning out there.'

'Are you going to tell him that?'

'I am. Not that it will do any good.' Judith sighed. 'Martine says "he's stubborn", as if that makes it all right. And that he feels morally responsible. As if we didn't have enough to contend with. Come on. I could do with some back-up. I'll be bad cop,' she said, 'just in case you were wondering.'

***

James was sitting, hands clasped together, staring at the floor, when Judith and Constance entered. Judith began to walk forward, then checked her own progress and sat down, taking out her notebook and pen.

'In case you wanted to know, everything today was as expected. Nothing we can't deal with,' she began.

'Thank you.' James spoke to the floor.

'But the things I talked to the witnesses about, the sensor, whether you were holding the steering wheel, they're hardly revelatory. Have you really told us all you can?'

James sat in silence. Judith flicked through her notes again and Constance took advantage of the hiatus to approach James herself.

'This is a difficult case, I know,' Constance said. 'And the lives of one family have been changed forever. And it's rubbish. I know that. And you probably feel you can't walk along the street and look people in the eye because they all think it was your fault. That you need to endure some kind of punishment to redress the balance. But you have a family, too. You have a wife and two sons. If we don't do enough to raise the doubt that you were responsible, then you will go to prison. How will that be for Martine? How will that be for *your* children?'

'You're not really making things better. Do you know that?' James looked up for the first time.

'Well I am sorry for that!' Constance's voice was gradually increasing in volume. 'But some things have to be said. Judith and I are fighting to defend you, but it's like climbing a mountain in a…a pair of slippers. Are you really going to stand up in court and say that you "must have been" driving in manual mode, even though you don't remember what happened? That's just opting out, and the jury will see that too.'

Constance was unstoppable in full flow.

'You think that sounds better than putting your hands up and saying, "I'm guilty. I wasn't looking where I was going. I killed those kids." Well it's not better, it's worse,' she said. 'It's accepting you killed them, but you don't even have the courage to admit it. Is that really what you want your legacy to be? After all your years of hard work?'

'Leave me!' James leapt to his feet, his voice reverberating around the tiny room and Constance sprang backwards.

Judith rose and collected her things. She took Constance's arm and led her towards the door.

'We've had a long day,' she said to James, 'all of us. We'll email you over some areas where we would welcome your input overnight. Back here around 8.30 tomorrow would be good, if you can manage.'

61

JUDITH OPENED up her mail box around 6am, on arrival at Constance's office, to find an email from James with a list entitled 'Questions you could ask Mr Abrams about his report'. She beckoned Constance over.

'Connie. Come and look.'

Constance, bleary-eyed through lack of sleep, ran over.

'Well done you!' Judith said, as she hurriedly devoured its contents.

'I thought I'd gone too far, calling him a coward,' Constance said.

'So did I, if I'm honest. I thought there was a good chance he might decide to plead guilty and we'd have the rest of the week off.'

'I know it was risky. I was just suddenly really angry with him. It all came tumbling out.'

'And now we have this. Not a magnum opus, but some extremely helpful pointers. I can use some of them this morning, I hope. And if I didn't say yesterday, I liked your slipper analogy.

I may use it myself.'

Judith poured out her first coffee of the day. 'You did well challenging James in that way,' she repeated. 'But you know what?'

'Yes. I know. Don't ever do it again. I won't. I promise. If you forward the email on to me, I'll get started on some of those leads.'

***

'Mr Abrams. Good morning. Picking up on where we left off yesterday,' Judith began the day loud and enthusiastic. 'Are you aware of research carried out, at the government's request, over the last five years or so, regarding the interface between autonomous and manual mode in these level three vehicles?'

'Yes.'

'Can you summarise that research and what it established?'

'It was inconclusive.'

'Let's take a look, as I think you will find there were some conclusions. The paper is entitled "Re-establishing control" and dated 2nd February 2017. It summarises its conclusions as follows: "Tests showed that most drivers took longer than was predicted, when instructed to re-take control of an autonomous vehicle without prior warning. The average driver took around five seconds to tune in and focus on all aspects of the driving process and while around 20% of drivers were able to manage the transition more quickly than this, a large minority took significantly longer. Around 3% of drivers tested took more than 20 seconds to readjust." Are you familiar with these conclusions?'

'I don't remember them, word for word, but, in general terms, yes.'

'So you are aware that the government recently acknowledged

that it took the average driver around five seconds to, let's say, marshal his or her thoughts and become a real driver again?'

'Yes I am.'

'Can you explain why the figures came back like this?'

'I suppose the people were relaxed, so it took them time to jump into action.'

'They were relaxed; you mean, they were not expecting to be, literally, *in the driving seat*?'

'Yes.'

'And the people who were used in the research, were they special in any way?'

'No. I don't believe so.'

'They were not particularly skilled at driving, had taken more advanced driving tests.'

'No. They were ordinary people.'

'Ordinary people, like James Salisbury.'

'Yes.'

'So why are you judging James Salisbury to a much higher standard than those other ordinary people?'

'I…I don't think I am.'

'If VERA, the voice activated software, had invited him to take control at that point in the road you have indicated, he would have had, how long before impact?'

'At 150 metres it's around nine seconds, but he actually took control at seventy metres, more like four and a half seconds.'

'And you based that on…?'

'Time equals distance over speed. At 36mph the car is travelling at around sixteen metres every second and the traffic light was seventy metres before the collision site.'

'And what precisely would Mr Salisbury have had to do, in

those four and a half seconds, to regain control?'

'He would have pressed the manual button, taken the steering wheel in his hands, looked through the windscreen to assess the situation, put his foot on the brake and steered away from the family.'

'What's the stopping distance at 36mph? It's a while since I studied my highway code.'

'Around thirty metres. It's, say, ten metres of thinking time and the rest is the braking mechanism itself.'

'So unless my client was fully in control of that vehicle, pushing out of his mind all his work thoughts or personal thoughts, what information he required for his next meeting – all of which he was perfectly entitled to do while being chauffeur-driven in style – more than thirty metres or two seconds before the crossing, he was doomed to hit the family?'

'No. He might still have steered away from them. But he could only have stopped the car before reaching them, if he applied the brake more than thirty metres away.'

'Yes, thank you. I see that. But in order to come to a standstill before hitting the family, Mr Salisbury would have had to *tune in* all those things we just talked about and had his foot firmly down on the brake in two and a half seconds after taking control.'

'Yes.'

'When the average person only does this within five seconds. Do you see my point?'

'Yes.' Mr Abrams fiddled with the button on his jacket and glanced over at Celia. The left side of his face contracted again, briefly, just as on his arrival the previous day.

'Are you aware of research written up by a distinguished Professor Stein, entitled "The problems of transition: driverless cars," published last year?'

'Yes.'

'And what does he conclude on this particular issue?'

'He concludes that the time taken to regain control is a problematic aspect of vehicles which can operate in both modes. He recommends that we drive either/or.'

'Either/or?'

'Yes. Either drive manually, where the driver knows throughout the journey that he is in control and remains alert or in autonomous mode, where the car is in control, but not both.'

'And why has everyone ignored Professor Stein?'

'I'm not sure they have.'

'All right. Why are the cars being trialled in the UK these level three transitional vehicles? Why have we not simply moved to fully autonomous vehicles?'

'Two reasons I know of. First, the Department of Transport's view, as advised by many experts, was that it's too big a leap for the public to make all at once, to move from all manual to all autonomous. The Department was advised it would be preferable to take things in stages.'

'And the other reason?'

'Extreme caution. These cars have been extensively tested, but there are always residual concerns that something might malfunction.'

'And cause an accident?'

'And cause an accident, yes.'

'Has research been carried out on how autonomous vehicles recognise road signs?'

'Yes.'

'Why?'

'There was some evidence, from the USA, that road signs were not always correctly interpreted, leading to a small number of minor accidents.'

'That makes the issue sound of little importance. It's more than that, isn't it? I can take you to the relevant studies if you wish?'

Mr Abrams frowned.

'It is an area that I know is being worked on,' he said. 'If signs were dirty or positioned in badly lit areas, or if they had been graffitied, then cars sometimes did not notice them or failed to read them correctly.'

'Or if they were at an angle?'

'Yes, if they were not face-on they were more difficult for autonomous vehicles to read.'

'Was there one specific sign that was highlighted as most problematic?'

'No, but word signs are better understood generally, as long as they are in the language the car understands.'

'And the temporary traffic light sign which appeared on the road at around 150 metres before the collision site, that is a symbol sign, isn't it?'

'Yes.'

'What about hacking?'

'I saw no evidence that this car's software had been hacked.'

'But autonomous cars can be hacked?'

'Theoretically.'

'And why is that?'

'They are not self-contained. They send signals back to a central server, usually via the internet or cellular connections. Often the entertainment system or GPS is a way for a hacker to gain entry. They communicate with each other too.'

'It isn't just theoretical then?'

'Well. In my view, it is.'

'How much is the UK government currently spending on this theoretical hacking concern?'

'Around £5 million.'

'So the government, including its specialist IT advisers, does not share your view. They see it as a realistic worry, or they would not be spending £5 million of public funds on it?'

'Look, the government has to be sure. But the educated view is that there isn't a real risk. And £5 million is a drop in the ocean, really.'

Judith saw Celia hovering, half-standing in protest, but ploughed on regardless.

'Were all UK 2016 SEDAs programmed in the same way?'

'Yes. As far as I know.'

'Who worked on the underlying software programmes?'

'Skilled software technicians at the Essex factory. I was given access to them and it's in my report.'

'Access?'

'I talked to them.'

Judith glanced fleetingly at Celia, who was now studiously ignoring her. She tried to keep the excitement from infiltrating her voice.

'They didn't actually show you any of the underlying software.'

'There was no reason for them to do that. I'm not interrogating their entire autonomous car programme and I wouldn't have the know-how even if I wanted to. I just checked a couple of parameters with them. They had given me the data from the EDR and that was all I needed in my report.'

Judith stood up straight and frowned so hard her eyebrows

joined in the middle.

'Can you just repeat that last sentence.'

'Yes. I said "they had given me the data from the EDR and that was all I needed".'

'SEDA technicians extracted the data from the EDR and gave it to you?'

'Yes. But that's usual. There are tools on the market to extract the data, but it's still safer for the manufacturer to do it. Then they can't argue that you've messed things up and tried to blame them. And sometimes you need a security code to access it too.'

Celia's eyes narrowed, and her poisonous glance to her solicitor suggested this might have been news to her too.

'How do we know, then, that the data you have seen is the original, unadulterated data? How do we know that this car did not malfunction and you were given the data from another vehicle?'

Mr Abrams also looked at Celia's solicitor.

'We don't. We have to trust them.'

Judith paused for maximum impact before continuing.

'Your honour. Can I explain to the court for a moment, that there was a tussle of sorts in the civil courts regarding who should first access the EDR. Mr Salisbury's application to the police was rejected. Instead, the Department of Transport intervened and obtained access to the data first, on the basis of there being a necessary public interest.'

'I see.'

'The defence had therefore assumed, wrongly it now seems, that the Department of Transport had accessed the data in a supervised fashion, together with Mr Abrams. Perhaps my learned friend can assist.'

Celia had recovered her composure sufficiently to return to attack mode.

'Your honour. First of all, this is not a matter for court today. If Ms Burton had real concerns about the integrity of the data, these should have been raised weeks ago when she was provided with a copy of Mr Abrams' report. Second, while the Ministry gained permission to access the data, it was felt that the most prudent method, in the circumstances, was for a SEDA representative to extract the data under the watchful eye of Mr Abrams and…'

'He didn't.' Mr Abrams interrupted Celia.

'I beg your pardon,' Celia almost choked.

'The SEDA representative didn't "extract the data under the watchful eye of Mr Abrams".' Judith and Constance each smothered a giggle as Abrams had mimicked Celia when he spoke, although he seemed completely oblivious to his offence.

'How do you know that?' Judith stepped in.

'When I arrived at the SEDA factory, they'd already done it. The senior technician, a Mr Herrera, had some other important work to do, so he had "got on with it" before I arrived. I have to say, though, it didn't appear to have been tampered with in any way and I was present very shortly afterwards.'

'That still doesn't deal with my first point, which is timing,' Celia said.

'Ms Burton. Before I have to rule on this, can you give me some inkling of where you are going with it?'

'Your honour, Mr Abrams' conclusion that Mr Salisbury was in control of the vehicle relies on two things; the cameras mounted on the chassis of the car, and data relating to speed, steering, braking – all provided by studying the EDR. As I understand it, the camera footage was left intact pending examination by Mr

Abrams, and he was able to access that himself. But, as we've just heard, the EDR data was not.'

'Mr Abrams. Is it possible to manipulate the data from the EDR? So that, for example, you change the speed recorded by the vehicle to 36 mph rather than 26?' Judge Wilson turned to the witness.

'Your honour, with technology, anything is possible,' he replied. 'But the injuries were consistent with a collision at above 35 mph.'

'Ms Burton. Are you asking me to do something, as a result of this potential difficulty?'

'Your honour. This is a *real* difficulty and it will come up again and again in the future, unless a formal mechanism is put in place to compel manufacturers to provide access to the EDR under controlled conditions.'

'Your malaise may well be justified, but what are you suggesting I do about it *now*?'

'I don't see how we can possibly continue this trial. The prosecution is relying on data from the car which cannot possibly be trusted to make assertions that the car was performing correctly. Lack of oversight of the data at the crucial moment makes it totally unreliable, and therefore, inadmissible.'

'Your honour, I must object,' Celia said. 'Ms Burton is impugning the data without any basis. The fact that data could, theoretically, have been changed does not mean it was changed. I say we ask the technician to come in. Surely it will only take a moment.'

'Your honour. Mr Herrera is unlikely to admit to having altered the data, so we will take up court time but be back to square one. This should not have been allowed to happen in the first place.'

Judge Wilson held up his hand. Judith and Celia both sat down.

James was staring intently over at Martine.

'Ms Burton, there is some weight in what you say. However, I tend to think that this would not necessarily render the evidence inadmissible. It would be more a question of how much weight to attach to it. It does seem sensible, before we proceed much further, though, to call this Mr Herrera. He could also assist with the issue on which Mr Abrams has limited knowledge; namely why this vehicle made the decisions it did.'

'You honour. I will accept that for now, as long as you please note that I have not withdrawn my application for the case against my client to be dropped.'

'Noted Ms Burton. That's settled then. Ms Mansome, see if you can arrange this and send me a revised timetable. I'll review it when I can. Ms Burton. Do you have any further questions for this witness?'

'Just a few.'

'Well, we are nearing lunchtime. Let's break now. Back at 2pm.

***

'Where did you get to with the traffic lights?' Judith asked Constance as they reviewed their notes in the break.

'Bit of a dead end. I found the contractors, called them and left a message, finally managed to speak to someone.'

'And?'

'They did log a call from a man, a Mr Senior, who said the lights had been completely out when he passed at around 2.30, so just before the accident. They had an engineer nearby. By the time he got there the accident had happened, so he had to park and walk the last bit. But they found his report, which was that the lights were working perfectly well when he attended.'

'Are they able to look back and see if the lights malfunctioned in the past?'

'I asked and he said it's not possible.'

'All right. You tried. What about the CCTV?'

'I am still waiting for it. Dawson's got someone digging it out. I should get access by this evening at the latest.'

'OK. So priority now is Mr Herrera.'

'Mr Herrera?'

'SEDA's technician. Get up there now and speak to him. I've hardly anything else left for Abrams.'

'But what kind of things should I ask?'

'First you ask him about the EDR. And then see what else you can find out. We need to understand more about how these vehicles navigate. I'm sure we're missing a trick.'

'OK. There's also something I must ask James too. It may be nothing, but I suddenly had a thought about the car, just now when Abrams was speaking. I'll prioritise Herrera though. See you later.'

62

Juan met Constance in the foyer of SEDA's offices an hour later, and he led her to the technicians' lab. He had pumped her hand energetically when they met and she found she had to run to keep up with him as he strode out along the corridor. She watched him key in a long code on the keypad and swipe his security pass up and then down before the door opened to allow them access to the lab.

'Now,' he said, sitting down at his desk and politely ignoring her breathlessness, 'I got a call. Is everything going OK at the trial?'

'As well as we could expect, for now.'

'What's so urgent then? They said I needed to go to court. Anything to help James.'

Constance was about to launch into her prepared questions about the EDR and the extraction of the data, when she noticed the monitor behind Juan, with lines criss-crossing the screen in a myriad of colours, and rectangular boxes moving horizontally and vertically across the display.

'What's that?' she asked.

Juan turned around.

'Aha,' he said. 'That is how an autonomous vehicle sees the world.'

'Really?'

'Yes. It's the combination of laser and radar signals and the mapping system which has been programmed in. Look.'

As Constance watched he switched on a second screen. Now Constance could see the digital display alongside a view of a road.

'That's incredible,' she said. 'So real life is turned into all those boxes. Is this what you do all day?'

'Part of it. We get live feed from our vehicles, we record it, analyse it and we check it for any problems. I think all manufacturers have these kind of programmes now.'

'So, each box is, what, a car?'

'A car, a person, a cyclist, a lorry, a tree.'

'And when you say "it's how the vehicle sees the world", it doesn't have eyes, like a human?'

'No. This comes from the LIDAR, the laser and radar sending out signals in all directions.'

'Then this turquoise box here…' Constance pointed to a rectangle in the middle of the screen, '…is this lorry here?' She moved her finger across to the corresponding point on the next screen.

'Yes. But what is amazing is that the laser and radar pick up obstacles much earlier than they come into view for a human driver. The green square is the car I'm tracking. It will be aware of your lorry, well before the driver sees it. That's why this is the way of the future.'

Constance realised how close to Juan she was sitting and

shuffled back in her chair.

'Can you connect to James' car too, like this?'

'All our test vehicles can be connected, if the engine is running.'

'And you're sitting here all day, watching to see what they all do?' she said.

'Yes. I'm watching, but not all day. I have other things I'm working on too. Was that what you wanted to ask?'

'No. I need to ask you a few questions about the EDR from James' car. And then we'd better head off to court. They've put you in, provisionally, at 4pm.'

63

'MR ABRAMS, we are nearly finished now, you'll be pleased to hear,' Judith resumed her questions in the afternoon, hoping that Constance would bring something back from Juan which she could use.

'Are there laws about tampering with the software on these cars?' she began.

'Yes. Well, there will be in the new government Bill.'

'What about updating the software?'

'The technology is moving on very quickly, so there will be an obligation on every autonomous car owner to install updates.'

'And how do they do that?'

'The manufacturer sends the updates regularly and the owner has to accept them. All very straightforward.'

'Perhaps not if you're blind or disabled or old, as some of the users of these vehicles will be.'

Judge Wilson frowned, and scribbled a note in the margin of his papers.

'When you talk about *fault* in your report, what do you mean?' Judith continued, on a new topic.

'I mean the person responsible for something having taken place.'

'Precisely. You say, your honour, this is page 16. "Clearly, as Mr Salisbury was ordered to take control at a distance of 150 metres from the collision site, and did indeed take control, as indicated by pressure on the steering wheel at around 70 metres or four and a half seconds before the collision site, it was his fault that the car then collided with the family." So, in your report, you are saying this is his responsibility and his alone?'

'I am.'

'But, if you cast your mind back, it was this morning, but I reminded you then, how long an ordinary person, like Mr Salisbury, would normally take to even begin to tune in – most likely five seconds but possibly even seven seconds – do you remember that?'

'Yes, I do.'

'And yet you stand here now, hand on heart, before his honour, the jury, the public, the media. You stand here and tell us that, in your expert opinion, the accident was *all* Mr Salisbury's fault?'

'Well, I...'

'Are you certain, beyond reasonable doubt, that *you* would have been able to stop that car safely, without injury, in four and a half seconds, if you had been sitting at the wheel, in the same conditions?'

'No, I...'

'You're not certain?'

'Ms Burton. Your passion is commendable but do not badger the witness. It is not helping your cause,' Judge Wilson intervened laconically.

'Mr Abrams. Please take your time. Do I need to repeat the question?'

'No,' he replied curtly. 'I remember the question. I believe I would have taken control in sufficient time to avoid the accident, but I accept on reflection that, perhaps, it is an overestimation to characterise this accident as wholly Mr Salisbury's fault.'

'Because?' Judith held her breath and her tongue.

'Because I accept that he may have been disorientated, not completely focused, when a complex road situation required negotiation very quickly.'

'Thank you. Mr Abrams, do you know how often the average person blinks?'

'No, I don't.'

'Every four and a half seconds. You are asking this court to accept that Mr Salisbury drove *dangerously* because he could not do all those things, look up, take in and understand a complicated road scene unfolding at speed before him, take the wheel, brake and steer away from a moving hazard, all in the blink of an eye.'

Mr Abrams, in one last passively defiant move, stared at Judith without blinking.

'Thank you. No further questions.'

***

'Are you really going to press for the trial to be abandoned?' Constance was rehydrating with her second bottle of aloe vera water, having raced back to court to update Judith.

'No. Not now, when I have five good explanations for why James' car could have got things so badly wrong. Not unless

Herrera confesses to changing the data.'

'Take it from me, he won't,' Constance chipped in.

'Not unexpected. I thought it was definitely worth dipping my toe in with Wilson, but he was clear that he's not having it. The jury will remember though, and store it away. And far better to look like we're confident that there are so many other reasons why James is not guilty that we don't care too much about this one.'

'Are you sure? I mean, we could finish it all now?'

'Trust me. Wilson doesn't like it. And this is a huge case. If it ends up being thrown out because the Department of Transport allowed the EDR to be reviewed unsupervised, after making a court application based on public interest, well, you can imagine the repercussions.'

'It's worse than that, actually.'

'What? How worse?'

Constance finished her drink and tossed it into the bin in the corner.

'The EDR had been removed even before the Ministry's court application. I checked with James just now. It had already gone when I visited the car in the lock-up. I took photos and it's clearly not there.'

'Ah well. Overzealous police officers maybe. Or more time to do a switch. It could be something.' Judith watched Constance out of the corner of her eye. 'Maybe I can make mileage from it in closing,' she said. 'But that's challenging the police again, and we saw what happened last time I hinted that our boys in blue may not be perfect.'

Constance looked away.

'I don't want you to think I don't value your efforts, Connie, I really do.'

'It's OK. I understand.'

'I just don't want to go for the no trial and lose. It makes us look desperate. What did you make of Herrera?'

'Clever, charming, knows his stuff. Wants to help James. And adamant that he did nothing wrong.'

'OK. Anything else useful?'

'Lots of other stuff but not useful for today. He showed me this elaborate digital programme they have, which turns a road scene into lines and shows what SEDA cars can see when they're driving. Very futuristic.'

'Hm. Sounds like you're quite taken with him. One other thing, I forgot to mention. There's a chap hanging around the back of the public gallery. He is something to do with the Department of Transport. Martine says his name is Peter Mears. Can you find out a bit about him too, after court, that is? Ask Toby to start with.'

'Will do. Any particular focus?'

'Yes. Ask him about Cinderella.'

64

THE PROSECUTION's next witness was Dr Novis, a Home Office pathologist. His testimony encompassed the injuries suffered by each of the children, and confirmed they had been in good health prior to the accident. Bertie had died from compression injuries; his vital organs had been crushed under the wheels of the car. Georgia's skull had smashed on impact with the tarmac. Mrs Layton's injuries were minor by comparison, but, even so, her shattered pelvis had required complex surgery. She was still in pain when walking and was undergoing intensive physiotherapy.

SEDA's dark-haired Mexican technician took the stand late afternoon, in an open-necked shirt and chinos.

'Mr Herrera. Your full name is Juan Carlos Herrera?'

'Yes, but my friends call me Juan. Well most of them call me "Wan" like I'm from China. But I don't mind.' He smiled at Celia, but she was in no mood for friendliness at this advanced stage of the day.

'You are the senior technician at SEDA?' Celia continued.

'Yes.'

'How many years have you been there?'

'I only started last June.'

'And what does your role entail?'

'It's a really broad role, as SEDA is such a small company. I am working as a software engineer, also configuring the networks which need to work together, and I have a project management role too, on more than one project.'

'Were you approached by someone at the Department of Transport to assist with extracting data from Mr Salisbury's car?'

'Yes. A man called Peter Mears. He called me and said he had the EDR from Mr Salisbury's car. He said it was password-protected and could I provide the password.'

Judith could sense Constance's intake of breath at the mention, again, of Peter Mears' name.

'And did you?' Celia said.

'I can't do that. I told him. But I said I could extract the data myself, download it to a laptop. I offered to do the diagnostics, but he said he had a man to do that, so I said I would put it all on a memory stick.'

'Is that what you did?'

'Yes. The EDR came over. It's like a small metal box. I entered the password and extracted the data and when Mr Abrams arrived, I gave him the memory stick. I also returned the EDR.'

'Thank you. That's all clear. Please wait for Ms Burton to ask you some questions.'

'Mr Herrera, do you like your job?' Judith began quietly.

'Yeah. It's very interesting. I love it.'

'And your wide-ranging role, does it involve ensuring these cars are safe on the roads?'

'Yes. I monitor data which comes back from the cars, checking it looks good, nothing unusual.'

'So if a car has a crash, would that, therefore, be your fault?'

'It would be good if things were so simple,' Juan said. 'Well, maybe not for me. In the car, you have all the things you know about, that people understand, that you can see from the outside, like brake and accelerator pedal and lights and wheels. The things you can see and touch. Then you have things in the engine that you can see, if you look underneath the hood. But in these cars you also have a lot of sensors, to make sure the car doesn't hit things, and they are all connected to each other and controlled by the central computer.'

'But aren't you responsible for making sure these sensors all work properly?'

'We test them; that's why we do all the test drives and we monitor the data that comes back. But we don't create the programmes in the first place. It's too expensive. We buy them in or licence them from the big guys. And no one person writes the code; Google may have hundreds of programmers working on writing the software. Sometimes they take code other people have written and they use bits of it and write over the rest. It might begin in a straightforward way that is easy for a human programmer to understand, but it has to end up in a form that a machine can read.'

'I see. So if I asked you to identify who had programmed the software of the car involved in this accident, could you tell me?'

'No. But I don't understand why you would want to know this. With a regular car, you don't want to know which person in the factory built it.'

'But regular cars don't make judgments about how to drive, Mr

Herrera. These cars do.'

Juan stood before Judith, momentarily silenced.

'I spoke yesterday and today to Mr Abrams, the forensic crash expert. You've met him?' Judith said.

'Yes. I gave him the memory stick.'

'Why didn't you wait for Mr Abrams to arrive before you downloaded the data?'

'No one asked me. The EDR arrived. I picked it up from reception. I was in early and I had a lot of work to do.'

'Did you look at the data yourself?'

'Of course I did. I also wanted to know if anything had gone wrong.'

'Was anyone else present when you were downloading the data?'

'Look. I didn't change anything. I didn't go and hide anywhere. I sat at my desk. The other technicians come in and out. I downloaded it. I copied it to the memory stick. I looked at it. I had a chat to Mr Abrams when he arrived. He asked me a few questions. I told him I couldn't see anything wrong, but he was the expert.'

'Is it possible that the EDR you were given did not come from Mr Salisbury's car?'

'No. I checked the serial numbers.'

Judith swallowed her disappointment and moved swiftly on.

'Is it possible the EDR was tampered with before you accessed it?'

'These questions are intolerable,' Celia's pinched expression revealed her displeasure. 'Now Ms Burton is accusing the police or the CPS of dishonesty.'

'It's possible,' Juan said, 'but they would need the password.

And then they wouldn't have needed me.'

'Do you know who removed the EDR from the vehicle?' Judith ignored Celia as the judge appeared content for her to continue.

'No. I don't know that.'

'Mr Abrams told us yesterday that the data confirmed that the car failed to slow down when it passed a road sign, indicating that roadworks and a temporary traffic light were ahead. Instead, it appeared to ask Mr Salisbury to take control. The car then continued at its existing speed of 36mph. Can you explain why this might have happened?'

'I can have ideas, but I can't say for sure. The software running these cars is very complex. And it learns, just like humans.'

'What do you mean "it learns"?'

'It isn't static. By being out on the road and interacting with people, with other road users, road hazards, new routes, it learns and improves its performance. The car which leaves the factory on day one, it comes back different. Just like a human. It looks the same from the outside, but it has learned new things from the experiences of the day, every day.'

'So you are telling me that you are not able, even with the EDR or any other resources available to you, to pinpoint why the car failed to slow down?'

Judith held her breath. This was where she wanted Herrera to put flesh on the bones of Abrams' evidence, to expound on the principles Greg had explained to Constance.

'There was a lot of talk, I know, and it continues, about whether these systems should be transparent, so that you could look back at how "decisions" were made,' Herrera explained. 'But if you want a transparent system, one where you can see every single evaluation, then the system together, it won't work very well. It must be better to have a brilliant system, which hardly ever goes wrong.'

'But then, when it does go wrong, you can't find out why?'

'Usually the EDR will show something up or we'll see, afterwards, that a component has obviously failed. If not, we can use our knowledge to say what we think happened. That's what happens with humans trying to explain things, isn't it? We don't go inside someone's brain. I'll give you an example. You just asked me a question. Why did you use those exact words?'

Judith stared at Herrera before continuing.

'I am used to asking the questions, Mr Herrera,' she said. 'But, to help with your illustration, I am using the words which come to me, which seem to be the most appropriate in all the circumstances, to achieve my objective.'

'And that's what these cars do, when they're driving. And just like you can't tell me which bit of your brain got all fired up and which bit powered down, to make those words come out the way they did, I can't do that with Mr Salisbury's car either. But that's OK, isn't it? I mean, why do we want something better from a car than from a human being?'

Constance congratulated herself. This was good and confirmed everything Greg had told her. And Juan was a compelling witness, so the jury should be following it. She looked up at Judge Wilson and saw he was making detailed notes; probably a good sign.

'In your view, then, using your knowledge and, given that you viewed the EDR from Mr Salisbury's car, are you able to say why the car did not slow down, of its own accord?'

Juan shrugged and opened his hands wide.

'Like I've just explained, I can't tell you for sure. I've read Mr Abrams' report. There's lots of things we can exclude, things we know didn't happen. My best guess, based on my knowledge of these vehicles, is that it couldn't read the sign properly. I don't know why. It's a standard sign. Sometimes light has an impact. There's been a lot of work on what happens when these cars go in and out of tunnels.

'Just like humans, it takes the sensors time to readjust to different light settings. Maybe the height of the sensors was important. But the car performed sensibly, cautiously, as it has been set up to do. It knew there was a problem and it invited the driver to take control. So the backup worked correctly. It was then down to the driver to take over in time, if he could.'

'Thank you, Mr Herrera. That's all I wanted to ask. Your honour, I will withdraw my application for the trial to be adjourned, based on Mr Herrera's testimony, but I do wish it to be recorded that there is a question mark over the authenticity of the data, to which I will make reference in closing.'

'Very well. Thank you, Mr Herrera. You are free to go. Tomorrow 9.30 please.'

***

Constance caught up with Toby at the end of the day and led him along one of the quieter corridors. As they walked side by side, Martine appeared, hurrying in the opposite direction, her eyes lingering on Toby's angst-ridden face, before she rushed off. Toby stopped and watched her, until she had disappeared from sight. Constance sat down on the nearest bench and waited for him to follow.

'What can I do to help?' Toby asked, finally sitting next to her, crossing and uncrossing his legs, his face unnaturally flushed.

'You didn't want to speak to Martine?' Constance asked him.

'She was in a hurry, probably wants to see James.'

'Hm. Probably. There are a couple of things I think you can help us with.'

'Juan was good, wasn't he? Explaining about the cars and the EDR?'

'Yes. He was a very convincing witness. I wanted to ask you about Cinderella?'

Toby crossed his legs again.

'It's one of our projects, the main one I suppose. Trying to get on the government list. I'm not sure what it has to do with any of this.'

'And you have meetings?'

'James has had meetings for as long as I can remember, but the project goes back about five years, since the government was serious about autonomous vehicles. The government organised for car manufacturers to have access to lots of specialists: engineers, energy companies, design, communication. But James set up a project group: just him, someone from insurance, a cyclist organisation and a government man.'

'And the government man is called Peter Mears?'

'Yes.'

'Are he and James friends?'

'You'd have to ask James. I know James meets him for coffee sometimes, or they go out. I went to the last Cinderella meeting, on the day James was arrested.'

'Why do you think Peter is in court?'

'Probably to hear what James has to say. At that meeting, James wanted to know if SEDA would be on the list, and Peter wanted him to say the accident was definitely his fault, before he would agree.'

'And what did James say?'

'That he couldn't say that yet.'

'Do you have notes of that meeting?'

'Yes.'

'Can you send them to me?'

'If James agrees, yes.'

'And why do you call it Cinderella?'

Toby stood up to go.

'It's just a name,' he said. 'Can I go? Juan's probably waiting. I said I'd share a taxi home with him.'

'One more question,' Constance said, 'then you can go.'

65

'Where were you last night? I tried calling you lots.' Judith and Constance were cosseted in the smallest room, just behind the stairs leading to one of the courts, the following morning.

'I had a drink at a wine bar near Bow. You should try it some time. They have a happy hour that lasts all night on Tuesdays.'

'Don't you usually wait till the end of the trial to have a drink?'

'But this was for a good cause.'

'And which cause was that?'

'The "get your own back on Celia Mansome" cause.'

'What?' Judith stopped tidying her papers.

'I had a drink with Sarah, my counterpart, the prosecution solicitor. She told me a few interesting things about Celia.'

'Connie, I'm not sure...'

'We were just old friends, sharing a few experiences. She told me that they were asked to advise on whether to go for corporate manslaughter too, you know, join SEDA into the trial – belt and braces and all that.'

'I thought they must have some killer point against James, although they haven't disclosed anything that seems remotely fatal.'

'They never did. Just the expert report. Sarah said that she and Celia talked it over and they were agreed that it would be sensible to add SEDA and the companies which had manufactured all the major parts too. That way, at least, someone would be found guilty. It was the best way for the Laytons to get resolution.'

'What happened?'

'She said Celia called her late that evening and said she'd changed her mind. She thought it better to focus on James, that it looked like they were more confident of a conviction.'

'It's a valid point and the same one Judge Wilson made in court. I can see that if a jury was given the choice, they might prefer to blame the company in a case like this. And even I've been known to change my mind.'

'I know that. But Sarah also said that, immediately after their meeting, Celia had been going to the Department of Transport. She knew because she asked Sarah to get her a cab, and Celia forwarded her diary entry to show the address. And guess who her meeting was with?'

'I have no idea? Should I know?'

'Peter Mears. The man you told me to investigate. The man who's been in court this week.'

'So you are assuming something Peter said made her change her mind and decide to just focus on James. She won't have liked that, not one bit! Why do you think your friend told you this?'

'I think she's seriously pissed off. This is a huge case for her, her first really big one. And everyone thinks *she* advised them not to prosecute SEDA. If James walks, she'll take the blame.'

'You think she wanted you to do something about it?'

'What can we do? I think it was more she wanted me to know she wasn't an idiot. She shouldn't have told me, of course. But the bucks fizz slipped down really easily.'

'I did think I got away with a lot of questions yesterday without Celia objecting. Maybe she wanted to give me the floor to reveal information to enable her to build a new case against SEDA once this is all over. Well, that's not our business, although James won't thank us for it.'

'What about building a case against the Department of Transport, diverting things from SEDA?'

'And how might we do that?'

'When we first met, James told us that SEDA had been working on making their cars stronger. Do you remember?'

'Vaguely. Clearly you do.'

'I found a useful article online last night about super-reinforced cars. It might give James another line of defence, and it clearly shifts the focus onto whoever authorised it. I asked Toby about it yesterday too, and he gave me some more background.'

Judith leaned back against the wall.

'I'll take a look,' she said. 'And, naturally, I have to tread very carefully with Celia and not mislead her in any way, however attractive a proposition that may be. I don't know who's been teaching you, but clearly you've listened hard.'

'Thanks.' Constance beamed. 'Can you spare me for a couple of hours this morning again, do you think?'

'If I must. You know it's better if you're behind me, keeping me on the straight and narrow.'

'It's important. I've just got the CCTV through from Dawson and I think there might be something there we can use.'

66

THE DEFENCE began with two medical doctors. Dr Pamela Edwards, consultant neurologist, testified that James had sustained a mild traumatic brain injury, which appeared to have been caused by impact with the headrest and the steering wheel. She explained that, even at 36mph, the effect of coming to a sudden stop was equivalent to being hit on the head by a 10kg weight.

James had also broken two ribs; a consequence, she believed, of not wearing the seat belt properly. Her view was that James had leaned over to the passenger seat or the back of the car and, in doing so, had pushed the belt down, so that it did not restrict his upper body. She had seen this a few times before and it would account for the broken ribs and the relatively severe head injury for a low speed crash, with the airbag having been deployed. Other than that, James' physical injuries were minor – just cuts and bruises.

She also confirmed that concussion could lead to memory

loss, if certain areas of the brain were affected. Alternatively, and if James began to remember parts of what happened, that tended to support a traumatic loss of memory. With trauma, James' brain still retained knowledge of past events, she opined, but he was being prevented from accessing that knowledge. It was not possible to be certain which of these diagnoses was correct or, if the latter, whether he would ever access those memories.

Dr Ian Branston, consultant psychiatrist, confirmed that traumatic events could certainly lead to problems recalling past events lasting for weeks, months or sometimes years, even without serious brain injury. When cross-examined by Celia, he accepted it was possible to feign amnesia but, in his expert opinion, concluded James was not shamming.

***

Judith prepared herself for James to be sworn in. Her eyes scoured the public gallery. Toby was not in court this morning, but Peter shuffled in after the doctors had finished, this time seating himself in the penultimate row. Martine was there as usual, and Neil and Therese Layton. She was about to switch off her phone, when she received a message from Constance.

You need to get James to talk about the trolley problem, it said. *I've found something!*

Judith looked around her for inspiration. She understood the message, but getting a textbook ethical and theoretical dilemma into James' testimony could be difficult with a stickler like Celia on the other side. If only she could persuade Celia to allow her to do it, she was certain Judge Wilson would be interested. And it was an example the jury would understand too. But Celia was never going to do anything to jeopardise the prosecution case or help James.

She took a deep breath, switched off her phone and thrust it deep into her pocket, closing her eyes to try to shut out the background shuffling and coughing and murmuring, and really focus.

'Some people might say it was a mistake to have kept the parameters of the trial so narrow.' She leaned over and spoke quietly to Celia, when Celia returned to her seat.

'What?' Celia said.

'Not me, of course. But they might question whether it was prudent to have let SEDA off the hook so easily.'

'I don't know what you're talking about.'

'And the others, the manufacturers. When James walks, those same people will be asking who could have possibly given such ill-considered legal advice. You know how people are with hindsight.'

'You don't know what you're talking about.' Celia glanced around her, but her solicitor had also disappeared at the end of the doctors' testimony and not yet returned.

'I understand you have to say that. Don't worry,' Judith said. 'But I can see now why you've let me go on so much about SEDA and its product, when you said you wouldn't.'

'Perhaps you persuaded me with your fabulous rhetoric.'

'I doubt that. Here's the olive branch. It's up to you whether you take it or not.'

'Olive branch?'

'James isn't going down for this. There are more and more uncertainties. You won't get a conviction.'

'I don't agree but do go on.'

'He's up next. I'm going to get him to address a few, *incidental* things about his cars. It will help you with the fallout, afterwards, when he's acquitted.'

'And what "incidental things" are these?'

'He'll mention advanced safety features when he answers my questions. You'll be able to use it, at the appropriate time, to divert attention from your own shortcomings. It will allow you to pass the buck along to one of your favourite people, should you wish to do so.' As she spoke Judith turned and stared at Peter, in the public gallery, and Celia followed her gaze.

'You have nothing to lose,' Judith continued. 'James's not going to prison anyway.'

'And what do you want in return?'

'Nothing. I'm just giving you a heads-up of where I will be going with James.'

'Why would you want to help me out?'

Judith looked at Peter again. This time he was scratching enthusiastically underneath his armpit.

'Old times' sake?' she said.

67

James cut an imposing figure in the witness box; tall and immaculately turned out. He resembled the head of a major financial institution, rather than a car manufacturer. Celia certainly appeared impressed, as she fussed with her collar while he was sworn in.

'Mr Salisbury. I think it would assist all of us, please, if you would take a couple of minutes to explain a little about your company, SEDA. Can you do that please?' Judith began.

'Certainly. SEDA is the company I built from scratch. It's an acronym for Self Drive Autonomy. I began the company seventeen years ago, working from home and now we have manufacturing centres in six countries and we employ a hundred and fifty staff.'

'And your product, what is it?'

'An autonomous vehicle. We only build autonomous vehicles. We have focused on cars so far, although we have the intention to diversify in the future into taxis, vans, buses and lorries.'

'And you are not the only autonomous vehicle manufacturer

in the UK?'

'No. We have many competitors who want to sell their products here, although we are the only British-owned company manufacturing here.'

'And what's your USP?'

'Our safety record. Before this accident, we had never had any incident, not even a minor bump, in more than 600,000 miles of road-testing.'

'I see.'

'We have added a number of safety features to our cabin. And we are very good value for money, too.'

'You're mass-market rather than high-end?'

'Yes.'

'Is it correct that the government is, almost as we speak, working on new legislation which will regulate a number of issues regarding autonomous vehicles?'

'Yes, that's correct.'

'Covering a range of things, from charging stations to power these cars, to insurance, to hacking controls, to whether certain road signs will need changing?'

'Yes.'

'But that, attached to that legislation, there will be a list of car manufacturers whose cars are authorised on our roads?'

'Yes.'

'And when will that list be published?'

'It was supposed to be coming out in October, but I heard recently it will not be before March.'

'So, it should have been October last year, around the time of the awful, tragic accident which forms the basis for today's proceedings, but now it's been postponed some six months. Do you know why?'

'Why it's been delayed? You'd have to ask someone in the Department of Transport.' James' eyes ranged over Judith's head to take in the area in which Peter was sitting.

Judith turned the page of her notebook and paused for a moment before moving on to the issue she had canvassed with Celia.

'Mr Salisbury, the injuries sustained by Mrs Layton and her children were severe relative to the speed at which your car was travelling. Why do you think that was the case?'

'Your honour. Mr Salisbury is a witness of fact; his opinion is not valuable here.' Celia, lying in wait for this line of questioning, had leaped to her feet.

'I'll rephrase the question to ensure Mr Salisbury sticks to the facts. Are there any particular features of your cars in general, or this car in particular, which might have compounded the severity of the injuries suffered by the children and Mrs Layton?'

James' eyes flitted towards Celia before returning to Judith.

'We have some advanced safety elements,' he said.

'Can you elaborate?'

'SEDA was asked by the Department for Transport to develop a number of advanced safety elements, focusing on passenger safety. This project was known as Hercules. The flipside is that there is a correspondingly greater impact on external factors.'

Judith hesitated again before continuing.

'I'm sorry, Mr Salisbury, for the silence. I'm trying to deconstruct your reply and make sense of it for the members of the jury. Perhaps I have it? Are you, first of all, saying that, at the direction of the Department of Transport, you have made SEDA cars stronger, more capable of withstanding impact, in order to improve passenger safety?'

Celia jumped up again. 'This testimony is completely irrelevant. It is immaterial how strong Mr Salisbury's car was or might have been. He is responsible for driving it safely and responsibly. Of course, a bigger, heavier car will cause more damage than a smaller, lighter one, if it hits a child.'

'Your honour, if Ms Mansome would allow my client to explain his answer, then she would see why it is of particular relevance. I am not in the habit of wasting valuable court time.'

'Very well, Mr Salisbury, please answer Ms Burton's question. She asked you about a direction you might have received from the Department of Transport, I believe.'

'Yes your honour. We now use titanium rods in the side bars running vertically up the front of the car. And reinforced steel in the bumper, to endure greater forces in a head-on collision.'

'But one consequence of that is that if your stronger, safer-for-the-passenger car, hits a pedestrian, the pedestrian is worse off than before?' Judith was back in control again.

'Yes.'

'How much worse off than before?'

'It's hard to quantify.'

Celia stood up again. 'Mr Salisbury is being asked again to give expert evidence when he is not an expert and certainly not independent and I repeat that he cannot absolve himself from responsibility for this car, however "armour plated" it might have been.'

Judge Wilson frowned at Celia's words and held up his pen.

'I have a question for Mr Salisbury. Your company must have done some research into this matter before it made modifications to its design. In terms of the force hitting those children, hitting

Mrs Layton, how did it compare with a traditional car?'

'You can compare it in many ways, your honour.'

'Let's use speed, shall we, as that is something we can all easily understand. How does the impact on a pedestrian at 36 mph compare between your old model and your newer reinforced model?'

'It probably adds about five miles per hour on.'

'You mean that the impact at 36 mph in a SEDA is more like forty-one in a conventional car?'

'Yes.'

A low wave of chatter rose and then fell as the public tried to process what they had just heard. Judge Wilson made more notes in his book and waved at Judith to continue.

'Why did the Department for Transport ask you to make these changes?' Judith asked.

Celia rose again. 'Your honour, the reasons for the proposed changes are of even less relevance than the changes themselves.'

Judge Wilson sat back in his chair. 'Ms Mansome. I am aware of the wider repercussions of this trial. And, on that basis, I think we need to have a little more latitude than I would normally give in terms of questioning this witness. Continue please.'

'It goes back to what I was saying earlier,' James said. 'The focus, rightly, is on fewer accidents and fatalities in the future, dramatically fewer. Once everyone has autonomous cars and they are all being driven in autonomous mode, there will almost never be accidents involving pedestrians or cyclists or motorcyclists. So the focus shifts to protecting the passengers, especially if we move to car pooling, where all cars will carry four or five passengers at a time.'

'Was yours the only company which has developed these

fortified vehicles?'

'I don't know, but I know other manufacturers were consulted.'

'Ms Mansome, Ms Burton can you wait a moment while I ask another question. Mr Salisbury, if these strengthened cars have more impact on collision, then speed limits must be amended accordingly, mustn't they?'

'I can't speak for the Department of Transport, but I believe it is on the agenda.'

'Reviewing speed limits is "on the agenda" in the light of your new brood of super-toughened cars?'

'Yes.'

'And is this common knowledge?'

'Within government and manufacturing circles, yes. I can't say how much the public knows.'

'Thank you, Mr Salisbury. Ms Burton, let's move on to another topic now, shall we?'

'Yes your honour. Turning now to your car, a SEDA from 2016. We have already heard from Mr Abrams that your car is a hybrid?'

'Yes. It can operate in autonomous mode, meaning the car does the driving, or manual mode when the human drives.'

'In the same way as a regular car?'

'Yes, it has an automatic gear box, so like a regular automatic car.'

'And which mode do you usually choose?'

'I always drive in autonomous mode. It's the safest way to travel.'

'And, what, you get on with work during your journey?'

'Yes. I must sit in the driver's seat but, as long as the car is in autonomous mode, I can work, answer emails, take calls.'

'Does the car alert you to dangers on the road in advance?'

'Yes. Just like your conventional satnav may show traffic jams or speed cameras, you get a constant update of what is on the road.'

'So you can, perhaps, choose to go by another route?'

'You can. I prefer to leave the driving to the car, generally. I let the car decide how best to get somewhere. I'm not one of those people who is constantly searching for a quicker route. It's very time-consuming and defeats the object, for me, of having the car doing all the work in the first place.'

'So just take us through a typical journey. When you first switch on the ignition, the car is in autonomous mode?'

'Yes. I have VERA, the voice-activated technology, switched on. Some people find it annoying, the voice can drone on a bit, but I like it. I say my destination and off we go.'

'If you want to move from autonomous mode to manual mode, what must you do?'

'There is a button on the dashboard clearly marked "manual". You press that button. But, like I said, it's not something I have ever done before. I am being forced to accept, from Mr Abrams' report, that I may have applied pressure to it on this occasion, but I don't remember doing so.'

'Have you ever been asked by the car to take control previously?'

'No. I haven't.'

'So in two years of driving that vehicle, you've never been asked to take control, yet this happened on 10th October, just as you approached the temporary traffic light.'

'Apparently so, yes.'

'Did you hear Mr Herrera's possible explanation for why your car did not slow down and, instead, asked you to resume control?'

'Yes.'

‘Do you agree with him?’

‘I agree that what he said is plausible. Whether it is what happened, I can’t say.’

‘Let’s just examine that for a moment…’

‘Your honour.’ Celia was standing up, her left hand, palm upwards, pointing in Judith’s direction. ‘I really don’t see how a masterclass in controlling autonomous vehicles is advancing Mr Salisbury’s defence. Next we’ll be treated to a TED talk on the long-term drawbacks of AI.’

Judith smiled politely to acknowledge Celia’s intervention.

‘Ms Burton. Explain where are you going with all this.’ Judge Wilson’s face was crinkled like a prune.

‘Your honour. I need fifteen minutes only of the court’s time to develop this line of defence. It will be fruitful I assure you.’

‘All right. But I’ll be watching the clock.’

‘I’m grateful. Mr Salisbury, if your car, while driving along in autonomous mode, which you have testified is how you always travel, encounters an unexpected obstacle in the road, what would you expect it to do?’

‘Your honour. Forgive my interruption so soon,’ Celia was on her feet again and she stole a quick sideways glance at Judith as she spoke. ‘The car was not in autonomous mode. The expert evidence is that Mr Salisbury put it into manual mode. This can’t possibly be remotely relevant.’

‘Given Mr Abrams’ testimony that the only way he can assess whether the car was in manual mode is because Mr Salisbury had his hands on the steering wheel and his foot on the brake, I will be challenging that conclusion in my summing up. If I am right, we need to explore the behaviour of the car in autonomous mode.’

Judge Wilson squinted at the two lawyers.

'Fifteen minutes, that's all. Continue.'

'I was asking what your car would do when meeting an obstacle.'

'SEDA's car is designed to avoid obstacles if at all possible.'

'What if it's not possible?'

'Well, then a collision will occur.'

'I touched on this yesterday with Mr Abrams. The vehicle itself – much as a human would in manual mode – the vehicle itself must make a decision on how to steer the car. How does it do that?'

'Through the interaction of the various pieces of software under which it operates. Mr Herrera talked about that too. He is right that we can't identify exactly how each component acts. Clearly though, the car has been programmed to travel from its point of origin to its point of destination, in accordance with any speed restrictions, without colliding with anything.'

'Are you familiar with what's known colloquially as the trolley problem?'

'Yes.'

'Members of the jury, just to explain, in this hypothetical scenario, a trolley (or we can substitute if easier to visualise, a train) is hurtling along some tracks, totally out of control and there are five people on the line, let's say they are tied up and unable to move, rather like in an old black and white Western film. But the tracks split, shortly before the train will reach those helpless individuals, and *you are in control of the points*; you can divert the train to the second limb of the track and save those five people.

'However, what you can see, up ahead, is that there is one person tied up on the second limb of the track and, if you do succeed in diverting the train onto that second limb, that person, who would otherwise remain alive, will die, solely because of *your* intervention. So what do you do?'

'Your honour. Much as I am sure this primary school ethics problem is fascinating for Ms Burton, it's rather boring for the rest of us who want to hear evidence relevant to this most serious charge,' Celia interrupted again.

'And it's not possible to answer the charge, without understanding a little more of how these complex vehicles operate,' Judith said.

'That's not correct. If the car was in manual mode, which it was, then Mr Salisbury was driving it and that's the end of the story. The rest is a diversion.'

'Your honour I have explained why this is highly relevant testimony for the witness and I am still well within my fifteen minutes and will remain within it, if I am not continually interrupted. Mr Salisbury is on trial here on a very serious charge. I must be allowed to conduct his defence!'

Judith waited for Judge Wilson.

'Ms Mansome. I agree this appears tenuous, but I have also agreed to allow Ms Burton time to complete her argument. I suggest you do the same.'

'Thank you. Mr Salisbury. Back to the speeding trolley; five people on one track, one on the other. What do you do?'

'Are you asking me what I would do?'

'It is correct, is it not, that this trolley problem and similar problems have had to be grappled with by those designing the algorithms which go into the cars you make?'

'Yes.'

'Because you need there to be a sensible and ethical solution provided to your vehicle, *in advance*, if it happens to come across its own modern version of the trolley problem, when it's out on the road?'

'Yes.'

'And, I'm sure you can see where I am going with this, the layout of the road at the accident site was one version of the trolley problem. To the right of the northbound carriageway, there was the Layton family, halfway across the road, sheltering in the limited refuge of the central reservation, Mrs Layton pushing her three children in front of her. Immediately ahead, there was a temporary, high-sided concrete barrier and further to the right there was the southbound carriageway where, usually, traffic would be coming along from the other direction.

'If your car had, for example, hit the concrete barrier, the Laytons may have been saved but you would almost certainly have suffered more severe injuries, perhaps even death. And the car itself would probably have been written off?'

'Perhaps.'

'Your honour. This is confusing,' Celia was on her feet once more. 'This isn't an objection but an observation. It's patently obvious that there was a third option available to Mr Salisbury; to transition onto the southbound carriageway, as directed by the road signs and as every other vehicle passing through the contraflow over the previous week had successfully done,' Celia sat down. Judith ignored her.

'What was your 2016 SEDA supposed to do, when faced with an imminent collision, like this one?'

'The software we installed has been programmed to take the path which leads to least injury. In this case that would have been to steer away from the family, onto the other carriageway.'

'Are you absolutely certain of that? I will repeat what you said. That this car, left to its own devices, well, in accordance with the manner in which it had been programmed, would have a hundred per cent steered away from the people crossing the road?'

'Yes.'

'Do the algorithms only deal with quantitative measures?'

'I don't know what you mean?'

'I mean, is "least injury" only measured quantitatively. So, for example, it's "better" to kill one person rather than three. Or does the car also consider the age of the people, their gender, race, profession, health?'

'I imagine it is possible, theoretically, to input that kind of information into the software, but it isn't part of the software in our cars.'

'Isn't it true that, over the last five years or so, in preparation for the time when these cars would be let loose on our roads, large numbers of people have been invited to make these kinds of decisions online, in a huge data collection exercise?'

'Yes.'

'They might be asked, *if you had no choice, no way out, would you kill three old women or one child, two doctors or four nurses, one pregnant woman or a Nobel prize-winning scientist, a teacher or a burglar*; that kind of thing?'

James sighed and nodded.

'You need to speak up please.'

'Yes, those tests were carried out.'

'The public were asked their views and their answers were analysed?'

'Yes.'

'How much did your company, alone, spend on this analysis,

finding out what people thought they should do in these situations?'

'It was a lot of money; perhaps as much as £2 million, but it wasn't just us. It was a consortium; we shared the work product.'

'And what happened to the results of those tests?'

'They were used to help develop policy.'

'Policy on what?'

'On how autonomous vehicles should respond to real life versions of this problem.'

'But those tests I have just described are qualitative, aren't they? Who is worth more; a doctor or a nurse? A teacher or a burglar? You said "least injury" meant something quantitative only.'

'To my knowledge, no programmer wrote code which included those kinds of criteria. Who can say if a doctor is more deserving of life than a nurse, an old man or a young woman?'

'I see. No one wanted to play King Solomon.'

'Yes.'

'Does the driver count in all this?'

'How do you mean?'

'Well, when people were asked to choose between their own life and that of, say, a pregnant woman, what did they choose?'

'Perhaps surprisingly, it was around fifty-fifty.'

'That does surprise me. When interpreting the data, did you *believe* those selfless people who declared publicly that they would rather die themselves than kill another person?'

'Personally, no.'

'So just to complete this point, as I can see his honour's generous fifteen minutes is coming to an end, you are certain that your 2016 SEDA car, driving in autonomous mode, made decisions purely based on how to keep the most people alive, in an unfortunate situation?'

James chewed his bottom lip. He looked out at Martine, then he sighed deeply.

'No. I can't be certain.'

'Why not?' Judith asked.

'You heard Mr Herrera. The computers which power these vehicles are programmed to get from A to B safely and efficiently, but they are not static. They interact with their environment and learn; that's why we call them intelligent. They might, theoretically, pick up and learn, themselves, that humans prize the lives of, say, doctors, above all else, and that might then form part of their own criteria for decision making.'

'Well. I have to say, Mr Salisbury, that I have been defending cases for more than twenty years now and I have never had to deal with so many complicated issues in a road-traffic matter. I think what you are saying is that we will never know, for certain, why your car hit the family.'

James drew himself up to his full height and his eyes roamed the public gallery.

'The public has to decide what it wants, and it can't have it all,' James spoke earnestly. 'Does it want far-reduced levels of accidents, injuries and fatalities on the road, back to maybe a handful only? Does it want a system where people who cannot hold a driving licence now, through illness or disability, will be able to travel around more freely and independently? Does it want to build a community where people no longer feel they have to live in heavily populated and expensive areas because they cannot face a long commute to work?

'Does it want the ability to have certainty about journey times because traffic jams and accidents are eradicated? Does it want to cut carbon emissions dramatically and halt global warming because these vehicles are electric and because, if they can be pooled, thereby also enhancing community spirit, we will need far fewer of them on the roads? If so, then all of those enormous benefits, towards which we, supported by the Department of Transport, have been working ceaselessly for fifteen years or so, are only available if we allow the vehicles *full autonomy*.

'If, instead, the public insists on a post mortem after every collision which will trace the cause back to a particular manufacturer or component or even back to a live human being, the programmer, the code writer, then the vehicles will be less effective and there will be more accidents and more people will die.'

'Mr Salisbury. Is what you are saying, about sacrificing transparency for performance, is this common knowledge?' Judge Wilson was peering myopically at James and his expression was grave.

'Your honour. It is something which is being discussed at the moment within government at the highest level so that the right decisions can be made. And it's certainly well known within the AI community.'

The Judge frowned, made a note and waved at Judith to continue.

'Thank you, Mr Salisbury. I have no further questions.'

68

CELIA TUCKED her hair behind her ear and stared at James for a full ten seconds before she spoke.

'Your honour, I have a few short questions only, as the known facts speak for themselves, unless the witness has suddenly recovered his memory. Let's see, shall we? Mr Salisbury, is it still the case that you do not remember the crash which killed Georgia and Bertie Layton and injured Therese Layton?'

'That's right.'

'What is the last thing you remember, before the collision?'

'I remember getting into my car. That's all.'

'So you can't deny Mrs Layton's evidence that you had your phone in your hand, shortly before impact or Mr Abrams' evidence that you were travelling throughout at 36mph, that you pumped the brake with your foot and gripped the steering wheel?'

'I can't deny it, but I can say that I have always driven in autonomous mode on every other occasion, which includes necessarily complying with all speed limits. That's all.'

'Thank you, Mr Salisbury. As I thought, then...' Celia allowed herself a shallow smirk. 'We just heard some useful testimony from you about how you had made your cars stronger than before, indeed stronger than similar conventional vehicles.'

'Yes.'

'So you were aware at all times and, specifically, on 10th October, that the force of your car colliding with a pedestrian at 36mph was equivalent, in conventional terms, to a collision at 41mph?'

'Well, it wasn't in the forefront of my mind all the time, and I don't remember that journey, as I've said. Here, today, when the judge asked me the question, I knew the figures.'

'But you knew those figures today and you knew them on 10th October?'

'Yes.'

'And why do we have speed limits on our roads, do you think?'

'To protect all road users from the consequences of excessive speed.'

'Thank you. So why on earth, knowing what you do about your vehicles, did you not drive more slowly?'

'I don't know.'

'You didn't actively think, my car is stronger, I must drive a bit slower in order to protect pedestrians?'

'No.'

'Or I should tell my other test drivers to modify their speed accordingly?'

'No.'

'Why on earth not?'

'I don't know.'

'That would have been the prudent thing to do, wouldn't it?

Is it correct that you have regular meetings with the government and other manufacturers?'

'Yes, with the Department for Transport.'

'Why did you never mention in one of those meetings your concerns about your "super-charged" cars?'

James winced. 'We generally focused on other matters which appeared higher priority,' he said.

Celia's eyes were wide and she threw her head back.

'The fact that modifications you had made to your cars transformed them into child-killers at 36 miles per hour was not high priority?' she said.

'Your honour. Ms Mansome's question is unfair as it is conflating a number of matters and includes a huge dose of hindsight,' Judith objected.

'Mr Salisbury is on trial for driving *dangerously*, which necessarily includes consideration of his speed,' Celia replied. 'The fact that he drove this modified vehicle means that, in effect, and by his own admission, he was over the speed limit. And he knew he was potentially breaking the law every time he got into his car. Hardly the behaviour of a prudent, careful driver.'

'Your honour. My learned friend is blaming my client for following a direction of the Department for Transport itself, the very body which, together with local councils, sets those speed limits in the first place.'

'Your client is to blame because he ignored clear warning signs on the road, was travelling much too fast and drove his car straight into helpless pedestrians!' Celia was shouting to be heard above the significant level of noise which had risen in the court room since Judith's intervention. Judge Wilson banged his hand down and stared hard at both women.

'This combative approach is unhelpful to the administration of justice,' he said, with one eye on two journalists, who were edging their way out of the court. 'Ms Mansome, move on please.'

For the next hour, Celia re-hashed a number of arguments raised by previous witnesses and tried to get James to accept he had definitely moved into manual mode and that any consideration of how his car would behave as an autonomous vehicle was irrelevant. He remained steadfast. Eventually, and after checking with Sarah, her solicitor, she conceded she would make no further progress and sat down.

***

'Well done James. You were brilliant, wasn't he Judith?'

Constance had returned from her secret mission and was keen to share her news with Judith. She found her with James, in the usual holding cell. On this occasion he was picking at a cheese sandwich Judith had brought him.

'Yes, very impressive.' Judith pondered how Constance could possibly comment on James' performance, given that she had been absent throughout, but as he was clearly buoyed up by the praise, she decided not to mention that in his company.

'Thank you, both,' he said, in between mouthfuls. 'I'm pleased it's all over.'

'The journalists were all busy taking down your comments about transparency and ethical dilemmas. They love that sort of thing, sells lots of papers,' Constance continued. 'I was at the back of the court for the last bit of your evidence, and outside, and I could hear what they were saying. It'll be headlines tonight.'

'Yes, I was lucky to get all that in,' Judith said. 'The transparency stuff is fascinating and I imagine the broadsheets will love it. The trolley problem will more likely major in the tabloids, although I'm hoping you are going to reveal to me now why I needed to go to so much trouble to mention it.'

'I don't understand why Celia didn't object more to any of that,' Constance said.

'She tried but she'd used up a lot of goodwill with the judge on the earlier stuff, bouncing up and down, trying to stop James talking about the reinforced cars. I knew she would.'

'How did you know that?'

'Oh, I might have suggested to her that it would be in the interests of justice and, to a lesser degree her own personal interest, to allow James to talk about them. I knew then that she would object as much as she possibly could, just to spite me.'

'Wasn't that a bit risky?'

'Not really. I spent my formative years with her. People never change, you know. And I decided that even her objecting would help wake the jury up and get the judge's ear. It was a win-win situation. To be fair, she had very little opportunity to assess whether it was going to help or hinder the prosecution and she had a jolly good go at spinning it the other way around, when she got hold of James.'

'So was it good for me in the end, all the "armoured car" stuff?'

'It was good for you,' Judith said. 'It shifts the blame onto the Transport guys, for ordering you to make the cars stronger without telling the public or changing speed limits. That will be up there in the media too and I predict some heads may roll. OK, Celia tried to spin it that you should have driven slower because your car was stronger, but I don't think anyone will buy that, especially when, earlier, she had gone to great pains to point out that some people have little, lightweight cars and others great big MPVs. They're all subject to the same speed limit. I'll bring that out in closing. So now, Connie, spill the beans. Why the trolley problem?'

'Yes.' Constance grinned broadly. 'It's about the CCTV, and I think it changes everything.'

69

'YOUR HONOUR. I should like to mention a recent but important occurrence, if I may, which necessitates me asking if I can interpose a new witness,' Judith said, after a hurried ten minutes briefing from Constance. 'This matter has only just come to light and I have not yet had an opportunity to discuss it with my learned friend.'

'Go on.'

'CCTV from the scene of the accident was reviewed by the police some time ago, but discounted as irrelevant. The defence has now had access to this and has concluded differently. From this CCTV footage, the police have traced an eye witness. He is a Mr Bukowski and I should like to call him as my next witness.'

Mr Bukowski, a forty-something, broad-shouldered gentleman with at least an 18-inch collar, had the air of someone eager to please, as he bowed and smiled in every direction on his journey across the floor of the court. Martine stared at James, who acknowledged her blankly and then focused on a spot on the floor halfway across the court room. Constance crossed her fingers as Judith began her questioning.

'Mr Bukowski. Were you in your car travelling on Common Lane on the 10th October last year?'

'Yes, I was.'

'Where had you been before you got into your car?'

'I was working on building a house, just along the road from there. We finished early and we were called to go to another site.'

'When you say we, who else was in the car?'

'I was taking four men with me in the car.'

'And what happened?'

'There was a car crash, just in front of me.'

'Can you describe things in a little more detail?'

'There was a traffic light and some roadworks. I had been through there a few times. It was my way to work. The digging was on my right, where I had to stop.'

'You were coming south down the road, the opposite direction to Mr Salisbury.'

'Yes. On that day, as I drove forward, I saw a blue car, with all kinds of stuff on its roof, just for a second, then it was gone to the side.' Mr Bukowski frowned hard at the judge. When he received no feedback, he continued. 'I slowed down and drove on slowly,' he said. 'Then I saw the blue car had a crash.'

'When you say you saw the car, then it was "gone to the side", what do you mean?'

'I saw it and then it moved away so sudden, I couldn't see it any more.' Mr Bukowski held his hand out in front of him and then quickly threw it out to his right.

'So, the blue car was directly in front of you, coming towards you on your side of the road for a short period of time. Is that correct?'

'Yes.'

'Then it moved quickly away to your right and you were not able to see it any more, until you came level with the scene of the crash?'

'Yes.'

'And what colour was the traffic light when you travelled through it?'

'Green. What do you think of me? It was a green light.'

'Good, thank you. I am going to show the CCTV from the street now. What kind of car is yours?'

'It's a red polo.'

'Thank you. Your honour, this is the street CCTV.'

The film had been taken from a camera facing north. The central reserve, where the Layton family had waited, was just at the very bottom of its field of vision and they were not visible. Presumably, that was why the police had discounted the film as unhelpful.

Mr Bukowski's red Polo could, however, be seen clearly, moving at a constant speed towards the camera. Then, as it approached the central reserve, the tip of the bonnet of the SEDA appeared at the bottom left of the screen, but then quickly shifted out of the frame and disappeared.

'Your honour. This is very significant,' Judith announced sombrely.

Judge Wilson frowned. He had been watching carefully, but he was not certain yet of the importance of this film, especially as so little of James' car had been visible.

'How so?'

'Mr Bukowski had drawn almost level with the crossing when

the accident occurred.'

'Yes, I saw that.'

'Mr Bukowski is testifying that he went through a green light.'

'Yes.'

'Mr Salisbury also passed through a green light.'

'Perhaps Mr Salisbury jumped the light?'

'Oh no, your honour, if you remember we have the camera from the chassis of his car, I can play it again for you if you wish. It clearly showed the SEDA passing a green light, at the same time as Mr Bukowski had a green light on his side of the road.'

'You are saying that the traffic lights malfunctioned?'

'Yes, your honour, just as the old man referred to by Inspector Dawson two days ago, reported. Your honour we, and no doubt you, have been struggling with why the SEDA car, shifted, albeit very late, over towards the right-hand side of the road, but then, most crucially, suddenly veered back towards the family.'

'Yes.'

'We have the answer now. The SEDA or my client – actually I think it is immaterial which – saw or detected the oncoming vehicle driven by Mr Bukowski and moved quickly to avoid it.'

'I see. Just give me a moment to make a note…yes thank you. Continue.'

'Your honour, the point here is that Mr Salisbury would have navigated the contraflow safely, had it not been for the fact that the traffic lights malfunctioned. At the last moment, he was forced back onto the northbound carriageway, otherwise he would have had a head-on collision with a car containing five working men, and any cars following might also have been involved. Sadly, lulled into a false sense of security, the Layton family had already begun to cross the northbound carriageway. Clearly, all the evidence now shows that, far from driving dangerously, Mr Salisbury did everything he could to avoid loss of life, in a difficult situation. I have no further questions.'

Celia was chewing on the end of her pen as Judith sat down. She whispered hurriedly to her solicitor and asked for a ten-minute recess, to allow her time to view the CCTV. Returning after the break, she launched straight into her questions.

'Mr Bukowski, what did you do when you saw the accident?'

'I slowed down and I stopped.'

'We can't see that on the CCTV?'

'No. It must be further down the road.'

'Did you get out of your car?'

Mr Bukowski was slow to reply.

'Hm, yes.'

'Did you go back to the scene?'

'No.'

'I see. Why not?'

Judith stood up to challenge the question. 'Your honour, this is wholly irrelevant.'

'Not entirely,' Judge Wilson replied. 'You have introduced this witness late and without notice and Ms Mansome is entitled to test his credibility. I will allow the question, but there will be a limit, Ms Mansome.'

'Understood your honour. Mr Bukowski, why did you not run back to the scene?'

'I looked back and there were other people already running. And someone was already calling on their phone.'

'Who were they calling?'

'I thought it must be an ambulance. That's what you do, isn't it, when you see an accident?'

'But you didn't check for yourself?'

'No.'

'Was there any other reason why you didn't go back to the scene?'

'No. Well, I didn't want to be late for my next job. It would make us all late. And other people were helping.'

'Did you go to the police then, afterwards, that evening or the next day, to tell them what you saw?'

'No.'

'Why not?'

'I just didn't.'

'Was it because you were worried about anything?'

Judith's insides twisted furiously but, to the world she maintained her cool exterior. This was what happened when you worked on the hoof and had a clever opponent.

'No,' Mr Bukowski said, but his enormous frame seemed suddenly dwarfed by the lectern.

'I see. Just returning to the CCTV again, and contrary to what Ms Burton suggested might have happened, there don't appear to be any cars following you through the light. Is that correct?'

'I don't remember.'

'Well, if we look at the film, we can just see that the car behind you is stationary at the light.'

Mr Bukowski shrugged.

'It appears to have stopped, we can only assume because the light is at red.'

'I don't know what you want me to say. He's behind me. I don't know what was happening behind me.'

'But you are adamant that the light was green when you went through it?'

'The light was green, yes.'

'Thank you, no more questions.'

Judith gathered her thoughts, smiled to herself and took in Mr Bukowski, who clearly desired nothing more now, than to be gone as soon as humanly possible, his earlier enthusiasm having been dampened by Celia's pointed accusations.

'Just two more questions,' she said.

'What would have happened to you and the other men in your car, if you'd been late to your next job that day?'

'We might have lost the job, certainly lost some pay.'

'And where do you live?'

'I live in Uxbridge.'

'In Uxbridge. How far is that from the site of the crash?'

'It's a forty-five mile round-trip for me.'

'So you live a long way from the scene, and from any local police station?'

'Yes.'

'Thank you. I have no more questions. Your honour, that is the end of the defence case.'

***

'I'm sorry.' Constance whispered to Judith, as they each tidied their papers. 'I didn't think to ask him about why he didn't stop or give his name to police.'

'It's all right. So it's not perfect and I can't conclude by saying the lights definitely failed; I'll fudge it a bit. And, anyway, just because Mr Bukowski didn't stop and he didn't volunteer his story, doesn't mean he ran a red light. The jury get that. He didn't want to get involved then, but he was prepared to come forward now. That means something. He disappeared pretty quickly from the court room, though, did you see?'

'I know,' Constance giggled. 'I didn't think he could move that fast. You didn't link his evidence to the trolley problem?'

'No.'

'Wasn't that the point though?' Constance asked.

'Not if the car was being controlled by James right at the end, it wasn't,' Judith said. 'Better to have the jury think he swerved courageously to avoid an oncoming vehicle with five men inside, than the car did it for him, I think? Hardly the actions of a reckless driver.'

***

Martine approached Judith and Constance only once she had seen James disappear downstairs.

'I thought you did a very good job, thank you,' she said.

'Let's hope it was enough,' Judith said.

'Yes. I'm going outside for half an hour. It's stifling in here. Call me if anything else is going to happen, will you please?'

'Don't you want to see James?'

A frown passed across Martine's forehead.

'Maybe later,' she said. 'I know James will have a lot to say about that last witness. I want him to be able to speak to you, openly and freely. I won't be long. My head is pounding.'

Constance rested her hand gently on Judith's shoulder.

'Calm now,' she said.

'So I'm not the only one to find that woman infuriating. "My head is pounding". She never replies to any of your requests for help and then she doesn't want to be with her husband, when he's probably desperate for her company, or at least someone to distract him from what's coming next.'

'She's been here every day for him. She might also have helped with the expert report. And maybe for once, she is being sensible. James always has one eye on Martine when she's around.'

'Perhaps I am being too harsh on her. It can't be easy for her either, her husband being branded a "child killer". Did you ever find out anything more about her background?'

'She did hold a couple of beauty-queen titles, like she said, regional titles. And she had a company registered in her name, when she met James, as well as the modelling. It doesn't exist any more, so I didn't bother checking up on it.'

'Hm. And you say she's a co-director of SEDA?'

'With Toby and the company lawyer who recommended me. She owns shares too.'

'Fairly standard for a spouse, I suppose,' Judith said. 'Having been so disparaging, I think I will take five minutes' walk around the block, myself, too, just to clear my head. See you shortly.'

70

CELIA BEGAN her closing speech half an hour later. While Judith could not imagine Celia feeling remotely confident, given the way the evidence had emerged, she knew better than to underestimate such an accomplished adversary.

'James Salisbury has had a difficult time these last three months,' Celia began. 'No one can deny that. He has been injured in a car accident. His doctors say he is suffering still from the trauma associated with the accident and from *some* loss of memory. He is also potentially facing serious questions regarding the cars he put on the roads. That he gave his evidence articulately in court is admirable. And there may be some members of the jury who have sympathy with him. I have only one response to that: don't.

'Therese Layton was generous in her evidence. Despite coming face to face with the killer of her children, she refused to totally condemn the defendant, but she did testify that she saw him with a mobile phone, raised up in his hand, shortly before the crash. The defence does not deny that Mr Salisbury had his phone with him in the car at the time. If he was looking at his phone, then he could not have been concentrating sufficiently on the road.

'Mr Abrams, our crash specialist, gave crystal clear evidence. The car data establishes beyond doubt that the defendant was invited to take control of the vehicle 150 metres before the collision and was in control at seventy metres; that's more than three times the length of this court room. Whatever happened before that point is immaterial. From then on, James Salisbury must be judged as any competent driver. He failed to slow down when he passed the roadworks sign, failed to slow at the traffic light, failed to move over into the other carriageway until very late and then swerved back into the closed lane. All this is clear from the recovered data and the cameras on the bodywork of the car and the CCTV. The camera never lies, as they say.

'On top of that, he admitted to knowingly driving a car reinforced with extra steel rods, which had the effect of adding five miles per hour to his driving speed, compounding the severity of the injuries to his victims. He accepted he never adjusted his driving speed, despite this knowledge.

'Why did he fail to slow down in time or heed the clear signs? We will never know for certain and perhaps, if we believe that the defendant has indeed suffered extensive amnesia, he will never know either. But when we can't be certain, in a court room, we have to offer up the most likely reasons, guided by experience, common sense and the facts which are clear and incontrovertible.

'The defence has tried to confuse this case with hours of diversionary material, statistics for reaction times and stopping distances, school room ethics problems and late, unconvincing witnesses. Don't be side-tracked. James Salisbury lost control of his car, in circumstances where it was clearly marked that there were impending hazards. He had ample time to respond to the road signs, but he failed to do so, because he was too bothered checking his social diary. As a result, Georgia and Bertie Layton lost their lives and Therese Layton will never be free from pain. There is only one possible verdict in this case; guilty of causing death and guilty of causing serious injury by dangerous driving.'

***

Judith glanced at James before she spoke. While she had been delighted with his charismatic performance earlier, she had told him in no uncertain terms, that now things had to be different.

'*Humble* is what I need from you now, James. Do you understand?'

'Yes.'

'I know you're a proud man, and rightly so, but you are being judged by those twelve jury members and they will have the images of those children pasted across their souls. Any hint of arrogance, conceit, ego, even of your "man of vision" persona, and you may lose them.'

James nodded.

'Thank you, Judith. I will definitely do as I am told this time.'

Judith had hesitated before leaving him, reflecting on whether to say anything more, to ask if he was satisfied that what had unfolded gave him reassurance that he was not to blame. It was an unusual situation to be in, where not only did you have to convince the jury of a man's innocence, you had to convince the man himself too.

***

'James Salisbury, Therese Layton, her husband Neil, Georgia and Bertie Layton. They all have something in common,' Judith began. 'They are all victims. Victims of a car accident, yes. But victims also of circumstance. When things go wrong, we naturally want someone to blame. It has to be someone's fault. We try cases in this court to reach a decision; guilty or not guilty, that is the question.'

'So what were the circumstances which led to this accident? Well, you have heard at least part of the story, and it's a complicated tale with many interwoven facts. A new vehicle, not yet cleared for general release on the streets of our city. Mr Salisbury, whose company, SEDA, designed and built it, incorporating components from many other companies, himself confirming that he prefers to drive in autonomous mode. He has no faith in these hybrid vehicles which can also operate like conventional cars. But he has been compelled by the government, albeit for admirable reasons (taking innovation one step at a time) to produce and trial this "mongrel" car.

'The government has also compelled him to add features to his vehicles, with an eye on passenger safety, and he complied. The natural consequence of this is that pedestrians may be more at risk, but the government has not yet reached a decision about making any consequential changes to the rules of the road. You cannot possibly penalise Mr Salisbury for following instructions he was given by a government body, with a view to saving lives. And, as my learned friend helpfully pointed out herself, there are a wide range of vehicles travelling on our roads, from bicycles to articulated lorries. They all abide by the same speed limits, whatever their weight or composition.

'Was Mr Salisbury even driving the car when it crashed? Mr Abrams, the prosecution's expert, says he was, but he has no hard proof. He can only say that Mr Salisbury's foot hit the brake and his hands applied pressure to the steering wheel shortly before the crash, and the car appeared to respond. Ms Mansome, for the prosecution, concedes that, if Mr Salisbury was not in control at the moment of impact, then he must be acquitted and that is our primary line of defence, which his honour will explain to you further in his summing up.

'If, members of the jury, on the contrary, you have *no doubt* that Mr Salisbury *had* tried to take control of the vehicle before the crash, then you need to consider if he was really in control. Mr Abrams, the expert, confirmed how short a time frame James had; nine seconds to impact at most from the earliest prompt, four and a half seconds, the blink of an eye, in reality, to conclude a series of complicated manoeuvres. The statistics say most of us would have failed to take control within such a short time frame.

'But we have also heard that the data the prosecution relies upon for most of its conclusions may not be genuine. It was extracted by SEDA's own representative, unsupervised and handed to Mr Abrams. Clearly, while I have stopped short of accusing anyone of improper conduct, this should not have happened, and reliance on this evidence alone should be treated with utmost caution.

'Why did Mr Salisbury's car not slow down as it approached the Layton family? Mr Abrams confirmed that a crucial sensor in the driver's side bumper was crushed and that he could not say with certainty that it had been fully intact before the crash.

And both he and Mr Herrera, chief technician at SEDA, have confirmed that there is no precise way of establishing this. Mr Herrera's best educated guess is that the car failed to recognise the temporary traffic light sign. What we know, therefore, is that something failed on the car, leaving Mr Salisbury to do what he could in an impossibly short time frame.

'You may well have formed the view that Mr Salisbury's conduct was blameless, right up to the moment when the car swerved back onto the northbound carriageway. That might be the only time when you judge his behaviour to have been potentially at fault. But what did we hear from Mr Bukowski? A potentially malfunctioning traffic light put Mr Salisbury's car on a collision course with another vehicle. We saw with our own eyes, from the CCTV footage, Mr Bukowski's car heading straight for Mr Salisbury.

'Mr Salisbury had a stark choice to make and only fractions of a second in which to make it. Either stay where he was and collide with a car carrying five working men, or take evasive action which might avoid an accident, but would return him to the closed northbound carriageway. He could not have anticipated that the Layton family would choose *that very moment* to rush out into the road. These are not the actions of someone driving dangerously; much more a cautious driver, trying to make the best of an impossible Catch-22, a real-life application of the trolley problem Mr Salisbury explained to us earlier.

'The prosecution's case has been torn to shreds. The defence case has been verified and reinforced. There is only one possible verdict, members of the jury, and that is *not guilty*.'

Judith sat quietly during the judge's summing up to the jury. She usually hung on every word, eager to ensure there was no misdirection, either to correct on the spot or leave for an appeal. But today she had no appetite for any of it.

After a few minutes, she dared to steal a glance at James who was surprisingly composed, leaning back in his seat, listening serenely to the tail end of the proceedings, which would determine his fate. His expression was not quite "humble" but it would certainly do for now.

71

THE COURT WAS packed for the verdict which came first thing next morning. Martine and Toby sat in the front row and Neil and Therese Layton three rows behind. Peter was not there.

When the foreman rose to his feet, Judith noticed a number of jury members looking at James, rather than out into the public gallery. She hoped it was a good sign, but she couldn't be certain.

James was sitting with his eyes closed and his lips were moving slowly. It was impossible to tell whether he was praying or trying to reassure himself with some distraction technique, but he certainly wanted the moment to be over as quickly as possible.

'Oh God,' Constance whispered to Judith. 'I hate this bit.'

Judith was silent. She had spent much of the night thinking up potential grounds of appeal, if James were convicted. The newspapers would help. They had already filled many pages with all the arguments she had raised during the trial and more still analysing James' discourse on what choices the public faced. She had also thought, more than she had wanted, about the Layton children and their broken bodies lying on the road. The foreman stood up.

'On the count of causing death by dangerous driving, how do you find the defendant?'

'Not guilty.'

Constance dug her fingernails hard into the palms of each hand. James flinched but kept his eyes closed.

'And on the charge of causing serious injury by dangerous driving.'

'Not guilty.'

James' eyes snapped open and searched out Martine, who blew him a kiss before hugging Toby close to her. James remained in his seat, taking deep breaths, his attention now directed, once more, at the floor. Celia muttered something inaudible to herself and closed her notebook. Judge Wilson dismissed the jury and told James he was free to go.

'Well done,' Constance tapped Judith lightly on the shoulder.

'Thank you. And to you. You go to James,' Judith added. 'See if he wants to make a statement, although, if he does, keep it very short and very bland. You know the kind of thing – no *sword of truth*, nothing like that.'

'Sword of truth?'

'Oh, don't worry. Before your time. On reflection, I would advise no statement. If James disagrees, muzzle him. I'll join you in a moment.'

'Well done Judith,' Celia formally conceded defeat. 'Given your client's selective memory, you did very well indeed.'

'That's very gracious of you, Celia,' Judith said. 'But you've paved the way for some further investigation of what really happened, what decisions were made in the background in high places – if the police has any stomach for it.'

'Yes, I have, haven't I?'

'Celia…' Judith chewed her lip, uncharacteristically. 'If I did say anything to you, when we were girls, which was unfair or which hurt you, I am sorry,' she said.

'What?' Celia straightened up and tucked her books under her arm. Her clerk, a young man who could not have been more than sixteen years old, had just arrived, and she pointed at various boxes and files for him to remove.

'I'm trying to apologise if I ever said anything hurtful when we were younger,' Judith forced the words out, with some difficulty.

'I don't know what you're talking about,' Celia said. 'Oh that stuff from the first day? I was just trying to put you off your stride. Nearly worked, didn't it?'

***

Neil and Therese remained seated in the courtroom as the rest of the public filed out. Neil was weeping openly, Therese sat staring at her hands. Celia noticed them, contemplated approaching them and then thought better of it. They were not her clients and there was little she could say to them. Instead, she directed her clerk to wheel away her boxes, and decided she would consider next steps after a stiff drink.

In the end, they were the only two people remaining in the empty room, which somehow appeared so much smaller now everyone had gone. It was impossible to believe that so many people had been thrown together in this airless, sterile space. All that remained were a few discarded papers littering the lawyers' benches, the microphones knocked awry, the judge's chair askew.

Therese reached across and took her husband's hand. Then, with her other hand, she stroked his face.

'It's OK,' she said.

'I don't know what to do now,' Neil spoke between sobs. 'It's been all about today, for so long.'

Therese pulled him close.

'I know,' she said. 'But it wouldn't have made any difference, sending him to jail,' Therese fought back her own tears. 'He didn't do it on purpose. He wasn't drunk or on drugs. He didn't steal the car. He didn't try to hit us.'

'But he was on his phone, you said, not paying attention. You said.'

'I just said that,' Therese said, 'because I was angry. I don't know if he was on his phone. I don't remember anything about the car or who was driving. I didn't even remember what colour it was before I watched the video. But I do remember what happened just before.

'I remember it was a lovely afternoon, sunny and bright and we were walking along the road and Bertie was in such a hurry. Georgia was whingeing, she wanted to be first but she was being so slow and she was talking about what she ate for lunch, something about cutting her sandwiches into quarters.

'And I was tired, so tired from getting up early and ironing my clothes and washing my hair. Trying to look normal. Pah. That was a joke, as if anyone cared what I was wearing. And organising everything for Mum. And my head was filled with nonsense from the surgery. I was thinking about what stocks were low and how I could reorganise the shelves next time I was there, and I saw the roadworks and I thought about crossing at the proper crossing, just like his lawyer said. I really did.

'But Bertie was whining and he kept jumping on the buggy board and it was heavy and Georgia was hanging back on my other arm. And, do you know what? Ruby was smiling at me. Just waving at her mobile and gurgling and smiling and even that made me angry. I thought "what are you smiling at?" And I wondered what my life would be like if I didn't have them, any of them. Only for a moment but I did. I thought about all the things I could do if I wasn't weighed down so low with our children.'

Neil frowned but he didn't interrupt.

'I didn't think that I was blessed with three, beautiful, healthy children, like I should have done.' Therese clasped her hand to her mouth before continuing.

'So we crossed there and we huddled in the middle with the pram sticking out and we waited, except Bertie couldn't wait. And, as I was cursing him for being so impatient, and scowling at Georgia for delaying us and dragging her forward for not keeping up, and fuming at Ruby for being so happy, Bertie slipped out of my hand.'

Neil let out a low moan.

'I've been waiting all through the trial for someone to say that, you know. They've been busy looking at so many details about the car. I kept thinking they would say "Mrs Layton. When we stop the video, you can clearly see your son runs out into the road. Why didn't you stop him?"'

'He should've seen you. He should've been driving more slowly.' Neil spoke softly.

'Have you not been listening to what has been said in this room? Because I have, all of it. He's a man too. He did his best. It wasn't his fault. It was an accident. I read one child pedestrian dies every week on our roads. We lost two in one go. We were unlucky, desperately unlucky. But that means someone else's children were saved.'

'Tay.'

'No don't. It helps me to think like that. When I see other children Bertie and Georgia's age I don't feel so bad any more. And the papers say he has two sons, one still at school. What would be the point of sending him to prison for fifteen years, to take his life away too? Especially when all his work is to reduce road accidents.'

'He's taken you in. He wants to make money selling his cars. That's all he cares about.'

'We all have to live. There are worse things he could do. I'm not angry with him any more.'

Neil wiped his eyes and stood up. Therese stood up too, pulled Neil closer and she held him tight.

'You've done your bit,' she whispered. 'You've had your say. It's over. I want to go home now, quietly, no more speeches, no more newspapers, no more Twitter, and I want us to be a family again. You and me and Ruby.'

PART FOUR

72

James was sitting at his desk when Juan knocked and entered. He was pleased at the distraction; he had insisted on coming in to the office today, despite Martine's protestations that he should 'take at least one day off'. But once he had got here, he had found it almost impossible to concentrate on work.

First of all, he had trawled the internet for coverage of the trial and the verdict, related features and editorials. Then he had allowed at least fifteen minutes to elapse, staring out at the driving rain and at his employees heading in, with a variety of interesting mechanisms to cope with the inclement weather. *Why did no one use an umbrella any more?* he queried, before appreciating his own inactivity and shaking his head violently to engage his brain.

His inbox was full, but not overflowing. Toby had played his part in keeping things under control and diverting the more mundane traffic to his own account. But James could not bring himself to delve into any of it; not quite yet. He could not completely erase recent events by putting on a clean shirt and opening a new day in his diary. It wasn't like shaking the Etch A Sketch and beginning anew.

'Mr Salisbury, you must be so busy, but I wondered if you had a minute?' Juan's usual jovial manner was absent as he closed the door behind him. James was slow to respond and Juan took that as encouragement, crossing the room to sit down. As he leaned back and fingered the arms of his chair, there was a second knock and Toby's face appeared around the door. He froze when he saw Juan.

'I'm here for our catch-up but I can come back later if you're busy,' Toby said. 'You did say "no one was to come in before eleven", I thought, so you could get through your messages.'

James surveyed the two men.

'Don't panic, Toby,' he said, 'you haven't missed anything. Juan has only just arrived. Is it about Connect?'

'No.' Juan turned around and frowned at Toby. 'It's something else, but maybe Toby should stay and hear it.'

James laughed uneasily. 'All right. That sounds ominous. Out with it then. If it's something bad, I'd really rather know now.'

Toby sat down, his eyes scanning Juan's face.

'It's something I should have picked up earlier,' Juan said. 'I only thought about it after I came to the court.'

'This is about my car?'

'Yes. And the last witness at the trial. And the EDR.'

Juan shot a quick glance at Toby. Toby deliberately focused on James.

'Go on,' James said.

'Well, if there was a car coming in the opposite direction, like the CCTV showed, then why was there no record of it on the EDR?'

'Yes. That crossed my mind too, although I'm sure it can be explained.'

'I know it wasn't a live feed from your car, like I'm used to watching, but we should have been able to see data from the LIDAR, detecting that car coming towards you on the EDR, even if it was some distance away.'

'Have you checked?'

'I've been back through the copy the police gave me and there's nothing there.'

'So, the EDR malfunctioned?'

Juan looked at Toby again before speaking.

'It's possible, yes. It's possible that it failed to record all the data correctly, to retain it for review afterwards. And your car is an older model. Or…' Juan trailed off.

James sat forward in his seat. 'You're saying someone could have deleted that data from the EDR?'

Juan nodded. 'If they didn't want anyone to know about the other car. I swear it wasn't me. I wouldn't have had the time, anyway. I got the call from your friend, I collected it, unlocked it, downloaded it and gave it to the Abrams guy.'

'When you say "my friend" you mean Peter Mears?'

'Yes.'

James turned to Toby. 'You're quiet,' he said.

Juan stared at Toby too. 'I think it's time we told James about the calls,' he said.

'What calls? What else don't I know?' James stood up and marched around his desk, so he stood looming over Toby.

'I had some messages and a call…asking to meet up, in the weeks before your crash,' Juan continued.

'Who called you?' James' face was working its way through the gamut of emotions.

'We didn't want to worry you,' Toby finally spoke. 'You had the trial and everything.' And then to Juan, 'You think it's connected?'

Juan's lips were set tight.

'Who was it who called you? Some crackpot?' James was losing his patience.

'No. I'm sorry James.' Toby was desolate beneath James' penetrating stare. 'I thought it would be a good thing to do, to meet him. I thought it would help, what with the Cinderella project stalling.'

'Who did you meet behind my back?'

'Him. Peter. Peter Mears.'

73

Constance and Judith travelled together to James' house that evening. The invitation to join him at a celebration of his acquittal had been low-key, as James was keen that he should not be seen to be gloating in any way. He had invited all his London staff, a few friends and business associates and the two of them.

'Why didn't you tell me about Greg?' Constance had been waiting for an opportunity to broach the subject with Judith and, seated in the back of their taxi, this seemed as good a time as any.

'About Greg? There's nothing to tell, is there?'

'That he's moved out.'

'Ah. He never really moved in,' Judith said. 'Well it was never forever. Just a trial and, well, now both trials are finished.'

'I don't think he sees it that way.'

'You two have been talking? I knew it was a mistake to introduce you; ganging up on me, are you?'

'He called me to ask if the information he had given me, given us, was useful.'

'That was nice of him.'

'He's very upset.'

'He told you that, did he?'

'I could tell. Maybe you should call him.'

'And maybe I shouldn't. It's really not your business, you know.'

'Did he do something wrong?'

'Connie. Don't push our friendship. I don't do confidences.'

Constance tapped the fingers of one hand lightly against the other.

'My brother, Jermain, was arrested for resisting being searched on the street, when he was seventeen. They gave him a caution, so he lost his apprenticeship place. Now he flits around doing jobs here and there. Calls me every six months or so, usually when he needs money or a favour.'

'How old is he?'

'Twenty-six.'

'It's not too late for him to study, to train for something. Maybe Greg could help him, with his new venture?'

'You see. You like dishing out advice but not receiving it.'

'All right. Point taken.' Judith sighed and stared out of the window. 'Perhaps I have made a mistake with Greg, but I just felt suffocated. I think he wants more of me than I am prepared to give. I'm quite good at being on my own, you see. I am not sure I really need anyone else.'

'You should talk to him, meet him for a drink. I'm sure if you explained you could work something out. Being on your own, that's OK when we've got a trial, loads to do, rushing around. But when things quieten down again, won't you be lonely?'

'It's hard for me to change. I have been trying, like Greg suggested, to be more empathetic, to see the other person's side of things. All that's happened is now I feel guilty about a whole lot of things I never cared about before. You never went back to Mike?'

'No. I still see him, at parties and things, when I go to them. His new girlfriend's a waitress. Bit less challenging for him. Less controversial. We've moved on.'

'Great team aren't we? Married to our work. Growing old together.'

Constance shuffled around on the leather seat, crossing and uncrossing her legs. 'I never got back to you about Peter Mears, the man at the back of the court,' she said.

'You had other more important leads, from what I remember. And I did a little of my own research, which suggested Mears may not be the kindest soul. I plan a quick debrief with James when we arrive – get it over with. And I confess I'd be looking forward to the whole evening more, if we didn't have to speak to Martine again.'

'I did finally manage to get round to checking up on her today,' Constance said. 'Not that it matters now.'

'And?'

'More interesting than we thought. She dabbled in acting too, had a small part in a low-budget film. And the company she ran organised photoshoots for models.'

'Oh.'

'It was doing well for a few years but then it folded in 2012. I found a local newspaper article reporting that a rival accused Martine's company of trying to steal its client lists, but it never got any further than that.'

'Hilarious. What tools do you think she used? A hairdryer and a lipstick?'

'And I think Martine and Toby must have had a fling,' Constance fiddled with her seat belt.

'Must have?'

'He can't even look at her without crumbling.'

'Ah. Poor boy. That will end in tears.'

'And one of the receptionists, Carol, she told me Martine is always hanging around the IT lab and spending a lot of time with Juan.'

'So perhaps it already has…ended, that is. I suspect Mr Herrera can look after himself though. So, her conquests: The toy boy, the technician and the video security man. That sounds like the title for a film. Do you think he knows? James, that is.'

'I think at least two of them are going to be there tonight.'

'And with a few drinks inside them…'

'He doesn't drink, James. He was an alcoholic. Toby said.'

'Hm. That's a shame. I rather liked him in the end, you know.'

'No!'

'Yes. He believes in his product, not just because of the prospect of making a killing – oh, excuse the unfortunate pun – but also because of the predictions for reduced accidents, once these cars go live. He is a true visionary.'

'Gosh. Smitten aren't you? Are you sure that isn't why you've ditched Greg?'

'I will ignore that comment as unworthy of you.'

As they exited the taxi and sauntered up the drive, Judith caught Constance's arm. The patio doors had been flung wide and guests were spilling out into the garden, where a small awning had been erected and chains of coloured lights danced in the breeze, interspersed with towering heaters blasting their flames skyward. The sound of soothing music floated out from the lounge. Judith pointed towards a rotund, bald man who was rushing inside, tucking his mobile phone back in his jacket pocket.

'That's him, Peter Mears,' Judith said.

'What?'

'The man from court. James must have invited him too. Ooh, this evening looks like it might be even more fun than I had imagined.'

74

James was finishing up in his study when Peter entered.

'Your own party and you're still working?' Peter began, all the time, circling the rim of his glass over and again with his forefinger.

'Just finalising arrangements for a trip to France next week,' James said. 'It's done now.' He switched off his laptop and closed the lid. 'I might be able to drum up support for your review of data security after all, if it's still on the table?'

'I have to hand it to you,' Peter said, striding towards James and making himself comfortable in the nearest chair, 'you are a real "glass half-full" man.' He took a sip from his drink and giggled. 'It's over though, don't you see that?'

'What's over?'

'All of it. Alan has gone, well, he'll be gone by the end of today, and, without him, your precious Bill is unlikely to get through this time around.'

'Alan has been sacked?'

'I think the correct term for Alan is "shuffled". I've been sacked,' Peter said.

'What? Why?'

'I supported the Bill, I tried to help you. There're a lot of people in high places feeling embarrassed right now, because of the speeches you made in that court room. We're all paying the price. Did you forget everything we agreed?'

'I told the truth, that's all.'

'You talked about the things you agreed never to talk about in public; transparency versus performance, reinforced bodywork, autonomous versus manual. You even talked about the fucking trolley problem. It was like a red devil was sitting on your shoulder feeding you all the most incendiary material.'

'I suppose I did get carried away. But SEDA was exonerated. I don't understand why the Bill has to be shelved.'

'SEDA wasn't exonerated,' Peter said. 'Your own programmer argued that its sensors failed to recognise a simple traffic-light sign, and you agreed with him.'

'I said it was plausible. We don't know that's what happened.'

'No, we don't. Because you and your lawyers created this impossible maze with no way out, this tantalising prospect of things going wrong and no one ever knowing why. The British public will never accept that. They demand reasons, explanations, resolution.'

'Why did you call Toby?'

'What?'

'Toby Barnes. You contacted him without telling me.'

'I'm not sure I even remember now. It was weeks ago and things were stalling with the project. I thought he could help get them moving again. And he's a nice lad, young, ambitious, very malleable, open to new ideas.'

'And Juan Herrera?'

'You wouldn't let us in through the front door to audit your data security, I thought the back might be left open.'

'Oh my God. It was you. All along it was you.'

'Now you're being overly dramatic.'

'It was you who kept delaying things, putting the date back. It wasn't Alan or the lawyers. It was you. Why would you do that?'

Peter finished his drink and put the glass down on James' desk. He patted his belly twice. 'I might have used my influence to advise caution once or twice,' he replied.

'I thought you wanted progress. We were on the journey together. I trusted you.'

'You think you're such a fantastic champion for the car industry. Frankly, James, you're a royal pain in the neck. Always getting in the way of what was necessary. For an entrepreneur, you really don't like moving with the times, but you can't see it. And you carried a lot of the others with you. I was merely contemplating possible, less rigid alternatives for your company's future. Toby was one of them. That's all.'

James stared at Peter. He reached across the desk. Peter flinched. Then he picked up Peter's glass and moved it onto a coaster.

'Still keeping up the pretence that you were, somehow, doing the right thing, defending the moral high ground,' James said. 'I know about the data which was deleted from the EDR. Why did you do that? Why did you remove evidence that pointed to my innocence?'

'I have no idea what you're talking about.'

'That car coming the other way. It was deleted from the EDR. I suppose you thought that if I was in prison, you could steal my company. Was that it? Were you in cahoots with Bruce? Two children died on that road.'

'Now you're straying into fantasy,' Peter said. 'I didn't delete anything. What a ridiculous, slanderous idea.'

'Someone erased material from the EDR. It wasn't Juan, I hardly think it was your expert; that leaves you, and you've just admitted you wanted me out of the way. And you had ample opportunity. My solicitor told me the EDR was removed from my car well before the court application.'

'You were the one who rang me up and asked me to *help* make sure the investigation came to the *right conclusion*.'

'That was before I knew you were mounting a takeover of my company.'

Peter stood up and leaned over James.

'This conversation is demeaning to both of us,' he said. 'I have always acted with the interests of the Department of Transport and the public firmly in mind. I will only say this once more. I did not delete any material from your car's EDR. And I warn you, if you repeat your horrible accusation, I will sue. It's going to be hard enough for me to find another position after all your public, self-serving pontification.

'And don't get all moralistic with me, either, about the Layton children. In government, decisions are made every day which have far-reaching consequences and affect millions of lives of ordinary people, quite often condemning them to death. And what do we all do? Sob into our handkerchiefs, wave our hands theatrically, pretend they're random acts, unconnected with us, because the link isn't so obvious.

'So you've got caught out this time because you were personally involved and you can't handle it. That's what this is really about.

My advice to you is to leave it alone. You've been lucky. Accept the hand you've been dealt this time and move on. You know, better than most, the long-term benefits of your vehicles. Those two deaths, sad as they are, are merely a drop in the ocean. Will you forgive me if I leave now? I think if I stay any longer, I may say something I really regret.'

75

JUAN WAS SCREENED by two overflowing cocktails when Constance and Judith entered the lounge. He swooped towards them with a wide grin, handed them each a drink and instructed them to stay put, while he sourced another for himself. As Juan returned with two more glasses, Constance found herself alone with him, Judith abruptly steaming off in the opposite direction.

'Did I interrupt you?' Constance asked.

'Interrupt? You? Never.'

Constance pointed at the drinks. 'You have two.'

'Ha! No. Shhh! They're both for me. I think James asked the barman to make them very small. He's probably worried about his carpets. I would be. So I have to double up. You'll see. Try it.'

Constance eyed her cocktail suspiciously.

'Have you been to this house before?' Constance asked, and Juan frowned. 'What's the matter?'

'It just sounded a bit like you were still being the lawyer,' he said, 'asking questions, and I thought this was supposed to be a party.'

'OK. I was only going to say how lovely it looks with the lights outside and all the colours in here. I came once in the day and it seemed so stark and cold. Sorry. It's never that easy to switch off, I suppose.'

Juan drained one glass and moved the second to his lips. His eyes wandered to Martine, who was chatting animatedly to Jeremy and Will at the far side of the room.

'If you want to go and talk to Martine, that's fine with me,' Constance said, following his gaze.

'I'm happy with the company I have here,' he said. 'Why do you think I want to talk to Martine?'

Constance took a large gulp of her drink and noticed, for the first time, that a faint scar ran across Juan's left cheek, ending at his top lip. She mused on how it might have been inflicted; an unfriendly pet, a nasty fall, a flashing blade.

'There's one more thing I have been thinking about, since the court,' Juan said.

Constance felt her joy at being out for the evening evaporating. And Juan had berated her for talking shop. She lowered her drink.

'It only came into my head this afternoon, since I talked to James and Toby about deleting data from the EDR. I don't have any "proof" – is that what you say?'

'Wait a minute. You deleted data from the EDR?'

'Not me, and I don't know it was deleted. I can't be sure. But there was nothing on there about the other car, coming the other way. Mr Bukowski.'

'And James knows this?'

'He believes it was Peter, the guy from the government. The one who gave me the EDR. Especially because he kept calling me and Toby and trying to get us to tell him stuff, before the crash. But that's not what I wanted to tell you.'

'It isn't?'

'I was thinking again about why James' car might have crashed. It's not very likely, but you asked me to tell you about anything. James always says, in public, that it's not a risk at all, in all his meetings with the other guys but, privately, he has me working on it. Just me. No one else. James understands it's a really big risk.'

Constance found herself leaning in towards Juan and the pungent aroma of vanilla he was exuding was more welcome than she wanted to admit.

'What risk?' she asked.

'Hacking,' he said. 'James' car was the old model, far less secure. It could have been hacked.'

'Is that difficult to do?'

'You need to know your way around a computer and understand the software controlling the cars, but it can be done. You just find a way in, usually through an internet connection, like the GPS or stereo. Once you're in, you can migrate to any other parts of the vehicle that are computer-controlled.'

'Would it need to be someone near the car?'

'No. You can sit with a laptop a hundred miles away and do it, if you know how. Of course, it's easier if you can see what you're doing.'

'And what happens when you hack the computer?'

'Anything. You can take control of the brakes, the steering, the acceleration.'

'The driver loses control?'

'Of whatever part the hacker takes over.'

'Why did James stick with his older car, if he knew it could be hacked?'

'Toby says he loves that car and, look, just because a car *can* be hacked by a very determined person, doesn't mean it ever *will* be. All our home computers can be hacked, our phones, but it doesn't stop us all using them.'

'Yes but the consequences aren't the same.'

'Agreed. Look. I'm just doing what you asked. I don't know that's what happened. But it would explain the crash.'

Constance nodded slowly, the gears of her mind turning slowly around.

'I see that,' she said. 'But who on earth would want to hack James' car and why?'

76

James was still seated at his desk when Judith knocked and entered, all in one move.

'Lovely party,' she said. 'Aren't you joining in?'

'I am trying,' James replied. 'But things keep coming up. Are you intending to drag me along or did you want a private audience?'

'The latter, I'm afraid, but I promise not to be too long-winded.'

James motioned to her to sit down.

'I can't deny you anything,' he said. 'I owe you, and Constance, so much. I doubt many lawyers, many people, would have tried so hard on my behalf.'

'I'm curious about Toby, your "marketing assistant"?' Judith began.

'His mother was my partner, business partner, Imogen Walsh.'

'I didn't know that.'

'She died, too young. We were skiing. It was just like that

actress; she fell and hit her head, said she felt fine, went back to the hotel for a rest and never woke up. He found her – Toby. He was ten years old.'

'How did he come to work for you?'

'Imogen and I were fifty-fifty partners in the business. Under the terms of our agreement, I could have bought her shares for next to nothing, but it didn't feel right. Her husband – he was already her ex-husband by then, I should say – arranged for them to be held on trust for Toby. Toby went to live with him in Kent, and when he finished school and was looking for work, he asked me if I would take him into the business.'

'That's good of you.'

'Not really. I was thinking about it only today. I haven't been very nice to Toby, although Imogen would probably have been harder on him. He wanted to help, to be part of SEDA. It isn't just a job for him, it's a connection to his mother. I've treated him more like a secretary, running errands, booking rooms. I finally took him to a meeting a few weeks back and he really surprised me, rose to the occasion, researched things before we went, was focused and articulate when we were there, wrote up a plan afterwards – not that we've been able to implement it yet, if we ever will, now.

'But I misjudged him. Just because he didn't have qualifications and because he wasn't quite like his mother. She was a...a very extraordinary woman, let's say. He also came under considerable pressure in recent weeks to...betray me and he remained loyal. He's impressed me, after all.'

'So will he be your successor?' Judith asked.

James grunted. 'I think I have a few years in me yet. Not quite the dinosaur they make me out to be. Was that all? As you say,

I have other guests.'

'I thought I saw Peter Mears in here?'

'You know Peter?'

'Only by reputation.'

'He came to tell me he's lost his job. Said it was because he supported me.'

'That's rubbish.'

'He said the Bill won't happen any day soon and it's all my fault. You disagree?'

'I know one or two government lawyers, and I put some feelers out. I discovered that your friend, Peter, was known to be more opinionated and vociferous than he likes people to believe. It's often easier to deliver a bitter pill if you can pretend it's prescribed by someone else.'

James was silent.

'And I also heard they were planning to let him go, but not because he backed you. He wrote some papers maintaining it would be a simple process to determine fault if autonomous vehicles crashed. The Ministry had been relying on them to shape policy. He was also a staunch supporter of the hybrid. And I heard that he'd been trying to acquire information illicitly from manufacturers. Just a whisper, that last one.'

'I asked him if he'd deleted data from the EDR, which would have exonerated me, data showing the car coming the other way,' James said. 'He denied it, of course, only after hinting it might have been the right thing to do. Sanctimonious prig! But he made it clear he would sue me if I repeated it.'

'Why would he delete the data?'

'He told me he didn't like me, said he wanted to groom Toby to take over. That would have been easier if I was in jail. And looking back, after the accident, he pressed me to admit it was my fault – me, personally. That data showed it wasn't, so he hid it. The more I think about it, the more I believe the whole thing may have been staged, the roadworks, the traffic light, just to get me out and he's trying to dress it all up now as being for the public good. I know it's far-fetched but I've watched *House of Cards*. I know that anything is possible if you have enough influence!'

A drop of perspiration ran down the side of James' cheek and he crossed the room, ferreting around in a cupboard until he found a bottle of water. He poured himself a glass and drank it down.

'It's unlikely that Peter would arrange for your car to crash, even if he could,' Judith replied. 'The impact on the industry of any accident involving one of your vehicles was always going to be huge, especially at this critical stage. It would be a very brave – or a very stupid – man who would plan an accident now, even one that was carefully choreographed. From what I've heard, Peter does not strike me as either brave or stupid. Erasing data afterwards is less fantastical but, presumably, you have no proof?'

'Smarmy bastard. All the times I took him and his wife out and he was planning my demise.'

James returned to his chair, but his thoughts were elsewhere.

'Would you like me to say anything to Inspector Dawson, about your…concerns?' Judith asked.

James ran his hands across the surface of his laptop and focused on her again.

'You're probably right,' he said. 'I'm not able to think clearly about this yet. No, thank you. I'll sleep on it in any event.'

Judith walked towards the door, then she returned and sat down again.

'Can I ask you one further question?' she said. 'You don't have to answer, but it will haunt me forever if I don't ask it at least one more time.'

'I couldn't have that happen, could I? Not when I am so tremendously in your debt.'

'What do you really think went wrong on October 10th?'

James smiled sadly.

'Understandably, you and Constance have suspected me of holding things back but, truly, I'm still not certain. And I've looked at the film many times, I can assure you. I see it in my dreams as well as in many of my waking hours. Most likely the temporary traffic light sign was positioned in such a way that VERA didn't read it, failed to notice it. We're already working on that, like many other manufacturers. And then, when it was necessary to move over to the other carriageway, with so little time to spare, VERA had to choose; she was suddenly on the trajectory to hit that car with the Polish workers – five of them – so she swerved away.

'If the family had stayed in the central reserve they would have been safe. VERA would still have missed them. Perhaps she should have anticipated they would move forward, try to cross to the far side, that children would behave impetuously.'

'A human driver might have.'

'Possibly. That's another area we are focusing on.'

'So this was one of those accidents that will still happen in the future?'

'If we can perfect the issue with the road signs, the likelihood of something like this happening again is very low. Predicting the impulses of a human child correctly – I challenge you to find any system that can do that.'

Judith finished her drink and stood up again. 'Interesting, isn't it,' she said, 'that now you seem so sure that VERA was in charge all the time – right up to the moment of impact – when you couldn't remember just a few days ago. Of course, that would be consistent for a man who "always drives in autonomous mode" and would also explain why you couldn't bring yourself to plead guilty.'

James was no longer smiling.

'I suppose if you really believe that your cars will change the world, you might be able to justify to yourself lying on oath, on this occasion. It was only a "white lie" after all, saying you couldn't remember. Or perhaps what you said just now was a slip of the tongue,' Judith continued. 'You must be very tired. I'm going back to the party.' She stood up slowly. 'This has been a very enlightening but not entirely satisfactory conversation.'

'If I could turn back the clock and do anything to prevent those children being hurt, you know I would,' James said.

Judith handed him her empty glass and glided out of the room.

77

As Juan disappeared off to the kitchen in search of more drinks, Toby approached Constance and, lurching against her heavily, he mumbled that he needed to show her around the garden. Constance squinted out into the night, stifled the comment that it would be difficult to see anything in the dark that they couldn't see from the lounge, but Toby was most insistent, and she was forced to comply. Once he was certain they were out of earshot of the house, he began to speak.

'Did you ask Peter, find out if he erased the data? Is that what Juan was telling you?' he said.

'I can't really discuss it with you, Toby, I'm sorry.'

'I thought of something else, something that means it must have been Peter. I can see it now. But I never did then.' Toby rubbed his hand across his face and gazed blankly back at the house. 'He seemed so friendly. I never believed he would do something like this. He told me he wanted to help James, help SEDA, said if only I would persuade James to do what he wanted, SEDA would be on the list and selling its cars by the end of October.'

'He was playing on your loyalty to James.'

Toby smiled. He was pleased Constance understood.

'Have you met Martine?' he asked suddenly.

'James' wife? Yes. Why?'

'Of course you have. I'm just so messed up by all this. She and I…at least I think, oh God. If you're his lawyer, do you have to tell him everything I say?' He stumbled towards a bench and sat down, breathing heavily. Constance followed him. The cold was rapidly chilling her bones.

'I'm not James' lawyer any more,' she said. 'He just invited us here to say thank you. But if you tell me something about a crime having been committed, I would have to report it to the police, like anyone would.' As she spoke, she feared she was almost certainly going to stem Toby's flow, but she couldn't allow him to think that any secrets were safe with her.

Toby took a deep breath.

'I don't care if you do tell,' he said, shaking his head from side to side. 'Not any more. It's eating me up, keeping it inside. I would have said sooner, it's just…I told Peter something when we met.'

'You met Peter?'

'Just for coffee.'

'What did you tell him?'

'It was a silly idea. I never thought he would do anything about it.'

'What did you tell him?'

'I told him about this plan. I didn't mean it as something real to happen. It was just an idea.'

Constance waited. Judith had taught her about the power of silence, if used appropriately. And, after a few seconds she was rewarded.

'It was an idea I had,' Toby continued, 'that maybe if there was a road accident, a big pile-up and a SEDA car was involved but it didn't hit anything – then the people in the SEDA car would go on the News and tell everyone how all the others had a crash, but their SEDA car had saved them. It would be great publicity.'

'And you mentioned this idea to Peter?'

'Yes.'

'And what did he say?'

'Nothing at the time, but two weeks later, bang! James has the crash.'

'Why didn't you tell me this earlier? We've been through the investigation and the trial.'

Toby looked back towards the house and his eyes eventually focused on Martine, who was laughing raucously with Juan and some other men, in the centre of the lounge.

'I didn't believe any of it was linked, until we were standing in James' office today and Juan said that someone had messed with the EDR, and we know Peter had the EDR. He gave it to Juan. I couldn't say it then. I couldn't tell James. I thought he would be so...disappointed in me. It's bad enough that I had to tell him I met Peter in secret.'

Constance's eyes also flicked across to Juan and Martine before returning to Toby. Juan had one arm tightly around Martine's waist, before she disentangled herself and grabbed the arm of another companion.

'How well do you know Juan?' she said.

'We live together...housemates.'

'But he's not been with SEDA long?'

'No. But, look. It's not Juan. Why would he tell us about the data being deleted if he was the one who did it?'

'Maybe it's only a matter of time before someone else works it out. Far better to get in first.'

'No!' Toby shook his head violently. 'I told Peter about the plan. It must be Peter. Somehow, I don't know how, Peter made the accident happen, and then he had to delete the data to cover up whatever he did.'

Martine had left the gathering and Juan was now standing very close to Carol, and they were drinking their drinks with their arms linked around each other. At least half of Carol's drink sloshed over the edge of her glass and she giggled flirtatiously and sucked at her fingers.

'I heard from Carol, your receptionist, that Juan is working on other secret projects,' Constance said.

'Not *that* secret. I mean, I know about them too,' Toby pouted.

At that moment a couple exited the front door of the house and began to argue in the driveway. Their words were mostly drowned out by the music and the crunching of their feet on the gravel, but it was clear that the man was demanding something and the woman was refusing. As their gesticulating became wilder, Constance concentrated more on them.

'Is that Peter?' she peered through the darkness.

'Yes. Looks a bit cross, doesn't he?'

Peter shouted some parting comment, marched off up the drive and climbed into his car. The woman turned around and Constance saw her face for the first time, as she folded her arms around her body and dabbed at her eyes. Then, with a change of heart, she twisted around again and began to run up the drive after the departing vehicle, now positioned by the gates, waiting for a break in the traffic. On another day, in less vertiginous heels, she might have made it. This time, she was a metre short of the bumper when Peter sped out of the drive and into the night.

'And that's his wife?' Constance asked.

'Fiona. I think she's a friend of Martine's.'

'That might be awkward,' Constance muttered, 'or perhaps not. I need to go and find Judith,' she told Toby. 'Listen. Don't say anything to anyone else about the plan and the crash. Not till I've had a chance to think about it a bit more.'

Toby slumped over the arm of the bench, but he managed an appreciative smile.

'I won't,' he replied.

Constance stood up. She felt that she was inching her way towards the truth, but she still had some way to go.

'There's something else,' Toby said, suddenly pensive, and then his mobile phone rang. He ferreted around in his pocket, holding one finger up to indicate to Constance she should wait. Then he laughed out loud as he pressed the phone to his ear. 'Dad!' he shouted, and this time he succeeded in sitting up straight. 'Just wait one second. Don't go anywhere!' He muted his phone and covered the screen with his hand.

'I'm sure it can wait. You take your call,' Constance said.

'You asked me about the name, the project. Why it was called Cinderella,' Toby insisted on one more confession. 'James didn't understand. He thought it was just a name, but that's stupid. The one about the cars talking is called *Connect* and the one about them being made stronger is called *Hercules*. But *Cinderella*? It wasn't called that at the beginning. It's the name I gave it. I wanted him to understand why I called it that, why I gave it the name of a story about a poor motherless child, who was never allowed to show what she could do, who was always put down and made to sweep the floors.

'My mother used to read me that story and tell me it was an example of never giving up, of persevering and achieving the big prize in the end, even if you were small and unimportant and overlooked. It was a really clever name for the project! But James didn't even ask. He just said "Very good Toby, put it in my diary," and that's what I did.'

***

Constance ran inside and through the lounge to the kitchen, where she located Judith talking earnestly to Juan.

'Toby isn't feeling so well,' Constance said pointedly.

'I told him to stick to the beer,' Juan laughed.

'He's at the far end of the garden,' Constance persisted, 'and I think he might need some help getting back to civilisation, and quickly, before he gets hypothermia.'

'All right,' Juan handed his glass to Constance. 'I'll save him. It won't be the first time, but don't disappear again, either of you. We've still got loads to talk about.'

***

'What is it? You look excited,' Judith said, as Constance dragged her into the hallway and then to a quiet spot at the foot of the stairs.

'Fiona Mears is here.'

'Peter's wife?'

'Yep.'

'I suppose that fits. James says they used to go out a lot together, the two couples; corporate hospitality. He would host them, theatre, concerts. He was just complaining to me how he always paid. Where is Fiona now?'

'She just had a big row with Peter in the garden – massive. He left and she stayed. She's still outside somewhere, cooling off.'

'She got all dressed up and wanted to stay for the cake.'

'Actually, she changed her mind and wanted to leave, but he had already driven off. Oh what's he doing here?'

Dean McQueen had appeared in the doorway. He was wearing a black shirt and black jeans, with an iridescent dinner jacket. He stepped inside, his eyes sweeping the room.

'Who is that?' Judith asked.

'That, is Dean McQueen. You remember?'

'Oh yes. I remember. He's scrubbed up quite nicely. Do you think he's working tonight, or on the guest list? He's clearly looking for someone.'

'Should I introduce you?'

'No.' Judith caught Constance's arm and pulled her back, so they were out of his line of vision. 'Or at least, not yet. He looks like a man with a mission and we don't want it being aborted because we're here.'

Dean sidled over to the corner of the room and drained a drink from one of the trays. He nodded to a couple of guests, then began tapping at his phone, before hurrying out again.

'Ah, there she is!'

As Dean left, Fiona floated in and Constance nudged Judith.

'Fiona Mears?' Judith said. 'So she and Martine are friends. So what?'

'I think it's more than that,' Constance whispered. 'Toby says Peter deleted data from the EDR.'

'James thinks that too, but I'm not sure. He's looking for answers when they may simply not exist.'

'And he thinks Peter planned James' accident.'

Judith shook her head. 'Oh dear,' she said.

'You knew?'

'He's just spouting what James said.'

'No, I don't think so. He says he told Peter about a plan for a crash, and then it happened.'

Judith flung a quick glance in Fiona's direction. She was tucking her hair behind her ear and listening earnestly to another guest. 'So, what has this all got to do with his wife?' she said.

'Maybe she's the link. Peter couldn't get information from Toby, so he used Fiona to get it from Martine instead.'

***

Constance and Judith had just agreed to mingle with the guests and re-group later, when they became aware of a loud, high-pitched screeching noise, coming from outside. It happened to coincide with a lull in the music, and everyone rushed over to the window, the braver souls streaming out into the garden to see what on earth was going on.

Toby was lying on the ground in the driveway, in front of the house, hands over his ears, screaming loudly. His shirt was untucked and one of his shoes had fallen off. Juan was nowhere to be seen.

Dean was bending low over Toby, admonishing him in colourful language. When he saw that an audience had assembled, he straightened up, pointed an accusatory finger at Toby, shouted, 'You're the one who doesn't know how to behave, posh boy wanker!' before getting into his van and driving off at speed.

Constance tapped Judith's arm. James was standing at the window of his study, watching the altercation, a solemn expression etched across his face.

78

FIONA SAUNTERED into the kitchen and pilfered a sausage from the top of the tray, as a waitress hurried past. Martine turned around and greeted her with a kiss on each cheek.

'So pleased you're here. I wanted to come over, but I kept having to talk to other people. You know how it is when you're the hostess,' Martine said.

'You must be pleased with how it's all worked out,' Fiona said, helping herself also to a new drink. 'Everyone wants a piece of James; he's the man of the moment.'

'Is that how it looks? I'm just so relieved. It's been a terrible nightmare,' Martine said. 'And it's been so hard for James. It's changed him.'

Martine had James in her line of vision, out in the hallway and, as if on cue, he turned around and raised his orange juice to the two women. Martine smiled in return and blew him a kiss. Fiona threw her head back and snorted.

'I have to hand it to you,' she said. 'You play the part to

perfection. Peter was right that I should have used you in one of my commercials. You'd have been fantastic.'

'I don't know what you're talking about.'

'The devoted wife. It's all a pretence. I saw you and Juan earlier. I was at the end of the driveway. You were in the bushes.'

'Oh.' Martine poured herself a drink and fiddled with her waistband. 'It wasn't how it looked,' she said. 'Just a kiss, and then I reminded him I was married – and to his boss. He's drunk and he got the wrong idea. I said "maybe people do this in Cancún but not in Hadley Wood".' She forced a laugh but Fiona refused to share it. 'Oh come on, Fi. We've all done it. A stray kiss now and again at a party. It doesn't mean anything.'

Fiona looked again in James' direction, but he was now talking animatedly to some of his guests.

'I know I said I didn't care about Peter, when I told you all the things he said about James, that he was a fossil and he had to be removed,' Fiona used the cocktail stick from her sausage to prod at an array of debris on the draining board. 'I always thought James was a very proper, honest person, and that he didn't deserve to be backstabbed like that. I told you that.' Fiona's voice was steadily increasing in volume, 'But that was before I realised you would fuck things up quite so royally for Peter. He's lost his job, you know.'

'I didn't.'

'I think I feel too sorry for him to leave him now.' She snapped the cocktail stick in half.

'Why do you think I had anything to do with Peter losing his job?'

'Oh don't!' Fiona refilled her glass from another. 'OK. Once James had his accident, it was always going to be damage limitation for Peter. But that wasn't enough for you. You wanted to get your own back, big-time. Someone's been spreading rumours about him. They told him when they sacked him. Saying he was trying to steal secrets, mentioning names at SEDA. I told you about that in confidence.'

'You told me your husband was a shit and you wanted to leave him.'

'We were going through a rough patch. A real friend might have encouraged me to stick with it; you kept inviting me over and telling me to ditch him. Is that what you were planning to do, if James went to jail?'

'I supported James when he needed me. You're the one who gave your husband's secrets away – things he told you in confidence, because you were his wife and he trusted you. What will everyone think if they find out that's what you did? So my advice to you, and I've been dying for the last year to give you some advice, while I had to sit here night after night and listen to you dishing it out, is to keep your memories of what you told me to yourself, and your fingers crossed that your now-unemployed husband can get himself a new job that will help keep up the mortgage payments and your children's school fees.'

The light clinking sound of metal on glass attracted Martine's attention. She peered out into the corridor to see James was standing at the far side of the lounge, tapping his favourite pen against his glass.

'I must go. James is going to say something.'

Fiona caught her arm.

'Does he know, James, about all your other male…friends?' she asked.

'James and Imogen, Toby's mum, were very close,' Martine said, 'and if I asked around, I know I would find at least one "Vera" in each of his frequent overseas destinations. He isn't the saint you would like him to be.' She finished her drink and placed it down next to Fiona's. 'I make James happy when he's here,' she said. 'He doesn't ask questions. I don't either.' She disentangled herself from Fiona's grip. 'Excuse me, I'm going to be with my husband. And I think it's probably time you went to find yours.'

As Martine hurried out, Judith shrank back further into the shadow of the open door, behind which she had been concealing herself. And as Martine raised her glass with all the others, and chanted 'to James' and 'to SEDA' and everyone cheered, she pressed her glass against her lips, without drinking and pondered everything she had seen and heard.

***

Judith and Constance sat in the back of their taxi as it sped through the quiet streets towards central London.

'Well, I think that evening delivered even more than it promised,' Judith was reflecting on the night's events.

'Did you manage to speak to Fiona in the end?' Constance asked, leaning heavily on the central armrest. She had consumed more alcohol than she had intended, after months of lonely restraint.

'No. She left while James was making his speech.'

'That's a shame.'

'I did, however, overhear a conversation between Fiona and Martine, which suggested that Martine might have a reason for her amorous encounters with other men.'

'What?'

'She thinks James had an affair with Imogen Walsh and with someone called Vera; hence the name for his talking computer.'

'Sounds like an excuse to me,' Constance muttered, 'and not a very good one.'

Judith stared out of the window.

'What should we do about Peter?' Constance asked.

'Part of me says that we should do absolutely nothing. The Laytons don't need another investigation, the safety features of the cars will be checked and re-checked until they get it right, it makes no difference to the trial verdict and Peter no longer has the influence he once had.'

'But what about James?'

'What about James?'

'He's our client. Don't we have a duty to him, to investigate it further?'

'Our duty was to defend James and we've done that. Anyway, I asked him. He said to leave it alone. And he's not our client any more.'

'You've changed your mind about him, haven't you?' Constance snapped, 'now you know about his other women; Vera whoever she is. You don't admire him quite so much. You think they deserve each other, him and Martine.'

Judith's face pinched tight.

'It's OK,' Constance ploughed on. 'I understand why you think that. I'm not sure I agree, but we could forget everything we learned tonight, if that's what you want.'

'That's right, we could,' Judith snapped. 'But you didn't let me finish. Just because I said I was tempted, I didn't mean that was what we should do. If we suspect Peter of criminal activity, we should tell Dawson. Let him decide what's next, but we can always nudge him towards particular places of interest.'

'I'm sorry,' Constance's face crinkled with her apology. 'I thought you meant...'

'I know what you thought. You made it very clear.' Judith sighed. 'Look. We are partners in all this. And partners need to be honest with each other, at all times, even when it's hurtful.'

Now Constance stared out of the opposite window.

'It's really OK, Connie,' Judith said.

Constance nodded slowly. 'There's one other thing I forgot to tell you.' She found herself bending in low towards Judith, even though she hadn't intended to. Her head felt so heavy after all those cocktails. 'It was something Juan said. Probably nothing.'

'I'm surprised he had time to speak to you, he was so busy spreading his charms around, but, go ahead. What did our Latin lothario have to say for himself?'

'He has a new theory for why James' car crashed. He thinks it might have been hacked! He says it's easy if you know how, and even easier with older models like James'.'

'And does his theory extend to who did this hacking or why?'

'No. Although Peter is still top of the list. But it would explain James losing control suddenly, on a dry day and a quiet street.'

Judith sat forward, pressing her hands down on her seat and squeezing hard. She closed her eyes.

'Are you all right?' Constance felt compelled to ask, after a few minutes passed in silence.

'I wonder,' Judith said, with a flush of colour flooding her cheeks.

'What?'

'I just had a revelation. I could be right. Toby told you about the "plan" he had for a big accident, an almighty smash and the

SEDA rising from the ashes like a phoenix.'

'Yes.'

'Why didn't he tell James about it? Juan told James about the deleted data, they both admitted they were approached by Peter. Toby confessed he met Peter and that Peter tried to bribe him. Why didn't he tell James *then*, about the plan?'

'He said he felt ashamed. He…' Constance recalled how Toby's eyes had wandered over to the party guests when he had talked about the plan.

'It wasn't *his* plan in the first place, was it?' she said. 'So what does that mean?'

'That means we wait,' Judith said. 'In my experience, if you are patient, someone gives something crucial away. Like when robbers pull off the perfect heist, but one of them can't resist buying a pink Cadillac with the proceeds. Toby's probably disclosed all his secrets to you, and well done for gaining his confidence. But the others may need a little more time. We let them all reflect on the week's events and see what happens. Someone might remember something. And, importantly, because James isn't going to let this go now – he has the bit between his teeth – he may try shaking the apple tree himself. Of course, we have no obligation to do any of this. Like I said, our job is done.'

She finally sat back in her seat.

'You know I should feel sorry for James. After all, he was in a terrible predicament, torn between his belief in the ability of his product to save the world, to reduce road deaths in their thousands, and his need to explain what happened that afternoon on Common Lane but, perhaps surprisingly, I find that I don't. He hasn't learned from this tragedy, he wants to go on just like before.'

'You said you liked him?'

'Did I? Surely not.'

'On the way out, this evening.'

'I think the alcohol has affected your short-term memory.'

'Should I still tell Dawson about Peter then?' Constance said. 'I think it should be me. He's still feeling bruised by your fierce cross-examination in court.'

'I regret what happened with Dawson. This case has been difficult in so many ways,' Judith confessed, sighing and wiping the window so she could see out. 'Great party though,' she continued, suddenly livening up. 'What a way to finish off! I don't know if you tried one, but the barman mixed me this incredible gin that starts off a subtle shade of blue and, when you stir in the tonic, it turns flamingo pink. Did you have one?'

'No, I didn't.'

'Next time we go out, we have to find somewhere that does it. You need to Google the name. You'll be amazed.'

'I'll have a look online and find somewhere.'

Judith checked her watch. 'Oh. It's still early. I'll get home in time to watch *Game of Thrones*.'

'You watch *Game of Thrones*?'

'Of course not. Too much like real life, plus a few cloaks and jerkins. But I might start, tonight, tomorrow, on Tuesday. That's the incredible thing about living alone,' Judith said, patting Constance on the hand companionably. 'I can do whatever I want.'

79

JUAN WAS SITTING at the kitchen bar of Toby's flat, sipping at a mug of coffee, the following morning, staring at the screen of his laptop. Toby stumbled from his room, groaning and holding his head.

'Good party?' Juan asked.

'Was it?' Toby replied, rolling his tongue around his mouth and grimacing. 'How did we get home?'

'In a taxi. I had to give my watch to the driver, and, if you were sick, I said he could keep it.'

Toby squinted at Juan's wrist, where his timepiece nestled comfortably.

'Thanks,' Toby said. 'You're a mate.'

'It's not genuine, so don't thank me too much.'

'You're up early?'

'Ah. I was thinking about lots of things.'

'That sounds like woman trouble. I told you Carol wasn't interested.'

Juan laughed. 'Who says I'm interested in Carol?' he said. 'I'm taking your advice and keeping away from office romances.' He fidgeted on the stool and took another slug of coffee. 'Do you remember much about last night?' he asked. 'Something happened and you got quite upset. That was when I decided to bring you home.'

'Oh God!' Toby lowered his head until it nudged the edge of the bar. 'I was hoping it was a bad dream. You mean that arsehole in the white van was really there in the flesh?'

'Did he hurt you?'

'I don't think so. I pissed on his car. I was desperate,' Toby giggled. 'I was trying to follow the pattern of the letters on the side. It seemed like a good idea at the time, but it made him a bit cross. Did James see?'

'I think most people did. You made so much noise we thought he'd stabbed you. But I didn't see James come out of the house, so maybe not. And he had the sense to drive off. It was the security guy, you know, we see him around the office sometimes, checking on all the cameras.'

'Who invited him?'

'James I expect. Tobes, I'm sorry. I need to ask you this. Where were you when James' accident happened?' Juan wrapped his hands around his mug and he stared earnestly at Toby.

Toby rested his elbows on the bar.

'That's a bit random and on top of my hangover. Anyway, you know where I was,' Toby said. 'Out at that meeting, to talk about bodywork changes on the new models.'

'What time did you get back?'

'From the meeting? I can't remember now, but it was ages after the crash. I told the police.'

'But didn't the meeting get cancelled? You had to go another time, didn't you?'

Toby reddened. 'I didn't know it had been cancelled. No one told me. I went all the way there and I got delayed coming back. Where were you anyway?'

'You know where I was. I went to pick up the new brochures in Enfield. Look, don't get all defensive. I'm just trying to help James. He really wants to find out what happened.'

'I thought it was Peter.'

'I did too. But, if it was Peter, how did he do it? I had some more thoughts last night and I talked to Constance, James' lawyer. Then I went online this morning. I looked back at 10th October. My login history says I was logged-in to Connect from around 2.25 for twenty minutes. That's exactly when James' accident happened.'

'So?'

'You're not listening. I was in Enfield, stuck in traffic. I can't log in to Connect from my phone and my laptop was in the lab. Someone went into the lab and logged in as me, at the same time James crashed. They could have connected to his car.'

'Well, it wasn't me.' Toby's lip trembled.

Juan stared hard at him before shoving his coffee away.

'It's OK. I believe you,' he said. 'No offence, but I'm not sure you know how to. But whoever it was had access to the lab, and you know how tight security is.'

'It could have been Chris or Mark.'

'No. They were both on a course. A friend of mine saw them there.' Juan rose from the bar, folded his arms and walked around the room. 'Listen. We should tell someone, about my log-in being used. We might be able to check the cameras in the atrium, in the car park, see if anyone strange was hanging around, although it's months ago now. Should we tell the police?'

'No,' Toby said. 'And we shouldn't tell James yet. We don't want to get his hopes up when it could be nothing. We tell her, Constance. She'll know what to do.'

***

'Hello Dean.' Constance stood on Dean McQueen's doorstep, with Dawson beside her. Dean was wearing pyjama bottoms and a white vest and his face was grey. 'You remember me, I'm Constance Lamb. I came to see you a few weeks ago, about James Salisbury, after we met at his house. This is Chief Inspector Dawson. Can we come in please?'

'If this is about last night, I swear I didn't hit him,' Dean danced around, his eyes darting past them to the police car parked across his drive. 'I wanted to, but I didn't. I just touched him and he fell over.'

'It's not about last night,' Constance said. 'We need your help.'

'And we really need to come inside,' Dawson added gruffly.

Dean stood back and allowed them in. There were cardboard boxes in the hallway, piled up almost to the ceiling and the small sitting room was filled with laptops, wires, cameras, sensors, brackets and screws and black plastic boxes of varying shapes and sizes.

'What's all this stuff?' Dawson asked.

'It's my work. Security. Look. You said you needed my help.' Dean sat down on the sofa and removed a cigarette from his back pocket. He cradled it between his fingers. Constance sat down next to him. Dawson remained standing.

'When we met last time, you told me you installed security at Mr Salisbury's office?' she began.

'Yeah, that's right.'

'You said you put in hidden cameras, well-hidden.'

'James likes to know what his staff are doing.'

'He doesn't trust them?'

'He's just careful. He's not the only one.'

'Are there cameras in the corridor leading up to the IT lab?'

'Why don't you ask James?'

'Just answer the question.' Dawson picked up one of the cameras and began scrutinising it through its packaging.

'We want to see if it's possible to go back to the afternoon of 10th October, to look at who was in the IT lab around 2.30pm,' Constance said. 'Do you have a camera in the corridor? You said you kept records for six months.'

'Is that when the accident happened?'

'Yes.'

Dean looked from Constance to Dawson.

'It might take me a while to find,' he said. 'And I'm supposed to be at another job in half an hour.'

'Do you have receipts for all this stuff?' Dawson opened the package in his hand and shook the camera out so that it fell heavily to the floor. Dean picked it up and placed it next to him on the sofa. 'Some of it looks very high grade...' Dawson persisted.

'I think it would be good if you postponed your other job and did your best to find us the camera footage, please,' Constance advised, scowling at Dawson.

'All right.' Dean nodded and headed towards the back of the house, gesturing to them to follow. In the kitchen, he grabbed a laptop and placed it on the table.

'All right,' he repeated. 'It's going to take a while to find the exact date and time. Make yourself tea if you want to stay and watch. You asked for the corridor leading to the lab.' He suddenly smiled. 'I can do better than that. I have three cameras in the lab itself. Only people know about them is me and Mr Salisbury. Will that do for you?'

It took around 45 minutes for Dean to locate what they wanted. Then Constance and Dawson both crowded around him, as he pressed 'play'.

At first, all they could see was the empty lab in semi-darkness. Constance recognised Juan's desk, where she had sat to ask him questions, before bringing him to James' trial. All the monitors were switched off. Then, two minutes in, the door of the lab opened and the lights came on. It was Dawson who was first to voice the surprise they all felt, when they saw who had entered.

'Oh,' he said. 'I really didn't expect that. Looks like I need to pay someone a visit. And the sooner the better.'

LONDON, 10 OCTOBER 2018

80

MARTINE ENTERED the lab with a bag over her shoulder. She sat down at Juan's desk and unlocked the screen of his PC. She opened up the Connect software and located James' car from the drop-down list of vehicles. Another click and its position was pinpointed on the map, in the car park of an East London office complex.

Then Martine opened her own laptop and connected it up to Juan's PC. She chose 'LIDAR' from the menu and the left-hand screen was immediately populated with coloured boxes. She switched on Juan's second monitor, to its right, selected 'dashcam' and the area in front of James' car sprang to life on this screen. All of these steps were achieved within seconds and with minimal fuss.

Then she pulled on some headphones and checked out the various buttons on the Connect tool bar, until she located a live street-view of Common Lane in Haringey. For the last two months, SEDA had been allowed to tap directly into the CCTV in certain London boroughs, to enable it to assess its cars' performance. That meant that, in addition to the dashcam view, she should be able to watch James from above, via CCTV cameras, at least along part of his route back to the office.

Martine stiffened and jumped back. James had just crossed in front of one of the dashcams. She held her breath and waited for him to enter the car and settle himself down.

'Come on James, come on my darling. Hurry up. Turn that stereo on,' she whispered, leaning closer to the screen. 'Come on. Let me in.'

She extracted a small black box from her bag and placed it next to her laptop. She stroked its surface and fiddled with its dial. It was the key for what was to happen next. As long as she chose the right frequency, it would jam the radar sensors on James' car. All the obstacles in its path, the other cars, bikes, lorries, would all disappear. He would be driving 'blind'. And all this for £36.99 with free delivery.

Now James was moving off, out of the car park and onto the road. Martine adjusted the height of her chair, so that she was at eye-level with the dash cam, living James' journey with him. She turned the volume up, just a touch, on the live feed, and she could hear James talking to VERA. 'Hello VERA. You sound as perky as ever. It's James. Back to the office please.'

Martine's phone pinged suddenly and she pulled it from her pocket. A message from James.

Just thought I saw you on a ten-foot billboard, he had written. *Had to check. She is your double. Take a look. She could be your sister.*

Martine could not help but smile. James was thinking of her

in the middle of his busy day, even if he'd been prompted by a roadside advertisement. She tapped on the link he had sent through and an image emerged of a young woman grinning enthusiastically, a pizza slice hovering close to her gaping mouth. At first Martine frowned, the woman was selling fast food, which was not the persona she, herself, would ever try to cultivate, but she had to admit that the glow radiating out from the image was pleasing and the model was very pretty.

Not sure I'm pleased you're looking at pictures of other women! Where r u? she messaged back.

On the road. Might be back late. Don't wait for me to eat. You know I only have eyes for you. She heard James chuckle into his phone and a lump formed in her throat. *Maybe she shouldn't do this after all. It would be so difficult for James to bear, his photo in the papers for all the wrong reasons.* But she could never have let him in on her plan; he would never have agreed and the accident must look authentic for it to have the desired effect. And the aftermath too; she had always thought James a terrible liar.

Martine checked the time. She had at least four more minutes until James' car would reach the place she had chosen for the accident. A tricky spot to navigate, with a contraflow and temporary traffic light and, of course, that solid, impenetrable concrete barrier. That would help justify things after the event. But she also knew it would be quiet at this time of day, especially because people were being urged to avoid the roadworks.

Martine checked the coordinates on the black box, her eyes darting from one screen to another, her feet, crossed beneath the desk, tapping out a lively tune, her breathing laboured.

She thought briefly of Juan and the huge amount she had learned just by sitting next to him, these last weeks, together with the odd 'random' question. He had been so keen to impress her and she had taken full advantage of his enthusiasm. And the two courses on hacking he had recommended to his colleagues had been invaluable to her too.

She checked the time again, closed her eyes, opened them, coughed once and then flicked the switch on the black box.

The effect was amazing. Most of the coloured shapes on the Connect screen disappeared immediately, the ones representing the road signs Martine knew lined that stretch of road, the street lights, the temporary traffic light, the zebra crossing. It was as if they no longer existed.

She watched the dashcam. Nothing yet. She could hear James humming along to the music and the rustling of paper in his hand. She began to apply pressure, gently but firmly, to a button on the keyboard, which was now connected to James' accelerator pedal, and his speed increased correspondingly. She needed to find the right balance, sufficient for a crash into the barrier which would look terrifying to the outside world but not enough for him to notice any sudden change or to be seriously injured. Naturally, he would be out of action for a week or two afterwards, just long enough for her to work her magic, quietly, behind the scenes. And Toby was unlikely to object, given their recent interaction. No, she was surer than ever that she could count on his support.

Reluctantly, SEDA would blame James, of course, "human error" which would well and truly keep the Cinderella project on track, if a little delayed. And James would have to swallow his pride. She could just see the headline now. *If only I'd let the car drive! SEDA king reflects from hospital bed.*

Now Martine had to stop thinking too far ahead and focus on the task in hand. She mustn't overdo it. Not only would skid marks on the road give away any excessive speed and lead to more questions, she had to ensure James was not badly hurt.

Suddenly the dashcam witnessed a rapid shift to the right, followed by a jolt to the left. Martine heard James call out.

On Common Lane, Bertie Layton had broken his cover and darted into the road. Georgia trailed him, calling his name. Therese pursued them both, flinging the pram forward as James' car tossed her up in the air, like the ragdoll tucked into Georgia's backpack.

Martine saw their blurred figures cross the right-hand screen, she saw something, someone, a bundle of clothes and flesh and hair smash against the dashcam for an instant with a sickening thud. 'Whoosh!' she heard the air bag engage and more moans from James as he hit it at 36mph.

'No!' Martine screamed, slamming her free hand down on the table.

Then everything stopped.

The dashcam showed the car, stationary, at an angle, just short of the target concrete barrier. Trembling, she called up the CCTV, but in this area there was little coverage. It revealed a line of cars progressing steadily towards James on the other carriageway, but that was all. On the left-hand screen there was almost nothing, the green square representing James' car, sitting alone in the road, surrounded by black.

Martine held her breath. Nothing. She could hear voices around James' car, shouts and crying out and hooting. A minute passed and she waited. A man crossed the path of the dashcam and crouched down in front of the grille. He stood up again with blood coating his hands.

Martine opened her mouth and closed it again. Then, she

disconnected her laptop from Juan's machine, she switched off Juan's second screen, logged out of Connect and locked his first screen. Finally, although it mattered little now, she flicked the jamming switch to 'off' and planted Juan's security pass, which she had filched from his pocket less than half an hour earlier, in the centre of his desk. If he had any sense, he would keep quiet about "leaving it behind" (a breach of James' stringent security code) and no one would know that she had used it to gain entry to the lab.

Outside, in the car park, Martine sat in her car, staring straight ahead. When she saw Juan heading back in from his jaunt to Enfield, she started up the engine and pulled slowly out of the complex and onto the road, wondering why she had the noise of a baby crying in her head, and when it might go away.

On Common Lane, only the pram lay intact. When Bertie was struck, it had been sent into a violent spin. Now it rested, upright, part in the gutter, part clambering its way back up to normality, rocking gently forward and back, its occupant blinking her eyes once, twice, before letting out a tentative cry, which quickly became more persistent, when no one came.

THE END

ACKNOWLEDGEMENTS

My thanks go to all the team at Lightning Books: to Dan Hiscocks for his continued support and belief in my abilities, to Scott Pack for his incredible editing skills and guidance, to Sue Amaradivakara and Simon Edge for their tremendous efforts in publicity and marketing, to Hugh Brune for his enthusiastic sales campaign, to Nell Wood for the fabulous cover design, to Clio Mitchell for her meticulous copyediting and typesetting, and Rosemarie Malyon for her equally meticulous proofreading.

I must, of course, also acknowledge the enormous contribution of my parents, Jacqie and the late Sidney Fineberg, both inspirational teachers, who encouraged me and my sisters to spend all our waking hours reading.

Special thanks for his input into *The Cinderella Plan*, at various stages of its journey, go to a particular police officer and serious collision investigator, who spent many hours answering my questions about stopping distances, catastrophic injuries caused by cars and event data recorders. He has asked me not to reveal his identity, but he knows who he is and that I could not have written this story so convincingly without him. And to my dear, wise friend, Pen Vogler (aka @PenfromPenguin), for being so generous with her time, including reading more than one early draft, and for being brave enough to make some (very valid) suggestions for improvement; I am hugely grateful.

Finally, a gigantic thank you goes to everyone who has reviewed *The Cinderella Plan*, *The Aladdin Trial* and my first novel, *The Pinocchio Brief*, for taking the time to read my books and share their views in a variety of ways; including in radio broadcasts, space in some of our most prestigious national publications, for hosting me on their blogs and websites and for taking the time to post online reviews. Their support has provided me with the confidence to continue writing and, without their backing, I would not have been able to reach such a wide audience; I am forever indebted.

ABOUT THE AUTHOR

Yorkshire-bred, Abi Silver is a lawyer by profession. She lives in Hertfordshire with her husband and three sons. Her first courtroom thriller featuring the legal duo Judith Burton and Constance Lamb, *The Pinocchio Brief*, was published by Lightning Books in 2017 and was shortlisted for the Waverton Good Read Award. Her follow-up, *The Aladdin Trial*, featuring the same legal team, was published in 2018.

If you have enjoyed *The Cinderella Plan*, do please help us spread the word – by posting a review on Amazon (you don't need to have bought the book there) or Goodreads; by posting something on social media; or in the old-fashioned way by simply telling your friends or family about it.

Book publishing is a very competitive business these days, in a saturated market, and small independent publishers such as ourselves are often crowded out by the big houses. Support from readers like you can make all the difference to a book's success.

Many thanks.

Dan Hiscocks
Publisher
Lightning Books

Other books in the Burton & Lamb series